THE DROLL STORIES
OF BALZAC

THE
DROLL STORIES
OF
HONORÉ DE BALZAC

*With new illustrations especially made for this
edition by* STEELE SAVAGE

BLUE RIBBON BOOKS

Garden City, N. Y.

1932
BLUE RIBBON BOOKS
14 WEST 49TH STREET, NEW YORK, N. Y.

CL
PRINTED IN THE UNITED STATES OF AMERICA

TABLE OF CONTENTS

v

TRANSLATOR'S PREFACE

WHEN, in March, 1832, the first volume of the now famous *Contes Drolatiques* was published by Gosselin of Paris, Balzac, in a short preface, written in the publisher's name, replied to those attacks which he anticipated certain critics would make upon his hardy experiment. He claimed for his book the protection of all those to whom literature was dear, because it was a work of art—and a work of art, in the highest sense of the word, it undoubtedly is. Like Boccaccio, Rabelais, the Queen of Navarre, Ariosto, and Verville, the great author of *The Human Comedy* has painted an epoch. In the fresh and wonderful language of the Merry Vicar of Meudon, he has given us a marvellous picture of French life and manners in the sixteenth century. The gallant knights and merry dames of that eventful period of French history stand out in bold relief upon his canvas. The background to these life-like figures is, as it were, "Sketched upon the spot." After reading the *Contes Drolatiques,* one could almost find one's way about the towns and villages of Touraine, unassisted by map or guide. Not only is this book a work of art from its historical information and topographical accuracy; its claims to that distinction rest upon a broader foundation. Written in the nineteenth century in imitation of the style of the sixteenth, it is a triumph of literary archæology. It is a model of that which it professes to imitate; the production of a writer who, to accomplish it, must have been at once historian, linguist, philosopher, archæologist, and anatomist, and each in no ordinary degree. In France his work has long been regarded as a classic—as a faithful picture of the last days of the *moyen âge,* when kings and princesses, brave gentlemen and haughty ladies, laughed openly at stories and jokes which are considered disgraceful by their more fastidious descendants. In England the difficulties of the language employed, and the quaintness and peculiarity of its style, have placed it beyond the reach of all but those thoroughly acquainted with the French of the sixteenth century. Taking into consideration the vast amount of historical information enshrined in its pages, the archæological value which it must always possess for the student, and the dramatic interest of its stories, the translator has thought that an English edition of Balzac's chef-d'œuvre would be acceptable to many. It has, of course, been impossible to reproduce in all its vigour and freshness the language of the original. Many of the quips and cranks and puns have been lost in the process of Anglicizing. These unavoidable blemishes apart, the writer ventures to hope that he has treated this great masterpiece in a reverent spirit, touched it with no sacrilegious hand, but, on the contrary, given as close a translation as the dissimilarities of the two languages permit. With this idea, no attempt has been made to polish or round many of the awkwardly constructed sentences which are characteristic of this volume. Rough, and occasionally obscure, they are far more in keeping with the spirit of the original than the polished periods of modern romance. Taking into consideration the many difficulties which he has had to overcome, and which those best acquainted with the French edition will best appreciate, the translator claims the indulgence of the critical reader for any shortcomings he may discover. The best plea that can be offered for such indulgence is the fact that, although *Les Cent Contes Drolatiques* were completed and published in 1837, the present is the first English version ever brought before the public.

LONDON, *January*, 1874.

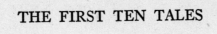

THE FIRST TEN TALES

PROLOGUE

THIS is a book of the richest flavour, full of right hearty merriment, spiced to the palate of the illustrious and very precious tosspots and drinkers, to whom our worthy compatriot, François Rabelais, the eternal honour of Touraine, addressed himself. Be it nevertheless understood, the author has no other desire than to be a good Tourainian, and joyfully to chronicle the merry doings of the famous people of this sweet and productive land, more fertile in cuckolds, dandies, and witty wags than any other, and which has furnished a good share of men of renown to France, as witness the departed Courier of piquant memory; Verville, author of the *Moyen de parvenir,* and others equally well known, among whom we will specially mention the Sieur Descartes, because he was a melancholy genius, and devoted himself more to brown studies than to drinks and dainties, a man of whom all the cooks and confectioners of Tours have a wise horror, whom they despise, and will not hear spoken of, and say, "Where does he live?" if his name is mentioned. Now this work is the product of the joyous leisure of the good old monks, of whom there are many vestiges scattered about the country, at Grenadière-les-Saint-Cyr, in the village of Sacchés-les-Azay-le-Rideau, at Marmoutiers, Veretz, Roche-Corbon, and in certain storehouses of good stories, which are old canons and wise dames, who remember the good old days when you could enjoy a hearty laugh without being afraid to shake your belly, not like the young women of the present day, who

3

wish to take their pleasure gravely—a custom which suits
our gay France as much as a water-jug would the head of
a queen. Since laughter is a privilege granted to man alone,
and he has sufficient causes for tears within his reach, without adding to them by books, I have considered it a thing
most patriotic to publish a drachm of merriment for these
times, when weariness falls like a fine rain, wetting us, soaking into us, and dissolving those ancient customs which
make the people to *reap public* amusement from the *Republic*. But of those old pantagruelists who allowed God
and the king to conduct their own affairs without putting of
their finger in the pie oftener than they could help, being
content to look on and laugh, there are very few left. They
are dying out day by day in such manner that I fear greatly
to see these illustrious fragments of the ancient breviary
spat upon, staled upon, set at naught, dishonoured, and
blamed, the which I should be loth to see, since I have and
bear great respect for the refuse of our Gallic antiquities.

Bear in mind also, ye wild critics, ye scrapers-up of
words, harpies who mangle the intentions and inventions
of every one, that as children only do we laugh, and as we
travel onward laughter sinks down and dies out, like the
light of the oil-lit lamp. This signifies, that to laugh you
must be innocent, and pure of heart, lacking which qualities
you purse your lips, drop your jaws, and knit your brow,
after the manner of men hiding vices and impurities. Take,
then, this work as you would a group or statue, certain
features of which an artist cannot omit, and he would be
the biggest of all big fools if he put leaves upon them, seeing
that these said works are not, any more than is this book,
intended for nunneries. Nevertheless, I have taken care,
much to my vexation, to weed from the manuscripts the
old words, which, in spite of their age, were still strong,

and which would have shocked the ears, astonished the eyes, reddened the cheeks, and sullied the lips of maidenly young men, and Madame Virtue with three lovers; for certain things must be done to suit the vices of the age, and a periphrase is much more agreeable than the word. Indeed, we are old, and find long trifles better than the short follies of our youth, because at that time our taste was better. Then spare me your slanders, and read this rather at night than in the daytime, and give it not to young maidens, if there be any, because this book is inflammable. I will now rid you of myself. But I fear nothing for this book, since it is extracted from a high and splendid source, from which all that has issued has had a great success, as is amply proved by the royal orders of the Golden Fleece, of the Holy Ghost, of the Garter, of the Bath, and by many notable things which have been taken therefrom, under shelter of which I place myself.

Now make ye merry, my hearties, and gaily read with ease of body and rest of reins, and may a cancer carry you off if you disown me after having read me. These words are those of our good Master Rabelais, before whom we must all stand, hat in hand, in token of reverence and honour to him, prince of all wisdom, and king of comedy.

THE FAIR IMPERIA

THE Archbishop of Bordeaux had added to his suite when going to the Council at Constance quite a good-looking little priest of Touraine whose ways and manner of speech were so charming that he passed for a son of La Soldée and the Governor. The Archbishop of Tours had willingly given him to his confrère for his journey to that town, because it was usual for archbishops to make each other presents, they well knowing how sharp are the itchings of theological palms. Thus this young priest came to the Council and was lodged in the establishment of his prelate, a man of good morals and great science.

Philippe de Mala, as he was called, resolved to behave well and worthily to serve his protector, but he saw in this mysterious Council many men leading a dissolute life and yet not making less, nay—gaining more indulgences, gold crowns and benefices than all the other virtuous and well-behaved ones. Now during one night—dangerous to his virtue—the devil whispered into his ear that he should live more luxuriously, since every one sucked the breasts of our Holy Mother Church and yet they were not drained, a miracle which proved beyond doubt the existence of God. And the little priest of Touraine did not disappoint the devil. He promised to feast himself, to eat his bellyful of roast meats and other German delicacies, when he could do so without paying for them, as he was poor. As he remained quite continent (in which he followed the example of the poor old archbishop, who sinned no longer because he was

6

unable to, and passed for a saint), he had to suffer from intolerable desires followed by fits of melancholy, since there were so many sweet courtezans, well developed, but cold to the poor people, who inhabited Constance, to enlighten the understanding of the Fathers of the Council. He was savage that he did not know how to make up to these gallant sirens, who snubbed cardinals, abbots, councilors, legates, bishops, princes, and margraves, just as if they had been penniless clerks. And in the evening, after prayers, he would practice speaking to them, teaching himself the breviary of love. He taught himself to answer all possible questions, but on the morrow if by chance he met one of the aforesaid princesses dressed out, seated in a litter and escorted by her proud and well-armed pages, he remained open-mouthed, like a dog in the act of catching flies, at the sight of the sweet countenance that so much inflamed him. The secretary of Monseigneur, a gentleman of Perigord, having clearly explained to him that the Fathers, procureurs, and auditors of the Rota bought by certain presents, not relics or indulgences, but jewels and gold, the favour of being familiar with the best of these pampered cats who lived under the protection of the lords of the Council; the poor Tourainian, all simpleton and innocent as he was, treasured up under his mattress the money given him by the good archbishop for writings and copying—hoping one day to have enough just to see a cardinal's lady-love, and trusting in God for the rest. He was hairless from top to toe and resembled a man about as much as a goat with a night-dress on resembles a young lady, but prompted by his desires he wandered in the evenings through the streets of Constance, careless of his life, and, at the risk of having his body halberded by the soldiers, he peeped at the cardinals entering the houses of their sweethearts. Then he saw the wax-candles lighted in the houses and suddenly the doors and the windows closed. Then he heard the blessed abbots or others jumping about, drinking, enjoying themselves, love-making, singing the secret *Alleluia* and applauding the music with which they were being regaled. The kitchen performed miracles, the Offices said were fine rich pots-full, the Matins sweet little hams, the Vespers luscious mouthfuls, and the Laudes delicate sweetmeats, and after their little carouses, these brave priests were silent, their pages diced upon the stairs, their mules stamped restively in the streets; everything went well—but faith and religion were there. That is how it came to pass the good man Huss was burned. And the reason? He put his finger in the pie without being asked. Then why was he a Huguenot before the others?

To return, however, to our sweet little Philippe, not unfrequently did he receive many a thump and hard blow, but the devil sustained him, inciting him to believe that sooner or later it would come to his turn to play the cardinal to some lovely dame. This ardent desire gave him the boldness of a stag in autumn, so much so that one evening he quietly tripped up the steps and into one of the first houses in Constance where often he had seen officers, seneschals, valets, and pages waiting with torches for their masters, dukes, kings, cardinals, and archbishops.

"Ah!" said he, "she must be very beautiful and amiable, this one."

A soldier well armed allowed him to pass, believing him to belong to the suite of the Elector of Bavaria, who had just left, and that he was going to deliver a message on behalf of the above-mentioned nobleman. Philippe de Mala mounted the stairs as lightly as a greyhound in love, and was guided by a delectable odour of perfume to a certain chamber where, surrounded by her handmaidens, the lady of the house was

divesting herself of her attire. He stood quite dumbfounded
like a thief surprised by sergeants. The lady was without
petticoat or head-dress. The chamber-maids and the servants, busy taking off her stockings and undressing her, so
quickly and dexterously had her stripped, that the priest,
overcome, gave vent to a long *Ah!* which had a flavour of
love about it.

"What want you, little one?" said the lady to him.

"To yield my soul to you," said he, flashing his eyes upon
her.

"You can come again to-morrow," said she, in order to
be rid of him.

To which Philippe replied, blushing, "I will not fail."

Then she burst out laughing. Philippe, struck motionless,
stood quite at his ease, letting wander over her his eyes that
glowed and sparkled with the flame of love. What lovely
thick hair hung over her ivory white back, showing sweet
white places, fair and shining between the many tresses! She
had upon her snow-white brow a ruby circlet, less fertile in
rays of fire than her black eyes, still moist with tears from
her hearty laugh. She even threw her slipper at a statue
gilded like a shrine, twisting herself about from very
ribaldry, and allowed her bare foot, smaller than a swan's
bill, to be seen. This evening she was in a good humour,
otherwise she would have had the little shaven-crown put
out by the window without more ado than her first bishop.

"He has fine eyes, Madame," said one of the handmaids.

"Where does he come from?" asked another.

"Poor child!" cried Madame, "his mother must be looking for him. Show him his way home."

The Tourainian, still sensible, gave a movement of delight
at the sight of the brocaded bed where the sweet form was
about to repose. This glance, full of amorous intelligence,

awoke the lady's fantasy, who, half laughing and half smitten, repeated "To-morrow," and dismissed him with a gesture which the pope Jehan himself would have obeyed, especially as he was like a snail without a shell, since the Council had just deprived him of the holy keys.

"Ah, Madame, there is another vow of chastity changed into an amorous desire," said one of her women; and the chuckles commenced again thick as hail.

Philippe went his way, bumping his head against the wall like a hooded rook as he was. So giddy had he become at the sight of this creature, even more enticing than a siren rising from the water. He noticed the animals carved over the door but could make no more than four of them: and as that was full of diabolical longings and his entrails sophisticated. Once in his little room he counted his coins all night long, and returned to the house of the archbishop with his head all his treasure, he counted upon satisfying the fair one by giving her all he had in the world.

"What is it ails you?" said the good archbishop, uneasy at the groans and "oh! oh's!" of his clerk.

"Ah! my lord," answered the poor priest, "I am wondering how it is that so light and sweet a woman can weigh so heavily upon my heart."

"Which one?" said the archbishop, putting down his breviary which he was reading for others—the good man.

"Oh! Mother of God! you will scold me, I know, my good master, my protector, because I have seen the lady of a cardinal at the least, and I am weeping because I lack more than one little crown to enable me to convert her."

The archbishop, knitting the circumflex accent that he had about his nose, said not a word. Then the very humble priest trembled in his skin to have confessed so much to his superior. But the holy man directly said to him, "She must be very dear then——"

"Ah!" said he, "she has swallowed many a mitre and stolen many a cross."

"Well, Philippe, if thou wilt renounce her, I will present thee with thirty crowns from the poor-box."

"Ah! my lord. I should be losing too much," replied the lad, emboldened by the treat he promised himself.

"Ah! Philippe," said the good prelate, "thou wilt then go to the devil and displease God, like all our cardinals," and the master, with sorrow, began to pray St. Gatien, the patron saint of Innocents, to save his servant. He made him kneel down beside him, telling him to recommend himself also to St. Philippe, but the wretched priest implored the saint beneath his breath to prevent him from failing if on the morrow the lady should receive him kindly and mercifully; and the good archbishop, observing the fervour of his servant, cried out to him, "Courage, little one, and Heaven will exorcise thee."

On the morrow, while Monsieur was declaiming at the Council against the shameless behaviour of the apostles of Christianity, Philippe de Mala spent his crowns—acquired with so much labour—in perfumes, baths, fomentations, and other fooleries. He played the fop so well, one would have thought him the fancy cavalier of a gay lady. He wandered about the town in order to find the residence of his heart's queen; and when he asked the passers-by to whom belonged the aforesaid house, they laughed in his face, saying—

"Whence comes this precious fellow that has not heard of La Belle Imperia?"

He was very much afraid that he and his money were gone to the devil when he heard the name, and knew into what a nice mess he had voluntarily fallen.

Imperia was the most precious, the most fantastic girl in the world, although she passed for the most dazzlingly beautiful, and the one who best understood the art of bamboozling the cardinals and softening the hardest soldiers and oppressors of the people. She had brave captains, archers, and nobles, ready to serve her at every turn. She had only to breathe a word, and the business of any one who had offended her was settled. A free fight only brought a smile to her lips, and often the Sire de Baudricourt—one of the King's Captains—would ask her if there was any one he could kill for her that day—a little joke at the expense of the abbots. With the exception of the potentates among the high clergy with whom Madame Imperia managed to accommodate her little tempers, she ruled every one with a high hand in virtue of her pretty babble and enchanting ways, which enthralled the most virtuous and the most unimpressionable. Thus she lived beloved and respected, quite as much as the real ladies and princesses, and was called Madame, concerning which the good Emperor Sigismund replied to a lady who complained of it to him, "That they, the good ladies, might keep to their own proper way and holy virtues, and Madame Imperia to the sweet naughtiness of the goddess Venus"—Christian words which very wrongly shocked the good ladies.

Philippe, then thinking over in his mind that which on the preceding evening he had seen with his eyes, doubted if more did not remain behind. Then was he sad, and without taking bite or sup, strolled about the town waiting the appointed hour, although he was well-favoured and gallant enough to find others less difficult to overcome than was Madame Imperia.

The night came; the little Tourainian, exalted with pride, caparisoned with desire, and spurred by his "alacks" and

"alases" which nearly choked him, glided like an eel into
the domicile of the veritable Queen of the Council—for
before her bowed humbly all the authority, science, and
wisdom of Christianity. The *major domo* did not know him,
and was going to bundle him out again, when one of the
chamber-women called out from the top of the stairs—"Eh,
M. Imbert, it is Madame's young fellow," and poor Philippe,
blushing like on a wedding night, ran up the stairs, shaking
with happiness and delight. The servant took him by the
hand and led him into the chamber where sat Madame,
lightly attired, like a brave woman who awaits her con-
queror.

The dazzling Imperia was seated near a table covered
with a shaggy cloth ornamented with gold, and with all the
requisites for a dainty carouse. Flagons of wine, various
drinking glasses, bottles of hippocras, flasks full of the good
wine of Cyprus, pretty boxes full of spices, roast peacocks,
green sauces, little salt hams—all that would gladden the
eyes of the gallant if he had not so madly loved Madame
Imperia. She saw well that the eyes of the young priest were
all for her. Although accustomed to the curl-paper devotion
of the churchmen, she was well satisfied that she had made a
conquest of the young priest who all day long had been in
her head.

The windows had been closed; Madame was decked out
and in a manner fit to do the honours to a prince of the
Empire. Then the rogue, beatified by the holy beauty of
Imperia, knew that emperor, burgraf, nay, even a cardinal
about to be elected pope, would willingly for that night have
changed places with him, a little priest who, beneath his
gown, had only the devil and love.

He put on a lordly air, and saluted her with a courtesy

by no means ungraceful; and then the sweet lady said to him, regaling him with a piercing glance—

"Come and sit close to me, that I may see if you have altered since yesterday."

"Oh, yes," said he.

"And how?" said she.

"Yesterday," replied the artful fellow, "I loved you: to-day, we love each other, and from a poor sinner I have become richer than a king."

"Oh, little one, little one!" cried she, merrily; "yes, you are indeed changed, for from a poor priest I see well you have turned into an old devil." And side by side they sat down before a large fire, which helped to spread their ecstasy around. They remained always ready to begin eating, seeing that they only thought of gazing into each other's eyes, and never touched a dish. Just as they were beginning to feel comfortable and at their ease, there came a great noise at Madame's door, as if people were beating against it, and crying out.

"Madame," cried the little servant, hastily, "here's another of them."

"Who is it?" cried she in a haughty manner, like a tyrant, savage at being interrupted.

"The Bishop of Coire wishes to speak with you."

"May the devil take him!" said she, looking at Philippe gently.

"Madame, he has seen the lights through the chinks, and is making a great noise."

"Tell him I have the fever, and you will be telling him no lie, for I am ill of this little priest who is torturing my brain."

But just as she had finished speaking, and was pressing with devotion the hand of Philippe who trembled in his skin, appeared the fat Bishop of Coire, indignant and angry. The officers followed him, bearing a trout canonically dressed, fresh drawn from the Rhine, and shining in a golden platter, and spices contained in little ornamental boxes, and a thousand dainties, such as liqueurs and jams, made by the holy nuns at his Abbey.

"Ah, ah," said he, with his deep voice, "I haven't time to go to the devil, but you must give me a touch of him in advance, eh! my little one."

"Your belly will one day make a nice sheath for a sword," replied she, knitting her brows above her eyes, which from being soft and gentle had become mischievous enough to make one tremble.

"And this little choir-boy? Has he already made his sacrifice?" said the bishop, insolently turning his great rubicund face towards Philippe.

"Monseigneur, I am here to confess Madame."

"Oh, oh, do you not know the canons? To confess to the ladies at this time of night is a right reserved to bishops, so take yourself off; go and herd with simple monks, and never come back here again under pain of excommunication."

"Do not move," cried the blushing Imperia, more lovely with passion than she was with love, because now she was possessed both with passion and love. "Stop, my friend. Here you are in your own house." Then he knew that he was really loved by her.

"Is it not in the breviary, and an evangelical regulation, that you shall be equal before God in the valley of Jehoshaphat?" asked she of the bishop.

"'Tis an invention of the devil, who has adulterated the holy book," replied the great numbskull of a bishop, in a hurry to fall to.

"Well, then, be equal now before me, who am here below your goddess," replied Imperia, "otherwise one of these days I will have you delicately strangled between the head and shoulders; I swear it by the power of my tonsure, which is as good as the pope's." And wishing that the trout should be added to the feast as well as the sweets and other dainties, she added, cunningly, "Sit you down and drink with us." But the artful minx, being up to a trick or two, gave the little one a wink which told him plainly not to mind the German, whom she would soon find a means to be rid of.

The servant-maid seated the bishop at the table and tucked him up, while Philippe, wild with a rage that closed his mouth, because he saw his plans ending in smoke, gave the archbishop to more devils than there ever were monks alive. Thus they got half way through the repast, which the young priest had not yet touched, hungering only for Imperia, near whom he was already seated, but speaking that sweet language which the ladies so well understand, that has neither stops, commas, accents, letters, figures, characters, notes, nor images. The fat bishop, sensual and careful enough of the sleek ecclesiastical garment of skin for which he was indebted to his late mother, allowed himself to be plentifully served with hippocras by the delicate hand of Madame, and it was just at his first hiccough that the sound of an approaching cavalcade was heard in the street. The number of horses, the "Ho, ho!" of the pages, showed plainly that some great prince hot with love was about to arrive. In fact, a moment afterwards the Cardinal of Ragusa, against whom the servants of Imperia had not dared to bar the door, entered the room. At this terrible sight the poor courtezan and her young lover became ashamed and embarrassed, like fresh cured lepers; for it would be tempting the devil to try and oust the cardinal, the more so as at that time it was not known who would be pope, three aspirants having resigned their hoods for the benefit of Christianity. The cardinal, who was a cunning Italian, long bearded, a great sophist, and the life and soul of the Council, guessed, by the feeblest exercise of the faculties of his understanding, the alpha and omega of the adventure. He only had to weigh in his mind one little thought before he knew how to proceed in order to be able to hypothecate his manly vigour. He arrived with the appetite of a hungry monk, and to obtain its satisfaction he was just the man to stab two monks and sell his bit of the true cross, which was wrong.

"Holloa! friend," said he to Philippe, calling him towards him.

The poor Tourainian, more dead than alive, and expecting the devil was about to interfere seriously with his arrangements, rose and said, "What is it?" to the redoubtable cardinal.

He taking him by the arm led him to the staircase, looked him in the white of the eye and said, without any nonsense—

"Ventredieu! you are a nice little fellow, and I should not like to have to let your master know the weight of your carcase. My revenge might cause me certain pious expenses in my old age, so choose to espouse an abbey for the remainder of your days, or to marry Madame to-night and die to-morrow."

The poor little Tourainian in despair murmured, "May I come back when your passion is over?"

The cardinal could scarcely keep his countenance, but he said sternly, "Choose the gallows or a mitre."

"Ah!" said the priest, maliciously; "a good fat abbey."

Thereupon the cardinal went back into the room, opened

an escritoire, and scribbled upon a piece of parchment an
order to the envoy of France.

"Monseigneur," said the Tourainian to him while he was
spelling out the order, "you will not get rid of the Bishop
of Coire so easily as you have got rid of me, for he has
as many abbeys as the soldiers have drinking shops in the
town; besides, he is in the favour of his lord. Now I fancy
to show you my gratitude for this so fine abbey I owe you
a good piece of advice. You know how fatal has been and
how rapidly spread this terrible pestilence which has cruelly
harassed Paris. Tell him that you have just left the bedside
of your old friend the Archbishop of Bordeaux; thus you
will make him scutter away like straw before a whirlwind."

"Oh, oh," cried the cardinal, "thou meritest more than
an abbey. Ah, Ventredieu! my young friend, here are 100
golden crowns for thy journey to the abbey of Turpenay,
which I won yesterday at cards, and of which I make you
a free gift."

Hearing these words, and seeing Philippe de Mala dis-
appear without giving her the amorous glances she expected,
the beautiful Imperia, puffing like a dolphin, denounced all
the cowardice of the priest. She was not then a sufficient
good Catholic to pardon her lover deceiving her, by not
knowing how to die for her pleasure. Thus the death of
Philippe was foreshadowed in the viper's glance she cast at
him to insult him, which glance pleased the cardinal much,
for the wily Italian saw he would soon get his abbey back
again. The Tourainian, heeding not the brewing storm,
avoided it by walking out silently and with his ears down,
like a wet dog being kicked out of church. Madame drew a
sigh from her heart. She must have had her own ideas of
humanity for the little value she held it in. The fire which
possessed her had mounted to her head, and scintillated in

rays about her, and there was good reason for it, for this was the first time that she had been humbugged by a priest. Then the cardinal smiled, believing it was all to his advantage: was not he a cunning fellow? Yes, he was the possessor of a red hat.

"Ah! ah! my friend," said he to the bishop, "I congratulate myself on being in your company, and I am glad to have been able to get rid of that little wretch unworthy of Madame, the more so as if you had gone near him, my lovely and amiable creature, you would have perished miserably through the deed of a simple priest."

"Ah! How?"

"He is the secretary of the Archbishop of Bordeaux. The good man was seized this morning with the pestilence."

The bishop opened his mouth wide enough to swallow a Dutch cheese.

"How do you know that?" asked he.

"Ah!" said the cardinal, taking the good German's hand, "I have just administered to him, and consoled him; at this moment the holy man has a fair wind to waft him to paradise."

The Bishop of Coire demonstrated immediately how light fat men are; for when men are big-bellied, a merciful providence, in the consideration of their works, often makes their internal tubes as elastic as balloons. The aforesaid bishop sprang backwards with one bound, burst into a perspiration, and coughed like a cow who finds feathers mixed with her hay. Then becoming suddenly pale, he rushed down the stairs without even bidding Madame adieu. When the door had closed upon the bishop, and he was fairly in the street, the Cardinal of Ragusa began laughing fit to split his sides.

"Ah, my fair one, am I not worthy to be pope, and better than that, thy lover this evening?"

But seeing Imperia thoughtful, he approached her to take her in his arms, and pet her after the usual fashion of cardinals, men who embrace better than all others, even the soldiers, because they are leisurely, and do not waste their essential properties.

"Ha!" said she, drawing back, "you wish to cause my death, you ecclesiastical idiot. The principal thing for you is to enjoy yourself; my sweet carcase, a thing accessory. Your pleasure will be my death, and then you'll canonize me perhaps? Ah, you have the plague, and you would give it to me. Go somewhere else, you brainless priest. Ah! touch me not," said she, seeing him about to advance, "or I will stab you with this dagger."

And the clever hussy drew from her armoire a little dagger which she knew how to use with great skill when necessary.

"But, my little paradise, my sweet one," said the other, laughing, "don't you see the trick? Wasn't it necessary to get rid of that old bullock of Coire?"

"Well, then, if you love me, show it," replied she. "I desire that you leave me instantly. If you are touched with the disease, my death will not worry you. I know you well enough to know at what price you will put a moment of pleasure at your last hour. You would drown the earth. Ah! ah! you have boasted of it when drunk. I love only myself, my treasures, and my health. Go, and if to-morrow your veins are not frozen by the disease, you can come again. To-day, I hate you, my good cardinal," said she, smiling.

"Imperia!" cried the cardinal, on his knees, "my blessed Imperia, do not play with me thus."

"No," said she, "I never play with blessed and sacred things."

"Ah! ribald woman, I will excommunicate thee to-morrow."

"And now you are out of your cardinal sense."

"Imperia, cursed daughter of Satan! Oh, my little beauty —my love——"

"Respect yourself more. Don't kneel to me, fie for shame!"

"Wilt thou have a dispensation *in articulo mortis?* Wilt thou have my fortune—or better still, a bit of the veritable true cross?—Wilt thou?"

"This evening, all the wealth of heaven above and earth beneath would not buy my heart," said she, laughing. "I should be the blackest of sinners, unworthy to receive the Blessed Sacrament if I had not my little caprices."

"I'll burn the house down. Sorceress, you have bewitched me. You shall perish at the stake. Listen to me, my love— my gentle dove—I promise you the best place in heaven. Eh? No. Death to you then—death to the sorceress."

"Oh! oh! I will kill you, Monseigneur."

And the cardinal foamed with rage.

"You are making a fool of yourself," said she. "Go away, you'll tire yourself."

"I shall be pope, and you shall pay for this!"

"Then you are no longer disposed to obey me?"

"What can I do this evening to please you?"

"Get out."

And she sprang lightly like a wagtail into her room, and locked herself in, leaving the cardinal to storm that he was obliged to go. When the fair Imperia found herself alone, seated before the fire, and without her little priest, she exclaimed, snapping angrily the gold links of her chain, "By the double triple horn of the devil, if the little one has made me have this row with the cardinal, and exposed me to the danger of being poisoned to-morrow, unless I pay him over to my heart's content. I will not die till I have seen him burnt alive before my eyes. Ah!" said she, weeping, this time real tears, "I lead a most unhappy life, and the little pleasure I have costs me the life of a dog, let alone my salvation."

As she finished this jeremaid, wailing like a calf that being slaughtered, she beheld the blushing face of the young priest, who had hidden himself, peeping at her from behind her large Venetian mirror.

"Ah!" said she, "thou art the most perfect monk that ever dwelt in this blessed and amorous town of Constance. Ah! ah! come, my gentle cavalier, my dear boy, my little charm, my paradise of delectation, let me drink thine eyes, eat thee, kill thee with love. Oh! my ever-flourishing, evergreen sempiternal god; from a little monk I would make thee a king, emperor, pope, and happier than either. There, thou canst put anything to fire and sword, I am thine, and thou shalt see it well; for thou shall be all a cardinal, even when to redden thy hood I shed all my heart's blood." And with her trembling hands all joyously she filled with Greek wine the golden cup, brought by the Bishop of Coire, and presented it to her sweetheart, whom she served upon her knees, she whose slipper princes found more to their taste than that of the pope.

But he gazed at her in silence, with his eye so greedy with love, that she said to him, trembling with joy, "Ah, be quiet, little one. Let us have supper."

THE VENIAL SIN

HOW THE GOODMAN BRUYN TOOK A WIFE

MESSIRE BRUYN, he who completed the Castle of Roche-Corbon-les-Vouvray, on the banks of the Loire, was a boisterous fellow in his youth. When quite little, he squeezed the young ladies, turned the house out of windows, and played the devil with everything, when he was called upon to put his sire the Baron of Roche-Corbon some few feet under the turf. Then he was his own master, free to lead a life of wild dissipation, and indeed he worked very hard to get a surfeit of enjoyment. Now by making his crowns sweat and proving his virility, draining his land, and bleeding his hogsheads, and regaling frail wenches, he found himself excommunicated from decent society, and had for his friends only the plunderers of towns and the Lombardians. But the usurers turned rough and bitter as chestnut husks, when he had no other security to give them than his said estate of Roche-Corbon, since the *Rupes Carbonis* was held from our lord the king. Then Bruyn found himself just in the humour to give a blow here and there, to break a collarbone or two, and quarrel with every one about trifles. Seeing which the Abbot of Marmoustiers, his neighbour, and a man liberal with his advice, told him that it was an evident sign of lordly perfection, that he was walking in the right road, but if he would go and slaughter, to the great glory of God, the Mahommedans who defiled the Holy Land, it would be better still, and that he would undoubtedly return full of wealth

23

and indulgences into Touraine, or into Paradise, whence all barons formerly came.

The said Bruyn, admiring the great sense of the prelate, left the country equipped by the monastery, and blessed by the abbot, to the great delight of his friends and neighbours. Then he put to the sack many towns of Asia and Africa, and fell upon the infidels without giving them warning, burning the Saracens, the Greeks, the English and others, caring little whether they were friends or enemies, or where they came from, since among his merits he had that of being in no way curious, and he never questioned them until after he had killed them. At this business, agreeable to God, to the King, and to himself, Bruyn gained renown as a good Christian and loyal knight, and enjoyed himself thoroughly in these lands beyond the seas, since he more willingly gave a crown to the girls than to the poor, although he met more poor people than perfect maids; but like a good Tourainian he made soup of anything. At length, when he was satiated with Turks, relics, and other blessings of the Holy Land, Bruyn, to the great astonishment of the people of Vouvrillons, returned from the Crusades laden with crowns and precious stones; rather differently from some who, rich when they set out, came back heavy with leprosy, but light with gold. On his return from Tunis, our Lord, King Philippe, made him a Count, and appointed him his seneschal in our country and in that of Poitou. There he was greatly beloved and properly thought well of, since over and above his good qualities he founded the Church of the Carmes-Deschaulx, in the parish of Egrignolles, as a peace-offering to Heaven for the follies of his youth. Thus was he cardinally consigned to the good graces of the Church and of God. From a wicked youth and reckless man, he became a good, wise man, and discreet in his dissipations and pleas-

ures; rarely was in anger, unless some one blasphemed God
before him, the which he would not tolerate because he had
blasphemed enough for every one in his wild youth. In short,
he never quarreled, because, being seneschal, people gave
up to him instantly. It is true that he at that time beheld all
his desires accomplished, the which would render even an
imp of Satan calm and tranquil from his horns to his heels.
And besides this he possessed a castle all jagged at the corners, and shaped and pointed like a Spanish doublet, situated
upon a bank from which it was reflected in the Loire. In the
rooms were royal tapestries, furniture, Saracen pomps,
vanities, and inventions which were much admired by the
people of Tours, and even by the archbishop and clerks of
St. Martin, to whom he sent as a free gift a banner fringed
with fine gold. In the neighbourhood of the said castle
abounded fair domains, wind-mills, and forests, yielding a
harvest of rents of all kinds, so that he was one of the
strongest knights-banneret of the province, and could easily
have led to battle for our lord the king a thousand men. In
his old days, if by chance his bailiff, a diligent man at hanging, brought before him a poor peasant suspected of some
offence, he would say, smiling—

"Let this one go, Breddiff, he will count against those
I inconsiderately slaughtered across the seas;" oftentimes,
however, he would let them bravely hang on a chestnut tree,
or swing on his gallows, but this was solely that justice
might be done, and that the custom should not lapse in his
domain. Thus the people on his lands were good and orderly,
like fresh veiled nuns, and peaceful since he protected them
from robbers and vagabonds whom he never spared, knowing by experience how much mischief is caused by these
cursed beasts of prey. For the rest, most devout, finishing
everything quickly, his prayers as well as good wine, he

managed the processes after the Turkish fashion, having a thousand little jokes ready for the losers, and dining with them to console them. He had all the people who had been hanged buried in consecrated ground like godly ones, some people thinking they had been sufficiently punished by having their breath stopped. He only persecuted the Jews now and then, and when they were glutted with usury and wealth. He let them gather their spoils as the bees do honey, saying that they were the best of tax-gatherers. And never did he despoil them save for the profit and use of the churchmen, the king, the province, or himself.

This jovial way gained for him the affection and esteem of every one, great and small. If he came back smiling from his judicial throne, the Abbot of Marmoustiers, an old man like himself, would say, "Ha! ha! messire, there is some hanging on since you laugh thus!" And when coming from Roche-Corbon to Tours he passed on horseback along the Faubourg St. Symphorien, the little girls would say, "Ah, this is the justice day, here is the good man Bruyn," and without being afraid they would look at him astride on a big white hack, that he had brought back with him from the Levant. On the bridge the little boys would stop playing with the ball, and would call out, "Good day, Mr. Seneschal," and he would reply, jokingly, "Enjoy yourselves, my children, until you get whipped." "Yes, Mr. Seneschal."

Also he made the country so contented and so free from robbers that during the year of the great overflowing of the Loire there were only twenty-two malefactors hanged that winter, not counting a Jew burned in the Commune of Chateau-Neuf for having stolen a consecrated wafer, or bought it, some said, for he was very rich.

One day in the following year about harvest time, or mowing time, as we say in Touraine, there came Egyptians,

Bohemians, and other wandering troupes who stole the holy
things from the Church of St. Martin, and in the place and
exact situation of Madame the Virgin, left by way of insult
and mockery to our Holy Faith a wicked, pretty little girl,
about the age of an old dog, stark naked, an acrobat, and of
Moorish descent like themselves. For this almost nameless
crime it was equally decided by the king, people, and the
churchmen that the Mooress, to pay for all, should be
burned and cooked alive in the square near the fountain
where the herb market is. Then the good man Bruyn clearly
and dexterously demonstrated to the others that it would be
a thing most profitable and pleasant to God to gain over this
African soul to the true religion, and if the devil were lodged
in this feminine body the faggots would be useless to burn
him, as said the said order. The which the archbishop sagely
thought most canonical and conformable to Christian charity and the gospel. The ladies of the town and other persons
of authority said loudly that they were cheated of a fine
ceremony, since the Mooress was crying her eyes out in the
gaol and would certainly be converted to God in order to
live as long as a crow, if she were allowed to do so, to which
the seneschal replied that if the foreigner would wholly
commit herself to the Christian religion there would be a
gallant ceremony of another kind, and that he would undertake that it should be royally magnificent, because he would
be her sponsor at the baptismal font, and that a virgin should
be his partner in the affair in order the better to please the
Almighty, while himself was reputed never to have lost the
bloom of innocence, in fact to be a *coquebin*. In our country
of Touraine thus are called the young virgin men, unmarried or so esteemed, to distinguish them from the husbands
and the widowers, but the girls always pick them out without

the name, because they are more lighthearted and merry
than those seasoned in marriage.

The young Mooress did not hesitate between the flaming
faggots and the baptismal water. She much preferred to be
a Christian and live than be an Egyptian and be burnt; thus
to escape a moment's baking, her heart would burn unquenched through all her life, since for the greater surety
of her religion she was placed in the convent of nuns near
Chardonneret, where she took the vow of sanctity. The said
ceremony was concluded at the residence of the archbishop,
where on this occasion, in honour of the Saviour of men, the
lords and ladies of Touraine hopped, skipped, and danced,
for in this country the people dance, skip, eat, flirt, have
more feasts and make merrier than any in the whole world.
The good old seneschal had taken for his associate the
daughter of the lord of Azay-le-Ridel, which afterwards became Azay-le-Bruslé, the which lord being a Crusader was
left before Acre, a far distant town, in the hands of a Saracen who demanded a royal ransom for him because the said
lord was of high position.

The lady of Azay having given his estate as security to
the Lombards and extortioners in order to raise the sum,
remained, without a penny in the world, awaiting her lord
in a poor lodging in the town, without a carpet to sit upon,
but proud as the Queen of Sheba and brave as a mastiff who
defends the property of his master. Seeing this great distress the seneschal went delicately to request this lady's
daughter to be the godmother of the said Egyptian, in order
that he might have the right of assisting the Lady of Azay.
And, in fact, he kept a heavy chain of gold which he had
preserved since the commencement of the taking of Cyprus,
and the which he determined to clasp about the neck of his
pretty associate, but he hung there at the same time his

domain, and his white hairs, his money and his horses; in short, he placed there everything he possessed, directly he had seen Blanche of Azay dancing a pavan among the ladies of Tours. Although the Moorish girl, making the most of her last day, had astonished the assembly by her twists, jumps, steps, springs, elevations, and artistic efforts, Blanche had the advantage of her, as every one agreed, so virginally and delicately did she dance.

Now Bruyn, admiring this gentle maiden whose toes seemed to fear the boards, and who amused herself so innocently for her seventeen years—like a grasshopper trying her first note—was seized with an old man's desire; a desire apoplectic and vigorous from weakness, which heated him from the sole of his foot to the nape of his neck—for his head had too much snow on the top of it to let love lodge there. Then the good man perceived that he needed a wife in his manor, and it appeared more lonely to him than it was. And what then was a castle without a chatelaine? As well have a clapper without its bell. In short, a wife was the only thing that he had to desire, so he wished to have one promptly, seeing that if the Lady of Azay made him wait, he had just time to pass out of this world into the other. But during the baptismal entertainment, he thought little of his severe wounds, and still less of the eighty years that had stripped his head; he found his eyes clear enough to see distinctly his young companion, who, following the injunctions of the Lady of Azay, regaled him well with glance and gesture, believing there could be no danger near so old a fellow, in such wise that Blanche—naïve and nice as she was in contradistinction to the girls of Touraine, who are as wide-awake as a spring morning—permitted the good man first to kiss her hand, and afterwards her neck, rather low down; at least so said the archbishop who married them the

week after; and that was a beautiful bridal, and a still more
beautiful bride.

The said Blanche was slender and graceful as no other
girl, and still better than that, more maidenly than ever
maiden was; a maiden all ignorant of love, who knew not
why or what it was; a maiden who wondered why certain
people lingered in their beds; a maiden who believed that
children were found in parsley beds. Her mother had thus
reared her in innocence, without even allowing her to consider, trifle as it was, how she sucked in her soup between
her teeth. Thus was she a sweet flower, and intact, joyous,
and innocent; an angel, who needed but the wings to fly
away to Paradise. When she left the poor lodgings of her
weeping mother to consummate her betrothal at the cathedral of St. Gatien and St. Maurice, the country people came
to feast their eyes upon the bride, and on the carpets which
were laid down all along the Rue de la Scellerie, and all said
that never had tinier feet pressed the ground of Touraine,
prettier eyes gazed up to heaven, or a more splendid festival
adorned the streets with carpets and with flowers. The
young girls of St. Martin and of the borough of Chateau-
Neuf all envied the long brown tresses with which doubtless
Blanche had fished for a count, but much more did they
desire the gold embroidered dress, the foreign stones, the
white diamonds, and the chains with which the little darling
played, and which bound her for ever to the said seneschal.
The old soldier was so merry by her side, that his happiness showed itself in his wrinkles, his looks, and his movements. Although he was hardly as straight as a billhook, he
held himself so by the side of Blanche, that one would have
taken him for a soldier on parade receiving his officer, and
he placed his hand on his diaphragm like a man whose pleasure stifles and troubles him. Delighted with the sound of the

swinging bells, the procession, the pomps and vanities of this said marriage, which was talked of long after the episcopal rejoicings, the women desired a harvest of Moorish girls, a deluge of old seneschals, and baskets full of Egyptian baptisms. But this was the only one that ever happened in Touraine, seeing that the country is far from Egypt and from Bohemia. The Lady of Azay received a large sum of money after the ceremony, which enabled her to start immediately for Acre to go to her spouse, accompanied by the lieutenant and soldiers of the Count of Roche-Corbon, who furnished them with everything necessary. She set out on the day of the wedding, after having placed her daughter in the hands of the seneschal, enjoining him to treat her well; and later on she returned with the Sire d'Azay, who was leprous, and she cured him, tending him herself, running the risk of being contaminated, the which was greatly admired.

The marriage ceremony finished and at an end—for it lasted three days, to the great contentment of the people —Messire Bruyn with great pomp led the little one to his castle, and, according to the custom of husbands, had her put solemnly to bed in his couch, which was blessed by the Abbot of Marmoustiers; then came and placed himself beside her in the great feudal chamber of Roche-Corbon, which had been hung with green brocade and ribbon of golden wire. When old Bruyn, perfumed all over, found himself side by side with his pretty wife, he kissed her first upon the forehead and then upon the little round, white breast, on the same spot where she had allowed him to clasp the fastenings of the chain, but that was all. The old fellow had too great confidence in himself in fancying himself able to accomplish more; so then he abstained from love in spite of the merry nuptial songs, the epithalamiums and jokes which were going on in the rooms beneath where the dancing was still kept up. He refreshed himself with a drink of the marriage beverage, which, according to custom, had been blessed and placed near them in a golden cup. The spices warmed his stomach well enough, but not the heart of his dead ardour. Blanche was not at all astonished at the demeanour of her spouse, because she was a virgin in mind, and in marriage she only saw that which is visible to the eyes of young girls—namely, dresses, banquets, horses, to be a lady and mistress, to have a country seat, to amuse oneself and give orders; so, like the child that she was, she played with the gold tassels of the bed, and marvelled at the richness of the shrine in which her innocence should be interred. Feeling, a little later in the day, his culpability, and relying on the future, which, however, would spoil a little every day that with which he pretended to regale his wife, the seneschal tried to substitute the word for the deed. So he entertained his wife in various ways, promised her the keys of his sideboards, his granaries and chests, the perfect government of his houses and domains without any control, hanging round her neck "the other half of the loaf," which is the popular saying in Touraine. She being like a young charger full of hay, found her good man the most gallant fellow in the world, and raising herself upon her pillow began to smile, and beheld with greater joy this beautiful green brocaded bed, where henceforward she would be permitted, without any sin, to sleep every night. Seeing she was getting playful, the cunning lord, who had not been used to maidens, but knew from experience the little tricks that women will practise, seeing that he had much associated with ladies of the town, feared those handy tricks, little kisses, and minor amusements of love which formerly he did not object to, but which at the present time would have found him cold as the obit of a pope. Then he drew back towards the edge of the bed, afraid of his happiness, and said to his too delectable spouse, "Well, darling, you are a seneschal's wife now, and very well seneschaled as well."

"Oh, no!" said she.

"How no!" replied he, in great fear; "are you not a wife?"

"No," said she. "Nor shall I be till I have a child."

"Did you while coming here see the meadows?" began again the old fellow.

"Yes," said she.

"Well, they are yours."

"Oh! oh!" replied she laughing, "I shall amuse myself much there catching butterflies."

"That's a good girl," said her lord. "And the woods?"

"Ah! I should not like to be there alone, you will take me there. But," said she, "give me a little of that liquor which La Ponneuse has taken such pains to prepare for us."

"And why, my darling? It would put fire into your body."

"Oh! that's what I should like," said she, biting her lips with vexation, "because I desire to give you a child as soon as possible; and I am sure that liquor is good for the purpose."

"Ah, my little one," said the seneschal, knowing by this that Blanche was a virgin from head to foot, "the goodwill of God is necessary for this business, and women must be in a state of harvest."

"And when shall I be in a state of harvest?" asked she, smiling.

"When nature so wills it," said he, trying to laugh.

"What is it necessary to do for this?" replied she.

"Bah! a cabalistical and alchemical operation which is very dangerous."

"Ah!" said she, with a dreamy look, "that's the reason why my mother cried when thinking of the said metamorphosis; but Bertha de Breuilly, who is so thankful for being made a wife, told me it was the easiest thing in the world."

"That's according to the age," replied the old lord. "But did you see at the stable the beautiful white mare so much spoken of in Touraine?"

"Yes, she is very gentle and nice."

"Well, I give her to you, and you can ride her as often as the fancy takes you."

"Oh, you are very kind, and they did not lie when they told me so."

"Here," continued he, "sweetheart: the butler, the chaplain, the treasurer, the equerry, the farrier, the bailiff, even the Sire de Montsoreau the young varlet whose name is Gauttier and bears my banner, with his men at arms, captains, followers, and beasts—all are yours, and will instantly obey your orders under pain of being incommoded with a hempen collar."

"But," replied she, "this mysterious operation—cannot it be performed immediately?"

"Oh, no!" replied the seneschal. "Because it is necessary above all things that both the one and the other of us should be in a state of grace before God; otherwise we should have a bad child, full of sins; which is forbidden by the canons of the Church. This is the reason there are so many incorrigible scapegraces in the world. Their parents have not wisely waited to have their souls pure, and have given wicked souls to their children. The beautiful and the virtuous come of immaculate fathers; that is why we cause our beds to be blessed, as the Abbot of Marmoustiers has done this one. Have you not transgressed the ordinances of the Church?"

"Oh, no," said she, quickly, "I received before Mass absolution for all my faults and have remained since without committing the slightest sin."

"You are very perfect," cried the cunning lord; "and I am delighted to have you for a wife; but I have sworn like an infidel."

"Oh! and why?"

"Because the dancing did not finish, and I could not have you to myself to bring you here and kiss you."

Thereupon he gallantly took her hands and covered them with kisses, whispering to her little endearments and superficial words of affection which made her quite pleased and contented.

Then, fatigued with the dance and all the ceremonies, she settled down to her slumbers, saying to the seneschal—

"I will take care to-morrow that you shall not sin," and she left the old man quite smitten with her white beauty, amorous of her delicate nature, and as embarrassed to know how he should be able to keep her in her innocence as to explain why oxen chew their food twice over. Although he did not augur to himself any good therefrom, it inflamed him so much to see the exquisite perfection of Blanche during her innocent and gentle sleep, that he resolved to preserve and defend this pretty jewel of love. With tears in his eyes he kissed her sweet golden tresses, her beautiful eyelids, and her ripe red mouth, and he did it softly for fear of waking her. That was all his fruition, the dumb delight which still inflamed his heart without in the least affecting Blanche. Then he deplored the snows of his leafless old age, the poor old man, and he saw clearly that God had amused himself by giving him nuts when his teeth were gone.

HOW THE SENESCHAL STRUGGLED WITH HIS
WIFE'S MODESTY

During the first days of his marriage the seneschal invented many fibs to tell his wife, whose so estimable innocence he abused. Firstly, he found in his judicial functions good excuses for leaving her at times alone; then he occupied himself with the peasants of the neighbourhood, and took them to dress the vines on his lands at Vouvray, and at length pampered her up with a thousand absurd tales.

At one time he would say that lords did not behave like common people, that the children were only planted at certain celestial conjunctions ascertained by learned astrologers; at another that one should abstain from begetting children on feast days because it was a great undertaking; and he observed the feasts like a man who wished to enter into Paradise without contest. Sometimes he would pretend that if by chance the parents were not in a state of grace, the children commenced on the day of St. Claire were blind, of St. Gatien had the gout, of St. Agnes were scaldheaded, of St. Roch had the plague, sometimes that those begotten in February were chilly; in March, too turbulent; in April, were worth nothing at all; and that handsome boys were conceived in May. In short he wished his to be perfect, to have his hair of two colours; and for this it was necessary that all the required conditions should be observed. At other times he would say to Blanche that the right of a man was to bestow a child upon his wife according to his sole and unique will, and that if she pretended to be a virtuous woman she should conform to the wishes of her husband; in fact, it was necessary to await the return of the Lady of

Azay in order that she should assist at the confinement; from all of which Blanche concluded that the seneschal was annoyed by her requests, and was perhaps right, since he was old and full of experience; so she submitted herself and thought no more, except to herself, of this so much-desired child, that is to say, she was always thinking of it, like a woman who has a desire in her head, without suspecting that she was behaving like a gay lady or a townwalker running after her enjoyment. One evening by accident Bruyn spoke of children, a discourse that he avoided as cats avoid water, but he was complaining of a boy condemned by him that morning for great misdeeds, saying for certain he was the offspring of people laden with mortal sins.

"Alas," said Blanche, "if you will give me one, although you have not got absolution, I will correct him so well that you will be pleased with him."

Then the count saw that his wife was bitten by a warm desire, and that it was time to dissipate her innocence in order to make himself master of it, to conquer it, to beat it, or to appease and extinguish it.

"What, my dear, you wish to be a mother?" said he; "you do not yet know the business of a wife, you are not accustomed to being mistress of the house."

"Oh! oh!" said she, "to be a perfect countess, and have in my loins a little count, must I play the great lady? I will do it, and thoroughly."

Then Blanche, in order to obtain issue, began to hunt the fawns and the stags, leaping the ditches, galloping upon her mare over valley and mountain, through the woods and the fields, taking great delight in watching the falcons fly, in unhooding them and while hunting always carried them gracefully upon her little wrist, which was what the senes-

chal had desired. But in this pursuit, Blanche gained an
appetite of nun and prelate, that is to say, wished to procreate, had her desires whetted, and could scarcely restrain
her hunger, when on her return she gave play to her teeth.
Now by reason of reading the legends written by the way,
and of separating by death the embraces of birds and wild
beasts, she discovered a mystery of natural alchemy, while
colouring her complexion, and superagitating her feeble
imagination, which did little to pacify her warlike nature,
and strongly tickled her desire which laughed, played, and
frisked unmistakably. The seneschal thought to disarm the
rebellious virtue of his wife by making her scour the country; but his fraud turned out badly, for the unknown lust
that circulated in the veins of Blanche emerged from these
assaults more hardly than before, inviting jousts and tour-
neys as a herald the armed knight.

The good lord saw then that he had grossly erred and
that he was now upon the horns of a dilemma; also he no
longer knew what course to adopt; the longer he left it
the more it would resist. From this combat, there must
result one conquered and one contused—a diabolical con-
tusion which he wished to keep distant from his physiognomy by God's help until after his death. The poor seneschal
had already great trouble to follow his lady to the chase,
without being dismounted; he sweated under the weight of
his trappings, and almost expired in that pursuit wherein
his frisky wife cheered her life and took great pleasure.
Many times in the evening she wished to dance. Now the
good man, swathed in his heavy clothing, found himself
quite worn out with these exercises, in which he was constrained to participate either in giving her his hand, when
she performed the vaults of the Moorish girl, or in holding
the lighted faggot for her, when she had a fancy to do the

torchlight dance; and in spite of his sciaticas, accretions, and rheumatisms, he was obliged to smile and say to her some gentle words and gallantries after all the evolutions, mummeries, and comic pantomimes which she indulged in to divert herself; for he loved her so madly that if she had asked him for an impossibility he would have sought one for her immediately.

Nevertheless one fine day he recognized the fact that his frame was in a state of too great debility to struggle with the vigorous nature of his wife, and humiliating himself before his wife's virtue, he resolved to let things take their course, relying a little upon the modesty, religion and bashfulness of Blanche, but he always slept with one eye open, for he suspected that God had made virginities to be taken like partridges, to be spitted and roasted. One wet morning, when the weather was that, in which the snails make their tracks, a melancholy time, and suitable to reverie, Blanche was in the house sitting in her chair in deep thought, because nothing produces more lively coctions of the substantive essences, and no receipt, specific or philtre is more penetrating, transpiercing, or doubly transpiercing and titillating than the subtle warmth which simmers between the nap of a chair and a maiden sitting during certain weather.

Now without knowing it, the countess was incommoded by her innocence, which gave her more trouble than it was worth to her brain, and gnawed her all over. Then the good man, seriously grieved to see her languishing, wished to drive away the thoughts which were ultra-conjugal principles of love.

"Whence comes your sadness, sweetheart?" said he.

"From shame."

"What then affronts you?"

"The not being a good woman; because I am without a child, and you without lineage! Is one a lady without progeny? Nay! look!... all my neighbours have it, and I was married to have it, as you to give it me; the nobles of Touraine are all amply furnished with children, and their wives give them lapfuls, you alone have none, they laugh at you there. What will become of your name and your fiefs and your seigniories? A child is our natural company; it is a delight to us to make a fright of it, to fondle it, to swaddle it, to dress and undress it, to cuddle it, to sing it lullabies, to cradle it, to get it up, to put it to bed, and to nourish it, and I feel that if I had only the half of one, I would kiss it, swaddle it and unharness it, and I would make it jump and crow all day long, as the other ladies do."

"Were it not that in giving them birth women die, and that for this you are still too delicate and too close in the bud, you would be already a mother," replied the seneschal, made giddy from the flow of words. "But will you buy one ready made—that will cost you neither pain nor labour."

"But," said she, "I want the pain and labour, without which it will not be ours. I know very well it should be the fruit of my body, because at church they say that Jesus was the fruit of the Virgin's womb."

"Very well, then pray God that it may be so," cried the seneschal, "and intercede with the Virgin of Egrignolles. Many a lady has conceived after the neuvaine; you must not fail to do one."

Then the same day Blanche set out towards Notre-Dame de l'Egrignolles, decked out like a queen, riding her beautiful mare, having on her a robe of green velvet, laced down with fine gold lace, open at the breast, having sleeves of scarlet, little shoes, and a high hat ornamented with precious stones, and a gold waistband that showed off her little waist.

as slim as a pole. She wished to give her dress to Madame the Virgin, and in fact promised it her, for the day of her churching. The Sire de Montsoreau galloped before her, his eye bright as that of a hawk, keeping the people back and guarding with his knights the security of the journey. Near Marmoustiers the seneschal, rendered sleepy by the heat, seeing it was the month of August, waggled about in his saddle, like a diadem upon the head of a cow, and seeing so frolicsome and so pretty a lady by the side of so old a fellow, a peasant girl, who was squatting near the trunk of a tree and drinking water out of her stone jug, inquired of a toothless old hag, who picked up a trifle by gleaning, if this princess was going to bury her dead.

"Nay," said the old woman, "it is our lady of Roche-Corbon, wife of the seneschal of Poitou and Touraine, in quest of a child."

"Ah! ah!" said the young girl, laughing like a fly just satisfied; then pointing to the handsome knight who was at the head of the procession—"he who marches at the head would manage that; she would save the wax-candles and the vow."

"Ha! my little one," replied the hag, "I am rather surprised that she should go to Notre-Dame de l'Egrignolles, seeing that there are no handsome priests there. She might very well stop for a short time beneath the shadow of the belfry of Marmoustiers; she would soon be fertile, these good fathers are so lively."

"By a nun's oath!" said a tramp walking up, "look; the Sire de Montsoreau is lively and delicate enough to open the ladies' heart, the more so as he is well formed to do so."

And all commenced to laugh. The Sire de Montsoreau wished to go to them and hang them to a lime-tree by the road as a punishment for their bad words, but Blanche cried out quickly—

"Oh, sir, do not hang them yet. They have not said all they mean; and we shall see them on our return."

She blushed, and the Sire de Montsoreau looked at her eagerly, as though to shoot into her the mystic comprehensions of love, but the clearing out of her intelligence had already been commenced by the sayings of the peasants, which were fructifying in her understanding—her innocence was like touchwood, there was only need for a word to inflame it.

Thus Blanche perceived now the notable and physical differences between the qualities of her old husband and the perfections of the said Gauttier, a gentleman who was not over affected with his twenty-three years, but held himself upright as a ninepin in the saddle, and as wideawake as the matin chimes, while in contrast to him, slept the seneschal; he had courage and dexterity there where his master failed. He was one of those smart fellows whom the jades would sooner wear at night than a leather garment, because they then no longer fear the fleas; there are some who vituperate them, but no one should be blamed, because every one should sleep as he likes.

So much did the seneschal's lady think, and so imperially well, that by the time she arrived at the bridge of Tours she loved Gauttier secretly, as a maiden loves, without suspecting that it is love. From that she became a proper woman, that is to say, she desired the good of others, the best that men have, she fell into a fit of lovesickness, going at the first jump to the depth of her misery, seeing that all is flame between the first coveting and the last desire, and she knew not how she then learnt that by the eyes can flow in a subtle essence, causing such powerful corrosions in all the veins of the body, recesses of the heart, nerves of the members, roots of the hair, perspiration of the substance, limbo of the brain, orifices of the epidermis, windings of the pluck, tubes of the hypochondriac and other channels, which in her were suddenly dilated, heated, tickled, envenomed, clawed, narrowed and disturbed, as if she had a basketful of needles in her inside. This was a maiden's desire, a well-conditioned desire, which troubled her sight to such a degree that she no longer saw her old spouse, but clearly the young Gauttier, whose nature was as ample as the glorious chin of an abbot. When the good man entered Tours, the *Ah! Ah!* of the crowd woke him up, and he came with great pomp with his suite to the church of Notre-Dame de l'Egrignolles, formerly called *la greigneur,* as if you said that which has the most merit. Blanche went into the chapel where children are asked of God and of the Virgin and went there alone, as was the custom, always however in presence of the seneschal, of his varlets and the loiterers who remained outside the grill. When the countess saw the priest come who had charge of the masses said for children, and who received the said vows, she asked him if there were many barren women. To which the good priest replied, that he must not complain, and that the children were good revenue to the Church.

"And do you often see," said Blanche, "young women with such old husbands as my lord?"

"Rarely," said he.

"But have those obtained offspring?"

"Always," replied the priest, smiling.

"And the others whose companions are not so old?"

"Sometimes."

"Oh! oh!" said she, "there is more certainty than with one like the seneschal?"

"To be sure," said the priest.

"Why?" said she.

"Madame," gravely replied the priest, "before that age God alone interferes with the affair, after, it is the men." At this time it was a true thing that all the wisdom had gone to the clergy. Blanche made her vow, which was a very profitable one, seeing that her decorations were worth quite two thousand gold crowns.

"You are very joyful!" said the old seneschal to her when on the home journey she made her mare prance, jump and frisk.

"Yes, yes!" said she. "There is no longer any doubt about my having a child, because any one can help me, the priest said; I shall take Gauttier."

The seneschal wished to go and slay the monk, but he thought that was a crime which would cost him too much, and he resolved cunningly to arrange his vengeance with the help of the archbishop; and before the housetops of Roche-Corbon came in sight he had ordered the Sire de Montsoreau to seek a little retirement in his own country, which the young Gauttier did, knowing the ways of his lord. The seneschal put in the place of the said Gauttier the son of the Sire de Jallanges, whose fief was held from Roche-Corbon. He was a young boy named René, approaching fourteen years, and he made him a page, awaiting the time when he should be old enough to be equerry, and gave the command of his men to an old cripple, with whom he had knocked about a great deal in Palestine and other places. Thus the good man believed he would avoid the horned trappings of cuckoldum, and would still be able to girth, bridle and curb the factious innocence of his wife, which struggled like a mule held by a rope.

THAT WHICH IS ONLY A VENIAL SIN

The Sunday following the arrival of René at the manor of Roche-Corbon, Blanche went out hunting without her goodman, and when she was in the forest near Les Carneaux, saw a monk who appeared to be pushing a girl about more than was necessary, and spurred on her horse, saying to her people, "Ho there! don't let him kill her." But when the seneschal's lady arrived close to them, she turned her horse's head quickly and the sight she beheld prevented her from hunting. She came back pensive, and then the lantern of her intelligence opened, and received a bright light, which made a thousand things clear, such as church and other pictures, fables, and lays of the troubadours, or the domestic arrangements of birds; suddenly she discovered the sweet mystery of love written in all languages, even in that of the Carps'. Is it not silly thus to seal this science from maidens? Soon went Blanche to bed, and soon said she to the seneschal—

"Bruyn, you have deceived me, you ought to behave as the monk of the Carneaux behaved with the girl."

Old Bruyn suspected the adventure, and saw well that his evil hour was at hand. He regarded Blanche with too much fire in his eyes for the same ardour to be lower down, and answered her softly—

"Alas! sweetheart, in taking you for my wife I had more love than strength, and I have taken advantage of your clemency and virtue. The great sorrow of my life is to feel all my capabilities in my heart only. This sorrow hastens my death little by little, so that you will soon be free. Wait for my departure from this world. That is the sole request that he makes of you, he who is your master, and who could command you, but who wishes only to be your prime minis-

ter and slave. Do not betray the honour of my white hairs!
Under these circumstances there have been lords who have
slain their wives."

"Alas! you will not kill me?" said she.

"No," replied the old man, "I love thee too much, little
one; why, thou are the flower of my old age, the joy of my
soul. Thou art my well-beloved daughter; the sight of thee
does good to mine eyes, and from thee I could endure anything, be it a sorrow or a joy; I give thee full license in
everything, provided that thou dost not curse too much the
poor Bruyn who has made thee a great lady, rich and honoured. Wilt thou not be a lovely widow? And thy happiness
will soften the pangs of death."

And he found in his dried-up eyes still one tear which
trickled quite warm down his fir-cone coloured face, and
fell upon the hand of Blanche who, grieved to behold this
great love of her old spouse who would put himself under
the ground to please her, said laughing—

"There! there! don't cry, I will wait."

Thereupon the seneschal kissed her hands and regaled
her with little endearments, saying with a voice quivering
with emotion—

"If you knew, Blanche, my darling, how I devour thee
in thy sleep with caresses, now here, now there!" And the
old ape patted her with his two hands, which were nothing
but bones. And he continued, "I dared not awaken the cat
that would have strangled my happiness, since at this occupation of love I only embraced with my heart."

"Ah!" replied she, "you can fondle me thus even when
my eyes are open; that has not the least effect upon me."

At these words the poor seneschal, taking the little dagger
which was on the table by the bed, gave it to her, saying
with passion—

"My darling, kill me, or let me believe that you love me a little!"

"Yes, yes," said she, quite frightened, "I will try to love you much."

Behold how this young maidenhood made itself master of this old man, and subdued him, for in the name of the sweet face of Venus, Blanche, endowed with the natural artfulness of women, made her old Bruyn come and go like a miller's mule.

"My good Bruyn, I want this! Bruyn, I want that—go on Bruyn!" Bruyn! Bruyn! and always Bruyn in such a way that Bruyn was more worn out by the clemency of his wife than he would have been by her unkindness. She turned his brain, wishing that everything should be in scarlet, making him turn everything topsy-turvy at the least movement of her eyebrow, and when she was sad the seneschal, distracted, would say to everything from his judicial seat, "Hang him!" Another would have died like a fly at this conflict with the maid's innocence, but Bruyn was of such an iron nature that it was difficult to finish him off. One evening that Blanche had turned the house upside-down, upset the men and the beasts, and would by her aggravating humour have made the eternal father desperate—he who has such an infinite treasure of patience since he endures us—she said to the seneschal while getting into bed, "My good Bruyn, I have low down fancies, that bite and prick me; thence they rise into my heart, inflame my brain, incite me therein to evil deeds, and in the night I dream of the monk of the Carneaux."

"My dear," replied the seneschal, "these are deviltries and temptations against which the monks and nuns know how to defend themselves. If you will gain salvation, go and confess to the worthy Abbot of Marmoustiers, our neighbour; he will advise you well and will holily direct you in the good way."

"To-morrow I will go," said she.

And indeed directly it was day, she trotted off to the monastery of the good brethren, who marvelled to see among them so pretty a lady; committed more than one sin through her in the evening, and for the present led her with great ceremony to their reverend abbot.

Blanche found the said good man in a private garden near the high rock under a flowery arcade, and remained stricken with respect at the countenance of the holy man, although she was accustomed not to think much of grey hairs.

"God preserve you, Madame; what come you to seek of one so near death, you so young?"

"Your precious advice," said she, saluting him with a courtesy; "and if it will please you to guide so undutiful a sheep, I shall be well content to have so wise a confessor."

"My daughter," answered the monk, with whom old Bruyn had arranged this hypocrisy and the part to play, "if I had not the chills of a hundred winters upon this unthatched head, I should not dare to listen to your sins, but say on; if you enter paradise, it will be through me."

Then the seneschal's wife set forth the small fry of her stock in hand, and when she was purged of her little iniquities, she came to the postscript of her confession.

"Ah, my father!" said she, "I must confess to you that I am daily exercised by the desire to have a child. Is it wrong?"

"No," said the abbot.

But she went on, "It is by nature commanded to my husband not to draw from his wealth to bring about his poverty, as the old women say by the way."

"Then," replied the priest, "you must live virtuously and abstain from all thoughts of this kind."

"But I have heard it professed by the Lady of Jallanges, that it was not a sin when from it one derived neither profit nor pleasure."

"There always is pleasure," said the abbot, "but don't count upon the child as a profit. Now fix this in your understanding, that it will always be a mortal sin before God and a crime before men to bring forth a child through the embraces of a man to whom one is not ecclesiastically married. Thus those women who offend against the holy laws of marriage, suffer great penalties in the other world, are in the power of horrible monsters with sharp and tearing claws, who thrust them into flaming furnaces in remembrance of the fact that here below they have warmed their hearts a little more than was lawful."

Thereupon Blanche scratched her ear, and having thought to herself for a little while, she said to the priest, "How then did the Virgin Mary?"

"Ah!" replied the abbot, "that is a mystery."

"And what is a mystery?"

"A thing that cannot be explained, and which one ought to believe without inquiring into it."

"Well then," said she, "cannot I perform a mystery?"

"This one," said the abbot, "only happened once, because it was the Son of God."

"Alas! my father, is it then the will of God that I should die, or that from wise and sound comprehension, my brain should be turned? Of this there is great danger. Now in me something moves and excites me, and I am no longer in my senses. I care for nothing, and to find a man I would leap the walls, dash over the fields without shame and tear my things into tatters, only to see that which so much excited the monk of the Carneaux; and during these passions which work and prick my mind and body, there is neither God, devil, nor husband. I spring, I run, I smash up the wash-tubs, the pots, the farm implements, the fowl-house, the household things, and everything, in a way that I cannot describe. But I dare not confess to you all my misdeeds, because speaking of them makes my mouth water, and the thing with which God curses me makes me itch dreadfully. If this folly bites and pricks me, and slays my virtue, will God who has placed this great love in my body, condemn me to perdition?"

At this question it was the priest who scratched his ear, quite dumbfounded by the lamentations, profound wisdom, controversies and intelligence that this virginity secreted.

"My daughter," said he, "God has distinguished us from the beasts and made us a paradise to gain, and for this given us reason, which is a rudder to steer us against tempests and our ambitious desires, and there is a means of easing the imaginations in one's brains by fasting, excessive labours and other virtues; and instead of frisking and fretting like a child let loose from school, you should pray to the Virgin, sleep on a hard board, attend to your household duties, and never be idle."

"Ah! my father, when I am at church in my seat, I see neither the priest nor the altar, only the infant Jesus, who brings the thing into my head. But to finish, if my head is turned and my mind wanders, I am in the lime-twigs of love."

"If thus you were," said the abbot imprudently, "you would be in the position of Saint Lidoire, who in a deep sleep one day, one leg here and one leg there, through the great heat and scantily attired, was approached by a young man full of mischief, who dexterously gave her a child, and as of this trick the saint was thoroughly ignorant, and much surprised at being brought to bed, thinking that her unusual size was a serious malady, she did penance for it as a venial sin, as she had no pleasure in this wicked business, according to the statement of the wicked man, who said upon the scaffold where he was executed, that the saint had in nowise stirred."

"Oh, my father," said she, "be sure that I should not stir more than she did!"

With this statement she went away prettily and gracefully, smiling and thinking how she could commit a venial sin. On her return from the great monastery, she saw in the courtyard of her castle the little Jallanges, who under the superintendence of an old groom was turning and wheeling about on a fine horse, bending with the movements of the animal, dismounting, and mounting again by vaults and leaps most gracefully, and with lissome thighs, so pretty, so dexterous, so upright as to be indescribable, so much so, that he would have made the Queen Lucre long for him, she who killed herself from being contaminated against her will.

"Ah!" said Blanche, "if only this page were fifteen, I would go to sleep comfortably very near to him."

Then, in spite of the too great youth of this charming servitor, during the collation and supper, she eyed frequently the black hair, the white skin, the grace of René, above all his eyes, where was an abundance of limpid warmth and a great fire of life, which he was afraid to shoot out—child that he was.

Now in the evening, as the seneschal's wife sat thoughtfully in her chair in the corner of the fireplace, old Bruyn interrogated her as to her trouble.

"I am thinking," said she, "that you must have fought

the battles of love very early, to be thus completely broken up."

"Oh!" replied he, smiling like all old men questioned upon their amorous remembrances, "at the age of thirteen and a half I had overcome the scruples of my mother's waiting woman."

Blanche wished to hear nothing more, but believed the page René should be equally advanced, and she was quite joyous, and practised little allurements on the good man, and wallowed silently in her desire, like a cake which is being floured.

HOW AND BY WHOM THE SAID CHILD WAS PROCURED

The seneschal's wife did not think long over the best way quickly to awaken the love of the page, and had soon discovered the natural ambuscade in the which the most wary are taken. This is how: at the warmest hour of the day the good man took his siesta after the Saracen fashion, a habit in which he had never failed since his return from the Holy Land. During this time Blanche was alone in the grounds, where the women work at their minor occupations, such as broidering and stitching, and often remained in the rooms looking after the washing, putting the clothes tidy, or running about at will. Then she appointed this quiet hour to complete the education of the page, making him read books and say his prayers. Now on the morrow, when at the midday hour the seneschal slept, succumbing to the sun which warms with its most luminous rays the slopes of Roche-Corbon, so much so that one is obliged to sleep, unless annoyed, upset, and continually roused by an uneasy virginity. Blanche then gracefully perched herself in the great seignorial chair of her good man, which she did not find any too high, since she counted upon the chances of perspective. The cunning jade settled herself dexterously therein, like a swallow in its nest, and leant her head maliciously upon her arm like a child that sleeps; but in making her preparations, she opened fond eyes, that smiled and winked in advance of the little secret thrills, sneezes, squints, and trances of the page who was about to lie at her feet, separated from her by the jump of an old flea; and in fact she advanced so much and so near the square of velvet where the poor child should kneel, whose life and soul she trifled with, that had he been a saint of stone, his glance would have been constrained to follow the flexuosities of the dress in order to admire and readmire the perfections and beauties of the shapely leg, which moulded the white stocking of the seneschal's lady. Thus it was certain that a weak varlet would be taken in a snare, wherein the most vigorous knight would willingly have succumbed. When she had turned, returned, placed, and displaced her body, and found the snare would be most effective, she cried, gently, "René!" René who she well knew was in the guardroom, did not fail to run in and quickly thrust his brown head between the tapestries of the door.

"What do you please to wish?" said the page. And he held with great respect in his hand his shaggy scarlet cap, less red than his fresh dimpled cheeks.

"Come hither," replied she, under her breath, for the child attracted her so strongly that she was quite overcome. And forsooth there were no jewels so sparkling as the eyes of René, no vellum whiter than his skin, no woman more exquisite in shape—and so near to her desire, she found him still more sweetly formed—and was certain that the merry frolics of love would radiate well from all this youth, the warm sun, the silence, *et cetera*.

"Read me the litanies of Madame the Virgin," said she

to him, pushing an open book to him on her priedieu. "Let me see if you are well taught by your master."

"Do you not think the Virgin beautiful?" asked she of him, smiling when he held the illuminated prayer-book in which glowed the silver and the gold.

"It is a painting," replied he, timidly, and casting a litle glance upon his so gracious mistress.

"Read! read!"

Then René began to recite the so sweet and so mystic litanies, but you may imagine that the *"Ora pro nobis"* of Blanche became still fainter and fainter, like the sound of the horn in the woodlands, and when the page went on, "Oh, Rose of mystery," the lady, who certainly heard distinctly, replied by a gentle sigh. Thereupon René suspected that his mistress slept. Then he commenced to cover her with his regard, admiring her at his leisure, and had then no wish to utter any anthem save the anthem of love. His happiness made his heart leap and bound into his throat; thus, as was but natural, these two innocences burned one against the other, but if they could have foreseen never would have intermingled. René feasted his eyes, planning in his mind a thousand fruitions of love that brought the water into his mouth. In his ecstasy he let his book fall, which made him feel as sheepish as a monk surprised at a child's tricks; but also from that he knew that Blanche was sound asleep, for she did not stir, and the wily jade would not have opened her eyes even at the greatest dangers, and reckoned on something else falling as well as the book of prayer.

There is no worse longing than the longing of woman in a certain condition. Now, the page noticed his lady's foot, which was delicately slippered in a little laced shoe of a delicate blue colour. She had angularly placed it on a footstool, since she was too high in the seneschal's chair.

This foot was of narrow proportions, delicately curved, as broad as two fingers, and as long as a sparrow, tail included, small at the top—a true foot of delight, a virginal foot that merited a kiss as a robber does the gallows; a roguish foot; a foot wanton enough to damn an archangel; an ominous foot; a devilishly enticing foot, which gave one a desire to make two new ones just like it to perpetuate in this lower world the glorious works of God. The page was tempted to take the shoe from this persuasive foot. To accomplish this his eyes, glowing with the fire of his age, went swiftly, like the clapper of a bell, from this said foot of delectation to the sleeping countenance of his lady and mistress, listening to her slumber, drinking in her respiration again and again, and did not know where it would be sweetest to plant a kiss —whether on the ripe red lips of the seneschal's wife or on this speaking foot. At length, from respect or fear, or perhaps from great love, he chose the foot, and kissed it hastily, like a maiden who dares not. Then immediately he took up his book, feeling his red cheeks redder still, and exercised with his pleasure, he cried like a blind man—"*Janua cœli,* gate of Heaven." But Blanche did not move, making sure that the page would go from foot to knee, and thence to "Janua cœli, the gate of Heaven." She was greatly disappointed when the litanies finished without any other mischief, and René, believing he had had enough happiness for one day, ran out of the room quite lively, richer from this hardy kiss than a robber who has robbed the poor-box.

When the seneschal's lady was alone, she thought to herself that the page would be rather a long time at his task if he amused himself with singing of the *Magnificat* at matins. Thus she determined on the morrow to raise her foot a little, and then to bring to light those hidden beauties that are called perfect in Touraine, because they take no hurt in the open air, and are always fresh. You can imagine that the page, burned by his desire and his imagination, heated by the day before, awaiting impatiently the hour to read in this breviary of gallantry, and was called; and the conspiracy of the litanies commenced again, and Blanche did not fail to fall asleep. This time the said René fondled with his hand the pretty limb, and even ventured so far as to verify if the polished knee and something else were satin. At this sight the poor child, armed against his desire, so great was his fear, dared only make brief devotion and curt caresses, and although he kissed softly this fair surface, he remained bashful, the which, feeling by the senses of her soul and the intelligence of her body, the seneschal's lady who took great care not to move, called out to him—"Ah, René, I am asleep."

Hearing what he believed to be a stern reproach, the page frightened ran away, leaving the books, the task, and all. Thereupon, the seneschal's better half added this prayer to the litany—"Holy Virgin, how difficult children are to make."

At dinner her page perspired all down his back while waiting on his lady and her lord; but he was very much surprised when he received from Blanche the most shameless of all glances that ever woman cast, and very pleasant and powerful it was, seeing that it changed this child into a man of courage. Now, the same evening Bruyn staying a little longer than was his custom in his own apartment, the page went in search of Blanche, and found her asleep, and made her dream a beautiful dream.

He relieved her of what weighed so heavily upon her, and so plentifully bestowed upon her the sweets of love, that the surplus would have sufficed to render two others blessed with the joys of maternity. So then the minx, seizing the

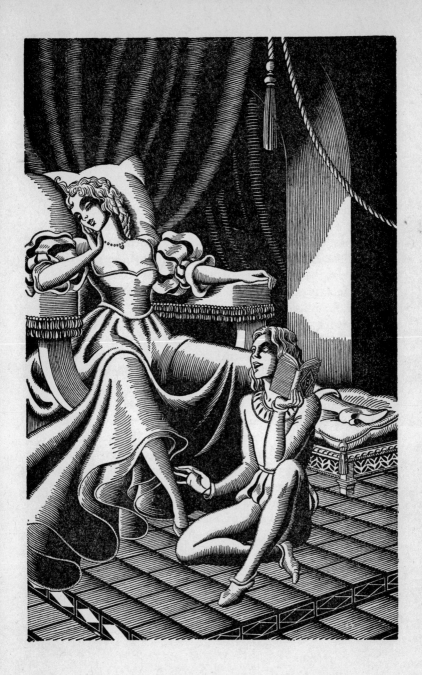

page by the head and squeezing him to her, cried out—
"Oh, René! thou hast awakened me!"

And in fact, there was no sleep could stand against it,
and they found that saints must sleep very soundly. From
this business, without other mystery, and by a benign faculty which is the assisting principle of spouses, the sweet
and graceful plumage, suitable to cuckolds, was placed upon
the head of the good husband without his experiencing the
slightest shock.

After this sweet repast, the seneschal's lady took kindly
to her siesta after the French fashion, while Bruyn took his
according to the Saracen. But by the said siesta she learned
how the good youth of the page had a better taste than that
of the old seneschal, and at night she buried herself in
the sheets far away from her husband, whom she found
strong and stale. And from sleeping and waking up in the
day, from taking siestas and saying litanies, the seneschal's
wife felt growing within her that treasure for which she
had so often and so ardently sighed; but now she liked more
the commencement than the fructifying of it.

You may be sure that René knew how to read, not only
in books, but in the eyes of his sweet lady, for whom he
would have leapt into a flaming pile, had it been her wish
he should do so. When well and amply, more than a hundred times, the train had been laid by them, the little lady
became anxious about her soul and the future of her friend
the page. Now one rainy day, as they were playing at touch-
tag, like two children, innocent from head to foot, Blanche,
who was always caught, said to him—

"Come here, René; do you know that while I have committed only venial sins because I was asleep, you have
committed mortal ones?"

"Ah! Madame!" said he, "where then will God stow away all the damned if that is to sin!"

Blanche burst out laughing, and kissed his forehead.

"Be quiet, you naughty boy; it is a question of paradise, and we must live there together if you wish always to be with me."

"Oh, my paradise is here."

"Leave off," said she. "You are a little wretch—a scapegrace who does not think of that which I love—yourself! You do not know that I am with child, and that in a little while I shall be no more able to conceal it than my nose. Now, what will the abbot say? What will my lord say? He will kill you if he puts himself in a passion. My advice is, little one, that you go to the Abbot of Marmoustiers, confess your sins to him, asking him to see what had better be done concerning my seneschal."

"Alas," said the artful page, "if I tell the secret of our joys, he will put his interdict upon our love."

"Very likely," said she; "but thy happiness in the other world is a thing so precious to me."

"Do you wish it, my darling?"

"Yes," replied she, rather faintly.

"Well, I will go, but sleep again that I may bid thee adieu."

And the couple recited the litany of Farewells as if they had both foreseen that their love must finish in its April. And on the morrow, more to save his dear lady than to save himself, and also to obey her, René de Jallanges set out towards the great monastery.

HOW THE SAID LOVE-SIN WAS REPENTED OF AND LED TO GREAT MOURNING

"Good God!" cried the abbot, when the page had chanted

the Kyrie eleison of his sweet sins, "thou art the accomplice
of a great felony, and thou hast betrayed thy lord. Dost
thou know, page of darkness, that for this thou wilt burn
through all eternity? and dost thou know what it is to lose
for ever the heaven above for a perishable and changeful
moment here below? Unhappy wretch! I see thee precipi-
tated for ever in the gulfs of hell unless thou payest to God
in this world that which thou owest him for such offence."

Thereupon, the good old abbot, who was of that flesh
of which saints are made, and who had great authority in
the country of Touraine, terrified the young man by a heap
of representations, Christian discourses, remembrances of
the commandments of the Church, and a thousand eloquent
things—as many as a devil could say in six weeks to seduce
a maiden—but so many that René, who was in the loyal
fervor of innocence, made his submission to the good abbot.
The said abbot, wishing to make for ever a good and virtuous man of this child, now in a fair way to be a wicked one,
commanded him first to go and prostrate himself before his
lord, to confess his conduct to him, and then if he escaped
from this confession, to depart instantly for the Crusades,
and go straight to the Holy Land, where he should remain
fifteen years of the time appointed to give battle to the
Infidels.

"Alas, my reverend father," said he, quite unmoved, "will
fifteen years be enough to acquit me of so much pleasure?
Ah! if you but knew, I have had joy enough for a thousand
years."

"God will be generous. Go," replied the old abbot, "and
sin no more. On this account *ego te absolvo.*"

Poor René returned thereupon with great contrition to
the castle of Roche-Corbon, and the first person he met was
the seneschal, who was polishing up his arms, helmets,

gauntlets, and other things. He was sitting on a great marble bench in the open air, and was amusing himself by making shine again the splendid trappings which brought back to him the merry pranks in the Holy Land, the good jokes, and the wenches, *et cetera*. When René fell upon his knees before him the good lord was much astonished.

"What is it?" said he.

"My lord," replied René, "order these people to retire."

Which the servants having done, the page confessed his fault, recounting how he had assailed his lady in her sleep, and that for certain he had made her a mother in imitation of the man and the saint, and came by order of the confessor to put himself at the disposition of the offended person. Having said which, René de Jallanges cast down his lovely eyes, which had produced all the mischief, and remained abashed, prostrate without fear, his arms hanging down, his head bare, awaiting his punishment, and humbling himself to God. The seneschal was not so white that he could not become whiter, and now he blanched like linen newly dried, remaining dumb with passion. And this old man, who had not in his veins the vital force to procreate a child, found in this moment of fury more vigour than was necessary to undo a man. He seized with his hairy right hand his heavy club, lifted it, brandished it, and adjusted it so easily that you could have thought it a bowl at a game of skittles, to bring it down upon the pale forehead of the said René, who, knowing that he was greatly in fault toward his lord, remained placid, and stretching his neck, thought that he was about to expiate his sin for his sweetheart in this world and in the other.

But his fair youth, and all the natural seductions of this sweet crime, found grace before the tribunal of the heart of this old man, although Bruyn was still severe, and throw-

ing his club away on to a dog who was catching beetles, he
cried out, "May a thousand million claws, tear during all
eternity, all the entrails of him, who made him, who planted
the oak, that made the chair, on which thou hast antlered me
—and the same to those who engendered thee, cursed page
of misfortune! Get thee to the devil, whence thou camest—
go out from before me, from the castle, from the country,
and stay not here one moment more than is necessary, otherwise I will surely prepare for thee a death by slow fire that
shall make thee curse twenty times in an hour thy villainous
and ribald partner!"

Hearing the commencement of these little speeches of the
seneschal, whose youth came back in his oaths, the page
ran away, escaping the rest: and he did well. Bruyn, burning with a fierce rage, gained the gardens speedily, reviling
everything by the way, striking and swearing; he even
knocked over three large pans held by one of his servants,
who was carrying the mess to the dogs, and he was so beside
himself that he would have killed a labourer for a "thank
you." He soon perceived his unmaidenly maiden, who was
looking towards the road to the monastery, waiting for the
page, and unaware that she would never see him again.

"Ah, my lady! by the devil's red three-pronged fork,
am I a swallower of tarrididdles and a child, to believe that
you are so fashioned that a page can behave in this manner
and you not know it? By the death! By the head! By the
blood!"

"Hold!" she replied, seeing that the mine was sprung,
"I knew it well enough, but as you had not instructed me
in these matters I thought that I was dreaming!"

The great ire of the seneschal melted like snow in the
sun, for the direst anger of God himself would have vanished at a smile from Blanche.

"May a thousand millions of devils carry off this alien child! I swear that——"

"There! there! do not swear," said she. "If it is not yours, it is mine; and the other night did you not tell me you loved everything that came from me?"

Thereupon she ran on with such a lot of arguments, hard words, complaints, quarrels, tears, and other pater-nosters of women; such as—firstly, the estates would not have to be returned to the king; that never had a child been brought more innocently into the world, that this, that that, a thousand things; until the good cuckold relented, and Blanche, seizing a propitious interruption, said——

"And where is the page?"

"Gone to the devil!"

"What, have you killed him?" said she. She turned pale and tottered.

Bruyn did not know what would become of him when he saw thus fall all the happiness of his old age, and he would to save her have shewn her this page. He ordered him to be sought, but René had run off at full speed, fearing he should be killed; and departed for the lands beyond the seas, in order to accomplish his vow of religion. When Blanche had learned from the above-mentioned abbot the penitence imposed upon her well beloved, she fell into a state of great melancholy, saying at times, "Where is he, the poor unfortunate, who is in the middle of great dangers for love of me?"

And always kept on asking, like a child who gives its mother no rest until its request be granted it. At these lamentations the poor seneschal, feeling himself to blame, endeavoured to do a thousand things, putting one out of the question, in order to make Blanche happy; but nothing was equal to the sweet caresses of the page. However, she had one day the child so much desired. You may be sure that was a fine festival for the good cuckold, for the resemblance to the father was distinctly engraved upon the face of this sweet fruit of love. Blanche consoled herself greatly, and picked up again a little of her old gaiety and flower of innocence, which rejoiced the aged hours of the seneschal. From constantly seeing the little one run about, watching its laughs answer those of the countess, he finished by loving it, and would have been in a great rage with any one who had not believed him its father.

Now as the adventure of Blanche and her page had not been carried beyond the castle, it was related throughout Touraine that Messire Bruyne had still found himself sufficiently in funds to afford a child. Intact remained the virtue of Blanche, and by the quintessence of instruction drawn by her from the natural reservoir of women, she recognized how necessary it was to be silent concerning the venial sin with which her child was covered. So she became modest and good, and was cited as a virtuous person. And then to make use of him she experimented on the goodness of her good man, and without giving him leave to go farther than her chin, since she looked upon herself as belonging to René, Blanche, in return for the flowers of age which Bruyn offered her, coddled him, smiled upon him, kept him merry, and fondled him with pretty ways and tricks, which good wives bestow upon the husbands they deceive; and all so well, that the seneschal did not wish to die, squatted comfortably in his chair, and the more he lived the more he became partial to life. But to be brief, one night he died without knowing where he was going, for he said to Blanche, "Ho! ho! my dear, I see thee no longer! Is it night?"

It was the death of the just, and he had well merited it as a reward for his labours in the Holy Land.

Blanche held for this death a great and true mourning, weeping for him as one weeps for one's father. She remained melancholy, without wishing to lend her ear to music of a second wedding, for which she was praised by all good people, who knew not that she had a husband in her heart, a life in hope; but she was the greater part of her time widow in fact and widow in heart, because hearing no news of her lover at the Crusades, the poor countess reputed him dead, and during certain nights seeing him wounded and lying at full length, she would wake up in tears. She lived thus for fourteen years in the remembrance of one day of happiness. Finally, one day when she had with her certain ladies of Touraine, and they were talking together after dinner, behold her little boy, who was at that time about thirteen and a half, and resembled René more than it is allowable for a child to resemble his father, and had nothing of the Sire Bruyn about him but his name— behold the little one, a madcap and pretty like his mother, who came in from the garden, running, perspiring, panting, jumping, scattering all things in his way, after the uses and customs of infancy, and who ran straight to his well-beloved mother, jumped into her lap, and interrupting the conversation, cried out—

"Oh, mother, I want to speak to you, I have seen in the courtyard a pilgrim, who squeezed me very tight."

"Ah!" cried the chatelaine, hurrying towards one of the servants who had charge of the young count and watched over his precious days, "I have forbidden you ever to leave my son in the hands of strangers, not even in those of the holiest man in the world. You quit my service."

"Alas! my lady," replied the old equerry, quite overcome

"this one wished him no harm for he wept while kissing him passionately."

"He wept?" said she; "ah! it's the father."

Having said which, she leaned her head upon the chair in which she was sitting, and which you may be sure was the chair in which she had sinned.

Hearing these strange words, the ladies were so surprised that at first they did not perceive that the seneschal's widow was dead, without its ever being known if her sudden death was caused by her sorrow at the departure of her lover, who, faithful to his vow, did not wish to see her, or from great joy at his return and the hope of getting the interdict removed which the Abbot of Marmoustiers had placed upon their loves. And there was great mourning for her, for the Sire de Jallanges lost his spirits when he saw his lady laid in the ground, and became a monk of Marmoustiers, which at that time was called by some Maimoustier, as much as to say *Maius Monasterium,* the largest monastery, and it was indeed the finest in all France.

THE KING'S SWEETHEART

THERE lived at this time at the forges of the Pont-au-Change, a goldsmith whose daughter was talked about in Paris on account of her great beauty, and renowned above all things for her exceeding gracefulness. There were those who sought her favours by the usual tricks of love, but others offerd large sums of money to the father to give them his daughter in lawful wedlock, the which pleased him not a little.

One of his neighbours, a parliamentary advocate, who by selling his cunning devices to the public had acquired as many lands as a dog has fleas, took it into his head to offer the said father a domain in consideration of his consent to this marriage, which he ardently desired to undertake. To this arrangement our goldsmith was nothing loth. He bargained away his daughter, without taking into consideration the fact that her patched-up old suitor had the features of an ape and had scarcely a tooth in his jaws. The smell which emanated from his mouth did not however disturb his own nostrils, although he was filthy and high flavoured, as are all those who pass their lives amid the smoke of chimneys, yellow parchment, and other black proceedings. Immediately the sweet girl saw him she exclaimed, "Great Heaven! I would rather not have him."

"That concerns me not," said the father, who had taken a violent fancy to the proffered domain. "I give him to you for a husband. You must get on as well as you can together.

That is his business now, and his duty is to make himself agreeable to you."

"Is it so?" said she. "Well then, before I obey your orders I'll let him know what he may expect."

And the same evening, after supper, when the lovesick man of law was pleading his cause, telling her he was mad for her, and promising her a life of ease and luxury, she, taking him up, quickly remarked—

"My father has sold me to you, but if you take me, you will make a bad bargain, seeing that I would rather offer myself to the passers-by than to you. I promise you a disloyalty that shall only finish with death—yours or mine."

Then she began to weep, like all young maidens will before they become experienced, for afterwards they never cry with their eyes. The good advocate took this strange behaviour for one of those artifices by which the women seek to fan the flames of love and turn the devotion of their admirers into the more tender caress and more daring osculation that speak a husband's right. So that the knave took little notice of it, but laughing at the complaints of the charming creature, asked her to fix the day.

"To-morrow," replied she, "for the sooner this odious marriage takes place the sooner I shall be free to have gallants and to lead the gay life of those who love where it pleases them."

Thereupon this foolish fellow—as firmly fixed as a fly in a glue pot—went away, made his preparations, spoke at the Palace, ran to the High Court, bought dispensations, and conducted his purchase more quickly than he had ever done one before, thinking only of the lovely girl. Meanwhile the king, who had just returned from a journey, heard nothing spoken of at court but the marvellous beauty of the jeweller's daughter who had refused a thousand crowns from this one, snubbed that one; in fact, would yield to no one, but turned up her nose at the finest young men of the city, gentlemen who would have forfeited their seat in paradise only to possess one day, this little dragon of virtue.

The good king, who was a judge of such game, strolled into the town, passed the forges, and entered the goldsmith's shop, for the purpose of buying jewels for the lady of his heart, but at the same time to bargain for the most precious jewel in the shop. The king not taking a fancy to the jewels, or they not being to his taste, the good man looked in a secret drawer for a big white diamond.

"Sweetheart," said he, to the daughter, while her father's nose was buried in the drawer, "sweetheart, you were not made to sell precious stones, but to receive them, and if you were to give me all the little rings in the place to choose from, I know one that many here are mad for; that pleases me; to which I should ever be subject and servant; and whose price the whole kingdom of France could never pay."

"Ah, sire!" replied the maid, "I shall be married to-morrow, but if you will lend me the dagger that is in your belt, I will defend my honour, and you shalt take it, that the gospel may be observed wherein it says, 'Render unto Cæsar the things which be Cæsar's.'"

Immediately the king gave her the little dagger, and her brave reply rendered him so amorous that he lost his appetite. He had an apartment prepared, intending to lodge his new lady-love in the Rue à l'Hirundelle, in one of his palaces.

And now behold my advocate, in a great hurry to get married, to the disgust of his rivals, leading his bride to the altar to the clang of bells and the sound of music, so timed as to provoke the qualms of diarrhœa. In the evening, after the ball, comes he into the nuptial chamber, where should be reposing his lovely bride. No longer is she a lovely bride—but a fury—a wild she-devil, who, seated in an arm-chair, refuses her share of her lord's couch, and sits defiantly before the fire warming at the same time her ire and her charms. The good husband, quite astonished, kneels down gently before her, inviting her to the first passage of arms in that charming battle which heralds a first night of love; but she utters not a word, and when he tries to raise her garment, only just to glance at the charms that have cost him so dear, she gives him a slap that makes his bones rattle, and refuses to utter a syllable.

This amusement, however, by no means displeased our friend the advocate, who saw at the end of his troubles that which you can as well imagine as did he; so played he his share of the game manfully, taking cheerfully the punish-ment bestowed upon him. By so much hustling about, scuffling, and struggling he managed at last to tear away a sleeve, to slit a petticoat, until he was able to place his hand upon the lovely spot he coveted. This bold endeavour brought Madame to her feet, and drawing the king's dagger, "What would you with me?" she cried.

"Everything," answered he.

"Ha! I should be a great fool to give myself against my inclinations! If you fancied you would find my virtue un-armed you made a great error. Behold the poniard of the king, with which I will kill you if you make the semblance of a step toward me."

So saying, she took a cinder, and having still her eye upon her lord she drew a circle on the floor, adding, "These are the confines of the king's domain. Beware how you pass them."

The advocate, with whose ideas of love-making the dagger sadly interfered, stood quite discomfited, but at the same time he heard the cruel speech of his tormentor he caught sight through the slits and tears in her robe of a sweet sample of a plump white thigh, and such voluptuous specimens of hidden mysteries, *et cetera,* that death seemed sweet to him if he could only taste of them a little. So that he rushed within the domain of the king, saying, "I mind not death." In fact he came with such force that his charmer fell backwards on to the bed, but keeping her presence of mind she defended herself so gallantly that the advocate enjoyed no further advantage than a knock at the door that would not admit him, and he gained as well a little stab from the poniard which did not wound him deeply, so that it did not cost him very dearly, his attack upon the realm of his sovereign. But maddened with this slight advantage, he cried, "I cannot live without the possession of that lovely body, and those marvels of love. Kill me then!"

And again he attacked the royal preserves. The young beauty, whose head was full of the king, was not even touched by this great love, said gravely, "If you menace me further, it is not you but myself I will kill." She glared at him so savagely that the poor man was quite terrified, and commenced to deplore the evil hour in which he had taken her to wife, and thus the night which should have been so joyous, was passed in tears, lamentations, prayers and ejaculations. In vain he tempted her with promises; she should eat out of gold, she should be a great lady, he would buy houses and lands for her. Oh! if she would only let him break one lance with her in the sweet conflict of love, he would leave her for ever and pass the remainder of his life according to her fantasy. But she, still unyielding, said she would permit him to die, and that was the only thing he could do to please her.

"I have not deceived you," said she. "Agreeable to my

promise, I shall give myself to the king, making you a present of the pedlars, chance passers, and street loungers with whom I threatened you."

When the day broke she put on her wedding garments and waited patiently till the poor husband had to depart to his offices on clients' business, and then ran out into the town to seek the king. But she had not gone a bowshot from the house before one of the king's servants who had watched the house from dawn, stopped her with the question, "Do you not seek the king?"

"Yes," said she.

"Good; then allow me to be your good friend," said the subtle courtier. "I ask your aid and protection, as now I give you mine."

With that he told her what sort of man the king was, which was his weak side, that he was passionate one day and silent the next, that she would be luxuriously lodged and well kept, but that she must keep the king well in hand; in short, he chatted so pleasantly that the time passed quickly until she found herself in the Hôtel de l'Hirundelle where afterwards lived Madame d'Estampes. The poor husband shed scalding tears, when he found his little bird had flown, and became melancholy and pensive. His friends and neighbours edified his ears with as many taunts and jeers as Saint Jacques had the honour of receiving in Compostella, but the poor fellow took it so to heart, that at last they tried rather to assuage his grief. These artful compeers by a species of legal chicanery, decreed that the good man was not a cuckold, seeing that his wife had refused consummation, and if the planter of horns had been any one but the king, the said marriage might have been dissolved; but the amorous spouse was wretched unto death at my lady's trick. However, he left her to the king, determining one day to

have her to himself, and thinking that a life-long shame
would not be too dear a payment for a night with her. One
must love well to love like that, eh? and there are many
worldly ones, who mock at such affection. But he, still
thinking of her, neglected his cases and his clients, his robberies and everything. He went to the palace like a miser
searching for a lost sixpence, bowed down, melancholy, and
absent-minded, so much so, that one day he relieved himself
against the robe of a counsellor, believing all the while
he stood against a wall. Meanwhile, the beautiful girl was
loved night and day by the king, who could not tear himself
from her embraces, because in amorous play she was so
excellent, knowing as well how to fan the flame of love as
to extinguish it—to-day snubbing him, to-morrow petting
him, never the same, and with a thousand little tricks to
charm an ardent lover.

A lord of Bridoré killed himself through her, because
she would not receive his embraces, although he offered her
his land, Bridoré in Touraine. Of these gallants of Touraine, who gave an estate for one tilt with love's lance,
there are none left. This death made the fair one sad, and
since her confessor laid the blame of it upon her, she determined for the future to accept all domains and secretly ease
their owners' amorous pains for the better saving of their
souls from perdition. 'Twas thus she commenced to build
up that great fortune which made her a person of consideration in the town. By this means she prevented many gallant
gentlemen from perishing, playing her game so well, and
inventing such fine stories, that his Majesty little guessed
how much she aided him in securing the happiness of his
subjects. The fact is, she had such a hold over him that she
could have made him believe the floor was the ceiling, which
was perhaps easier for him to think than any one else seeing

that at the Rue d'Hirundelle my lord king passed the greater portion of his time embracing her always as though he would see if such a lovely article would wear away: but he wore himself out first, poor man, seeing that he eventually died from excess of love. Although she took care to grant her favours only to the best and noblest in the court, and that such occasions were rare as miracles, there were not wanting those among her enemies and rivals who declared that for 10,000 crowns a simple gentleman might taste the pleasures of his sovereign, which was false above all falseness, for when her lord taxed her with it, did she not reply, "Abominable wretches! curse the devils who put this idea in your head! I never yet did have man who spent less than 30,000 crowns upon me."

The king, although vexed, could not repress a smile, and kept her on a month to silence scandal. At last, la demoiselle de Pisseleu, anxious to obtain her place, brought about her ruin. Many would have liked to be ruined in the same way, seeing she was taken by a young lord who was happy with her, the fires of love in her being still unquenched. But to take up my thread again. One day that the king's sweetheart was passing through the town in her litter to buy laces, furs, velvets, broideries, and other ammunition, and so charmingly attired, and looking so lovely, that any one, especially the clerks, would have believed the heavens were open above them, behold, her good man, who comes upon her near the old cross. She, at that time lazily swinging her charming little foot over the side of the litter, drew in her head as though she had seen an adder. She was a good wife, for I know some who would have proudly passed their husbands, to their shame and to the great disrespect of conjugal rights.

"What is the matter?" asked one M. de Lannoy, who humbly accompanied her.

"Nothing," she whispered; "but that person is my husband. Poor man, how changed he looks. Formerly he was the picture of a monkey; to-day he is the very image of Job."

The poor advocate stood open-mouthed. His heart beat rapidly at the sight of that little foot—of that wife so wildly loved.

Observing which, the Sire de Lannoy said to him, with courtly insolence—

"If you are her husband, is that any reason you should stop her passage?"

At this she burst out laughing, and the good husband, instead of killing her bravely, shed scalding tears at that laugh which pierced his heart, his soul, his everything, so much that he nearly tumbled over an old citizen whom the sight of the king's sweetheart had driven against the wall. The aspect of this sweet flower, which had been his in the bud, but far from him had spread its lovely leaves; of the fairy figure, the voluptuous bust—all this made the poor advocate more wretched and more mad for her than it is possible to express in words. You must have been madly in love with a woman who refused your advances thoroughly to understand the agony of this unhappy man. Rare indeed is it to be so infatuated as was he. He swore that life, fortune, honour—all might go, but that for once at least he would be flesh to flesh with her, and make so grand a repast of her dainty body as would suffice him all his life. He passed the night saying, "Oh, yes; ah! I'll have her!" and "Curses, am I not her husband?" and "Devil take me," striking himself on the forehead and tossing about. There are chances and occasions which occur so opportunely in this world that little-minded men refuse them credence, saying they are supernatural, but men of high intellect know them to be true because they could not be invented. One of the chances came to the poor advocate, even the day after that terrible one which had been so sore a trial to him. One of his clients, a man of good renown, who had his audiences with the king, came one morning to the advocate, saying that he required immediately a large sum of money, about 12,000 crowns. To which the artful fellow replied, 12,000 crowns were not so often met at the corner of a street as that which often is seen at the corner of a street; that besides the sureties and guarantees of interest, it was necessary to find a man who had about him 12,000 crowns, and that those gentlemen were not numerous in Paris, big city as it was, and various other things of a like character the man of cunning remarked.

"Is it true, my lord, that you have a hungry and relentless creditor?" said he.

"Yes, yes," replied the other, "it concerns the mistress of the king. Don't breathe a syllable; but this evening, in consideration of 20,000 crowns, and my domain of Brie, I shall take her measure."

Upon this the advocate blanched, and the courtier perceived he touched a tender point. As he had only lately returned from the wars, he did not know that the lovely woman adored by the king had a husband.

"You appear ill," he said.

"I have a fever," replied the knave.

"But is it to her that you give the contract and the money?"

"Yes."

"Who then manages the bargain? Is it she also?"

"No," said the noble; "her little arrangements are con-

cluded through a servant of hers, the cleverest little ladies'
maid that ever was. She's sharper than mustard, and these
nights stolen from the king have lined her pocket well."

"I know a Lombard who could accommodate you. But
nothing can be done; of the 12,000 crowns you shall not
have a brass farthing if this same ladies' maid does not
come here to take the price of the article that is so great
an alchemist, that turns blood into gold, by Heaven!"

"It will be a good trick to make her sign the receipt,"
replied the lord, laughing.

The servant came faithfully to the rendezvous with the
advocate, who had begged the lord to bring her. The ducats
looked bright and beautiful. There they lay, all in a row, like
nuns going to vespers. Spread out upon the table they would
have made a donkey smile, even if he were being gutted
alive; so lovely, so splendid, were those brave noble young
piles. The good advocate, however, had prepared this view
for no ass, for the little hand-maiden looked longingly at the
golden heap, and muttered a prayer at the sight of them.
Seeing which, the husband whispered in her ear these golden
words, "These are for you."

"Ah!" said she; "I have never been so well paid."

"My dear," replied the dear man, "you shall have them
without being troubled with me"; and, turning her round,
"Your client has not told you who I am, eh? No? Learn
then, I am the husband of the lady whom the king has
debauched, and whom you serve. Carry her these crowns,
and come back here. I will hand over yours to you on a
condition which will be to your taste."

The servant did as she was bidden, and being very curious to know how she could get 12,000 crowns without
sleeping with the advocate, was very soon back again.

"Now, my little one," said he, "here are 12,000 crowns.

With that sum I could buy lands, men, women, and the conscience of three priests at least; so that I believe if I give it you I can have you, body, soul; and toe nails. And I shall have faith in you like an advocate. I expect that you will go to the lord who expects to pass the night with my wife, and you will deceive him, by telling him that the king is coming to supper with her, and that to-night he must seek his little amusements elsewhere. By so doing I shall be able to take his place and the king's."

"But how?" said she.

"Oh!" replied he; "I have bought you, you and your tricks. You won't have to look at these crowns twice without finding me a way to have my wife. In bringing this conjunction about you commit no sin. It is a work of piety to bring together two people whose hands only have been put one into the other, and that by the priest."

"By my faith, come," said she; "after supper the lights will be put out, and you can enjoy Madame if you remain silent. Luckily, on these joyful occasions she cries more than she speaks, and asks questions with her hands alone, for she is very modest, and does not like loose jokes, like the ladies of the Court."

"Oh," cried the advocate, "look, take the 12,000 crowns and I promise you twice as much more if I get by fraud that which belongs to me by right."

Then he arranged the hour, the door, the signal, and all; and the servant went away, bearing with her on the back of the mules the golden treasure wrung by fraud and trickery from the widow and the orphan, and they were all going to that place where everything goes—save our lives, which come from it. Now behold my advocate, who shaves himself, scents himself, goes without onions for dinner that his breath may be sweet, and does everything to make himself as presentable as a gallant signor. He gives himself the airs of a young dandy, tries to be lithe and frisky and to disguise his ugly face; he might try all he knew, he always smelt of the musty lawyer. He was not so clever as the pretty washerwoman of Portillon who one day wishing to appear at her best before one of her loves, got rid of a disagreeable odour in a manner well known to young women of an inventive turn of mind. But our crafty fellow fancied himself the nicest man in the world, although in spite of his drugs and perfumes he was really the nastiest. He dressed himself in his thinnest clothes although the cold pinched him like a rope collar, and sallied forth, quickly gaining the Rue d'Hirundelle. There he had to wait some time. But just as he was beginning to think he had been made a fool of, and just as it was quite dark, the maid came down and opened the door to him and the good husband slipped gleefully into the king's apartment. The girl locked him carefully in a cupboard that was close to his wife's bed, and through a crack he feasted his eyes upon her beauty, for she undressed herself before the fire, and put on a thin nightgown, through which her charms were plainly visible. Believing herself alone with her maid she made those little jokes that women will when undressing. "Am I not worth 20,000 crowns to-night? Is that overpaid with a castle in Brie?"

And saying this she gently raised two white outposts firm as rocks, which had well sustained many assaults, seeing they had been furiously attacked and had not softened. "My shoulders alone are worth a kingdom; no king could make their equal. But I am tired of this life. That which is hard work is no pleasure." The little maid smiled, and her lovely mistress said to her, "I should like to see you in my place."

Then the maid laughed outright, saying—
"Be quiet, Madame, he is there."
"Who?"
"Your husband."
"Which?"
"The real one."
"Chut!" said Madame.

And her maid told her the whole story, wishing to keep her favour and the 12,000 crowns as well.

"Oh, well, he shall have his money's worth. I'll give his desires time to cool. If he tastes me may I lose my beauty and become as ugly as a monkey's baby! You get into bed in my place and thus gain the 12,000 crowns. Go and tell him that he must take himself off early in the morning in order that I may not find out your trick upon me, and just before dawn I will get in by his side."

The poor husband was freezing and his teeth were chattering, and the chambermaid coming to the cupboard on pretence of getting some linen, said to him, "Your hour of bliss approaches. Madame to-night has made grand preparations and you will be well served. But work without whistling, otherwise I shall be lost."

At last, when the good husband was on the point of perishing with cold, the lights were put out. The maid cried softly in the curtains to the king's sweetheart, that his lordship was there, and jumped into the bed, while her mistress went out as if she had been the chambermaid. The advocate, released from his cold hiding-place, rolled rapturously into the warm sheets, thinking to himself, "Oh, this is good!" To tell the truth, the maid gave him his money's worth—and the good man thought of the difference between the profusion of royal houses and the niggardly ways of the citizens' wives. The servant, laughing, played her part marvellously well, regaling the knave with gentle cries, shiverings, convulsions and tossings about, like a new-caught fish on the grass, giving little Ah! ah's! in default of other words; and as often as the request was made by her, so often was it complied with by the advocate, who dropped off to sleep at last, like an empty pocket. But before finishing, the lover, who wished to preserve a souvenir of this sweet night of love, by a dexterous turn plucked out some of his wife's hair, where from I know not, seeing I was not there, and kept in his hand this precious gage of the warm virtue of that lovely creature. Towards the morning, when the cock crew, the wife slipped in beside her husband, and pretended to sleep. Then the maid tapped gently on the happy man's forehead, whispering in his ear, "It is time, get into your clothes and off you go—it's daylight." The good man grieved to lose his treasure, and wished to see the source of his vanished happiness.

"Oh! oh!" said he, proceeding to compare certain things, "I've got light hair, and this is dark."

"What have you done?" said the servant; "Madame will see she has been duped."

"But, look."

"Ah!" said she, with an air of disdain, "do you not know, you who know everything, that that which is plucked dies and discolours?" and thereupon roaring with laughter at the good joke, she pushed him out of doors. This became known. The poor advocate, named Féron, died of shame, seeing that he was the only one who had not his own wife; while she, who from this was called La belle Féronière, married, after having the king, a young lord, Count of Buzançois. And in her old days she would relate the story, laughingly adding, that she had never scented the knave's favour.

This teaches us not to attach ourselves more than we can help to wives who refuse to support our yoke.

THE DEVIL'S HEIR

THERE once was a good old Canon of Notre Dame de Paris, who lived in a fine house of his own, near St. Pierre-aux-Bœufs, in the Parvis. This canon had come a simple priest to Paris, naked as a dagger without its sheath. But since he was found to be a handsome man, well furnished with everything, and so well constituted, that if necessary he was able to do the work of many without doing himself much harm, he gave himself up earnestly to the confessing of ladies, giving to the melancholy a gentle absolution, to the sick a drachm of his balm, to all some little dainty. He was so well known for his discretion, his benevolence, and other ecclesiastical qualities, that he had customers at Court. Then in order not to awaken the jealousy of the officials, that of the husbands and others, in short, to endow with sanctity these good and profitable practices, the Lady Desquerdes gave him a bone of St. Victor, by virtue of which all the miracles were performed. And to the curious it was said, "He has a bone which will cure everything"; and to this, no one found anything to reply, because it was not seemly to suspect relics. Beneath the shade of his cassock, the good priest had the best of reputations, that of a man valiant under arms. So he lived like a king. He made money with holy water; sprinkled and transmitted the holy water into good wine. More than that, his name lay snugly in all the *et ceteras* of the notaries, in wills or in caudicils, which certain people have falsely written CODICIL, seeing that the word is derived from *cauda,* as if to say the tail of the legacy.

In fact, the good old Long Skirts would have been made an archbishop if he had only said in joke, "I should like to put on a mitre for a head-kerchief in order to have my head warmer." Of all the benefices offered to him, he chose only a simple canon's stall, to keep the good profits of the confessional. But one day the courageous canon found himself weak in the back, seeing that he was all sixty-eight years old, and had held many confessionals. Then thinking over all his good works, he thought it about time to cease his apostolic labours, the more so, as he possessed about one hundred thousand crowns earned by the sweat of his body. From that day he only confessed ladies of high lineage, and did it very well. So that it was said at Court that in spite of the efforts of the best young clerks there was still no one but the canon of St. Pierre-aux-Bœufs to properly bleach the soul of a lady of condition. Then at length the canon became by force of nature a fine nonagenarian, snowy about the head, with trembling hands, but square as a tower, having spat so much without coughing, that he coughed now without being able to spit; no longer rising from his chair, he who had so often risen for humanity; but drinking dry, eating heartily, saying nothing but having all the appearance of a living Canon of Notre Dame. Seeing the immobility of the aforesaid canon; seeing the stories of his evil life which for some time had circulated among the common people, always ignorant; seeing his dumb seclusion, his flourishing health, his young old age, and other things too numerous to mention—there were certain people who to do the marvellous and injure our holy religion, went about saying that the true canon was long since dead, and that for more than fifty years the devil had taken possession of the old priest's body. In fact, it seemed to his former customers that the devil only could by his great heat have furnished those hermetic distillations, that they remembered to have obtained on demand from this good confessor, who always had *le diable au corps*. But as this devil had been undoubtedly cooked and ruined by them, and that for a queen of twenty years he would not have moved, well-disposed people and those not wanting in sense, or the citizens who argued about everything, people who found lice in bald heads, demanded why the devil rested under form of a canon, went to the church of Notre Dame at the hours when the canons usually go, and ventured so far as to sniff the perfume of the incense, taste the holy water, and a thousand other things. To these heretical propositions some said that doubtless the devil wished to convert himself, and others that he remained in the shape of the canon to mock at the three nephews and heirs of this said brave confessor and make them wait until the day of their own death for the ample succession of this uncle, to whom they paid great attention every day, going to look if the good man had his eyes open, and in fact found him always with his eye clear, bright, and piercing as the eye of a basilisk, which pleased them greatly, since they loved their uncle very much—in words. On this subject an old woman related that for certain the canon was the devil, because his two nephews, the procureur and the captain, conducting their uncle at night, without lamp or lantern, returning from a supper at the penitentiary's, had caused him by accident to tumble over a heap of stones gathered together to raise the statue of St. Christopher. At first the old man had struck fire in falling, but was, amid the cries of his dear nephews and by the light of the torches they came to seek at her house, found standing up as straight as a skittle and as gay as a weaving whirl, exclaiming that the good wine of the penitentiary had given him the courage to sustain this shock and that his bones were exceedingly hard and had sustained rude assaults. The good nephews, believing him dead, were much astonished, and perceived that the day that was to despatch their uncle was a long way off, seeing that at the business stones were of no use. So that they did not falsely call him their good uncle, seeing that he was of good quality. Certain scandalmongers said that the canon found so many stones in his path that he stayed at home not to be ill with the stone, and the fear of worse was the cause of his seclusion.

Of all these sayings and rumours, it remains that the old canon, devil or not, kept his house, refused to die, and had three heirs with whom he lived as with his sciaticas, lumbagos, and other appendage of human life. Of the said three heirs, one was the wickedest soldier ever born of woman, and he must have considerably hurt her in breaking his egg, since he was born with teeth and bristles. So that he ate twofold, for the present and the future, keeping wenches whose cost he paid; inheriting from his uncle the continuance, strength, and good use of that which is often of service. In great battles, he endeavoured always to give blows without receiving them, which is, and always will be, the only problem to solve in war, but he never spared himself there, and, in fact, as he had no other virtue except his bravery, he was captain of a company of lancers, and much esteemed by the Duke of Bourgoyne, who never troubled what his soldiers did elsewhere. This nephew of the devil was named Captain Cochegrue; and his creditors, the blockheads, citizens, and others, whose pockets he slit, called him the manucinge, since he was as mischievous as strong; but he had moreover his back spoilt by the natural infirmity of a hump, and it would have been unwise to attempt to mount thereon to get a good view, for he would incontestably have run you through.

The second had studied the laws, and through the favour of his uncle had become a procureur, and practised at the palace, where he did the business of the ladies, whom formerly the canon had the best confessed. This one was called *Pille-grue,* to banter him upon his real name, which was Cochegrue, like that of his brother the captain. Pille-grue had a lean body, seemed to throw off very cold water, was pale of face, and possessed a physiognomy like a polecat.

This notwithstanding, he was worth many a penny more than the captain, and had for his uncle a little affection, but since about two years his heart had cracked a little, and drop by drop his gratitude had run out, in such a way that, from time to time, when the air was damp, he liked to put his feet into his uncle's hose, and press in advance the juice of this good inheritance. He and his brother, the soldier, found their share very small, since loyally, in law, in fact, in justice, in nature, and in reality, it was necessary to give the third part of everything to a poor cousin, son of another sister of the canon, the which heir, but little loved by the good man, remained in the country, where he was a shepherd, near Nanterre.

The guardian of beasts, an ordinary peasant, came to town by the advice of his two cousins, who placed him in their uncle's house, in the hope that, as much by his silly tricks as his clumsiness, his want of brain, and his ignorance, he would be displeasing to the canon, who would kick him out of his will. Now this poor Chiquon, as the shepherd was named, had lived about a month alone with his old uncle, and finding more profit or more amusement in minding an abbot than looking after sheep, made himself the canon's dog, his servant, the staff of his old age, saying, "God keep you," when he passed wind, "God save you," when he sneezed, and "God guard you," when he belched;

going to see if it rained, where the cat was, remaining silent, listening, speaking, receiving the coughs of the old man in his face, admiring him as the finest canon there ever was in the world, all heartily and in good faith, knowing that he was licking him after the manner of animals who clean their young ones ; and the uncle, who stood in no need of learning which side the bread was buttered, repulsed poor Chiquon, making him turn about like a die, always calling Chiquon, and always saying to his other nephews that this Chiquon was helping to kill him, such a numskull was he. Thereupon, hearing this, Chiquon determined to do well by his uncle, and puzzled his understanding to appear better ; but as he had a behind shaped like a pair of pumpkins, was broad shouldered, large limbed, and far from sharp, he more resembled old Silenus than a gentle Zephyr. In fact, the poor shepherd, a simple man, could not reform himself, so he remained big and fat, awaiting his inheritance to make himself thin.

One evening the canon began discoursing concerning the devil and the grave agonies, penances, tortures, etc., which God will get warm for the accursed, and the good Chiquon hearing it, began to open his eyes as wide as the door of an oven, at this statement, without believing a word of it.

"What," said the canon, "are you not a Christian ?"

"In that, yes," answered Chiquon.

"Well, there is a paradise for the good ; is it not necessary to have a hell for the wicked ?"

"Yes, Mr. Canon ; but the devil's of no use. If you had here a wicked man who turned everything upside down, would you not kick him out of doors ?"

"Yes, Chiquon."

"Oh, well, mine uncle ; God would be very stupid to leave in this world, which he has so curiously constructed, an abominable devil whose special business it is to spoil everything for him. Pish! I recognise no devil if there be a good God; you may depend upon that. I should very much like to see the devil. Ha! ha! I am not afraid of his claws!"

"And if I were of your opinion I should have no care of my very youthful years in which I held confessions at least ten times a day."

"Confess again, Mr. Canon. I assure you that will be a precious merit on high."

"There, there! do you mean it?"

"Yes, Mr. Canon."

"Thou dost not tremble, Chiquon, to deny the devil?"

"I trouble no more about it than a sheaf of corn."

"The doctrine will bring misfortune upon you."

"By no means. God will defend me from the devil because I believe him more learned and less stupid than the learned men make him out."

Thereupon the other two nephews entered, and perceiving from the voice of the canon that he did not dislike Chiquon very much, and that the jeremiads which he made concerning him were simply tricks to disguise the affection which he bore him, looked at each other in great astonishment.

Then, seeing their uncle laughing, they said to him—

"If you make a will, to whom will you leave the house?"

"To Chiquon."

"And the quit rent of the Rue St. Denys?"

"To Chiquon."

"And the fief of Ville Parisis?"

"To Chiquon."

"But," said the captain, with his big voice, "everything then will be Chiquon's."

"No," replied the canon, smiling, "because I shall have

made my will in proper form, the inheritance will be to the sharpest of you three; I am so near to the future, that I can therein see clearly your destinies."

And the wily canon cast upon Chiquon a glance full of malice, like a decoy bird would have thrown upon a little one to draw him into her net. The fire of this flaming eye enlightened the shepherd, who from that moment had his understanding and his ears all unfogged, and his brain open, like that of a maiden the day after her marriage. The procureur and the captain, taking these sayings for gospel prophecies, made their bow and went out from the house, quite perplexed at the absurd designs of the canon.

"What do you think of Chiquon?" said Pille-grue to Mau-cinge.

"I think, I think," said the soldier, growling, "that I think of hiding myself in the Rue de'Hiérusalem, to put his head below his feet; he can pick it up again if he likes."

"Oh! oh!" said the procureur, "you have a way of wounding that is easily recognised, and people would say, 'It's Cochegrue.' As for me, I thought to invite him to dinner, after which, we would play at putting ourselves in a sack, in order to see, as they do at Court, who could walk best thus attired. Then, having sewn him up, we could throw him into the Seine, at the same time begging him to swim."

"This must be well matured," replied the soldier.

"Oh! it's quite ripe," said the advocate. "The cousin gone to the devil, the heritage would then be between us two."

"I'm quite agreeable," said the fighter, "but we must stick as close together as the two legs of the same body, for if you are fine as silk, I am strong as steel, and daggers are always as good as traps—you hear that, my good brother."

"Yes," said the advocate, "the cause is heard—now shall it be the thread or the iron?"

"Eh? ventre de Dieu! is it then a king that we are going to settle? For a simple numskull of a shepherd are so many words necessary? Come! 20,000 francs out of the heritage to the one of us who shall first cut him off: I'll say to him in good faith, 'Pick up your head.' "

"And I, 'Swim, my friend,' " cried the advocate, laughing like the gap of a pourpoint.

And then they went to supper, the captain to his wench, and the advocate to the house of a jeweller's wife, of whom he was the lover.

Who was astonished? Chiquon! The poor shepherd heard the planning of his death, although his two cousins had walked in the parvis, and talked to each other as every one speaks at church when praying to God. So that Chiquon was much troubled to know if the words had come up or if his ears had gone down.

"Do you hear, Mister Canon?"

"Yes," said he, "I hear the wood crackling in the fire."

"Ho! ho!" replied Chiquon, "if I don't believe in the devil, I believe in St. Michael, my guardian angel; I go there where he calls me."

"Go, my child," said the canon, "and take care not to wet yourself nor to get your head knocked off, for I think I hear more rain, and the beggars in the street are not always the most dangerous beggars."

At these words Chiquon was much astonished, and stared at the canon; found his manner gay, his eye sharp, and his feet crooked; but as he had to arrange matters concerning the death which menaced him, he thought to

himself that he would always have leisure to admire the
canon, or to cut his nails, and he trotted off quickly through
the town, as a little woman trots towards her pleasure.

His two cousins, having no presumption of the divina-
tory science, of which shepherds have had many passing
attacks, had often talked before him of their secret goings
on, counting his as nothing.

Now one evening to amuse the canon, Pille-grue had
recounted to him how had fallen in love with him the wife
of a jeweller on whose head he had adjusted certain carved,
burnished, sculptured, historical horns, fit for the brow
of a prince. The good lady was, to hear him, a right merry
wench, quick at opportunities, giving an embrace while her
husband was mounting the stairs, devouring the com-
modity as if she were swallowing a strawberry, only
thinking of love-making, always trifling and frisky, gay as
an honest woman who lacks nothing, contenting her husband, who cherished her as much as he loved his own
gullet; subtle as a perfume, so much so, that for five years
she managed so well his household affairs, and her own
love affairs, that she had the reputation of a prudent
woman, the confidence of her husband, the keys of the
house, the purse, and all.

"And when do you play upon this gentle flute?" said
the canon.

"Every evening, and sometimes I stay all the night."

"But how?" said the canon, astonished.

"This is how. There is in a room close to, a chest into
which I get. When the good husband returns from his
friend the draper's, where he goes to supper every evening,
because often he helps the draper's wife in her work, my
mistress pleads a slight illness, lets him go to bed alone, and
comes to doctor her malady in the room where the chest

is. On the morrow, when my jeweller is at his forge, I depart, and as the house has one exit on to the bridge, and
another into the street, I always come to the door where
the husband is not, on the pretext of speaking to him of
his suits, which commence joyfully and heartily, and I never
let them come to an end. It is an income from cuckoldom,
seeing that in the minor expenses and loyal costs of the
proceedings, he spends as much as on the horses in his
stable. He loves me well, as all good cuckolds should
love the man who aids them, to plant, cultivate, water,
and dig the natural garden of Venus, and he does nothing
without me."

Now these practices came back again to the memory
of the shepherd, who was illuminated by the light issuing
from his danger, and counselled by the intelligence of
those measures of self-preservation, of which every animal
possesses a sufficient dose to go to the end of his ball of life.
So Chiquon gained with hasty feet the Rue de la Calandre,
where the jeweller should then be supping with his companion, and after having knocked at the door, replied
to the question put to him through the little grill, that he
was a messenger on state secrets, and was admitted to the
draper's house. Now coming straight to the fact, he made
the happy jeweller get up from the table, led him into a
corner, and said to him, "If one of your neighbors had
planted a horn on your forehead, and he were delivered
to you, bound hand and foot, would you throw him into
the river?"

"Rather," said the jeweller, "but if you are mocking me
I'll give you a good drubbing."

"There, there!" replied Chiquon, "I am one of your
friends, and come to warn you that as many times as you
have conversed with the draper's wife here, as often has

your good wife been served the same way by the advocate Pille-grue, and if you will come back to your forge, you'll find a good fire there. On your arrival, he who looks after your you-know-what, to keep it in good order, gets into the big clothes chest. Now make a pretence that I have bought the said chest of you, and I will be upon the bridge with a cart, waiting your orders."

The said jeweller took his cloak and his hat, and parted company with his crony without saying a word, and ran to his hole like a poisoned rat. He arrives and knocks, the door is opened, he runs hastily up the stairs, finds two covers laid, sees his wife coming out of the chamber of love, and then says to her, "My dear, here are two covers laid."

"Well, my darling, are we not two?"

"No," said he, "we are three."

"Is your friend coming?" said she, looking towards the stairs with perfect innocence.

"No, I speak of the friend who is in the chest."

"What chest?" said she. "Are you in your sound senses? where do you see a chest? is it usual to put friends in chests? am I a woman to keep chests full of friends? How long have friends been kept in chests? are you come home mad to mix up your friends with your chests? I know no other friend than Master Cornille the draper, and no other chest than the one with our clothes in."

"Oh!" said the jeweller, "my good woman, there is a bad young man, who has come to warn me that you allow yourself to be embraced by our advocate, and that he is in the chest."

"I!" said she, "I would not put up with his knavery, he does everything the wrong way."

"There, there, my dear," replied the jeweller, "I know you to be a good woman, and won't have a squabble with

you about this paltry chest. The giver of the warning is
a box-maker, to whom I am about to sell this cursed chest
that I wish never again to see in my house, and for this
one he will sell me two pretty little ones, in which there
will not be space enough even for a child; thus the scandal and the babble of those envious of thy virtues will be
extinguished for want of nourishment."

"You give me great pleasure," said she; "I don't attach
any value to my chest, and by chance there is nothing in
it. Our linen is at the wash. It will be easy to have the mischievous chest taken away to-morrow morning. Will you
sup?"

"Not at all," said he, "I shall sup with a better appetite
without this chest."

"I see," said she, "that you won't easily get the chest out
of your head."

"Halloa there!" said the jeweller to his smiths and apprentices; "come down!"

In the twinkling of an eye his people were before him.
Then he, their master, having briefly ordered the handling
of the said chest, this piece of furniture dedicated to love
was suddenly tumbled across the room, but in passing,
the advocate, finding his feet in the air to which he was
not accustomed, tumbled over a little.

"Go on," said the wife, "go on, it's the lid shaking."

"No, my dear, it's the bolt."

And without any other opposition the chest slid gently
down the stairs.

"Ho there, carrier!" said the jeweller, and Chiquon
came whistling his mules, and the good apprentices lifted
the litigious chest into the cart.

"Hi! hi!" said the advocate.

"Master, the chest is speaking," said an apprentice.

"In what language?" said the jeweller, giving him a good kick between two features that luckily were not made of glass. The apprentice tumbled over on to a stair in a way that induced him to discontinue his studies in the language of chests. The shepherd, accompanied by the good jeweller, carried all the baggage to the waterside without listening to the high eloquence of the speaking wood, and having tied several stones to it, the jeweller threw it into the Seine.

"Swim, my friend," cried the shepherd, in a voice sufficiently jeering at the moment when the chest turned over, giving a pretty little plunge like a duck.

Then Chiquon continued to proceed along the quay, as far as the Rue-due-port, St. Laudry, near the cloisters of Notre Dame. There he noticed a house, recognized the door, and knocked loudly.

"Open," said he, "open by order of the king."

Hearing this, an old man who was no other than the famous Lombard, Versoris, ran to the door.

"What is it?" said he.

"I am sent by the provost to warn you to keep good watch to-night," replied Chiquon, "as for his own part he will keep his archers ready. The hunchback who has robbed you has come back again. Keep under arms, for he is quite capable of easing you of the rest."

Having said this, the good shepherd took to his heels and ran to the Rue des Marmouzets, to the house where Captain Cochegrue was feasting with La Pasquerette, the prettiest of town girls, and the most charming in perversity that ever was; according to all the gay ladies, her glance was sharp and piercing as the stab of a dagger. Her appearance was so tickling to the sight, that it would have put all paradise to rout. Besides which she was as bold as a woman who has no other virtue than her insolence. Poor Chiquon was greatly embarrassed while going to the quarter of the Marmouzets. He was greatly afraid that he would be unable to find the house of La Pasquerette, or find the two pigeons gone to roost, but a good angel arranged things speedily to his satisfaction. This is how. On entering the Rue des Marmouzets, he saw several lights at the windows, and nightcapped heads thrust out, and good wenches, gay girls, housewives, husbands, and young ladies, all of them just out of bed, looking at each other as if a robber were being led to execution by torchlight.

"What's the matter?" said the shepherd to a citizen who in great haste had rushed to the door with a chamber utensil in his hand.

"Oh! it's nothing," replied the good man. "We thought it was the Armagnacs descending upon the town, but it's only Mau-cinge beating La Pasquerette."

"Where?" asked the shepherd.

"Below there, at that fine house where the pillars have the mouths of flying frogs delicately engraved upon them. Do you hear the varlets and the serving maids?"

And in fact there were nothing but cries of "Murder! Help! Come, some one!" and in the house blows were raining down and the Mau-cinge said with his gruff voice, "Death to the wench! Ah, you sing out now, do you? Ah, you want money now, do you? Take that——"

And La Pasquerette was groaning, "Oh! oh! I die! Help! help! Oh! oh!" Then came the blow of a sword, and the heavy fall of the light body of the fair girl sounded, and was followed by a great silence, after which the lights were put out, servants, waiting women, roysterers, and others went in again, and the shepherd who had come opportunely mounted the stairs in company with them, but on beholding in the room above broken glasses, slit carpets, and the cloth on the floor with the dishes, every one remained at a distance.

The shepherd, bold as a man with but one end in view, opened the door of the handsome chamber where slept La Pasquerette, and found her quite exhausted, her hair dishevelled, and her neck twisted, lying upon a bloody carpet, and Mau-cinge frightened, with his tone considerably lower, and not knowing upon what note to sing the remainder of his anthem.

"Come, my little Pasquerette, don't pretend to be dead. Come, let me put you tidy. Ah! little minx, dead or alive, you look so pretty in your blood I'm going to kiss you." Having said which the cunning soldier took her and threw her upon the bed, but she fell there all of a heap, and stiff as the body of a man that had been hanged. Seeing which her companion found it was time for his hump to retire from the game; however, the artful fellow before slinking away said, "Poor Pasquerette, how could I murder so good a girl, and one I loved so much? But, yes, I have killed her, the thing is clear, for in her life never did her sweet breast hang down like that. Good God, one would say it was a crown at the bottom of a wallet." Thereupon La Pasquerette opened her eyes and bent her head slightly to look at her flesh, which was white and firm, and she brought herself to life again by a box on the ears, administered to the captain.

"That will teach you to speak ill of the dead," said she, smiling.

"And why did he kill you, my cousin?" asked the shepherd.

"Why? to-morrow the bailiffs seize everything that's here, and he who has no more money than virtue, reproached me because I wished to be agreeable to a handsome gentleman, who would save me from the hands of justice."

"Pasquerette, I'll break every bone in your skin."

"There! there!" said Chiquon, whom the Mau-cinge had just recognized, "is that all? Oh, well, my good friend, I bring you a large sum."

"Where from?" asked the captain, astonished.

"Come here, and let me whisper in your ear—if 30,000 crowns were walking about at night under the shadow of a pear-tree, would you not stoop down to pluck them, to prevent them spoiling?"

"Chiquon, I'll kill you like a dog if you are making game of me, or I will kiss you there where you like it, if you will put me opposite 30,000 crowns, even when it shall be necessary to kill three citizens at the corner of the Quay."

"You will not even kill one. This is how the matter stands. I have for a sweetheart in all loyalty, the servant of the Lombard who is in the city near the house of our good uncle. Now I have just learned on sound information that this dear man has departed this morning into the country, after having hidden under a pear-tree in his garden a good bushel of gold, believing himself to be seen only by the angels. But the girl who had by chance a bad toothache, and was taking the air at her garret window, spied the old crookshanks, without wishing to do so, and chattered of it to me in fondness. If you will swear to give me a good share I will lend you my shoulders in order that you may climb on to the top of the wall, and from there throw yourself into the pear-tree, which is against the wall. There, now do you say that I am a blockhead, an animal?"

"No, you are a right loyal cousin, an honest man, and if you have ever to put an enemy out of the way, I am there, ready to kill even one of my own friends for you. I am no

longer your cousin, but your brother. Ho there, sweetheart,"
cried Mau-cinge to La Pasquerette, "put the tables straight,
wipe up your blood, it belongs to me, and I'll pay you for
it, by giving you a hundred times as much of mine as I have
taken of thine. Make the best of it, shake the black dog off
your back, adjust your petticoats, laugh, I wish it, look to
the stew, and let us recommence our evening prayer where
we left it off. To-morrow I will make thee braver than a
queen. This is my cousin whom I wish to entertain, even
when to do so it were necessary to turn the house out of
windows. We shall get back everything to-morrow in the
cellars. Come, fall to."

Thus, and in less time than it takes a priest to say his
Dominus Vobiscum, the whole rookery passed from tears
to laughter as it had previously passed from laughter to
tears. It is only in these houses of ill-fame that love is made
with the blow of a dagger, and where tempests of joy rage
between four walls. But these are things ladies of the high-
necked dresses do not understand.

The said Captain Cochegrue was gay as a hundred schoolboys at the breaking up of class, and made his good cousin
drink deeply, who swilled everything country fashion, and
pretended to be drunk, spluttering out a hundred stupidities,
as, that "to-morrow he would buy Paris, would lend a hundred thousand crowns to the king, that he would be able to
roll in gold"; in fact, talked so much nonsense that the captain, fearing some compromising avowal and thinking his
brain quite muddled enough, led him outside with the good
intention, instead of sharing with him, of ripping Chiquon
open to see if he had not a sponge in his stomach, because
he had just soaked in a big quart of the good wine of
Suresne. They went along, disputing about a thousand theological subjects, which got very much mixed up, and fin-

ished by rolling quietly up against the garden where were
the crowns of the Lombard. Then Cochegrue, making a
ladder of Chiquon's broad shoulders, jumped on to the pear-
tree like a man expert in attacks upon towns, but Versoris,
who was watching him, made a blow at his neck; and repeated it so vigorously that with three blows fell the upper
portion of the said Cochegrue, but not until he had heard
the clear voice of the shepherd, who cried to him, *"Pick up
your head, my friend."* Thereupon the generous Chiquon, in
whom virtue received its recompense, thought it would be
wise to return to the house of the good canon, whose heritage was by the grace of God considerably simplified. Thus
he gained the Rue St. Pierre-aux-Bœufs with all speed, and
soon slept like a new-born baby, no longer knowing the
meaning of the word "cousin-german." Now on the morrow
he rose according to the habit of shepherds, with the sun,
and came into his uncle's room to inquire if he spat white,
if he coughed, if he had slept well; but the old servant told
him that the canon, hearing the bells of St. Maurice, the
first patron of Notre Dame, ring for matins, he had gone
out of reverence to the cathedral, where all the Chapter were
to breakfast with the Bishop of Paris; upon which Chiquon
replied, "Is his reverence the canon out of his senses thus
to disport himself, to catch a cold, to get rheumatism? does
he wish to die? I'll light a big fire to warm him when he
returns"; and the good shepherd ran into the room where
the canon generally sat, and to his great astonishment beheld him seated in his chair.

"Ah! ah! What did she mean, that fool of a Buyrette?
I knew you were too well advised to be shivering at this
hour in your stall."

The canon said not a word. The shepherd, who was like
all thinkers, a man of hidden sense, was quite aware that

sometimes old men have strange crotchets, converse with the essence of occult things, and mumble to themselves discourses concerning matters not under consideration : so that, from reverence and great respect for the secret meditations of the canon, he went and sat down at a distance, and waited the termination of these dreams ; noticing silently the length of the good man's nails, which looked like cobblers' awls, and looking attentively at the feet of his uncle, he was astonished to see the flesh of his legs so crimson, that it reddened his breeches and seemed all on fire through his hose.

He is dead, thought Chiquon. At this moment the door of the room opened, and he still saw the canon, who, his nose frozen, came back from church.

"Ho! ho!" said Chiquon, "my dear uncle, are you out of your senses? Kindly take notice that you ought not to be at the door, because you are already seated in your chair in the chimney corner, and that it is impossible for there to be two canons like you in the world."

"Ah! Chiquon, there was a time when I could have wished to be in two places at once, but such is not the fate of man, he would be too happy. Are you getting dimsighted? I am alone here."

Then Chiquon turned his head towards the chair, and found it empty ; and much astonished, as you will easily believe, he approached it, and found on the seat a little pat of cinders, from which ascended a strong odour of sulphur.

"Ah!" said he merrily, "I perceive that the devil has behaved well towards me—I will pray God for him."

And thereupon he related naïvely to the canon how the devil had amused himself by playing at providence, and had loyally aided him to get rid of his wicked cousins, the which the canon admired much, and thought very good, seeing that he had plenty of good sense left, and often had observed things which were to the devil's advantage. So the good old priest remarked that as much good was always met with in evil as evil in good, and that therefore one should not trouble too much after the other world, the which was a grave heresy, which many councils have put right.

And this was how the Chiquons became rich, and were able in these times, by the fortunes of their ancestors, to help to build the bridge of St. Michael, where the devil cuts a very good figure under the angel, in memory of this adventure now consigned to the veracious histories.

THE MERRY JESTS OF
KING LOUIS THE ELEVENTH

KING LOUIS THE ELEVENTH was a merry fellow, loving a
good joke, and—the interests of his position as king, and
those of the church on one side—he lived jovially, giving
chase to soiled doves as often as to hares, and other royal
game. Therefore, the sorry scribblers who have made him
out a hypocrite, show plainly that they knew him not, since
he was a good friend, good at repartee, and a jollier fellow
than any of them.

It was he who said when he was in a merry mood, that
four things are excellent and opportune in life—to keep
warm, to drink cool, to stand up hard, and to swallow soft.
Certain persons have accused him of taking up with dirty
trollops; this is a notorious falsehood, since all his mistresses, of whom one was legitimatized, came of good houses
and had notable establishments. He did not go in for waste
and extravagance, always put his hand upon the solid, and
because certain devourers of the people found no crumbs
at his table, they have all maligned him. But the real collec-
tors of facts know that the said king was a capital fellow in
private life, and even very agreeable; and before cutting off
the heads of his friends, or punishing them—for he did not
spare them—it was necessary that they should have greatly
offended him, and his vengeance was always justice; I have
only seen in our friend Verville that this worthy sovereign
ever made a mistake; but once does not make a habit, and
even for this his boon companion Tristan was more to blame

than he, the king. This is the circumstance related by the said Verville, and I suspect he was cracking a joke. I reproduce it because certain people are not familiar with the exquisite work of my perfect compatriot. I abridge it and only give the substance, the details being more ample, of which fact the savants are not ignorant.

Louis XI. had given the Abbey of Turpenay (mentioned in *Imperia*) to a gentleman who, enjoying the revenue, had called himself Monsieur de Turpenay. It happened that the king being at Plessis-les-Tours, the real abbot, who was a monk, came and presented himself before the king, and presented also a petition, remonstrating with him that, canonically and monastically, he was entitled to the abbey, and that the usurping gentleman wronged him of his right, and therefore he called upon his majesty to have justice done to him. Nodding his peruke, the king promised to render him contented. This monk, importunate as are all hooded animals, came often at the end of the king's meals, who, bored with the holy water of the convent, called friend Tristan and said to him, "Old fellow, there is here a Turpenay who angers me, rid the world of him for me." Tristan, taking a frock for a monk, or a monk for a frock, came to this gentleman, whom all the Court called Monsieur de Turpenay, and having accosted him managed to lead him on one side, and taking him by the button-hole gave him to understand that the king desired he should die. He tried to resist, supplicating and supplicating to escape, but in no way could he obtain a hearing. He was delicately strangled between the head and the shoulders, so that he expired; and, three hours afterward, Tristan told the king that he was discharged. It happened five days afterwards, which is the space in which souls come back again, that the monk came into the room where the king was, and when he saw him he was much astonished. Tristan was present; the king called him, and whispered into his ear—

"You have not done that which I told you to."

"Saving your Grace, I have done it. Turpenay is dead."

"Eh? I meant this monk."

"I understood the gentleman!"

"What, it is done then?"

"Yes, sire."

"Very well then"—turning towards the monk—"come here, monk." The monk approached. The King said to him, "Kneel down." The poor monk began to shiver in his shoes. But the king said to him, "Thank God that he has not willed that you should be killed as I had ordered. He who took your estates has been instead. God has done you justice. Go and pray for me, and don't stir out of your convent."

This proves the good-heartedness of Louis XI. He might very well have hanged the monk, the cause of the error. As for the said gentleman, he died in the king's service.

In the early days of his sojourn at Plessis-les-Tours King Louis, not wishing to hold his drinking-bouts and give vent to his rakish propensities in his chateau, out of respect to her Majesty (a kingly delicacy which his successors have not possessed) became enamoured of a lady named Nicole Beaupertuys, who was, to tell the truth, wife of a citizen of the town. The husband he sent into Ponent, and put the said Nicole in a house near Chardonneret, in that part where is the Rue Quincangrogne, because it was a lonely place, far from other habitations. The husband and the wife were thus both in his service, and he had by La Beaupertuys, a daughter, who died a nun. This Nicole had a tongue as sharp as a popinjay's, was of stately proportions, furnished with large beautiful cushions of nature, firm to the touch, white as the wing of an angel, and known for the rest to be fertile in peripatetic ways, which brought it to pass that never with her was the same thing encountered twice in love, so deeply had she studied the sweet solutions of the science, the manners of accommodating the olives of Poissy, the expansions of the nerves, and hidden doctrines of the breviary, the which much delighted the king. She was as gay as a lark, always laughing and singing, and never made any one miserable, which is the characteristic of women of this open and free nature, who have always an occupation—an equivocal one if you like. The king often went with the hail-fellows his friends to the lady's house, and in order not to be seen always went at night-time and without his suite. But being always distrustful, and fearing some snare, he gave to Nicole all the most savage dogs he had in his kennels, beggars that would eat a man without saying "By your leave," the which royal dogs knew only Nicole and the king. When the Sire came Nicole let them loose in the garden, and the door of the house being sufficiently barred and closely shut, the king put the keys in his pocket and in perfect security gave himself up, with his satellites, to every kind of pleasure, fearing no betrayal, jumping about at will, playing tricks, and getting up good games. Upon these occasions friend Tristan watched the neighborhood, and any one who had taken a walk on the Mall of Chardonneret would have been rather quickly placed in a position in which it would have been easy to give the passers-by a benediction with his feet, unless he had the king's pass, since often would Louis send out in search of lasses for his friends, or people to entertain him with the amusements suggested by Nicole or the guests. People of Tours were there for these little amusements, to whom he gently recommended silence, so that no one knew of these pastimes until after his death. The farce of "Baisez mon cul" was, it is said, invented by

the said Sire. I will relate it, although it is not the subject
of this tale, because it shows the natural comicality and humour of this merry monarch. There were at Tours three
well-known misers: the first was Master Cornelius, who is
sufficiently well known; the second was called Peccard, and
sold the gilt-work, coloured papers, and jewels used in
churches; the third was hight Marchandeau, and was a very
wealthy vine-grower. These three men of Touraine were
the founders of good families, notwithstanding their sordid-
ness. One evening that the king was with Beaupertuys, in a
good humour, having drunk heartily, joked heartily, and
offered early in the evening his prayer in Madame's oratory,
he said to Le Daim, his crony, to the Cardinal, La Balus, and
to old Dunois, who were still soaking, "Let us have a good
laugh! I think it will be a good joke to see misers before a
bag of gold without their being able to touch it. Hi, there!"

Hearing which, appeared one of his varlets.

"Go," said he, "seek my treasurer, and let him bring
hither six thousand gold crowns—and at once! And you
will go and seize the bodies of my friend Cornelius, of the
jeweller of the Rue de Cygnes, and of old Marchandeau,
and bring them here, by order of the king."

Then he began to drink again, and to judiciously wrangle
as to which was the better, a woman with a gamy odour or
a woman who soaped herself well all over; a thin one or a
stout one; and as the company comprised the flower of wisdom it was decided that the best was the one a man had all
to himself like a plate of warm mussels, at that precise moment when God sent him a good idea to communicate to her.
The cardinal asked which was the most precious thing to a
lady; the first or the last kiss? To which La Beaupertuys
replied, "that it was the last, seeing that she knew then what
she was losing, while at the first she did not know what she

would gain." During these sayings, and others which have most unfortunately been lost, came the six thousand gold crowns, which were worth all three hundred thousand francs of to-day, so much do we go on decreasing in value every day. The king ordered the crowns to be arranged upon a table, and well lighted up, so that they shone like the eyes of the company which lit up involuntarily, and made them laugh in spite of themselves. They did not wait long for the three misers, whom the varlet led in, pale and panting, except Cornelius, who knew the king's strange freaks.

"Now then, my friends," said Louis to them, "have a good look at the crowns on the table."

And the three townsmen nibbled at them with their eyes. You may reckon that the diamond of La Beaupertuys sparkled less than their little minnow eyes.

"These are yours," added the king.

Thereupon they ceased to admire the crowns to look at each other; and the guests knew well that old knaves are more expert in grimaces than any others, because their physiognomies become tolerably curious, like those of cats lapping up milk, or girls titillated with marriage.

"There," said the king, "all that shall be his who shall say three times to the two others, 'Baisez mon cul,' thrusting his hand into the gold; but if he be not as serious as a fly who has violated his lady-love, if he smile while repeating the jest, he will pay ten crowns to Madame. Nevertheless he can essay three times.'"

"That will be soon earned," said Cornelius, who, being a Dutchman, had his lips as often compressed and serious as Madame's mouth was often open and laughing. Then he bravely put his hand upon the crowns to see if they were good, and clutched them gravely, but as he looked at the others to say civilly to them, "Baisez mon cul," the two misers, distrustful of his Dutch gravity, replied, "Certainly, sir," as if he had sneezed. The which caused all the company to laugh, and even Cornelius himself. When the vine-grower went to take the crowns he felt such a commotion in his cheeks that his old scummer face let little laughs exude from all its pores like smoke pouring out of a chimney, and he could say nothing. Then it was the turn of the jeweller, who was a little bit of a bantering fellow, and whose lips were as tightly squeezed as the neck of a hanged man. He seized a handful of the crowns, looked at the others, even the king, and said, with a jeering air, "Baisez mon cul."

"Is it dirty?" asked the vine-dresser.

"Look and see," replied the jeweller, gravely.

Thereupon the king began to tremble for his crowns, since the said Peccard began again, without laughing, and for the third time was about to utter the sacramental word, when La Beaupertuys made a sign of consent to his modest request, which caused him to lose his countenance, and his mouth broke up into dimples.

"How did you do?" asked Dunois, "to keep a grave face before six thousand crowns?"

"Oh, my lord, I thought first of one of my cases which is tried to-morrow, and, secondly, of my wife who is a sorry plague."

The desire to gain this good round sum made them try again, and the king amused himself for about an hour at the expression of these faces, the preparations, jokes, grimaces, and other monkeys' paternosters that they performed; but they were baling their boats with a sieve, and for men who preferred closing their fists to opening them it was a bitter sorrow to have to count out, each one, a hundred crowns to Madame.

When they were gone, Nicole said boldly to the king, "Sire, will you let me try?"

"Holy Virgin!" replied Louis; "no! I can kiss you for less money."

That was said like a thrifty man, which indeed he always was.

One evening the fat Cardinal La Balue carried on gallantly with words and actions, a little farther than the canons of the Church permitted him, with this Beaupertuys, who luckily for herself, was a clever hussy, not to be asked with impunity how many holes there were in her mother's chemise.

"Look you here, Sir Cardinal!" said she; "the thing which the king likes is not to receive the holy oils."

Then came Olivier le Daim, whom she would not listen to either, and to whose nonsense she replied, that she would ask the king if he wished her to be shaved.

Now as the said shaver did not supplicate her to keep his proposals secret, she suspected that these little plots were ruses practised by the king, whose suspicions had perhaps been aroused by her friends. Now, not being able to revenge herself upon Louis, she at least determined to pay out the said lords, to make fools of them, and amuse the king with the tricks she would play upon them. One evening that they had come to supper, she had a lady of the city with her, who wished to speak with the king. This lady was a lady of position, who wished to ask of the king pardon for her husband, the which, in consequence of this adventure, she obtained. Nicole Beaupertuys having led the king aside for a moment into an antechamber, told him to make their guests drink hard and eat to repletion; that he was to make merry, and joke with them; but when the cloth was removed, he was to pick quarrels with them about trifles, dispute their words, and be sharp with them; and that then she would divert him by turning them inside out before him. But above all things, he was to be friendly to the said lady, and it was to appear genuine, as if she enjoyed the perfume of his flavour, because she had gallantly lent herself to this good joke.

"Well, gentlemen," said the king, re-entering the room, "let us fall-to; we have had a good day's sport."

And the surgeon, the cardinal, a fat bishop, the captain of the Scotch guard, a parliamentary envoy, and a judge loved of the king, followed the two ladies into the room where one rubs the rust off one's jawbones. And there they lined the mould of their doublets. What is that? It is to pave the stomach, to practise the chemistry of nature, to register the various dishes, to regale your tripes, to dig your grave with your teeth, play with the sword of Cain, to inter sauces, to support a cuckold. But more philosophically it is to make ordure with one's teeth. Now do you understand? How many words does it require to burst open the lid of your understanding?

The king did not fail to distil into his guests this splendid and first-class supper. He stuffed them with green peas, returning to the hotch-potch, praising the plums, commending the fish, saying to one, "Why do you not eat?" to another, "Drink to Madame"; to all of them, "Gentlemen, taste these lobsters; put this bottle to death! You do not know the flavour of this forcemeat. And these lampreys— ah! what do you say to them? And, by the Lord! the finest barbel ever drawn from the Loire! Just stick your teeth into this pasty. This game is my own hunting! he who takes it not offends me." And again, "Drink, the king's eyes are the other way. Just give me your opinion of these preserves, they are Madame's own. Have some of these grapes, they are my own growing. Have some medlars." And while in-

ducing them to swell out their abdominal protuberances, the
good monarch laughed with them, and they joked, and dis-
puted, and spat, and blew their noses, and kicked up just
as though the king had not been with them. Then so much
victuals had been taken on board, so many flagons drained
and stews spoilt, that the faces of the guests were the colour
of cardinals' gowns, and their doublets appeared ready to
burst, since they were crammed with meat like Troyes saus-
ages from the top to the bottom of their paunches. Going
into the salon again, they broke into a profuse sweat, began
to blow, and to curse their gluttony. The king sat quietly
apart; each of them was the more willing to be silent because all their forces were required for the intestinal digestion of the huge platefuls confined in their stomachs, which
began to wabble and rumble violently. One said to himself,
"I was stupid to eat of that sauce." Another scolded himself
for having indulged in a plate of eels cooked with capers.
Another thought to himself, "Oh! oh! the forcemeat is
serving me out." The cardinal, who was the biggest-bellied
man of the lot, snorted through his nostrils like a frightened
horse. It was he who was first compelled to give vent to a
loud sounding belch, and then he soon wished himself in
Germany, where this is a form of salutation, for the king
hearing this gastric language looked at the cardinal with
knitted brows.

"What does this mean?" said he, "am I a simple clerk?"

This was heard with terror, because usually the king
made much of a good belch well off the stomach. The other
guests determined to get rid in another way of the vapours
which were dodging about in their pancreatic retorts; and
at first they endeavoured to hold them for a little while in
the pleats of their mesenteries. It was then that some of

them puffed and swelled like tax-gatherers. Beaupertuys
took the good king aside and said to him—

"Know now that I have had made by the Church jeweller,
Peccard, two large dolls, exactly resembling this lady and
myself. Now when hard pressed by the drugs which I have
put in their goblets, they desire to mount the throne to
which we are now about to pretend to go, they will always
find the place taken; by this means you will enjoy their
writhings."

Thus having said, La Beaupertuys disappeared with the
lady to go and turn the wheel, after the custom of women,
and of which I will tell you the origin in another place. And
after an honest lapse of water, Beaupertuys came back
alone, leaving it to be believed that she had left the lady at
the little laboratory of natural alchemy. Thereupon the king,
singling out the cardinal, made him get up, and talked with
him seriously of his affairs, holding him by the tassel of
his amice. To all that the king said, La Balue replied, "Yes,
sir," to be delivered from this favour, and to slip out of the
room, since the water was in his cellars, and he was about
to lose the key of his back-door. All the guests were in a
state of not knowing how to arrest the progress of the fæcal
matter to which nature has given, even more than to water,
the property of finding a certain level. Their substances
modified themselves and glided working downward, like
those insects who demand to be let out of their cocoons, raging, tormenting, and ungrateful to the higher powers; for
nothing is so ignorant, so insolent as those cursed objects,
and they are importunate like all things detained to whom
one owes liberty. So they slipped at every turn like eels out
of a net, and each one had need of great efforts and science
not to disgrace himself before the king. Louis took great
pleasure in interrogating his guests, and was much amused

with the vicissitudes of their physiognomies, on which were reflected the dirty grimaces of their writhings. The counsellor of justice said to Olivier, "I would give my office to be behind a hedge for half a dozen seconds."

"Oh, there is no enjoyment to equal a good stool; and now I am no longer astonished at the sempiternal droppings of a fly," replied the surgeon.

The cardinal believing that the lady had obtained her receipt from the bank of deposit, left the tassels of his girdle in the king's hand, making a start as if he had forgotten to say his prayers, and made his way towards the door.

"What is the matter with you, Monsieur le Cardinal?" said the king.

"By my halidame, what is the matter with me? It appears that everything is on a grand scale here, sire!"

The cardinal slipped out, leaving the others astonished at his cunning. He proceeded gloriously towards the lower room, loosing a little the strings of his purse; but when he opened the blessed little door he found the lady at her functions upon the throne, like a pope about to be consecrated. Then restraining his impatience, he descended the stairs to go into the garden. However, on the last steps the barking of the dogs put him in great fear of being bitten in one of his precious hemispheres; and not knowing where to deliver himself of his chemical produce he came back into the room, shivering like a man who has been in the open air! The others, seeing the cardinal return, imagined that he had emptied his natural reservoirs, unburdened his ecclesiastical bowels, and believed him happy. Then the surgeon rose quickly, as if to take note of the tapestries and count the rafters, but gained the door before any one else, and relaxing his sphincter in advance, he hummed a tune on his way to the retreat; arrived there he was compelled, like La Balue, to murmur words of excuse to this student of perpetual motion, shutting the door with as much promptitude as he had opened it; and he came back burdened with an accumulation which seriously impeded his private channels. And in the same way went the guests one after the other, without being able to unburden themselves of their sauces, and soon again found themselves all in the presence of Louis the Eleventh, as much distressed as before, looking at each other slyly, understanding each other better with their tails than they ever understood with their mouths, for there is never an equivoque in the transactions of the parts of nature, and everything therein is rational and of easy comprehension, seeing that it is a science which we learn at our birth.

"I believe," said the cardinal to the surgeon, "that lady will go on until to-morrow. What was Le Beaupertuys about, to ask such a case of diarrhœa here?"

"She's been an hour working at what I would get done in a minute. May the fever seize her!" cried Olivier le Daim.

All the courtiers seized with colic were walking up and down to make their importunate matters patient, when the said lady reappeared in the room. You can believe they found her beautiful and graceful, and would willingly have kissed her, there where they so longed to go; and never did they salute the day with more favour than this lady, the liberator of their poor unfortunate bodies. La Balue rose; the others, from honour, esteem, and reverence of the church, gave way to the clergy, and, biding their time, they continued to make grimaces, at which the king laughed to himself with Nicole, who aided him to stop the respiration of these loose-bowelled gentlemen. The good Scotch captain, who had more than all the others eaten of a dish in which the cook had put an aperient powder, tried gently to break wind, and spoiled his trousers. He went ashamed into a corner, hoping that before the king, his mishap might escape detection. At this moment the cardinal returned horribly upset, because he had found La Beaupertuys on the episcopal seat. Now, in his torments, not knowing if she were in the room, he came back and gave vent to a diabolical "*Oh!*" on beholding her near his master.

"What do you mean?" exclaimed the king, looking at the priest in a way to give him the fever.

"Sire," said La Balue, insolently, "the affairs of purgatory are in my ministery, and I am bound to inform you that there is sorcery going on in this house."

"Ah! little priest, you wish to make game of me!" said the king.

At these words the company were in a terrible state.

"So, you treat me with disrespect?" said the king, which made them turn pale. "Ho, there! Tristan, my friend!" cried Louis XI. from the window, which he threw up suddenly, "come up here!"

The grand provost of the hotel was not long before he appeared; and as these gentlemen were all nobodies, raised to their present position by the favour of the king, Louis, in a moment of anger, could crush them at will; so that with the exception of the cardinal, who relied upon his cassock, Tristan found them all rigid and aghast.

"Conduct these gentlemen to the Pretorium, on the Mall, my friend, they have disgraced themselves through overeating."

"Am I not good at jokes?" said Nicole to him.

"The farce is good, but it is fetid," replied he, laughing.

This royal answer showed the courtiers that this time the king did not intend to play with their heads, for which

they thanked heaven. This monarch was partial to these
dirty tricks. He was not at all a bad fellow, as the guests
remarked while relieving themselves against the side of the
Mall with Tristan, who, like a good Frenchman, kept them
company, and escorted them to their homes. This is why
since that time the citizens of Tours have never failed to
defile the Mall of Chardonneret, because the gentlemen of
the court had been there.

I will not leave this great king without committing to
writing the good joke which he played upon La Godegrand,
who was an old maid, much disgusted that she had not, during the forty years she had lived, been able to find a lid to her
saucepan, enraged, in her yellow skin, that she was still as
virgin as a mule. This old maid had her apartments on the
other side of the house which belonged to La Beaupertuys,
at the corner of Rue de Hiérusalem, in such a position that,
standing on the balcony joining the wall, it was easy to see
what she was doing, and hear what she was saying in the
lower room where she lived; and often the king derived
much amusement from the antics of the old girl, who did
not know that she was so much within the range of his
majesty's culverin. Now one market day it happened that
the king had caused to be hanged a young citizen of Tours,
who had violated a noble lady of a certain age, believing
that she was a young maiden. There would have been no
harm in this, and it would have been a thing greatly to the
credit of the said lady to have been taken for a virgin; but
on finding out his mistake, he had abominably insulted her,
and suspecting her of trickery, had taken it into his head to
rob her of a splendid silver goblet, in payment of the present
he had just made her. This young man had long hair, and
was so handsome that the whole town wished to see him
hanged, both from regret and out of curiosity. You may

be sure that at this hanging there were more bonnets than hats. Indeed, the said young man swung very well; and, after the fashion and custom of persons hanged, he died gallantly with his lance erect, which fact made a great noise in the town. Many ladies said on this subject that it was a murder not to have preserved so fine a fellow from the scaffold.

"Suppose we were to put this handsome corpse in the bed of La Godegrand," said La Beaupertuys to the king.

"We should terrify her," replied Louis.

"Not at all, sire. Be sure that she will welcome even a dead man, so madly does she long for a living one. Yesterday I saw her making love to a young man's cap placed on the top of a chair, and you would have laughed heartily at her words and gestures."

Now while this forty-year-old virgin was at vespers, the king sent to have the young townsman, who had just finished the last scene of his tragic farce, taken down, and having dressed him in a white shirt, two officers got over the walls of La Godegrand's garden, and put the corpse into her bed, on the side nearest the street. Having done this they went away, and the king remained in the room with the balcony to it, playing with Beaupertuys, and awaiting the hour at which the old maid should go to bed. La Godegrand soon came back with a hop, skip, and jump, as the Tourainians say, from the church of St. Martin, from which she was not far, since the Rue d'Hiérusalem touches the walls of the cloister. She entered her house, laid down her prayer-book, chaplet, and rosary, and other ammunition which these old girls carry, then poked the fire, blew it, warmed herself at it, settled herself in her chair, and played with her cat for want of something better; then she went to the larder, supping and sighing, and sighing and supping, eating alone, with her eyes cast down upon the carpet; and after having drunk, behaved in a manner forbidden in court society.

"Ah! if the corpse said to her, 'God bless you!'"

At this joke of La Beaupertuys, both laughed heartily in their sleeves. And with great attention this very Christian king watched the undressing of the old maid, who admired herself while removing her things—pulling out a hair, or scratching a pimple which had maliciously come upon her nose; picking her teeth, and doing a thousand little things which, alas! all ladies, virgins or not, are obliged to do, much to their annoyance; but without these little faults of nature, they would be too proud, and one would not be able to enjoy their society. Having achieved her aquatic and musical discourse, the old maid got in between the sheets, and yelled forth a fine, great, ample, and curious cry, when she saw, when she smelt the fresh vigour of this hanged man and the sweet perfume of his manly youth: then sprang away from him out of coquetry. But as she did not know he was really dead, she came back again believing he was mocking her, and counterfeiting death.

"Go away, you bad young man!" said she.

But you can imagine that she preferred this request in a most humble and gracious tone of voice. Then seeing that he did not move, she examined him more closely, and was much astonished at this so fine human nature when she recognized the young fellow, upon whom the fancy took her to perform some purely scientific experiments in the interests of hanged persons.

"What is she doing?" said La Beaupertuys to the king.

"She is trying to reanimate him. It is a work of Christian humanity."

And the old girl rubbed and warmed this fine young man,

supplicating holy Mary the Egyptian to aid her to renew the life of this husband who had for her fallen so amorously from heaven, when, suddenly looking at the dead body she was so charitably rubbing, she thought she saw a slight movement in the eyes; then she put her hand upon the man's heart, and felt it beat feebly. At length, from the warmth of the bed and of affection, and by the temperature of old maids, which is by far more burning than the warm blasts of African deserts, she had the delight of bringing to life that fine handsome young fellow who by a lucky chance had been very badly hanged.

"See how my executioners serve me!" said Louis, laughing.

"Ah!" said La Beaupertuys, "you will not have him hanged again? he is too handsome."

"The decree does not say that he shall be hanged twice, but he shall marry the old woman."

Indeed, the good lady went in a great hurry to seek a master leech, a good bleeder, who lived in the Abbey, and brought him back directly. He immediately took his lancet, and bled the young man. And as no blood came out: "Ah!" said he, "it is too late, the trans-shipment of blood in the lungs has taken place."

But suddenly this good young blood oozed out a little, and then came in abundance, and the hempen apoplexy, which had only just begun, was arrested in its course. The young man moved and came more to life; then he fell, from natural causes, into a state of great weakness and profound sadness, prostration of flesh and general flabbiness. Now the old maid, who was all eyes, and followed the great and notable changes which were taking place in the person of this badly hanged man, pulled the surgeon by the sleeve, and pointing out to him, by a curious glance of the eye, the piteous case, said to him—

"Will he for the future be always like that?"

"Often," replied the veracious surgeon.

"Oh! he was much nicer hanged!"

At this speech the king burst out laughing. Seeing him at the window, the woman and the surgeon were much frightened, for this laugh seemed to them a second sentence of death for their poor victim. But the king kept his word, and married them. And in order to do justice he gave the husband the name of the Sieur de Mortsauf in the place of the one he had lost upon the scaffold. As La Godegrand had a very big basket full of crowns, they founded a good family in Touraine, which still exists and is much respected, since M. de Mortsauf faithfully served Louis the Eleventh on different occasions. Only he never liked to come across gibbets or old women, and never again made amorous assignations in the night.

This teaches us to thoroughly verify and recognize women, and not to deceive ourselves in the local difference which exists between the old and the young, for if we are not hanged for our errors of love, there are always great risks to run.

THE HIGH CONSTABLE'S WIFE

The high constable of Armagnac, desiring to rise in the world, espoused the Countess Bonne, who was already considerably enamoured of little Savoisy, son of the chamberlain to his majesty King Charles the Sixth.

The constable was a rough warrior, miserable in appearance, tough in skin, thickly bearded, always uttering angry words, always busy hanging people, always in the sweat of battles, or thinking of other stratagems than those of love. Thus this good soldier, caring little to favour the marriage stew, used his charming wife after the fashion of a man with more lofty ideas; of the which the ladies have a great horror, since they like not the joists of the bed to be the sole judges of their fondling and vigorous conduct.

Now the lovely countess, as soon as she was grafted on the constable, only nibbled more eagerly at the love with which her heart was laden for the aforesaid Savoisy, which that gentleman clearly perceived.

Wishing both to study the same music, they would soon harmonize their fancies, and decipher the hieroglyphic; and this was a thing clearly demonstrated to the Queen Isabella, that Savoisy's horses were oftener stabled at the house of her cousin of Armagnac than in the Hôtel St. Pol, where the chamberlain lived, since the destruction of his residence, ordered by the university, as every one knows.

This discreet and wise princess, fearing in advance some unfortunate adventure for Bonne—the more so as a constable was as ready to brandish his broadsword as a priest to bestow benedictions—the said queen, as sharp as a dirk, said one day, while coming out from vespers, to her cousin, who was taking the holy water with Savoisy—

"My dear, don't you see some blood in that water?"

"Bah!" said Savoisy to the queen. "Love likes blood, Madame."

This the queen considered a good reply, and put it into writing, and, later on, into action, when her lord the king wounded one of her lovers, whose business you will see settled in this narrative.

You know by constant experience, that in the early time of love each of two lovers is always in great fear of exposing the mystery of the heart, and as much from the flower of prudence as from the amusement yielded by the sweet tricks of gallantry they play at who can best conceal their thoughts. But one day of forgetfulness suffices to inter the whole virtuous past. The poor woman is taken in her joy as in a lasso; her sweetheart proclaims his presence, or sometimes his departure, by some article of clothing—a scarf, a spur, left by some fatal chance, and there comes a stroke of the dagger that severs the web so gallantly woven by their golden delights. But when one is full of days, he should not make a wry face at death, and the sword of a husband is a pleasant death for a gallant, if there be pleasant deaths. So may be will finish the merry amours of the constable's wife.

One morning Monsieur d'Armagnac having lots of leisure time in consequence of the flight of the Duke of Burgundy, who was quitting Lagnay, thought he would go and wish his lady good day, and attempted to wake her up in a pleasant enough fashion, so that she should not be angry; but she, sunk in the heavy slumbers of the morning, replied to the action—

"Leave me alone, Charles!"

"Oh, oh," said the constable, hearing the name of a saint who was not one of his patrons, "I have a Charles on my head!"

Then, without touching his wife, he jumped out of the bed, and ran upstairs with his face flaming and his sword drawn, to the place where slept the countess's maid-servant, convinced that the said servant had a finger in the pie.

"Ah, ah, wench of hell!" cried he, to commence the discharge of his passion, "say thy prayers, for I intend to kill thee instantly, because of the secret practices of Charles who comes here."

"Ah, Monseigneur," replied the woman, "who told you that?"

"Stand steady, that I may rip thee at one blow, if you do not confess to me every assignation given, and in what manner they have been arranged. If thy tongue gets entangled, if thou falterest, I will pierce thee with my dagger!"

"Pierce me through!" replied the girl; "you will learn nothing."

The constable, having taken this excellent reply amiss, ran her through on the spot, so mad was he with rage; and came back into his wife's chamber and said to his groom, whom, awakened by the shrieks of the girl, he met upon the stairs, "Go upstairs; I've corrected Billette rather severely."

Before he reappeared in the presence of Bonne he went to fetch his son, who was sleeping like a child, and led him roughly into her room. The mother opened her eyes pretty widely, you may imagine—at the cries of her little one; and was greatly terrified at seeing him in the hands of her husband, who had his right hand all bloody, and cast a fierce glance on the mother and son.

"What is the matter?" said she.

"Madame," asked the man of quick execution, "this child,

is he the fruit of my loins, or those of Savoisy, your lover?"

At this question Bonne turned pale, and sprang upon her son like a frightened frog leaping into the water.

"Ah, he is really ours," said she.

"If you do not wish to see his head roll at your feet confess yourself to me, and no prevarication. You have given me a lieutenant."

"Indeed!"

"Who is he?"

"It is not Savoisy, and I will never say the name of a man that I don't know."

Thereupon the constable rose, took his wife by the arm to cut her speech with a blow of the sword, but she, casting upon him with an imperial glance, cried—

"Kill me if you will, but touch me not."

"You shall live," replied the husband, "because I reserve for you a chastisement more ample than death."

And doubting the inventions, snares, arguments, and artifices familiar to women in these desperate situations, of which they study night and day the variations, by themselves, or betwen themselves, he departed with this rude and bitter speech. He went instantly to interrogate his servants, presenting to them a face divinely terrible; so all of them replied to him as they would to God the Father on the Judgment Day, when each of us will be called to his account.

None of them knew the serious mischief which was at the bottom of these summary interrogations and crafty interlocutions; but from all that they said, the constable came to the conclusion that no male in his house was in the business, except one of his dogs, whom he found dumb, and to whom he had given the post of watching the gardens; so taking him in his hands, he strangled him with rage. This fact incited him by induction to suppose that the other constable came into his house by the garden, of which the only entrance was a postern opening on to the water side.

It is necessary here to explain to those who are ignorant of it, the locality of the Hôtel d'Armagnac, which had a notable situation near to the royal houses of St. Pol. On this site has since been built the Hôtel of Longueville. Then, as at the present time, the residence of d'Armagnac had a porch of fine stone in the Rue St. Antoine, was fortified at all points, and the high walls by the river side, in face of the Ile du Vaches, in the part where now stands the port of La Grêve, were furnished with little towers. The design of this has for a long time been shown at the house of Cardinal Duprat, the king's chancellor. The constable racked his brains, and at the bottom, from his finest stratagems, drew the best, and fitted it so well to the present case, that the gallant would be certain to be taken like a hare in the trap. " 'Sdeath," said he, "my planter of horns is taken, and I have the time now to think how I shall finish him off."

Now this is the order of battle which this grand hairy captain who waged such glorious war against Duke Jean-sans-Peur commanded for the assault of his secret enemy. He took a goodly number of his most loyal and adroit archers, and placed them in the quay tower, ordering them under the heaviest penalties to draw without distinction of persons, except his wife, on those of his household who should attempt to leave the gardens, and to admit therein, either by night or by day, the favoured gentleman. The same was done on the porch side, in the Rue St. Antoine.

The retainers, even the chaplain, were ordered not to leave the house under pain of death. Then the guard of the two sides of the hotel having been committed to the soldiers of a company of ordnance, who were ordered to keep a sharp look out in the side streets, it was certain that the unknown lover, to whom the constable was indebted for his pair of horns, would be taken warm, when, knowing nothing, he should come at the accustomed hour of love to insolently plant his standard in the heart of the legitimate appurtenances of the said lord count.

It was a trap into which the most expert man would fall unless he were seriously protected by the fates, as was the good St. Peter by the Saviour when he prevented him going to the bottom of the sea the day when they had a fancy to try if the sea were as solid as *terra firma*.

The constable had business with the inhabitants of Poissy, and was obliged to be in the saddle after dinner, so that, knowing his intention, the poor Countess Bonne determined at night to invite her young gallant to that charming duel in which she was always the stronger.

While the constable was making round his hotel a girdle of spies and of death, and hiding his people near the postern to seize the gallant as he came out, not knowing where he would spring from, his wife was not amusing herself by threading peas or seeing black cows in the embers. First, the maid-servant who had been stuck, unstuck herself and dragged herself to her mistress; she told her that her outraged lord knew nothing, and that before giving up the ghost she would comfort her dear mistress by assuring her that she could have perfect confidence in her sister, who was laundress in the hotel, and was willing to let herself be chopped up as small as sausage-meat to please Madame. This she was the most adroit and roguish woman in the neighborhood, and renowned from the council chamber to the Trahoir cross among the common people, as fertile in invention for the desperate cases of love.

Then, while weeping for the decease of her good chamber-woman, the countess sent for the laundress, made her leave

her tubs and join her in rummaging the bag of good tricks,
wishing to save Savoisy, even at the price of her future
salvation.

First of all the two women determined to let him know
their lord and master's suspicions, and beg him to be careful.

Now behold the good washerwoman who, carrying her
tub like a mule, attempts to leave the hotel. But at the porch
she found a man-at-arms who turned a deaf ear to all the
blandishments of the wash-tub. Then she resolved, from her
great devotion, to take the soldier on his weak side, and she
tickled him so with her fondling that he romped very well
with her, although he was armourplated ready for battle;
but when the game was over he still refused to let her go
into the street, and although she tried to get herself a pass-
port sealed by some of the handsomest, believing them more
gallant: neither the archers, men-at-arms, nor others, dared
open for her the smallest entrance of the house. "You are
wicked and ungrateful wretches," said she, "not to render
me a like service."

Luckily at this employment she learned everything, and
came back in great haste to her mistress, to whom she recounted the strange machinations of the count. The two
women held a fresh council and had not considered the time
it takes to sing *Alleluia,* twice, these warlike appearances,
watches, defences, and equivocal, specious, and diabolical
orders and dispositions before they recognized by the sixth
sense with which all females are furnished, the special danger which threatened the poor lover.

Madame having learnt that she alone had leave to quit
the house, ventured quickly to profit by her right, but she
did not go the length of a bow-shot, since the constable
had ordered four of his pages to be always on duty ready
to accompany the countess, and two of the ensigns of his

company not to leave her. Then the poor lady returned to her chamber, weeping as much as all the Magdalens one sees in the church pictures, could weep together.

"Alas!" said she, "my lover must then be killed, and I shall never see him again!... he whose words were so sweet, whose manners were so graceful, that lovely head that has so often rested on my knees, will now be bruised.... What! can I not throw to my husband an empty and valueless head in place of the one full of charms and worth . . . a rank head for a sweet-smelling one; a hated head for a head of love."

"Ah, Madame!" cried the washerwoman, "suppose we dress up in the garments of a nobleman, the steward's son who is mad for me, and wearies me much, and having thus accoutred him, we push him out through the postern."

Thereupon the two women looked at each other with assassinating eyes.

"This marplot," said she, "one slain, all those soldiers will fly away like geese."

"Yes, but will not the count recognize the wretch?"

And the countess, striking her breast, exclaimed, shaking her head, "No, no, my dear, here it is noble blood that must be spilt without stint."

Then she thought a little, and jumping with joy, suddenly kissed the laundress, saying, "Because I have saved my lover's life by your counsel, I will pay you for his life until death."

Thereupon the countess dried her tears, put on the face of a bride, took her little bag and her prayer-book, and went towards the church of St. Pol, whose bells she heard ringing, seeing that the last Mass was about to be said. In this sweet devotion the countess never failed, being a showy woman, like all the ladies of the court. Now this was called the *full-dress Mass,* because none but fops, fashionables, young gentlemen and ladies puffed out and highly scented, were to be met there. In fact no dresses were seen there without armorial bearings, and no spurs that were not gilt.

So the Countess Bonne departed, leaving at the hotel the laundress much astonished, and charged to keep her eyes about her, and came with great pomp to the church, accompanied by her pages, the two ensigns and men-at-arms. It is here necessary to say that among the band of gallants who frisked round the ladies in church, the countess had more than one whose joy she was, and who had given his heart to her, after the fashion of youths who put down enough and to spare upon their tablets, only in order to make a conquest of at least one out of a great number.

Among these birds of fine prey who with open beaks looked oftener between the benches and the paternosters than towards the altar and the priests, there was one upon whom the countess sometimes bestowed the charity of a glance, because he was less trifling and more deeply smitten than all the others.

This one remained bashful, always stuck against the same pillar, never moving from it, but readily ravished with the sight alone of this lady whom he had chosen as his. His pale face was softly melancholy. His physiognomy gave proof of a fine heart, one of those which nourish ardent passions and plunge delightedly into the despairs of a love without hope. Of these people there are few, because ordinarily one likes more a certain thing than the unknown felicities lying and flourishing at the bottommost depths of the soul.

This said gentleman, although his garments were well made, and clean and neat, having even a certain amount of taste shown in the arrangement, seemed to the constable's wife to be a poor knight seeking fortune, and come from afar, with his nobility for his portion. Now partly from a suspicion of his secret poverty, partly because she was well beloved by him and a little because he had a good countenance, fine black hair, and a good figure, and remained humble and submissive in all, the constable's wife desired for him the favour of women and of fortune, not to let his gallantry stand idle, and from a good housewifely idea, she fired his imagination according to her fantasies, by certain small favours and little looks which serpented towards him like biting adders, trifling with the happiness of this young life, like a princess accustomed to play with objects more precious than a simple knight. In fact, her husband risked the whole kingdom as you would a penny at piquet. Finally it was only three days since, at the conclusion of vespers, that the constable's wife, pointing out to the queen this follower of love, said laughing—

"There's a man of quality."

This sentence remained in the fashionable language. Later it became a custom so to designate the people of the court. It was to the wife of the constable d'Armagnac, and to no other source, that the French language is indebted for this charming expression.

By a lucky chance the countess had surmissed correctly concerning this gentleman. He was a bannerless knight, named Julien de Boys-Bourredon, who not having inherited on his estate enough to make a toothpick, and knowing no other wealth than the rich nature with which his dead mother had opportunely furnished him, conceived the idea of deriving therefrom both rent and profit at Court, knowing how fond ladies are of these good revenues, and value them high and dear, when they can stand being looked at between two suns. There are many like him who have thus taken the narrow road of women to make their way; but he, far from arranging his love in measured quantities, spent funds and all, as soon as, come to the full-dress Mass, he saw the triumphant beauty of the Countess Bonne. Then he fell really in love, which was a grand thing for his crowns, because he lost both thirst and appetite. This love is of the worst kind, because it incites you to the love of diet, during the diet of love; a double malady, of which one is sufficient to extinguish a man.

Such was the young gentleman of whom the good lady had thought, and towards whom she came quickly to invite him to his death.

On entering, she saw the poor chevalier, who faithful to his pleasure, awaited her, his back against a pillar, as a sick man longs for the sun, the spring-time, and the dawn. Then she turned away her eyes, and wished to go to the queen and request her assistance in this desperate case, for she took pity on her lover, but one of the captains said to her, with great appearance of respect, "Madame, we have orders not to allow you to speak with man, or woman, even though it should be the queen or your confessor. And remember that the lives of all of us are at stake."

"Is it not your business to die?" said she.

"And also to obey," replied the soldier.

Then the countess knelt down in her accustomed place, and again regarding her faithful slave, found his face thinner and more deeply lined than ever it had been.

"Bah!" said she, "I shall have less remorse for his death; he is half dead as it is."

With this paraphrase of her idea, she cast upon the said gentleman one of those warm little ogles that are only allowable in princesses and harlots, and the false love which her lovely eyes bore witness to, gave a pleasant pang to the gallant of the pillar. Who does not love the warm attack of life when it flows thus round the heart and engulfs everything?

Madame recognized with a pleasure, always fresh in the minds of women, the omnipotence of her magnificent regard by the answer which, without saying a word, the chevalier made to it. And in fact, the blushes which empurpled his cheeks spoke better than the best speeches of the Greek and Latin orators, and was also well understood. At this sweet sight, the countess, to make sure that it was not a freak of nature, took pleasure in experimentalizing how far the virtue of her eyes would go, and after having heated her slave more than thirty times, she was confirmed in her belief that he would bravely die for her. This idea so touched her, that from three repetitions between her orisons she was tickled with the desire to put into a lump all the joys of man, and to dissolve them for him in one single glance of love, in order that she should not one day be reproached with having not only dissipated the life, but also the happiness of this gentleman. When the officiating priest turned round to sing the *Off you go* to this fine gilded flock, the constable's wife went out by the side of the pillar where her courtier was, passed in front of him and endeavoured to insinuate into his understanding by a speaking glance that he was to follow her, and to make positive the intelligence and significant interpretation of this gentle appeal, the artful jade turned round again a little after passing him to again request his company. She saw that he had moved a little from his place, and dared not advance, so modest was he, but upon this last sign, the gentleman, sure of not being over-credulous, mixed with the crowd with little and noiseless steps, like an innocent who is afraid of venturing in one of those good places people call bad ones. And whether he walked behind or in front, to the right or to the left, my lady be-

stowed upon him a glistening glance to allure him the more
and the better to draw him to her, like a fisher who gently
jerks the line in order to hook the gudgeon. To be brief:
the countess practised so well the profession of the daughters
of pleasure when they work to bring grist into their mills,
that one would have said nothing resembled a harlot so much
as a woman of high birth. And indeed, on arriving at the
porch of her hotel the countess hesitated to enter therein,
and again turned her face towards the poor chevalier to
invite him to accompany her, discharging at him so diabolical a glance, that he ran to the queen of his heart, believing
himself to be called by her. Thereupon she offered him her
hand, and both boiling and trembling from contrary causes
found themselves inside the house. At this wretched hour,
Madame d'Armagnac was ashamed of having done all these
harlotries to the profit of death, and of betraying Savoisy
the better to save him; but this slight remorse was lame as
the greater, and came tardily. Seeing everything ready, the
countess leant heavily upon her vassal's arm, and said to
him—

"Come quickly to my room; it is necessary that I should
speak with you."

And he, now knowing that his life was in peril, found
no voice wherewith to reply, so much did the hope of approaching happiness choke him.

When the laundress saw this handsome gentleman so
quickly hooked, "Ah!" said she, "these ladies of the court
are the best at such work." Then she honoured this courtier
with a profound salutation, in which was depicted the
ironical respect due to those who have the great courage to
die for so little.

"Picard," said the constable's lady, drawing the laundress to her by the skirt, "I have not the courage to con-

fess to him the reward with which I am about to pay his silent love and his charming belief in the loyalty of women."

"Bah! Madame: why tell him? Send him away well contented by the postern. So many men die in war for nothing, cannot this one die for something? I'll produce another like him if that will console you."

"Come along," cried the countess, "I will confess all to him. That shall be the punishment for my sin."

Thinking that his lady was arranging with her servant certain trifling provisions and secret things in order not to be disturbed in the interview she had promised him, the unknown lover kept at a discreet distance, looking at the flies. Nevertheless, he thought that the countess was very bold, but also, as even a hunchback would have done, he found a thousand reasons to justify her, and thought himself quite worthy to inspire such recklessness. He was lost in these good thoughts when the constable's wife opened the door of her chamber, and invited the chevalier to follow her in. There his noble lady cast aside all the apparel of her lofty fortune, and falling at the feet of this gentleman, became a simple woman.

"Alas, sweet sir!" said she, "I have acted vilely towards you. Listen. On your departure from this house, you will meet your death. The love which I feel for another has bewildered me, and without being able to hold his place here, you will have to take it before his murderers. This is the joy to which I have bidden you."

"Ah!" replied Boys-Bourredon, interring in the depths of his heart a dark despair, "I am grateful to you for having made use of me as of something which belonged to you. . . . Yes, I love you so much that every day I have dreamed of offering you in imitation of the ladies, a thing that can be given but once. Take, then, my life!"

And the poor chevalier, in saying this, gave her one glance to suffice for all the time he would have been able to look at her through the long days. Hearing these brave and loving words, Bonne rose suddenly.

"Ah! were it not for Savoisy, how I would love thee!" said she.

"Alas! my fate is then accomplished," replied Boys-Bourredon. "My horoscope predicted that I should die by the love of a great lady. Ah, God!" said he, clutching his good sword, "I will sell my life dearly, but I shall die content in thinking that my decease assures the happiness of her I love. I shall live better in her memory than in reality." At the sight of the gesture and the beaming face of this courageous man, the constable's wife was pierced to the heart. But soon she was wounded to the quick because he seemed to wish to leave her without even asking of her the smallest favour.

"Come, that I may arm you," said she to him, making an attempt to kiss him.

"Ha! my lady-love," replied he, moistening with a gentle tear the fire of her eyes, "would you render my death impossible by attaching too great a value to my life?"

"Come," cried she, overcome by this intense love, "I do not know what the end of all this will be, but come—afterwards we will go and perish together at the postern."

The same flame leaped in their hearts, the same harmony had struck for both, they embraced each other with rapture in the delicious access of that mad fever which you know well I hope; they fell into a profound forgetfulness of the dangers of Savoisy, of themselves, of the constable, of death, of life, of everything.

Meanwhile the watchmen at the porch had gone to inform the constable of the arrival of the gallant, and to tell

him how the infatuated gentleman had taken no notice of
the winks which, during Mass and on the road, the countess
had given him in order to prevent his destruction. They met
their master arriving in great haste at the postern, because
on their side the archers of the quay had whistled to him
afar off, saying to him—

"The Sire de Savoisy has passed in."

And indeed Savoisy had come at the appointed hour,
and like all the lovers, thinking only of his lady, he had
not seen the count's spies and had slipped in at the postern.
This collision of lovers was the cause of the constable's
cutting short the words of those who came from the Rue
St. Antoine, saying to them with a gesture of authority,
that they did not think wise to disregard—

"I know that the animal is taken."

Thereupon all rushed with a great noise through the
said postern, crying, "Death to him! death to him!" and
men-at-arms, archers, the constable, and the captains, all
rushed full tilt upon Charles Savoisy, the king's nephew,
whom they attacked just under the countess's window,
where by a strange chance, the groans of the poor young
man were dolorously exhaled, mingled with the yells of
the soldiers, at the same time as passionate sighs and cries
were given forth by the two lovers, who hastened up in
great fear.

"Ah!" said the countess, turning pale from terror,
"Savoisy is dying for me!"

"But I will live for you," replied Boys-Bourredon, "and
shall esteem it a joy to pay the same price for my happiness
as he has done."

"Hide yourself in the clothes chest," cried the countess;
"I hear the constable's footsteps."

And indeed M. d'Armagnac appeared very soon with

a head in his hand, and putting it all bloody on the mantel-shelf, "Behold, Madame," said he, "a picture which will enlighten you concerning the duties of a wife towards her husband."

"You have killed an innocent man," replied the countess, without changing colour. "Savoisy was not my lover."

And with this speech she looked proudly at the constable with a face marked by so much dissimulation and feminine audacity, that the husband stood looking as foolish as a girl who has allowed a note to escape her below, before a numer-ous company, and he was afraid of having made a mistake.

"Of whom were you thinking this morning?" asked he.

"I was dreaming of the king," said she.

"Then, my dear, why not have told me so?"

"Would you have believed me in the bestial passion you were in?"

The constable scratched his ear and replied—

"But how came Savoisy with the key of the postern?"

"I don't know," said she, curtly, "if you will have the goodness to believe what I have said to you."

And his wife turned lightly on her heel like a weather-cock turned by the wind, pretending to go and look after the household affairs. You can imagine that D'Armagnac was greatly embarrassed with the head of poor Savoisy, and that for his part Boys-Bourredon had no desire to cough while listening to the count, who was growling to himself all sorts of words. At length the constable struck two heavy blows over the table, and said, "I'll go and attack the inhabi-tants of Poissy." Then he departed, and when the night was come Boys-Bourredon escaped from the house in some dis-guise or other.

Poor Savoisy was sorely lamented by his lady, who had done all that a woman could do to save her lover, and later he was more than wept, he was regretted; for the countess having related this adventure to Queen Isabella, her majesty seduced Boys-Bourredon from the service of her cousin and put him to her own, so much was she touched with the qualities and firm courage of this gentleman.

Boys-Bourredon was a man whom danger had well recommended to the ladies. In fact he comported himself so proudly in everything in the lofty fortune, which the queen had made for him, that having badly treated King Charles one day when the poor man was in his proper senses, the courtiers, jealous of favour, informed the king of his cuckoldom. Then Boys-Bourredon was in a moment sewn in a sack and thrown into the Seine, near the ferry at Charenton, as every one knows. I have no need to add, that since the day when the constable took it into his head to play thoughtlessly with knives, his good wife utilized so well the two deaths he had caused and threw them so often in his face, that she made him as soft as a cat's paw and put him in the straight road of marriage; and he proclaimed her a modest and virtuous constable's lady, as indeed she was. As this book should, according to the maxims of great ancient authors, join certain useful things to the good laughs which you will find therein and contains precepts of high taste, I beg to inform you that the quintessence of this story is this: That women need never lose their heads in serious cases, because the God of Love never abandons them, especially when they are beautiful, young, and of good family: and that gallants when going to keep an amorous assignation should never go there like giddy young men, but carefully, and keep a sharp look-out near the burrow, to avoid falling into certain traps and to preserve themselves; for after a good woman the most precious thing is, certes, a pretty gentleman.

THE MAID OF THILOUSE

THE lord of Valennes, a pleasant place, of which the castle is not far from the town of Thilouse, had taken a mean wife, who by reason of taste or antipathy, pleasure or displeasure, health or sickness, allowed her good husband to abstain from those pleasures stipulated for in all contracts of marriage. In order to be just, it should be stated that the above-mentioned lord was a dirty and ill-favoured person, always hunting wild animals and not more entertaining than is a room full of smoke. And what is more, the said sports-man was all sixty years of age, on which subject, however, he was as silent as an hempen widow on the subject of rope. But nature, which the crooked, the bandy-legged, the blind, and the ugly abuse so unmercifully here below, and have no more esteem for her than the well-favoured,—since, like workers of tapestry, they know not what they do,—gives the same appetite to all, and to all the same mouth for pud-ding. So every beast finds a mate, and from the same fact comes the proverb, "There is no pot, however ugly, that does not one day find a cover." Now the lord of Valennes searched everywhere for nice little pots to cover, and often in addition to wild, he hunted tame animals; but this kind of game was scarce in the land, and it was an expensive affair to discover a maid. At length, however, by reason of much ferreting about and much inquiry, it happened that the lord of Valennes was informed that in Thilouse was the widow of a weaver who had a real treasure in the person of a little damsel of sixteen years, whom she had never

139

allowed to leave her apronstrings, and whom, with great maternal forethought, she always accompanied when the calls of nature demanded her obedience; she had her to sleep with her in her own bed, watched over her, got her up in the morning, and put her to such work that between the twain they gained about eight pennies a day. On fête days she took her to the church, scarcely giving her a spare moment to exchange a merry word with the young people; above all was she strict in keeping hands off the maiden.

But the times were just then so hard that the widow and her daughter had only bread enough to save them from dying of hunger, and as they lodged with one of their poor relations, they often wanted wood in winter and clothes in summer, owing enough rent to frighten sergeants of justice, men who are not easily frightened at the debts of others; in short, while the daughter was increasing in beauty, the mother was increasing in poverty and ran into debt on account of her daughter's virginity, as an alchemist will for the crucible in which his all is cast. As soon as his plans were arranged and perfect, one rainy day the said lord of Valennes by a mere chance came into the hovel of the two spinners, and in order to dry himself sent for some fagots to Plessis, close by. While waiting for them, he sat on a stool between the two poor women. By means of the grey shadows and half light of the cabin, he saw the sweet countenance of the Maid of Thilouse; her arms were red and firm, her breasts hard as bastions, which kept the cold from her heart, her waist round as a young oak, and all fresh and clean and pretty, like a first frost; green and tender as an April bud; in fact, she resembled all that is prettiest in the world. She had eyes of a modest and virtuous blue, with a look more coy than that of the Virgin, for she was less forward, never having had a child.

Had any one said to her, "Come, let us make love," she would have said, "Love! what is that?" she was so innocent and so little open to the comprehension of the thing.

The good old lord twisted about upon his stool, eyeing the maid and stretching his neck like a monkey trying to catch nuts, which the mother noticed, but said not a word, being in fear of the lord to whom the whole of the country belonged. When the fagot was put into the grate and flared up, the good hunter said to the old woman, "Ah, ah! that warms one almost as much as your daughter's eyes."

"But alas, my lord," said she, "we have nothing to cook on that fire."

"Oh, yes," replied he.

"What?"

"Ah, my good woman, lend your daughter to my wife, who has need of a good handmaiden: we will give you two fagots every day."

"Oh, my lord, what could I cook at such a good fire?"

"Why," replied the old rascal, "good broth, for I will give you a measure of corn in season."

"Then," replied the old hag, "where shall I put it?"

"In your dish," answered the purchaser of innocence.

"But I have neither dish nor flour-bins, nor anything."

"Well, I will give you dishes and flour-bins, saucepans, flagons, a good bed with curtains, and everything."

"Yes," replied the good widow, "but the rain would spoil them, I have no house."

"You can see from here," replied the lord, "the house of La Tourbellière, where lived my poor huntsman Pillegrain, who was ripped up by a boar?"

"Yes," said the old woman.

"Well, you can make yourself at home there for the rest of your days."

"By my faith!" cried the mother, letting fall her distaff, "do you mean what you say?"

"Yes."

"Well, then, what will you give my daughter?"

"All that she is willing to gain in my service."

"Oh! my lord, you are joking."

"No," said he.

"Yes," said she.

"By St. Gatien, St. Eleuther, and by the thousand million saints who move in heaven, I swear that——"

"Ah! well; if you are not jesting I should like those fagots to pass through the hands of the notary."

"By the blood of Christ and the charms of your daughter am I not a gentleman? is not my word good enough?"

"Ah, well, I don't say that it is not; but as true as I am a poor spinner I love my child too much to leave her; she is too young and weak at present, she would break down in service. Yesterday, in his sermon, the vicar said that we should have to answer to God for our children."

"There! there!" said the lord, "go and find the notary."

An old wood cutter ran to the scrivener, who came and drew up a contract, to which the lord of Valennes put his cross, not knowing how to write, and when all was signed and sealed—

"Well, old lady," said he, "now you are no longer answerable to God for the virtue of your child."

"Ah! my lord, the vicar said until the age of reason, and my child is quite reasonable." Then turning towards her, she added, "Marie Fiquet, that which is dearest to you is your honour, and there where you are going every one, without counting my lord, will try to rob you of it, but you see well what it is worth; for that reason do not lose it save willingly and in a proper manner. Now in order not to contaminate

your virtue before God and before man, except for a legitimate motive, take heed that your chance of marriage be
not damaged beforehand, otherwise you will go to the bad."

"Yes, dear mother," replied the maid.

And thereupon she left the poor abode of her relation,
and came to the chateau of Valennes, there to serve my lady,
who found her both pretty and to her taste.

When the people of Valennes, Saché, Villaines, and other
places, learned the high price given for the maid of Thilouse,
the good housewives recognized the fact that nothing is
more profitable than virtue, endeavoured to nourish and
bring up their daughters virtuous; but the business was as
risky as that of rearing silkworms, which are liable to
perish, since innocence is like a medlar, and ripens quickly
on the straw. There were, however, some girls noted for it
in Touraine, who passed for virgins in the convents of the
religious, but I cannot vouch for these, not having proceeded to verify them in the manner laid down by Verville,
in order to make sure of the perfect virtue of women. However, Marie Fiquet followed the wise counsel of her mother,
and would take no notice of the soft requests, honied words,
or apish tricks of her master, unless they were flavoured
with a promise of marriage.

When the old lord tried to kiss her, she would put her
back up like a cat at the approach of a dog, crying out, "I
will tell Madame!" In short, at the end of six months he
had not even recovered the price of a single fagot. From her
labour La Fiquet became harder and firmer. Sometimes she
would reply to the gentle request of her master, "When you
have taken it from me will you give it me back again?"
Another time she would say, "If I were as full of holes as
a sieve not one should be for you, so ugly do I think you."

The good old man took these village sayings for flowers

of innocence, and ceased not to make little signs to her, long harangues and a hundred vows and sermons, for by reason of seeing the fine big breasts of the maid, her plump hips, which at certain movements came into prominent relief, and could be seen through her dress, and by reason of admiring other things capable of inflaming the mind of a saint, this dear man became enamoured of her with an old man's passion, which augments in geometrical proportions as opposed to the passions of young men, because the old men love with their weakness which grows greater, and the young with their strength which grows less. In order to leave this headstrong no loophole for refusal, the old lord took into his confidence the steward, whose age was seventy odd years, and made him understand that he ought to marry in order to keep his body warm, and that Marie Fiquet was the very girl to suit him. The old steward, who had gained three hundred pounds by different services about the house, desired to live quietly without opening the front door again; but his good master begged him to marry to please him, assuring him that he need not trouble about his wife. So the good steward wandered out of sheer good nature into this marriage. The day of the wedding, bereft of all her reasons, and not able to find objections to her pursuer, she made him give her a fat settlement and dowry as the price of her conquest, and then gave the old knave leave to sleep with her as often as he could, promising him as many embraces as he had given grains of wheat to her mother. But at his age a bushel was sufficient.

The festivities over, the lord did not fail, as soon as his wife had retired, to wend his way towards the well-glazed, well-carpeted, and pretty room where he had lodged his lass, his money, his fagots, his house, his wheat, and his steward. To be brief, know that he found the maid of Thilouse the sweetest girl in the world, as pretty as anything, by the soft light of the fire which was gleaming in the chimney, snug between the sheets, with a sweet odour about her, as a young maiden should have, and in fact he had no regret for the great price of this jewel. Not being able to restrain himself from hurrying over the first mouthfuls of this royal morsel, the lord treated her more as a past master than a young beginner. So the happy man by too much gluttony, managed badly, and in fact knew nothing of the sweet business of love. Finding which, the good wench said, after a minute or two, to her old cavalier, "My lord, if you are there, as I think you are, give a little more swing to your bells."

From this saying, which became spread about, I know not how, Marie Fiquet became famous, and it is still said in our country, "She is a maid of Thilouse," in mockery of a bride, and to signify a "fricquenelle."

"Fricquenelle" is said of a girl I do not wish you to find in your arms on your wedding night, unless you have been brought up in the philosophy of Zeno, which puts up with anything, and there are many people obliged to be Stoics in this funny situation, which is often met with, for Nature turns, but changes not, and there are always good maids of Thilouse to be found in Touraine, and elsewhere. Now if you ask me in what consists, or where comes in, the moral of this tale? I am at liberty to reply to the ladies; that the Contes Drolatiques are made more to teach the moral of pleasure than to procure the pleasure of pointing a moral. But if it were a used-up old rascal who asked me, I should say to him, with all the respect due to his yellow or grey locks; that God wished to punish the lord of Valennes, for trying to purchase a jewel made to be given.

THE BROTHER-IN-ARMS

At the commencement of the reign of King Henry, second of the name, who loved so well the fair Diana, there existed still a ceremony of which the usage has since become much weakened, and which has altogether disappeared, like an infinity of the good things of the old times. This fine and noble custom was the choice which all knights made of a brother-in-arms. After having recognized each other as two loyal and brave men, each one of this pretty couple was married for life to the other; both became brothers, the one had to defend the other in battling against the enemies who threatened him, and at Court against the friends who slandered him. In the absence of his companion the other was expected to say to one who should have accused his good brother of any disloyalty, wickedness or dark felony, "You have lied by your throat," and so go into the field instantly, so sure was the one of the honour of the other. There is no need to add, that the one was always the second of the other in all affairs, good or evil, and that they shared all good or evil fortune. They were better than the brothers who are only united by the hazard of nature, since they were fraternized by the bonds of an especial sentiment, involuntary and mutual, and thus the fraternity of arms has produced splendid characters, as brave as those of the ancient Greeks, Romans, or others. . . . But this is not my subject; the history of these things has been written by the historians of our country, and every one knows them.

Now at this time two young gentlemen of Touraine, of

whom one was the Cadet of Maillé, and the other the Sieur de Lavallière, became brothers-in-arms on the day they gained their spurs. They were leaving the house of Monsieur de Montmorency, where they had been nourished with the good doctrines of this great Captain, and had shown how contagious is valour in such good company, for at the battle of Ravenna they merited the praises of the oldest knights. It was in the thick of this fierce fight that Maillé, saved by the said Lavallière, with whom he had had a quarrel or two, perceived that this gentleman had a noble heart. As they had each received slashes in their doublets, they baptized their fraternity with their blood, and were ministered to together in one and the same bed under the tent of Monsieur de Montmorency their master. It is necessary to inform you that, contrary to the custom of his family, which was always to have a pretty face, the Cadet of Maillé was not of a pleasing physiognomy, and had scarcely any beauty but that of the devil. For the rest, he was lithe as a greyhound, broad-shouldered and strongly built as King Pepin, who was a terrible antagonist. On the other hand, the Sieur de Chateau-Lavallière was a dainty fellow, for whom seemed to have been invented rich laces, silken hose, and cancellated shoes. His long dark locks were pretty as a lady's ringlets, and he was, to be brief, a child with whom all the women would be glad to play. One day the Dauphine, niece of the Pope, said laughingly to the Queen of Navarre, who did not dislike these little jokes, "that this page was a plaster to cure every ache," which caused the pretty little Tourainian to blush, because, being only sixteen, he took this gallantry as a reproach.

Now on his return from Italy the Cadet of Maillé found the slipper of marriage ready for his foot, the which his mother had obtained for him in the person of Mademoiselle d'Annebaut, who was a graceful maiden of good appearance, and well furnished with everything, having a splendid hotel in the Rue Barbette, with handsome furniture and Italian paintings and many considerable lands to inherit. Some days after the death of King Francis—a circumstance which planted terror in the hearts of every one because his said Majesty had died in consequence of an attack of the Neapolitan sickness, and that for the future there would be no security even with princesses of the highest birth—the above-named Maillé was compelled to quit the Court in order to go and arrange certain affairs of great importance in Piedmont. You may be sure that he was very loth to leave his good wife, so young, so delicate, so sprightly, in the midst of the dangers, temptations, snares and pitfalls of this gallant assemblage, which comprised so many handsome fellows, bold as eagles, proud of mien, and as fond of women as the people are partial to Paschal hams. In this state of intense jealousy everything made him ill at ease; but by dint of much thinking, it occurred to him to make sure of his wife in the manner about to be related. He invited his good brother-in-arms to come at daybreak on the morning of his departure. Now directly he heard Lavallière's horse in the courtyard, he leaped out of the bed, leaving his sweet and fair better-half sleeping that gentle, dreamy, dozing sleep so beloved by dainty ladies and lazy people. Lavallière came to him, and the two companions, hidden in the embrasure of the window, greeted each other with a loyal clasp of the hand, and immediately Lavallière said to Maillé—

"I should have been here last night in answer to thy summons, but I had a love suit on with my lady, who had given me an assignation; I could in no way fail to keep it, but I quitted her at dawn. Shall I accompany thee? I have told her of thy departure, she has promised me to remain without any amour; we have made a compact. If she deceives me—well, a friend is worth more than a mistress!"

"Oh, my good brother," replied Maillé, quite overcome with these words, "I wish to demand of thee a still higher proof of thy brave heart. Wilt thou take charge of my wife, defend her against all, be her guide, keep her in check and answer to me for the integrity of my head? Thou canst stay here during my absence, in the green-room, and be my wife's cavalier."

Lavallière knitted his brow and said—

"It is neither thee nor thy wife that I fear, but evil-minded people, who will take advantage of this to entangle us like skeins of silk."

"Do not be afraid of me," replied Maillé, clasping Lavallière to his breast. "If it be the divine will of the Almighty that I shall have the misfortune to be a cuckold, I should be less grieved if it were to your advantage. But by my faith, I should die of grief, for my life is bound up in my good, young, virtuous wife."

Saying which, he turned away his head, in order that Lavallière should not perceive the tears in his eyes; but the fine courtier saw this flow of water, and taking the hand of Maillé——

"Brother," said he to him, "I swear to thee on my honour as a man, that before any one lays a finger on thy wife, he shall have felt my dagger in the depths of his veins. And, unless I should die, thou shalt find her on thy return, intact in body if not in heart, because thought is beyond the control of gentlemen."

"It is then decreed above!" exclaimed Maillé, "that I shall always be thy servant and thy debtor!"

Thereupon the comrade departed, in order not to be in-

undated with the tears, exclamations, and other expressions
of grief which ladies make use of when saying "Farewell."
Lavallière having conducted him to the gate of the town,
came back to the hotel, waited until Marie d'Annebaut was
out of bed, informed her of the departure of her good husband, and offered to place himself at her orders, in such a
graceful manner, that the most virtuous woman would have
been tickled with a desire to keep such a knight to herself.
But there was no need of this fine paternoster to indoctrinate the lady, seeing that she had listened to the discourse
of the two friends, and was greatly offended at her husband's doubt. Alas! God alone is perfect! In all the ideas of
men there is always a bad side, and it is therefore a great
science in life, but an impossible science, to take hold of
everything, even a stick by the right end. The cause of the
great difficulty there is in pleasing the ladies is, that there
is in them a thing which is more woman than they are, and
but for the respect which is due to them, I would use another
word. Now we should never awaken the phantasy of this
malevolent thing. The perfect government of women is a
task to rend a man's heart, and we are compelled to remain
in perfect submission to them; that is, I imagine, the best
manner in which to solve the most agonizing enigma of
marriage.

Now Marie d'Annebaut was delighted with the bearing
and offers of the gallant; but there was something in her
smile which indicated a malicious idea, and, to speak plainly,
the intention of putting her young guardian between honour
and pleasure; to regale him so with love, to surround him
with so many little attentions, to pursue him with such warm
glances, that he would be faithless to friendship, to the advantage of gallantry.

Everything was in perfect trim for the carrying out of

her design, because of the companionship which the Sire de Lavallière would be obliged to have with her during his stay in the hotel, and as there is nothing in the world can turn a woman from her whim, at every turn the artful jade was ready to catch him in a trap.

At times she would make him remain seated near her by the fire, until twelve o'clock at night, singing soft refrains, and at every opportunity showing her fair shoulders, and the white temptations of which her corset was full, and casting upon him a thousand piercing glances, all without showing in her face the thoughts that surged in her brain.

At times she would walk with him in the morning, in the garden of the hotel, leaning heavily upon his arm, pressing it, sighing, and making him tie the laces of her little shoes, which were always coming undone in that particular place. Then it would be those soft words and things which the ladies understand so well, little attentions paid to a guest, such as coming in to see if he were comfortable, if his bed were well made, the room clean, if the ventilation were good, if he felt any draughts in the night, if the sun came in during the day, and asking him to forego none of his usual fancies and habits, saying—

"Are you accustomed to take anything in the morning in bed, such as honey, milk, or spice? Do the meal times suit you? I will conform mine to yours; tell me. You are afraid to ask me. Come——"

She accompanied these coddling little attentions with a hundred affected speeches; for instance, on coming into the room she would say—

"I am intruding, send me away. You want to be left alone—I will go." And always was she graciously invited to remain.

And the cunning Madame always came lightly attired,

showing samples of her beauty, which would have made a patriarch neigh, even were he as much battered by time as must have been Mr. Methuselah, with his nine hundred and sixty years.

The good knight being as sharp as a needle, let the lady go on with her tricks, much pleased to see her occupy herself with him, since it was so much gained; but like a loyal brother, he always called her absent husband to the lady's mind.

Now one evening—the day had been very warm—Lavallière, suspecting the lady's games, told her that Maillé loved her dearly, that she had in him a man of honour, a gentleman who doted on her, and was ticklish on the score of his crown.

"Why then, if he is so ticklish in this matter, has he placed you here?"

"Was it not a most prudent thing?" replied he. "Was it not necessary to confide you to some defender of your virtue? not that it needs one save to protect you from wicked men."

"Then you are my guardian?" said she.

"I am proud of it!" exclaimed Lavallière.

"Ah!" said she, "he has made a very bad choice."

This remark was accompanied by a little look, so lewdly lascivious that the good brother-in-arms put on, by way of reproach, a severe countenance, and left the fair lady alone, much piqued at this refusal to commence love's conflict.

She remained in deep meditation, and began to search for the real obstacle that she had encountered, for it was impossible that it should enter the mind of any lady, that a gentleman could despise that bagatelle which is of such great price, and so high value. Now these thoughts knitted and joined together so well, one fitting into the other, that out of little pieces she constructed a perfect whole, and found herself desperately in love; which should teach ladies never to play with a man's weapons, seeing that like glue, they always stick to the fingers.

By this means Marie d'Annebaut came to a conclusion which she should have known at the commencement—viz., that to keep clear of her snares, the good knight must be smitten with some other lady, and looking around her, to see where her young guest could have found a needle-case to his taste, she thought of the fair Limeuil, one of Queen Catherine's maids, of Mesdames de Nevers, d'Estrées, and de Giac, all of whom were declared friends of Lavallière's, and of the lot he must love one to distraction.

From this belief, she added the motive of jealousy to the other which tempted her to seduce her Argus, whom she did not wish to wound, but to perfume, kiss his head, and treat kindly.

She was certainly more beautiful, young, and more appetizing and gentle than her rivals; at least, that was the melodious decree of her imagination. So, urged on by the chords and springs of conscience, and physical causes which affect women, she returned to the charge, to commence a fresh assault upon the heart of the chevalier, for the ladies like to take that which is well fortified.

Then she played the pussy-cat, and nestled up close to him, became so sweetly sociable, and wheedled him so gently, that one evening when she was in a desponding state, although merry enough in her inmost soul, her guardian-brother asked her—

"What is the matter with you?"

To which she replied to him dreamily, being listened to by him as the sweetest music—

That she had married Maillé against her heart's will, and

that she was very unhappy; that she knew not the sweets of love; that her husband did not understand her, and that her life was full of tears. In fact, that she was a maiden in heart and all, since she confessed that in marriage she had experienced nothing but the reverse of pleasure. And she added, that surely this holy state should be full of the sweet-meats and dainties of love, because all the ladies hurried into it, and hated and were jealous of those who out-bid them, for it cost certain people pretty dear; that she was so curious about it that for one good day or night of love, she would give her life, and always be obedient to her lover without a murmur; but that he with whom she would sooner than all others try the experiment would not listen to her; that, nevertheless, the secret of their loves might be kept eternally, so great was her husband's confidence in him, and that finally if he still refused, it would kill her.

And all these paraphrases of the common canticle known to the ladies at their birth were ejaculated between a thousand pauses, interrupted with sighs torn from the heart, ornamented with quiverings, appeals to heaven, upturned eyes, sudden blushings, and clutchings at her hair. In fact, no ingredient of temptation was lacking in the dish, and at the bottom of all these words there was a nipping desire which embellished even its blemishes. The good knight fell at the lady's feet, and weeping took them and kissed them, and you may be sure the good woman was quite delighted to let him kiss them, and even without looking too carefully to see what she was going to do, she abandoned her dress to him, knowing well that to keep it from sweeping the ground it must be taken at the bottom to raise it; but it was written that for that evening she should be good, for the handsome Lavallière said to her with despair—

"Ah, madame, I am an unfortunate man, and a wretch."

"Not at all," said she.

"Alas, the joy of loving you is denied to me."

"How?" said she.

"I dare not confess my situation to you!"

"Is it then very bad?"

"Ah, you will be ashamed of me!"

"Speak, I will hide my face in my hands," and the cunning madam hid her face in such a way that she could look at her well-beloved between her fingers.

"Alas!" said he, "the other evening when you addressed me in such gracious words, I was so treacherously inflamed, that not knowing my happiness to be so near, and not daring to confess my flame to you, I ran to a Bordel where all the gentlemen go, and there for love of you, and to save the honour of my brother whose head I should blush to dishonour, I was so badly infected that I am in great danger of dying of the Italian sickness."

The lady, seized with terror, gave vent to the cry of a woman in labour, and with great emotion, repulsed him with a gentle little gesture. Poor Lavallière, finding himself in so pitiable a state, went out of the room, but he had not even reached the tapestries of the door, when Marie d'Annebaut again contemplated him, saying to herself, "Ah! what a pity!" Then she fell into a state of great melancholy, pitying in herself the gentleman, and became the more in love with him because he was fruit three times forbidden.

"But for Maillé," said she to him, one evening that she thought him handsomer than usual, "I would willingly take your disease. Together we should then have the same terrors."

"I love you too well," said the brother, "not to be good."

And he left her to go to his beautiful Limeuil. You can imagine that being unable to refuse to receive the burning glances of the lady, during meal times, and the evenings, there was a fire nourished that warmed them both, but she was compelled to live without touching her cavalier, otherwise than with her eyes. Thus occupied, Marie d'Annebaut was fortified at every point against the gallants of the Court, for there are no bounds so impassable as those of love, and no better guardian; it is like the devil, he whom it has in its clutches it surrounds with flames. One evening, Lavallière having escorted his friend's wife to a dance given by Queen Catherine, he danced with the fair Limeuil, with whom he was madly in love. At that time the knights carried on their amours bravely two by two, and even in troops. Now all the ladies were jealous of La Limeuil, who at that time was thinking of yielding to the handsome Lavallière. Before taking their places in the quadrille, she had given him the sweetest of assignations for the morrow, during the hunt. Our great Queen Catherine, who from political motives fomented these loves and stirred them up, like pastrycooks make their oven fires burn by poking, glanced at all the pretty couples interwoven in the quadrille, and said to her husband—

"When they combat here, can they conspire against you, eh?"

"Ah! but the Protestants?"

"Bah! have them here as well," said she, laughing. "Why, look at Lavallière, who is suspected to be a Huguenot; he is converted by my dear little Limeuil, who does not play her cards badly for a young lady of sixteen. He will soon have her name down in his list."

"Ah, Madame! do not believe it," said Marie d'Annebaut, "he is ruined through that same sickness of Naples which made you queen."

At this artless confession, Catherine, the fair Diana,

and the king, who were sitting together, burst out laughing, and the thing ran round the room. This brought endless shame and mockery upon Lavallière. The poor gentleman, pointed at by every one, soon wished somebody else in his shoes, for La Limeuil, whom his rivals had not been slow laughingly to warn of her danger, appeared to shrink from her lover, so rapid was the spread, and so violent the apprehensions of this nasty disease. Thus Lavallière found himself abandoned by every one like a leper. The king made an offensive remark, and the good knight quitted the ball-room, followed by poor Marie in despair at the speech. She had in every way ruined the man she loved; she had destroyed his honour, and marred his life, since the physicians and master surgeons advanced as a fact, incapable of contradiction, that persons Italianized by this love sickness, lost through it their greatest attractions, as well as their generative powers, and their bones went black.

Thus no woman would bind herself in legitimate marriage with the finest gentleman in the kingdom if he were only suspected of being one of those whom Master Francis Rabelais named *"his very precious scabby ones. . . ."*

As the handsome knight was very silent and melancholy, his companion said to him on the road home from Hercules House, where the fête had been held—

"My dear lord, I have done you a great mischief."

"Ah, Madame!" replied Lavallière, "my hurt is curable; but into what a predicament have you fallen? You should not have been aware of the danger of my love."

"Ah!" said she, "I am sure now always to have you to myself; in exchange for this great obloquy and dishonour, I will be forever your friend, your hostess, and your lady-love—more than that, your servant. My determination is to devote myself to you and efface the traces of this shame;

to cure you by watch and ward; and if the learned in these
matters declare that the disease has such a hold of you that
it will kill you like our defunct Sovereign, I must still have
your company in order to die gloriously in dying of your
complaint. Even then," said she, weeping, "that will not be
penance enough to atone for the wrong I have done you."

These words were accompanied with big tears; her virtuous heart waxed faint, she fell to the ground exhausted.
Lavallière, terrified, caught her and placed his hand upon
her heart, below a breast of matchless beauty. The lady,
revived at the warmth of this beloved hand, experienced
such exquisite delights as nearly to make her again uncon-
scious.

"Alas!" said she, "this sly and superficial caress will be
for the future the only pleasure of our love. It will still be a
hundred times better than the joys which poor Maillé
fancies he is bestowing on me. . . . Leave your hand there,"
said she; "verily it is upon my soul, and touches it."

At these words the knight was in a pitiful plight, and innocently confessed to the lady that he experienced so much
pleasure at this touch that the pains of his malady increased,
and that death was preferable to this martyrdom.

"Let us die then," said she.

But the litter was in the courtyard of the hotel, and as the
means of death were not handy, each one slept far from
the other, heavily weighed down with love, Lavallière having lost his fair Limeuil, and Marie d'Annebaut having
gained pleasures without parallel.

From this affair, which was quite unforeseen, Lavallière found himself under the ban of love and marriage
and dared no longer appear in public, and he found how
much it costs to guard the virtue of a woman; but the more
honour and virtue he displayed the more pleasure did he

experience in these great sacrifices offered at the shrine of brotherhood. Nevertheless his duty was very bitter, very ticklish, and intolerable to perform, towards the last days of his guard. And in this way.

The confession of her love, which she believed was returned, the wrong done by her to her cavalier, and the experience of an unknown pleasure, emboldened the fair Marie, who fell into a platonic love, gently tempered with those little indulgences in which there is no danger. From this cause sprang the diabolical pleasures of the game invented by the ladies, who since the death of Francis the First feared the contagion, but wished to gratify their lovers. To these cruel delights, in order to properly play his part, Lavallière could not refuse his sanction. Thus every evening the mournful Marie would attach her guest to her petticoats, holding his hands, kissing him with burning glances, her cheek placed gently against his, and during this virtuous embrace, in which the knight was held like the devil by a holy water brush, she told him of her great love, which was boundless since it stretched through the infinite spaces of unsatisfied desire. All the fire with which ladies endow their substantial amours, when the night has no other lights than their eyes, she transferred into the mystic motions of her head, the exultations of her soul, and the ecstasies of her heart. Then, naturally, and with the delicious joy of two angels united by thought alone, they intoned together those sweet litanies repeated by the lovers of the period in honour of love—anthems which the Abbot of Theleme has paragraphically saved from oblivion by engraving them on the walls of his abbey, situated, according to master Alcofribas, in our land of Chinon, where I have seen them in Latin, and have translated them for the benefit of Christians.

"Alas!" cried Marie d'Annebaut, "thou art my strength and my life, my joy and my treasure."

"And you," replied he, "you are a pearl, an angel."

"Thou art my seraphim."

"You my soul."

"Thou my God."

"You my evening star and morning star, my honour, my beauty, my universe."

"Thou my great, my divine master."

"You my glory, my faith, my religion."

"Thou my gentle one, my handsome one, my courageous one, my dear one, my cavalier, my defender, my king, my love."

"You my fairy, the flower of my days, the dream of my nights."

"Thou my thought at every moment."

"You the delight of my eyes."

"Thou the voice of my soul."

"You my light by day."

"Thou my glimmer in the night."

"You the best beloved among women."

"Thou the most adored of men."

"You my blood, a myself better than myself."

"Thou my heart, my lustre."

"You my saint, my only joy."

"I yield thee the palm of love, and how great soe'er mine be I believe thou lovest me still more, for thou art the lord."

"No; the palm is yours, my goddess, my Virgin Marie."

"No; I am thy servant, thine handmaiden, a nothing thou canst crush to atoms."

"No, no; it is I who am your slave, your faithful page, whom you can use as a breath of air, upon whom you can walk as on a carpet. My heart is your throne."

"No, dearest, for thy voice transfigures me."

"Your regard burns me."

"I see but thee."

"I love but you."

"Oh, put thine hand upon my heart—only thine hand—and thou wilt see me pale, when my blood shall have taken the heat of thine."

Then during these struggles their eyes, already ardent, flamed still more brightly, and the good knight was a little the accomplice of the pleasure which Marie d'Annebaut took in feeling his hand upon her heart. Now, as in this light embrace all their strength was put forth, all their desires strained, all their ideas of the thing concentrated, it happened that the knight's transport reached a climax. Their eyes wept warm tears, they seized each other hard and fast as fire seizes houses; but that was all. Lavallière had promised to return safe and sound to his friend the body only, not the heart.

When Maillé announced his return, it was quite time, since no virtue could avoid melting upon this gridiron; and the less licence the lovers had, the more pleasure they had in their fantasies.

Leaving Marie d'Annebaut, the good companion in arms went as far as Bondy to meet his friend, to help him to pass through the forest without accident, and the two brothers slept together, according to the ancient custom, in the village of Bondy.

There, in their bed, they recounted to each other, one the adventures of his journey, the other the gossip of the camp, stories of gallantry, and the rest. But Maillé's first question was touching Marie d'Annebaut, whom Lavallière swore to be intact in that precious place where the honour of husbands is lodged; at which the amorous Maillé was highly delighted.

On the morrow they were all three re-united, to the great disgust of Marie, who, with the high jurisprudence of women, made a great fuss with her good husband, but with her finger she indicated her heart in an artless manner to Lavallière, as one who said, "This is thine!"

At supper Lavallière announced his departure for the wars. Maillé was much grieved at this resolution, and wished to accompany his brother; but Lavallière refused him point blank.

"Madame," said he to Marie d'Annebaut, "I love you more than life, but not more than honour."

He turned pale, saying this, and Madame de Maillé blanched hearing him, because never in their amorous dalliance had there been so much true love as in this speech. Maillé insisted upon keeping his friend company as far as Meaux. When he came back, he was talking over with his wife the unknown reasons and secret causes of this departure, when Marie, who suspected the grief of poor Lavallière, said, "I know: he is ashamed to stop here because he has the Neapolitan sickness."

"He!" said Maillé, quite astonished. "I saw him when we were in bed together at Bondy the other evening, and yesterday at Meaux. There's nothing the matter with him; he is as sound as a bell."

The lady burst into tears, admiring this great loyalty, the sublime resignation to his oath, and the extreme sufferings of this internal passion. But as she still kept her love in the recesses of her heart, she died when Lavallière fell before Metz, as has been elsewhere related by Messire Bourdeilles de Brantôme in his tittle-tattle.

THE VICAR OF AZAY-LE-RIDEAU

In those days the priests no longer took any woman in legitimate marriage, but kept good mistresses as pretty as they could get; which custom has since been interdicted by the council, as every one knows, because, indeed, it was not pleasant that the private confessions of people should be retold to a wench who would laugh at them, besides the other secret doctrines, ecclesiastical arrangements, and speculations which are part and parcel of the politics of the Church of Rome. The last priest in our country who theologically kept a woman in his parsonage, regaling her with his scholastic love, was a certain Vicar of Azay-le-Ridel, a place later on most aptly named Azay-le-Brulé, and now Azay-le-Rideau, whose castle is one of the marvels of Touraine. Now this said period, when the women were not averse to the odour of the priesthood, is not so far distant as some may think, for Monsieur D'Orgemont, son of the preceding bishop, still held the see of Paris, and the great quarrels of the Armagnacs had not finished. To tell the truth, this vicar did well to have his vicarage in that age, since he was well shapen, of a high colour, stout, big, strong, eating and drinking like a convalescent, and, indeed, was always rising from a little malady that attacked him at certain times; and, later on, he would have been his own executioner, had he determined to observe the canonical continence. Add to this that he was a Tourainian, *id est,* dark, and had in his eyes flame to light, and water to quench all the domestic furnaces that required lighting or quenching;

163

and never since at Azay has been such vicar seen! A handsome vicar was he, square-shouldered, fresh-coloured, always blessing and chuckling, preferring weddings and christenings to funerals, a good joker, pious in church, and a man in everything. There have been many vicars who have drunk well and eaten well; others who have blessed abundantly and chuckled consumedly; but all of them together would hardly make up the sterling worth of this aforesaid vicar; and he alone has worthily filled his post with benedictions, has held it with joy, and in it has consoled the afflicted, all so well, that no one saw him come out of his house without wishing to be in his heart, so much was he beloved. It was he who first said in a sermon that the devil was not so black as he was painted, and who for Madame de Candé transformed partridges into fish, saying that the perch of the Indre were partridges of the river, and, on the other hand, partridges perch in the air. He never played artful tricks under the cloak of morality, and often said, jokingly, he would rather be in a good bed than in anybody's will, that he had plenty of everything, and wanted nothing. As for the poor and suffering, never did those who came to ask for wool at the vicarage go away shorn, for his hand was always in his pocket, and he melted (he who in all else was so firm) at the sight of all this misery and infirmity, and he endeavoured to heal all their wounds. There have been many good stories told concerning this king of vicars. It was he who caused such hearty laughter at the wedding of the lord of Valennes, near Sacché. The mother of the said lord had a good deal to do with the victuals, roast meats and other delicacies, of which there was sufficient quantity to feed a small town at least, and it is true, at the same time, that people came to the wedding from Montbazon, from

Tours, from Chinon, from Langeais, and from everywhere, and stopped eight days.

Now the good vicar, as he was going into the room where the company was enjoying themselves, met a little kitchen boy, who wished to inform Madame that all the elementary substances and fat rudiments, syrups, and sauces, were in readiness for a pudding of great delicacy, the secret compilation, mixing, and manipulation of which she wished herself to superintend, intending it as a special treat for her daughter-in-law's relations. Our vicar gave the boy a tap on the cheek, telling him that he was too greasy and dirty to show himself to people of high rank and that he himself would deliver the said message. The merry fellow pushes open the door, shapes the fingers of his left hand into the form of a sheath, and moves gently therein the middle finger of his right, at the same time looking at the lady of Valennes, and saying to her, "Come, all is ready." Those who did not understand the affair burst out laughing, to see Madame get up and go to the vicar, because she knew he referred to the pudding, and not to that which the others imagined.

But a true story is that concerning the manner in which this worthy pastor lost his mistress, to whom the ecclesiastical authorities allowed no successor; but, as for that, the vicar did not want for domestic utensils. In the parish every one thought it an honour to lend him theirs, the more readily because he was not the man to spoil anything, and was careful to clean them out thoroughly, the dear man. But here are the facts. One evening the good man came home to supper with a melancholy face, because he had just put into the ground a good farmer, whose death came about in a strange manner, and is still frequently talked about in Azay. Seeing that he only ate with the end of his teeth, and turned up his nose at a dish of tripe, which had been cooked in his own especial manner, his good woman said to him—

"Have you passed before the Lombard (see MASTER CORNELIUS *passim*), met two black crows, or seen the dead man turn in his grave, that you are so upset?"

"Oh! oh!"

"Has any one deceived you?"

"Ha! ha!"

"Come, tell me!"

"My dear, I am still quite overcome at the death of poor Cochegrue, and there is not at the present moment a good housewife's tongue or a virtuous cuckold's lips that are not talking about it."

"And what was it?"

"Listen! This poor Cochegrue was returning from market, having sold his corn and two fat pigs. He was riding his pretty mare, who, near Azay, commenced to caper about without the slightest cause, and poor Cochegrue trotted and ambled along counting his profits. At the corner of the old road of the Landes de Charlemagne they came upon a stallion kept by the Sieur de la Carte, in a field, in order to have a good breed of horses, because the said animal was fleet of foot, as handsome as an abbot, and so high and mighty that the admiral who came to see it, said it was a beast of the first quality. This cursed horse scented the pretty mare; like a cunning beast, neither neighed nor gave vent to any equine ejaculation, but when she was close to the road, leaped over forty rows of vines and galloped after her, pawing the ground with his iron shoes, discharging the artillery of a lover who longs for an embrace, giving forth sounds to set the strongest teeth on edge, and so loudly, that the people of Champy heard it and were much terrified thereat. Cochegrue, suspecting the affair, makes for the

moors, spurs his amorous mare, relying upon her rapid pace,
and indeed the good mare understands, obeys and flies—flies
like a bird, but a bowshot off follows the blessed horse,
thundering along the road like a blacksmith beating iron,
and at full speed, his mane flying in the wind, replying
to the sound of the mare's swift gallop with his terrible
pat-a-pan! pat-a-pan! Then the good farmer, feeling death
following him in the love of the beast, spurs anew his mare,
and harder still she gallops, until at last, pale and half dead
with fear, he reaches the outer yard of his farmhouse, but
finding the door of the stable shut he cries 'Help here!
wife!' Then he turned round on his mare, thinking to avoid
the cursed beast whose love was burning, who was wild with
passion, and growing more amorous every moment, to the
great danger of the mare. His family, horrified at the danger, did not go to open the stable door, fearing the strange
embrace and the kicks of the iron-shod lover. At last Cochegrue's wife went, but just as the good mare was half way
through the door, the cursed stallion seized her, squeezed
her, gave a wild greeting, with his two legs gripped her,
pinched her and held her tight, and at the same time so
kneaded and knocked about poor Cochegrue, that there was
only found of him a shapeless mass, crushed like a nut after
the oil has been distilled from it. It was shocking to see him
squashed alive and mingling his cries with the loud love-
sighs of the horse."

"Oh! the mare!" exclaimed the vicar's good wench.

"What!" said the priest, astonished.

"Certainly. You men wouldn't have cracked a plumstone
for us."

"There," answered the vicar, "you wrong me." The good
man threw her angrily upon the bed, attacked and treated
her so violently that she split into pieces, and died immedi-

ately without either surgeons or physicians being able to determine the manner in which the solution of continuity was arrived at, so violently disjointed were the hinges and mesial partitions. You can imagine that he was a proud man, and a splendid vicar as has been previously stated.

The good people of the country, even the women, agreed that he was not to blame, but that his conduct was warranted by the circumstances.

From this perhaps came the proverb so much in use at that time, *Que l'aze le saille!* The which proverb is really so much coarser in its actual wording, that out of respect for the ladies I will not mention it. But this was not the only clever thing this great and noble vicar achieved, for before this misfortune he did such a stroke of business that no robbers dare ask him how many angels he had in his pocket, even had they been twenty strong and over to attack him. One evening, when his good woman was still with him, after supper, during which he had enjoyed his goose, his wench, his wine and everything, and was reclining in his chair thinking where he could build a new barn for the tithes, a message came for him from the lord of Sacché, who was giving up the ghost and wished to reconcile himself with God, receive the Sacrament, and go through the usual ceremonies. "He is a good man and loyal lord. I will go," said he. Thereupon he passed into the church, took the silver box where the blessed bread is, rang the little bell himself in order not to wake his clerk, and went lightly and willingly along the road. Near the Gué-droit, which is a valley leading to the Indre across the moors, our good vicar perceived a high toby. And what is a high toby? It is a clerk of St. Nicholas. Well, what is that? That means a person who sees clearly on a dark night, instructs himself by examining and turning over purses, and takes his degrees on the high road. Do you understand now? Well then, this high toby waited for the silver box, which he knew to be of great value.

"Oh, oh!" said the priest, putting down the sacred vase on a stone at the corner of the bridge, "stop thou there without moving."

Then he walked up to the robber, tipped him up, seized his loaded stick, and when the rascal got up to struggle with him, he gutted him with a blow well planted in the middle of his stomach. Then he picked up the viaticum again, saying bravely to it, "Ah, if I had relied upon thy providence, we should have been lost." Now to utter these impious words upon the high road to Sacché was mere waste of breath, seeing that he addressed them not to God, but to the Archbishop of Tours, who had once severely rebuked him, threatened him with suspension, and admonished him before the Chapter for having publicly told certain lazy people that a good harvest was not due to the grace of God, but to skilled labour and hard work—a doctrine which smelt of the fagot. And indeed he was wrong, because the fruits of the earth have need both of one and the other; but he died in this heresy, for he could never understand how crops could come without digging, if God so willed it—a doctrine that learned men have since proved to be true, by showing that formerly wheat grew very well without the aid of man. I cannot leave this splendid model of a pastor without giving here one of the acts of his life, which proves with what fervour he imitated the saints in the division of their goods and mantles, which they gave formerly to the poor and the passers-by. One day, returning from Tours, where he had been paying his respects to the official, mounted on his mule, he was nearing Azay. On the way, just outside Ballan, he met a pretty girl on foot, and was grieved to see a woman travelling like a dog; the more so as she was visibly fatigued and could scarcely raise one foot before the other. He whistled to her softly, and the pretty wench turned round and stopped. The good priest, who was too good a sportsman to frighten the birds, especially the hooded ones, begged her so gently to ride behind him on his mule, and in so polite a fashion, that the lass got up; not without making those little excuses and grimaces they all make when one invites them to eat, or to take what they like. The sheep paired off with the shepherd, the mule jogged along after the fashion of mules, while the girl slipped now this way now that, riding so uncomfortably that the priest pointed out to her, after leaving Ballan, that she had better hold on to him; and immediately my lady put her plump arms around the waist of her cavalier, in a modest and timorous manner.

"There, you don't slip about now. Are you comfortable?" said the vicar.

"Yes, I am comfortable. Are you?"

"I?" said the priest; "I am better than that."

And, in fact, he was quite at his ease, and was soon gently warmed in the back by two projections which rubbed against it, and at last seemed as though they wished to imprint themselves between his shoulder blades, which would have been a pity, as that was not the place for those nice white things. By degrees the movement of the mule brought into conjunction the internal warmth of these two riders, and their blood coursed more quickly through their veins, seeing that it felt the motion of the mule as well as their own; and thus the good wench and the vicar finished by knowing each other's thoughts, but not those of the mule. When they were both acclimatized, he with her and she with him, they felt an internal disturbance which resolved itself into secret desires.

"Ah!" said the vicar, turning round to his companion,

"here is a fine cluster of trees which has grown very thick."

"It is too near the road," replied the girl. "Bad boys have cut the branches, and the cows have eaten the young leaves."

"Are you not married?" asked the vicar, trotting his animal again.

"No," said she.

"Not at all?"

"I' faith! No!"

"What a shame, at your age!"

"You are right, sir; but you see, a poor girl who has had a child is a bad bargain."

Then the good vicar taking pity on such ignorance, and knowing that the canons say among other things that pastors should indoctrinate their flock and show them the duties and responsibilities of this life, he thought he would only be discharging the functions of his office by showing her the burden she would one day have to bear. Then he begged her gently not to be afraid, for if she would have faith in his loyalty no one should ever know of the marital experiment which he proposed then and there to perform with her; and as, since passing Ballan the girl had thought of nothing else; as her desire had been carefully sustained and augmented by the warm movements of the animal, she replied harshly to the vicar, "If you talk thus I will get down." Then the good vicar continued his gentle requests so well that on reaching the wood of Azay the girl wished to get down, and the priest got down there too, for they would have to ride differently before this discussion could be finished. Then the virtuous maiden ran into the thickest part of the wood to get away from the vicar, calling out, "Oh, you wicked man, you will never find me."

The mule arrived in a glade where the grass was good, the girl tumbled down over a root and blushed. The good

vicar came to her, and there as he had rung the bell for mass
he went through the service for her, and both had a fine
foretaste of the joys of paradise. The good priest had it in
his heart to instruct her thoroughly, and found his pupil
very docile, as gentle in mind as soft in the flesh, a perfect
jewel. Therefore was he much grieved at having so much
abridged the lesson by giving it at Azay, seeing that he
would have been quite willing to recommence it, like all preceptors who say the same thing over and over again to their
pupils.

"Ah, little one," cried the good man, "why did you make
so much fuss that we only came to an understanding close
to Azay?"

"Ah!" said she, "I belong to Ballan."

To be brief, I must tell you that when this good man died
in his vicarage there was a great number of people, children
and others, who came, sorrowful, afflicted, weeping, and
grieved, and all exclaimed, "Ah, we have lost our father."
And the girls, the widows, the wives and the little girls
looked at each other, regretting him more than a friend, and
said, "He was more than a priest, he was a man!" Of these
vicars the seed is cast to the winds, and they will never be
reproduced in spite of the seminaries.

Why even the poor, to whom his savings were left, found
themselves still the losers, and an old cripple whom he had
succoured hobbled into the churchyard, crying, "I don't
die! I don't!" meaning to say, "Why did not death take me
in his place?" This made some of the people laugh, at which
the shade of the good vicar would certainly not have been
displeased.

THE REPROACH

THE fair laundress of Portillon-les-Tours, of whom a droll saying has already been given in this book, was a girl blessed with as much cunning as if she had stolen that of six priests and three women at least. She did not want for sweethearts, and had so many that one would have compared them, seeing them around her, to bees swarming of an evening towards their hive. An old silk dyer, who lived in the Rue Montfumier, and there possessed a house of scandalous magnificence, coming from his place at La Grenadière, situated on the fair borders of St. Cyr, passed on horseback through Portillon in order to gain the Bridge of Tours. By reason of the warmth of the evening, he was seized with a wild desire on seeing the pretty washerwoman sitting upon her doorstep. Now as for a very long time he had dreamed of this merry maid, his resolution was taken to make her his wife, and in a short time she was transformed from a washerwoman into a dyer's wife, a good townswoman with laces, fine linen, and furniture to spare, and was happy in spite of the dyer, seeing that she knew very well how to manage him. The good dyer had for a crony a silk-machinery manufacturer, who was small in stature, deformed for life, and full of wickedness. So on the wedding-day he said to the dyer, "You have done well to marry, my friend, *we* shall have a pretty wife;" and a thousand sly jokes, such as it is usual to address to a bridegroom.

In fact, this said hunchback courted the dyer's wife,

who from her nature caring little for badly built people, laughed to scorn the request of the mechanician, and joked him about the springs, engines, and spools of which his shop was full. However, this great love of the hunchback was rebuffed by nothing, and became so irksome to the dyer's wife that she resolved to cure it by a thousand practical jokes. One evening, after the sempiternal pursuit, she told her lover to come to the back-door and towards midnight she would open everything to him. Now note, this was on a winter's night; the Rue Montfumier is close by the Loire, and in this corner there continually blow, in winter, winds sharp as a hundred needle-points. The good hunchback, well muffled up in his mantle, failed not to come, and trotted up and down to keep himself warm while waiting for the appointed hour. Towards midnight he was half frozen, as fidgety as thirty-two devils caught in a stole, and was about to give up his happiness, when a feeble light passed by the cracks of the window and came towards the little door.

"Ah! it is she!" said he.

And this hope warmed him once more. Then he got close to the door, and heard a little voice—

"Are you there?" said the dyer's wife to him.

"Yes."

"Cough, that I may see."

The hunchback began to cough.

"It is not you."

Then the hunchback said aloud—

"How do you mean, it is not I? Do you not recognise my voice? Open the door!"

"Who's there?" said the dyer, opening the window.

"There, you have awakened my husband, who returned from Amboise unexpectedly this evening."

Thereupon the dyer, seeing by the light of the moon a

man at his door, threw a good big pot of cold water over
him, and cried out, "Thieves! thieves!" in such a manner
that the hunchback was forced to run away; but in his fear
he failed to clear the chain stretched across the bottom of
the road, and fell into the common sewer, which the sheriff
had not then replaced by a sluice to discharge the mud into
the Loire. In this bath the mechanician expected every
moment to breathe his last, and cursed the fair Tascherette,
for her husband's name being Taschereau, so was she called
by way of a little joke by the people of Tours.

Carandas—for so was named the manufacturer of machines to weave, to spin, to spool, and wind the silk—was
not sufficiently smitten to believe in the innocence of the
dyer's wife, and swore a devilish hate against her. But some
days afterwards, when he had recovered from his wetting
in the dyer's drain, he came to sup with his old comrade.
Then the dyer's wife reasoned with him so well, flavoured
her words with so much honey, and wheedled him with so
many fair promises, that he dismissed his suspicions.

He asked for a fresh assignation, and the fair Tascherette, with the face of a woman whose mind is dwelling
on the subject, said to him, "Come to-morrow evening;
my husband will be staying some days at Chenonceaux. The
queen wishes to have some of her old dresses dyed and
would settle the colours with him. It will take some time."

Carandas put on his best clothes, failed not to keep the
appointment, appeared at the time fixed, and found a good
supper prepared, lampreys, wine of Vouvray, fine white
napkins—for it was not necessary to remonstrate with the
dyer's wife on the colour of her linen—and everything so
well prepared that it was quite pleasant to him to see the
dishes of fresh eels, to smell the good odour of the meats,
and to admire a thousand nameless little things about the

room, and La Tascherette fresh and appetizing as an apple
on a hot day. Now the mechanician, excited to excess by
these warm preparations, was on the point of attacking the
charms of the dyer's wife, when Master Taschereau gave
a loud knock at the street door.

"Ha !" said madame, "what has happened? Put yourself
in the clothes-chest, for I have been much abused respecting
you; and if my husband finds you, he may undo you; he
is so violent in his temper."

And immediately she thrust the hunchback into the chest,
and went quickly to her good husband, who she knew well
would be back from Chenonceaux to supper. Then the dyer
was kissed warmly on both his eyes and both his ears, and
he caught his good wife to him and bestowed upon her two
hearty smacks with his lips that sounded all over the room.
Then the pair sat down to supper, talked together, and finished by going to bed; and the mechanician heard all, though
obliged to remain crumpled up, and not to cough or to make
a single movement. He was in with the linen, crushed up as
close as a sardine in a box, and had about as much air as he
would have had at the bottom of a river; but he had, to
divert him, the music of love, the sighs of the dyer, and the
little jokes of La Tascherette. At last, when he fancied
his old comrade was asleep, he made an attempt to get out
of the chest.

"Who is there?" said the dyer.

"What is the matter, my little one?" said his wife, lifting
her nose above the counterpane.

"I heard a scratching," said the good man.

"We shall have rain to-morrow; it's the cat," replied
his wife.

The good husband put his head back upon the pillow
after having been gently embraced by his spouse. "There,

my dear, ycu are a light sleeper. It's no good trying to make a proper husband of you. There, be good. Oh! oh! my little papa, your nightcap is on one side. There, put it on the other way, for you must look pretty even when you are asleep. There! are you all right?"

"Yes."

"Are you asleep?" said she, giving him a kiss.

"Yes."

In the morning the dyer's wife came softly and let out the mechanician, who was whiter than a ghost.

"Give me air, give me air!" said he.

And away he ran, cured of his love, but with as much hate in his heart as a pocket could hold of black wheat. The said hunchback left Tours and went to live in the town of Bruges, where certain merchants had sent for him to arrange the machinery for making hauberks.

During his long absence, Carandas, who had Moorish blood in his veins, since he was descended from an ancient Saracen left half dead after the great battle which took place between the Moors and the French in the commune of Ballan (which is mentioned in the preceding tale), in which place are the Landes of Charlemagne, where nothing grows because of the cursed wretches and infidels there interred, and where the grass disagrees even with the cows —this Carandas never rose up or lay down in the foreign land without thinking of how he could give strength to his desires of vengeance; and he was dreaming always of it, and wished nothing less than the death of the fair washerwoman of Portillon, and often would cry out, "I will eat her flesh! I will cook one of her breasts, and swallow it without sauce!" It was a tremendous hate of good constitution—a cardinal hate—a hate of a wasp or old maid. It was all known hates moulded into one single hate, which boiled

itself, concocted itself, and resolved itself into an elixir of
wicked and diabolical sentiments, warmed at the fire of the
most flaming furnaces of hell—it was, in fact, a master hate.

Now one fine day, the said Carandas came back into
Touraine with much wealth, that he brought from the country of Flanders, where he had sold his mechanical secrets.
He bought a splendid house in the Rue Montfumier, which
is still to be seen, and is the astonishment of the passers-by,
because it has certain very queer round humps fashioned
upon the stones of the wall. Carandas, the hater, found
many notable changes at the house of his friend the dyer,
for the good man had two sweet children, who, by a curious
chance, presented no resemblance either to the mother or to
the father. But as it is necessary that children bear a resemblance to some one, there are certain people who look for the
features of their ancestors, when they are good looking—
the flatterers. So it was found by the good husband that his
two boys were like one of his uncles, formerly a priest at
Notre Dame de l'Egrinolles, but, according to certain jokers,
these two children were the living portraits of a good-looking shaven crown officiating in the church of Notre Dame
la Riche, a celebrated parish situated between Tours and
Plessis. Now believe one thing, and inculcate it in your
minds, and when in this book you shall only have gleaned,
gathered, extracted and learned this one principle of truth,
look upon yourself as a lucky man—namely, that a man can
never dispense with his nose, *id est,* that a man will always
be snotty—that is to say, he will remain a man, and thus
will continue throughout all future centuries to laugh and
drink, to find himself in his shirt without feeling either
better or worse there, and will have the same occupations.
But these preparatory ideas are to better fix in the understanding that this two-footed soul will always accept as

true these things which flatter his passions, caress his hates, or serve his amours; from this comes logic. So it was that, the first day the above-mentioned Carandas saw his old comrade's children, saw the handsome priest, saw the beautiful wife of the dyer, saw Le Taschereau, all seated at the table, and saw to his detriment the best piece of lamprey given with a certain air by La Tascherette to her friend the priest, the mechanician said to himself, "My old friend is a cuckold, his wife intrigues with the little confessor, and the children have been begotten with his holy water. I'll show them that the hunchbacks have something more than other men."

And this was true—true as it is that Tours has always had its feet in the Loire, like a pretty girl who bathes herself and plays with the water, making a flick-flack, by beating the waves with her fair white hands; for this town is more smiling, merry, loving, fresh, flowery, and fragrant than all the other towns of the world, which are not worthy to comb her locks, or to buckle her waistband. And be sure if you go there you will find in the centre of it, a sweet place, in which is a delicious street where every one promenades, where there is always a breeze, shade, sun, rain, and love. Ha! ha! laugh away, but go there. It is a street always new, always royal, always imperial—a patriotic street, a street with two paths, a street open at both ends, a wide street, a street so large that no one has ever cried, "Out of the way!" there. A street which does not wear out, a street which leads to the abbey of Grand-Mont, and to a trench, which works very well with the bridge, and at the end of which is a fine fair ground. A street well paved, well built, well washed, as clean as a glass, populous, silent at certain times, a coquette with a sweet nightcap on its pretty blue tiles—to be short, it is the street where I was born; it is the queen of streets, always between the earth and the sky; a street with a fountain; a street which lacks nothing to be celebrated among streets; and, in fact, it is the real street, the only street of Tours. If there are others, they are dark, muddy, narrow, and damp, and all come respectfully to salute this noble street, which commands them. Where am I? For once in this street no one cares to come out of it, so pleasant it is. But I owed this filial homage, this descriptive hymn sung from the heart, to my natal street, at the corners of which there are wanting only the brave figures of my good master, Rabelais, and of Monsieur Descartes, both unknown to the people of the country. To resume: the said Carandas was, on his return from Flanders, entertained by his comrade, and by all those by whom he was liked for his jokes, his drollery, and quaint remarks. The good hunchback appeared cured of his old love, embraced the children, and when he was alone with the dyer's wife recalled the night in the clothes-chest, and the night in the sewer, to her memory, saying to her, "Ha! ha! what games you used to have with me."

"It was your own fault," said she, laughing. "If you had allowed yourself by reason of your great love to be ridiculed, made a fool of, and bantered a few more times, you might have made an impression on me, like the others." Thereupon Carandas commenced to laugh, though inwardly raging all the time. Seeing the chest where he had nearly been suffocated, his anger increased the more violently because the sweet creature had become still more beautiful, like all those who are permanently youthful from bathing in the waters of youth, which waters are naught less than the sources of love. The mechanician studied the proceedings in the way of cuckoldom at his neighbour's house, in order to revenge himself, for as many houses as there are so many varieties of manner are there in this business; and although all amours resemble each other in the same manner that all men resemble each other, it is proved to the abstractors of true things, that for the happiness of women, each love has its especial physiognomy, and if there is nothing that resembles a man so much as a man, there is also nothing differs from a man so much as a man. That it is, which confuses all things, or explains the thousand fantasies of women, who seek the best men with a thousand pains and a thousand pleasures, perhaps more than one than the other. But how can I blame them for their essays, changes, and contradictory aims? Why, Nature frisks and wriggles, twists and turns about, and you expect a woman to remain still! Do you know if ice is really cold? No. Well, then, neither do you know that cuckoldom is not a lucky chance, the produce of brains well furnished and better made than all others. Seek something better than ventosity beneath the sky. This will help to spread the philosophic reputation of this eccentric book. Oh, yes; go on. He who cries "vermin powder," is more advanced than those who occupy themselves with Nature, seeing that she is a proud jade and a capricious one, and only allows herself to be seen at certain times. Do you understand? So in all languages does she belong to the feminine gender, being a thing essentially changeable and fruitful and fertile in tricks.

Now Carandas soon recognized the fact that among cuckoldoms the best understood and the most discreet is ecclesiastical cuckoldom. This is how the good dyer's wife had laid her plans. She went always towards her cottage at Grenadière-les-St.-Cyr on the eve of the Sabbath, leaving her good husband to finish his work, to count up and check his books, and to pay his workmen; then Taschereau would join her there on the morrow, and always found a good

breakfast ready and his good wife gay, and always brought
the priest with him. The fact is, this damnable priest crossed
the Loire the night before in a small boat, in order to keep
the dyer's wife warm, and to calm her fancies, in order that
she might sleep well during the night, a duty which young
men understand very well. Then this fine curber of fantasies got back to his house in the morning by the time
Taschereau came to invite him to spend the day at La
Grenadière, and the cuckold always found the priest asleep
in his bed. The boatman being well paid, no one knew anything of these goings on, for the lover journeyed the night
before after nightfall, and on the Sunday in the early morning. As soon as Carandas had verified the arrangement and
constant practice of these gallant diversions, he determined
to wait for a day when the lovers would meet, hungry one
for the other, after some accidental abstinence. This meeting took place very soon, and the curious hunchback saw the
boatman waiting below the square, at the Canal St. Antoine, for the young priest, who was handsome, blond, slender, and well-shaped, like the gallant and cowardly hero of
love, so celebrated by Monsieur Ariosto. Then the mechanician went to find the old dyer, who always loved his wife
and always believed himself the only man who had a finger
in her pie.

"Ah! good evening, old friend," said Carandas to Taschereau; and Taschereau made him a bow.

Then the mechanician relates to him all the secret festi-
vals of love, vomits words of peculiar import, and pricks
the dyer on all sides.

At length, seeing he was ready to kill both his wife and
the priest, Carandas said to him, "My good neighbour,
I have brought back from Flanders a poisoned sword,
which will instantly kill any one, if it only make a scratch

upon him. Now, directly you shall have merely touched your wench and her paramour, they will die."

"Let us go and fetch it," said the dyer.

Then the two merchants went in great haste to the house of the hunchback, to get the sword and rush off to the country.

"But shall we find them *in flagrante delicto?*" asked Taschereau.

"You will see," said the hunchback, jeering his friend. In fact, the cuckold had not long to wait to behold the joy of the two lovers.

The sweet wench and her well-beloved were busy trying to catch, in a certain lake that you probably know, the little bird that never stays in it, and they were laughing and trying, and still laughing.

"Ah, my darling!" said she, clasping him, as though she wished to take an outline of him on her chest, "I love thee so much I should like to eat thee! Nay, more than that, to have you in my skin, so that you might never quit me."

"I should like it too," replied the priest, "but as you can't have me altogether, you must try a little bit at a time."

It was at this moment that the husband entered, his sword unsheathed and flourished above him. The beautiful Tascherette, who knew her lord's face well, saw what would be the fate of her well-beloved, the priest. But suddenly she sprang towards the good man, half naked, her hair streaming over her, beautiful with shame but more beautiful with love, and cried to him, "Stay, unhappy man! Wouldst thou kill the father of thy children?" Thereupon the good dyer, staggered by the paternal majesty of cuckoldom, and perhaps also by the fire of his wife's eyes, let the sword fall upon the foot of the hunchback, who had followed him, and thus killed him.

This teaches us not to be spiteful.

EPILOGUE

HERE endeth the first series of these Tales, roguish sample of the works of that merry Muse, born ages ago, in our fair land of Touraine, the which Muse is a good wench, and knows by heart that fine saying of her friend Verville, written in LE MOYEN DE PARVENIR: *It is only necessary to be bold to obtain favours*. Alas! mad little one, get thee to bed again, sleep; thou art panting from thy journey; perhaps thou hast been farther than the present time. Now dry thy fair naked feet, stop thine ears, and return to love. If thou dreamest other poesy interwoven with laughter to conclude these merry inventions, heed not the foolish clamour and insults of those who, hearing the carol of a joyous lark of other days, exclaim: Ah, the horrid bird!

END OF THE FIRST TEN TALES

THE SECOND TEN TALES

PROLOGUE

CERTAIN persons have reproached the Author for knowing no more about the language of the olden times than hares do of telling stories. Formerly these people would have been vilified, called cannibals, churls, and sycophants, and Gomorrah would have been hinted at as their natal place. But the Author consents to spare them these flowery epithets of ancient criticism; he contents himself with wishing not to be in their skin, for he would be disgusted with himself, and esteem himself the vilest of scribblers thus to calumniate a poor little book which is not in the style of any spoil-paper of these times. Ah! ill-natured wretches! you should save your breath to cool your own porridge! The Author consoles himself for his want of success in not pleasing every one by remembering that an old Tourainian, of eternal memory, had to put up with such contumely, that, losing all patience, he declared in one of his prologues, that he *would never more put pen to paper*. Another age, but the same manners. Nothing changes, neither God above nor men below. Therefore the Author continues his task with a light heart, relying upon the future to reward his heavy labours.

And certes, it is a hard task to invent A HUNDRED DROLL TALES, since not only have ruffians and envious men opened fire upon him, but his friends have imitated their example, and come to him, saying, "Are you mad? Do you think it possible? No man ever had in the depths of his imagination a hundred such tales. Change the hyperbolic title of your budget. You will never finish it." These people are neither misanthropes nor cannibals; whether they are ruffians I know not; but for certain they are kind, good-natured friends; friends, who have the courage to tell you disagreeable things all your life long, who are rough and sharp as currycombs, under the pretence that they are yours to command, in all the mishaps of life, and in the hour of extreme unction, all their worth will be known. If such people would only keep to these sad kindnesses: but they will not. When their terrors are proved to have been idle, they exclaim triumphantly, "Ha! ha! I knew it. I always said so."

In order not to discourage fine sentiments, intolerable though they be, the Author leaves to his friends his old shoes, and in order to make their minds easy, assures them that he has, legally protected and exempt from seizure, seventy droll stories, in that reservoir of nature, his brain. By the gods! they are precious yarns, well rigged out with phrases, carefully furnished with catastrophes, amply clothed with original humour, rich in diurnal and nocturnal effects, nor lacking that plot which the human race has woven each minute, each hour, each week, month, and year of the great ecclesiastical computation, commenced at a time when the sun could scarcely see, and the moon waited to be shown her way. These seventy subjects, which he gives you leave to call bad subjects, full of tricks and impudence, lust, lies, jokes, jests, and ribaldry, joined to the two portions here given, are, by the prophet! a small instalment of the aforesaid hundred.

Were it not now a bad time for bibliopolists, bibliomaniacs, bibliographers, and *bibliothèques* which hinder bibliolatry, he would have given them in a bumper, and not drop by drop as if he were afflicted with dysury of the

brain. He cannot possibly be suspected of this infirmity,
since he often gives good weight, putting several stories
into one, as is clearly demonstrated by several in this volume. You may rely on it, that he has chosen for the finish,
the best and most ribald of the lot, in order that he may not
be accused of a senile discourse. Put then more likes with
your dislikes, and dislikes with your likes. Forgetting the
niggardly behaviour of nature to storytellers, of whom
there are not more than seven perfect in the great ocean of
human writers, other, although friendly, have been of opinion that, at a time when every one went about dressed in
black, as if in mourning for something, it was necessary to
concoct works either wearisomely serious, or seriously
wearisome; that a writer could only live henceforward by
enshrining his ideas in some vast edifice, and that those who
were unable to reconstruct cathedrals and castles of which
neither stone nor cement could be moved, would die unknown, like the Pope's slippers. These friends were requested to declare which they liked best, a pint of good wine,
or a tun of cheap rubbish; a diamond of twenty-two carats,
or a flintstone weighing a hundred pounds; the ring of Hans
Carvel, as told by Rabelais, or a modern narrative pitifully
expectorated by a schoolboy. Seeing them dumbfoundered
and abashed, it was calmly said to them, "Do you thoroughly understand, good people? Then go your ways, and
mind your own businesses."

The following, however, must be added, for the benefit
of all whom it may concern:—The good man to whom we
owe fables and stories of sempiternal authority has only
used his tool on them, having taken his material from
others; but the workmanship expended on these little figures has given them a high value; and although he was,
like M. Louis Ariosto, vituperated for thinking of idle

pranks and trifles, there is a certain insect engraved by him
which has since become a monument of perennity more
assured than that of the most solidly built works. In the
especial jurisprudence of wit and wisdom the custom is to
esteem more dearly a leaf wrested from the book of Nature
and Truth, than all the indifferent volumes from which,
however fine they be, it is impossible to extract either a
laugh or a tear. The author has license to say this without
any impropriety, since it is not his intention to stand upon
tiptoe in order to obtain an unnatural height, but because
it is a question of the majesty of his art, and not of himself
—a poor clerk of the court, whose business it is to have ink
in his pen, to listen to the gentlemen on the bench, and take
down the sayings of each witness in this case. He is responsible for the workmanship, Nature for the rest, since from
the Venus of Phidias the Athenian, down to the little old
fellow Godenot, commonly called the Sieur Breloque, a
character carefully elaborated by one of the most celebrated
authors of the present day, everything is studied from the
eternal model of human imitations which belongs to all. At
this honest business, happy are the robbers that are not
hanged, but esteemed and beloved. But he is a triple fool,
a fool with ten horns on his head, who struts, boasts, and is
puffed up at an advantage due to the hazard of dispositions,
because glory lies only in the cultivation of the faculties, in
patience and courage.

As for the soft-voiced and pretty-mouthed ones, who
have whispered delicately in the author's ear, complaining
to him that they have disarranged their tresses and spoiled
their petticoats in certain places, he would say to them,
"Why did you go there?" To these remarks he is compelled,
through the notable slanders of certain people, to add a
notice to the well-disposed, in order that they may use it,

and end the calumnies of the aforesaid scribblers concerning him.

These droll tales are written—according to all authorities —at that period when Queen Catherine, of the house of Medicis, was hard at work; for during a great portion of the reign, she was always interfering with public affairs to the advantage of our holy religion. The which time has seized many people by the throat, from our defunct master, Francis, first of the name, to the Assembly at Blois, where fell M. de Guise. Now, even schoolboys who play at chuck-farthing, know that at this period of insurrections, pacifications, and disturbances, the language of France was a little disturbed also, on account of the inventions of the poets, who at that time, as at this, used each to make a language for himself, besides the strange Greek, Latin, Italian, German, and Swiss words, foreign phrases, and Spanish jargon, introduced by foreigners, so that a poor writer has plenty of elbow room in this Babelish language, which has since been taken in hand by Messieurs de Balzac, Blaise Pascal, Furetière, Menage, St. Evremond, de Malherbe, and others, who first cleaned out the French language, sent foreign words to the rightabout, and gave the right of citizenship to legitimate words used and known by every one, but of which the Sieur Ronsard was ashamed.

Having finished, the author returns to his lady-love, wishing every happiness to those by whom he is beloved; to the others, misfortune according to their deserts. When the swallows fly homeward, he will come again, not without the third and fourth volume, which he here promises to the Pantagruelists, merry knaves, and honest wags of all degrees, who have a wholesome horror of the sadness, sombre meditation and melancholy of literary croakers.

THE THREE CLERKS OF ST. NICHOLAS

THE Inn of the Three Barbels was formerly at Tours, the best place in the town for sumptuous fare; and the landlord, reputed the prince of cooks, went to prepare wedding breakfasts as far as Chatelherault, Loches, Vendôme, and Blois. This said man, an old fox, perfect in his business, never lighted lamps in the daytime, knew how to skin a flint, charged for wool, leather, and feathers, had an eye to everything, did not easily let any one pay with chaff instead of coin, and for a penny less than his account would have affronted even a prince. For the rest, he was a good banterer, drinking and laughing with his regular customers, hat in hand always before the persons furnished with plenary indulgences entitled *Sit nomen Domini benedictum,* running them into expense, and proving to them, if need were, by sound argument, that wines were dear, and that whatever they might think, nothing was given away in Touraine, everything had to be bought, and, at the same time, paid for. In short, if he could without disgrace have done so, he would have reckoned so much for the good air, and so much for the view of the country. Thus he built up a tidy fortune with other people's money, became as round as a butt, larded with fat, and was called Monsieur. At the time of the last fair three young fellows, who were apprentices in knavery, in whom there was more of the material that makes thieves than saints, and who knew just how far it was possible to go without catching their necks in the branches of trees, made up their minds to amuse themselves,

and live well, condemning certain hawkers or others in all
the expenses. Now these limbs of Satan gave the slip to
their masters, under whom they had been studying the
art of parchment scrawling, and came to stay at the hotel
of the Three Barbels, where they demanded the best rooms,
turned the place inside out, turned up their noses at everything, bespoke all the lampreys in the market, and announced themselves as first-class merchants, who never carried their goods with them, and travelled only with their
persons. The host bustled about, turned the spits, got out the
best of everything, and prepared a glorious repast for these
three dodgers, who had already made noise enough for a
hundred crowns, and who most certainly would not even
have given up the copper coins which one of them was jin-
gling in his pocket. But if they were hard up for money they
did not want for ingenuity, and all three arranged to play
their parts like thieves at a fair. Theirs was a farce in which
there was plenty of eating and drinking, since for five days
they so heartily attacked every kind of provision, that a
party of German soldiers would have spoilt less than they
obtained by fraud. These three cunning fellows made their
way to the fair after breakfast, well primed, gorged, and
big in the belly, and did as they liked with the greenhorns
and others, robbing, filching, playing, and losing, taking
down the writings and signs and changing them, putting
that of the toyman over the jeweller's, and that of the jeweller's outside the shoemaker's, turning the shops inside out,
making the dogs fight, cutting the ropes of tethered horses,
throwing cats among the crowd, crying "Stop thief!" and
saying to every one they met, "Are you not Monsieur D'En-
trefesse, of Angiers?" Then they hustled every one, making
holes in the sacks of flour, looking for their handkerchiefs

in ladies' pockets, raising their skirts, crying, looking for a lost jewel, and saying to them—

"Ladies, it has fallen into a hole!"

They directed the little children wrongly, slapped the stomachs of those who were gaping in the air, and prowled about, fleecing and annoying every one. In short, the devil would have been a gentleman in comparison with these blackguard students, who would have been hanged rather than do an honest action; as well have expected charity from two angry litigants. They left the fair, not fatigued, but tired of ill-doing, and spent the remainder of their time over their dinner until the evening, when they recommenced their pranks by torchlight. After the pedlars they commenced operations on the ladies of the town, to whom, by a thousand dodges, they gave only that which they received, according to the axiom of Justinian: *Cuicum jus tribuere.* "To every one his own juice;" and afterwards jokingly said to the poor wenches—

"We are in the right and you in the wrong."

At last, at supper-time, having nothing else to do, they began to knock each other about, and, to keep the game alive, complained of the flies to the landlord, remonstrating with him that elsewhere the innkeepers had them caught in order that gentlemen of position might not be annoyed by them. However, towards the fifth day, which is the critical day of fevers, the host not having been seen, although he kept his eyes wide open, the royal surface of a crown, and knowing that if all that glittered were gold it would be cheaper, began to knit his brows and go more slowly about that which his high-class merchants required of him. Fearing that he had made a bad bargain with them, he tried to sound the depth of their pockets; perceiving which the three clerks ordered him, with the assurance of a provost hanging his man, to serve them quickly with a good supper, as they had to depart immediately. Their merry countenances dismissed the host's suspicions. Thinking that rogues without money would certainly look grave, he prepared a supper worthy a canon, wishing even to see them drunk, in order the more easily to clap them in gaol in the event of an accident. Not knowing how to make their escape from the room, in which they were about as much at their ease as are fish upon straw, the three companions ate and drank immoderately, looking at the situation of the windows, waiting the moment to decamp, but not getting the opportunity. Cursing their luck, one of them wished to go and undo his waistcoat, on account of a colic, the other to fetch a doctor to the third, who did his best to faint. The cursed landlord kept dodging about from the kitchen into the room, and from the room into the kitchen, watching the nameless ones, going a step forward to save his crowns, and going to step back to save his crown, in case they should be real gentlemen; and he acted like a brave and prudent host who likes halfpence and objects to kicks; but under pretence of properly attending to them, he always had an ear in the room and a foot in the court; fancied he was always being called by them, came every time they laughed, showing them a face with an unsettled look upon it, and always said, "Gentlemen, what is your pleasure?" This was an interrogatory in reply to which they would willingly have given him ten inches of his own spit in his stomach, because he appeared as if he knew very well what would please them at this juncture, seeing that to have twenty crowns, full weight, they would each of them have sold a third of his eternity. You can imagine they sat on their seats as if they were gridirons, that their feet itched and their posteriors were rather warm. Already the host had put the pears, the cheese, and the preserves near their noses, but they, sipping their liquor and picking at the dishes, looked at each other to see if either of them had found a good piece of roguery in his sack, and they all began to enjoy themselves rather wofully. The most cunning of the three clerks, who was a Burgundian, smiled and said, seeing the hour of payment arrived, "This must stand over for a week," as if they had been at the Palais de Justice. The two others, in spite of the danger, began to laugh.

"What do we owe?" asked he who had in his belt the heretofore mentioned twelve sols, and he turned them about as though he would make them breed little ones by this excited movement. He was a native of Picardy, and very passionate; a man to take offence at anything in order that he might throw the landlord out of the window in all security of conscience. Now he said these words with the air of a man of immense wealth.

"Six crowns, gentlemen," replied the host, holding out his hand.

"I cannot permit myself to be entertained by you alone, Viscount," said the third student, who was from Anjou, and as artful as a woman in love.

"Neither can I," said the Burgundian.

"Gentlemen! gentlemen!" replied the Picardian, "you are jesting. I am yours to command."

"Sambreguoy!" cried he of Anjou. "You will not let us pay three times; our host would not suffer it."

"Well then," said the Burgundian, "whichever of us shall tell the worst tale shall justify the landlord."

"Who will be the judge?" asked the Picardian, dropping his twelve sols to the bottom of his pocket.

"Pardieu! our host. He should be capable, seeing that he is a man of taste," said he of Anjou. "Come along, great *chef,* sit you down, drink, and lend us both your ears. The audience is open."

Thereupon the host sat down, but not until he had poured out a gobletful of wine.

"My turn first," said the Anjou man. "I commence."

"In our duchy of Anjou, the country people are very faithful servants to our holy Catholic religion, and none of them would lose his portion of paradise for lack of doing penance or killing a heretic. If a professor of heresy passed that way, he quickly found himself under the grass, without knowing whence his death had proceeded. A good man of Larzé, returning one night from his evening prayer to the wine flasks of the Pomme-de-Pin, where he had left his understanding and memory, fell into a ditch full of water near his house, and found he was up to his neck. One of the neighbours finding him shortly afterwards nearly frozen, for it was winter time, said jokingly to him—

" 'Holloa! what are you waiting for there?'

" 'A thaw,' said the tipsy fellow, finding himself held by the ice.

"Then Godenot, like a good Christian, released him from his dilemma, and opened the door of the house to him, out of respect to the wine, which is lord of this country. The good man then went and got into the bed of the maid-servant, who was a young and pretty wench. The old bungler, bemuddled with wine, went ploughing in the wrong land, fancying all the time it was his wife by his side, and thanking her for the youth and freshness she still retained. On hearing her husband, the wife began to cry out, and by her terrible shrieks the man was awakened to the fact that he was not in the road to salvation, which made the poor labourer sorrowful beyond expression.

" 'Ah!' said he; 'God has punished me for not going to vespers at church.'

"And he began to excuse himself as best he could, saying, that the wine had muddled his understanding, and getting into his own bed he kept repeating to his good wife, that for his best cow he would not have had this sin upon his conscience.

" 'My dear,' said she, 'go and confess the first thing to-morrow morning, and let us say no more about it.'

"The good man trotted to confessional, and related his case with all humility to the rector of the parish, who was a good old priest, capable of being up above, the slipper of the holy foot.

" 'An error is not a sin,' said he to the penitent. 'You will fast to-morrow, and be absolved.'

" 'Fast—with pleasure,' said the good man. 'That does not mean go without drink.'

" 'Oh!' replied the rector, 'you must drink water, and eat nothing but a quarter of a loaf and an apple.'

"Then the good man, who had no confidence in his memory, went home, repeating to himself the penance ordered. But having loyally commenced with a quarter of a loaf and an apple, he arrived at home, saying, a quarter of apples, and a loaf.

"Then, to purify his soul, he set about accomplishing his fast, and his good woman having given him a loaf from the safe, and unhooked a string of apples from the beam, he set sorrowfully to work. As he heaved a sigh on taking the last mouthful of bread, hardly knowing where to put it, for he was full to the chin, his wife remonstrated with him, that God did not desire the death of a sinner, and that for lack of putting a crust of bread in his belly, he would not be reproached for having put things in their wrong places.

" 'Hold your tongue, wife!' said he. 'If it chokes me, I must fast.' "

"I've paid my share, it's your turn, Viscount," added he of Anjou, giving the Picardian a knowing wink.

"The goblets are empty. Hi, there! More wine."

"Let us drink," cried the Picardian. "Moist stories slip out easier."

At the same time he tossed off a glassful without leaving a drop at the bottom, and after a preliminary little cough, he related the following :—

"You must know that the maids of Picardy, before setting up housekeeping, are accustomed honestly to gain their linen, vessels, and chests; in short, all the needed household utensils. To accomplish this, they go into service in Péronne, Abbeville, Amiens, and other towns, where they are tire-women, wash up glasses, clean plates, fold linen, and carry up the dinner, or anything that there is to be carried. They are all married as soon as they possess something else besides that which they naturally bring to their husbands. These women are the best housewives, because they understand the business, and everything else thoroughly. One belonging to Azonville, which is the land of which I am lord by inheritance, having heard speak of Paris, where the people did not put themselves out of the way for any one, and where one could subsist for a whole day by passing the cooks' shops and smelling the steam, so fattening was it, took it into her head to go there. She trudged bravely along the road, and arrived with a pocket full of emptiness. There she fell in, at the Porte St. Denis, with a company of soldiers, placed there for a time as a vidette, for the Protestants had assumed a dangerous attitude. The sergeant seeing this hooded linnet coming, stuck his head-piece on one side, straightened his feather, twisted his moustache, cleared his throat, rolled his eye, put his hands on his hips, and stopped the Picardian to see if her ears were properly pierced, since it was forbidden to girls to enter otherwise into Paris. Then he asked her, by way of a joke, but with a serious face, what brought her there, he pretending to believe she had come to take the keys of Paris by assault. To which the poor innocent replied, that she was in search of a good situation, and had no evil intentions, only desiring to gain something.

" 'Very well; I will employ you,' said the wag. 'I am from Picardy, and will get you taken in here, where you will be treated as a queen would often like to be, and you will be able to make a good thing of it.'

"Then he led her to the guard-house, where he told her to sweep the floor, polish the saucepans, stir the fire, and keep a watch on everything, adding that she should have thirty sols a head for the men if their service pleased her. Now seeing that the squad was there for a month, she would be able to gain ten crowns, and at their departure would find fresh arrivals who would make good arrangements with her, and by this means she would be able to take back money and presents to her people. The girl cleaned the room and prepared the meals so well, singing and humming, that this day the soldiers found in their den the look of a monk's refectory. Then all being well content, each of them gave a sol to their handmaiden. Well satisfied, they put her into the bed of their commandant, who was in the town with his lady, and they petted and caressed her after the manner of philosophical soldiers, that is, soldiers partial to that which is good. She was soon comfortably ensconced between the sheets. But to avoid quarrels and strife, my noble warriors drew lots for their turn, arranged themselves in single file, playing well at Pique hardie, saying not a word, but each one taking at least twenty-six sols' worth of the girl's society. Although not accustomed to work for so many, the poor girl did her best, and by this means never closed her eyes the whole night. In the morning, seeing the soldiers were fast asleep, she rose happy at bearing no marks of the sharp skirmish, and although slightly fatigued, managed to get across the fields into the open country with her thirty sols. On the route to Picardy, she met one of her friends, who, like herself, wished to try service in Paris, and was hurrying thither, and seeing her, asked what sort of places they were.

"'Ah! Perrine; do not go. You want to be made of iron, and even if you were it would soon be worn away,' was the answer."

"Now, big-belly of Burgundy," said he, giving his neighbour a hearty slap, "spit out your story or pay!"

"By the queen of Antlers!" replied the Burgundian, "by my faith, by the saints, by God! and by the devil, I know only stories of the Court of Burgundy, which are only current coin in our own land."

"Eh, ventre Dieu! are we not in the land of Bauffremont?" cried the other, pointing to the empty goblets.

"I will tell you, then, an adventure well known at Dijon, which happened at the time I was in command there, and was worth being written down. There was a sergeant of justice named Franc-Taupin, who was an old lump of mischief, always grumbling, always fighting; stiff and starchy, and never comforting those he was leading to the hulks, with little jokes by the way; and in short, he was just the man to find lice in bald heads, and bad behaviour in the Almighty. This said Taupin, spurned by every one, took unto himself a wife, and by chance he was blessed with one as mild as the peel of an onion, who, noticing the peculiar humour of her husband, took more pains to bring joy to his house than would another to bestow horns upon him. But although she was careful to obey him in all things, and to live at peace would have tried to excrete gold for him, had God permitted it, this man was always surly and crabbed, and no more spared his wife blows, than does a debtor promises to the bailiff's man. This unpleasant treatment continuing in spite cf the carefulness and angelic behaviour of the poor woman, she being unable to accustom herself to it, was compelled to inform her relations, who thereupon came to the house. When they arrived, the husband declared to them that his wife was an idiot, that she displeased him in every possible way, and made his life almost unbearable; that she would wake him out of his first sleep, never came to the door when he knocked, but would leave him out in the rain and the cold, and that the house was always untidy. His garments were buttonless, his laces wanted tags. The linen was spoiling, the wine turning sour, the wood damp, and the bed was always creaking at unseasonable moments. In short, everything was going wrong. To this tissue of falsehoods, the wife replied by pointing to the clothes and things, all in a state of thorough repair. Then the sergeant said that he was very badly treated, that his dinner was never ready for him, or if it was, the broth was thin or the soup cold, either the wine or the glasses were forgotten, the meat was without gravy or parsley, the mustard had turned, he either found hairs in the dish or the cloth was dirty and took away his appetite, indeed nothing did she ever get for him that was to his liking. The wife, astonished, contented herself with stoutly denying the faults imputed to her. 'Ah,' said he, 'you dirty hussy! You deny it, do you! Very well then, my friends, you come and dine here to-day, you shall be witnesses of her misconduct. And if she can for once serve me properly, I will confess myself wrong in all I have stated, and will never lift my hand against her again, but will resign to her my halberd and my breeches, and give her full authority here.'

" 'Oh, well,' said she joyfully, 'I shall then henceforth be both wife and mistress!'

"Then the husband, confident of the nature and imperfections of his wife, desired that the dinner should be served under the vine arbour, thinking he would be able to shout at her if she did not hurry quickly enough from the table to the pantry. The good housewife set to work with a will. The plates were clean enough to see one's face in, the mustard was fresh and well made, the dinner beautifully cooked, as appetizing as stolen fruit; the glasses were clear, the wine was cool, and everything so nice, so clean and white, that the repast would have done honour to a bishop's chatterbox. Just as she was standing before the table, casting the last glance which all good housewives like to give to everything, her husband knocked at the door. At that very moment a cursed hen, who had taken it into her head to get on top of the arbour to gorge herself with grapes, let fall a large lump of dirt right in the middle of the cloth. The poor woman was half dead with fright; so great was her despair, she could think of no other way of remedying the thoughtlessness of the fowl than by covering the unseemly patch with a plate in which she put the fine fruits taken at random from her pocket, losing sight altogether of the symmetry of the table. Then, in order that no one should notice it, she instantly fetched the soup, seated every one in his place, and begged them to enjoy themselves.

"Now, all of them seeing everything so well arranged,

uttered exclamations of pleasure, except the diabolical husband, who remained moody and sullen, knitting his brows and looking for a straw on which to hang a quarrel with his wife. Thinking it safe to give him one for himself, her relations being present, she said to him, 'Here's your dinner, nice and hot, well served, the cloth is clean, the salt-cellars full, the plates clean, the wine fresh, the bread well baked. What is there lacking? What do you require? What do you desire? What else do you want?'

"'Dung!' said he, in a great rage.

"The good woman instantly lifted the plate, and replied—

"'There you are, my dear!'

"Seeing which, the sergeant was dumbfoundered, thinking that the devil was in league with his wife. He was immediately gravely reproached by the relations, who declared him to be in the wrong, abused him, and made more jokes at his expense than a recorder writes words in a month. From that time forward the sergeant lived comfortably and peaceably with his wife, who at the least appearance of temper on his part, would say to him—

"'Do you want some dung?'"

"Who has told the worst now?" cried the Anjou man, giving the host a tap on the shoulder.

"He has! he has!" said the two others. Then they began to dispute among themselves, like the holy fathers in council; seeking, by creating a confusion, throwing the glasses at each other, and jumping about, a lucky chance, to make a run of it.

"I'll settle the question," cried the host, seeing that whereas they had all three been ready with their own accounts, not one of them was thinking of his.

They stopped terrified.

"I will tell you a better one than all, then you will have to give me ten sols a head."

"Silence for the landlord," said the one from Anjou.

"In our faubourg of Notre-Dame la Riche, in which this inn is situated, there lived a beautiful girl, who besides her natural advantages, had a good round sum in her keeping. Therefore, as soon as she was old enough, and strong enough to bear the matrimonial yoke, she had as many lovers as there are sols in St. Gatien's money-box on the Paschal-day. This girl chose one who, saving your presence, was as good a worker, night and day, as any two monks together. They were soon betrothed, and the marriage was arranged; but the joy of the first night did not draw near without occasioning some slight apprehensions to the lady, as she was liable, through an infirmity, to expel vapours, which came out like bombshells. Now, fearing that when thinking of something else, during the first night, she might give the reins to her eccentricities, she stated the case to her mother, whose assistance she invoked. That good lady informed her that this faculty of engendering wind was inherent in the family; that in her time she had been greatly embarrassed by it, but only in the earlier period of her life. God had been kind to her, and since the age of seven, she had evaporated nothing except on the last occasion, when she had bestowed upon her dead husband a farewell blow. 'But,' said she to her daughter, 'I have a sure specific, left to me by my mother, which brings these surplus explosions to nothing, and exhales them noiselessly. By these means these sighs become odourless, and scandal is avoided.'

"The girl, much pleased, learned how to sail close to the wind, thanked her mother, and danced away merrily, storing up her flatulence like an organ-blower waiting the first note of mass. Entering the nuptial chamber, she determined to expel it when getting into bed, but the fantastic element was beyond control. The husband came; I leave you to imagine how they took part in that engagement where with two things you make a thousand, if you can. In the middle of the night, the bride arose under a false pretext, and quickly returned again; but when climbing into her place, the pent up force went off with such a loud discharge, that you would have thought with me that the curtains were split.

"'Ha! I've missed my aim!' said she.

"''Sdeath, my dear,' I replied, 'then spare your powder. You would earn a good living in the army with that artillery.'

"It was my wife."

"Ha! ha! ha!" went the clerks.

And they roared with laughter, holding their sides and complimenting their host.

"Did you ever hear a better story, Viscount?"

"Ah, what a story!"

"That is a story!"

"A master story!"

"The king of stories!"

"Ha! ha! It beats all the other stories hollow. After that I say there are no stories like the stories of our host."

"By the faith of a Christian, I never heard a better story in my life."

"Why, I can hear the report."

"I should like to kiss the orchestra."

"Ah, gentleman," said the Burgundian, gravely, "we cannot leave without seeing the hostess, and if we do not ask to kiss this famous wind-instrument, it is out of respect for so good a story-teller."

Thereupon they all exalted the host, his story, and his

wife's trumpet so well that the old fellow, believing in these knaves' laughter and pompous eulogies, called to his wife. But she not coming, the clerks said, not without frustrative intention, "Let us go to her."

Thereupon they all went out of the room. The host took the candle and went upstairs first, to light them and show them the way; but seeing the street door ajar, the rascals took to their heels, and were off like shadows, leaving the host to take in settlement of his account another of his wife's offerings.

THE CONTINENCE OF
KING FRANCIS THE FIRST

EVERY one knows through what adventure King Francis, the first of that name, was taken like a silly bird and led into the town of Madrid, in Spain. There the Emperor Charles V. kept him carefully locked up, like an article of great value, in one of his castles, in the which our defunct sire, of immortal memory, soon became listless and weary, seeing that he loved the open air and his little comforts, and no more understood being shut up in a cage than a cat would folding up lace. He fell into moods of such strange melancholy that his letters having been read in full council, Madame d'Angoulême, his mother; Madame Catherine, the Dauphine, Monsieur de Montmorency, and those who were at the head of affairs in France knowing the great lechery of the king, determined after mature deliberation, to send Queen Marguerite to him, from whom he would doubtless receive alleviation of his sufferings, that good lady being much loved by him, and merry, and learned in all necessary wisdom. But she, alleging that it would be dangerous for her soul, because it was impossible for her, without great danger, to be alone with the king in his cell, a sharp secretary, the Sieur de Fizes, was sent to the Court of Rome, with orders to beg of the Pontiff a papal brief of special indulgences, containing proper absolutions for the petty sins, which, looking at their consanguinity, the said queen might commit with a view to cure the king's melancholy.

At this time, Adrian VI., the Dutchman, still wore the

tiara, who, a good fellow, for the rest did not forget, in spite of the scholastic ties which united him to the emperor, that the eldest son of the Catholic Church was concerned in the affair, and was good enough to send to Spain an express legate, furnished with full powers, to attempt the salvation of the queen's soul, and the king's body, without prejudice to God. This most urgent affair made the gentlemen very uneasy, and caused an itching in the feet of the ladies, who, from great devotion to the crown, would all have offered to go to Madrid, but for the dark distrust of Charles the Fifth, who would not grant the king permission to see any of his subjects, nor even the members of his family. It was therefore necessary to negotiate the departure of the Queen of Navarre. Then, nothing else was spoken about but this deplorable abstinence, and the lack of amorous exercise so vexatious to a prince who was much accustomed to it. In short, from one thing to another, the women finished by thinking more of the king's condition, than of the king himself. The queen was the first to say that she wished she had wings. To this Monsigneur Odet de Châtillon replied, that she had no need of them to be an angel. One, that was Madame l'Amirale, blamed God that it was not possible to send by a messenger that which the poor king so much required; and every one of the ladies would have lent it in her turn.

"God has done very well to fix it," said the Dauphine, quietly; "for our husbands would leave us rather badly off during their absence."

So much was said and so much thought upon the subject, that at her departure the Queen of all Marguerites was charged, by these good Christians, to kiss the captive heartily for all the ladies of the realm; and if it had been permissible to prepare pleasure like mustard, the queen would have been laden with enough to sell to the two Castiles.

While Madame Marguerite was, in spite of the snow, crossing the mountains, by relays of mules, hurrying on to these consolations as to a fire, the king found himself harder pressed by unsatisfied desire than he ever had been before, or would be again. In this reverberation of nature, he opened his heart to the Emperor Charles, in order that he might be provided with a merciful specific, urging upon him that it would be an everlasting disgrace to one king to let another die for lack of gallantry. The Castilian showed himself to be a generous man. Thinking that he would be able to recuperate himself for the favour granted, out of his guest's ransom, he hinted quietly to the people commissioned to guard the prisoner, that they might gratify him in this respect. Thereupon, a certain Don Hiios de Lara y Lopez Barra di Ponto, a poor captain, whose pockets were empty in spite of his genealogy, and who had been for some time thinking of seeking his fortune at the court of France, fancied that by procuring his majesty a soft cataplasm of warm flesh, he would open for himself an honestly fertile door; and, indeed, those who know the character of the good king and his court, can decide if he deceived himself.

When the above mentioned captain came in his turn into the chamber of the French king, he asked him respectfully if it was his good pleasure to permit him an interrogation on a subject concerning which he was as curious as about papal indulgences? To which the prince, casting aside his hypochondriacal demeanour, and twisting round on the chair in which he was seated, gave a sign of consent. The captain begged him not to be offended at the license of his language, and confessed to him, that he the king was said to

be one of the most amorous men in France, and he would
be glad to learn from him if the ladies of his court were
expert in the science of love. The poor king, calling to mind
his many adventures, gave vent to a deep-drawn sigh, and
exclaimed, that no women of any country, including those
of the moon, knew better than the ladies of France the
secrets of this alchemy; and at the remembrance of the
savoury, gracious, and vigorous fondling of one alone, he
felt himself the man, were she then within his reach, to
clasp her to his heart, even on a rotten plank a hundred feet
above a precipice.

Saying which, this good king, a ribald fellow, if ever
there was one, shot forth so fiercely life and light from his
eyes, that the captain, although a brave man, felt a quaking
in his inside so fiercely flamed the sacred majesty of royal
love. But recovering his courage he began to defend the
Spanish ladies, declaring that in Castile alone was love
properly understood, because it was the most religious place
in Christendom, and the more fear the women had of
damning themselves by yielding to a lover, the more their
souls were in the affair, because they knew they must take
their pleasure then against eternity. He further added, that
if the Lord King would wager one of the best and most
profitable manors in the kingdom of France, he would give
him a Spanish night of love, in which a casual queen should,
unless he took care, draw his soul from his body.

"Done," said the king, jumping up from his chair. "I
will give thee, by God, the manor of Ville-aux-Dames in
my province of Touraine, with full privilege of chase, of
high and low jurisdiction."

Then the captain, who was acquainted with the Donna
of the Cardinal Archbishop of Toledo, requested her to
smother the King of France with kindness, and demon-

strate to him the great advantage of the Castilian imagination over the simple movement of the French. To which
the Marchesa of Amaesguy consented for the honour of
Spain, and also for the pleasure of knowing of what paste
God made kings, a matter in which she was ignorant, having
experience only of the princes of the church. Thus she came
passionate as a lion that has broken out of his cage, and
made the bones of the king crack, in a manner that would
have killed any other man. But the above-named lord was
so well furnished, so greedy, and so well bitten, that he no
longer felt a bite; and from this terrible duel the Marchesa
emerged abashed, believing that she had had the devil to
confess.

The captain, confident in his agent, came to salute his
lord, thinking to do homage for his fief. Thereupon the
king said to him, in a jocular manner, that the Spanish ladies
were of a passable temperature, and their system a fair one,
but that when gentleness was required they substituted
frenzy; that he kept fancying each thrill was a sneeze, or a
case of violence; in short, that the embrace of a French-
woman brought back the drinker more thirsty than ever,
tiring him never; and that with the ladies of his court, love
was a gentle pleasure without parallel, and not the labour
of a master baker in his kneading trough.

The poor captain was strangely piqued at this language.
In spite of the nice sense of honour which the king pretended to possess, he fancied that his majesty wished to
bilk him like a student, stealing a slice of love at a brothel
in Paris. Nevertheless, not knowing for the matter of that,
if the Marchesa had not overspanished the king, he demanded his revenge from the captive, pledging him his
word, that he should have for certain a veritable fay, and
that he would yet gain the fief. The king was too courteous

and gallant a knight to refuse this request, and even made a pretty and right royal speech, intimating his desire to lose the wager. Then, after vespers, the guard passed fresh and warm into the king's chamber, a lady most dazzlingly white —most delicately wanton, with long tresses and velvet hands, filling out her dress at the least movement, for she was gracefully plump, with a laughing mouth, and eyes moist in advance, a woman to beautify hell, and whose first word had such cordial power that the king's garment was cracked by it. On the morrow, after the fair one had slipped out after the king's breakfast, the good captain came radiant and triumphant into the chamber.

At sight of him the prisoner exclaimed—

"Baron de la Ville-aux-Dames! God grant you joys like to mine! I like my gaol! By'r lady, I will not judge between the love of our lands, but pay the wager."

"I was sure of it," said the captain.

"How so?" said the king.

"Sire, it was my wife."

This was the origin of Larray de la Ville-aux-Dames in our country, since from corruption of the names, that of Lara-y Lopez, finished by becoming Larray. It was a good family, delighting in serving the kings of France, and it multiplied exceedingly. Soon after, the Queen of Navarre came in due course to the king, who, weary of Spanish customs, wished to disport himself after the fashion of France; but the remainder is not the subject of this narrative. I reserve to myself the right to relate elsewhere how the legate managed to sponge the sin of the thing off the great slate, and the delicate remark of our Queen of Marguerites, who merits a saint's niche in this collection; she who first concocted such good stories. The morality of this one is easy to understand.

In the first place, kings should never let themselves be taken in battle any more than their archetype in the game of the Grecian chief Palamedes. But from this, it appears the captivity of its king is a most calamitous and horrible evil to fall upon the populace. If it had been a queen, or even a princess, what worse fate? But I believe the thing could not happen again, except with cannibals. Can there ever be a reason for imprisoning the flower of a realm? I think too well of Ashtaroth, Lucifer, and others, to imagine that did they reign, they would hide the joy of all the beneficent light, at which poor sufferers warm themselves. And it was necessary that the worst of devils, *id est,* a wicked old heretic woman, should find herself upon a throne, to keep a prisoner sweet Mary of Scotland, to the shame of all the knights of Christendom, who should have come without previous assignation to the foot of Fotheringay, and have left thereof no single stone.

THE MERRY TATTLE OF THE
NUNS OF POISSY

THE Abbey of Poissy has been rendered famous by old authors as a place of pleasure, where the misconduct of the nuns first began, and whence proceeded so many good stories calculated to make laymen laugh at the expense of our holy religion. The said abbey by this means became fertile in proverbs, which none of the clever folks of our day understand, although they sift and chew them in order to digest them.

If you ask one of them what the *olives of Poissy* are, they will answer you gravely that it is a periphrase relating to truffles, and that *the way to serve them,* of which one formerly spoke, when joking with these virtuous maidens, meant a peculiar kind of sauce. That's the way these scribblers hit on truth once in a hundred times. To return to these good recluses, it was said—by way of a joke, of course—that they preferred finding a harlot in their chemises to a good woman. Certain other jokers reproached them with imitating the lives of the saints, in their own fashion, and said that all they admired in Mary of Egypt was her fashion of paying the boatmen. From whence the raillery, *To honour the saints after the fashion of Poissy.* There is still the *crucifix of Poissy,* which kept the stomach warm; and the *matins of Poissy,* which concluded with a little chorister. Finally, of a hearty jade well acquainted with the ways of love, it was said—*She is a nun of Poissy.* That property of a man which he can only lend, was *The*

key of the Abbey of Poissy. What the *gate* of the said
abbey was can easily be guessed. This gate, door, wicket,
opening, or road was always half open, was easier to open
than to shut, and cost much in repairs. In short, at that
period, there was no fresh device in love invented, that had
not its origin in the good convent of Poissy. You may be
sure there is a good deal of untruth and hyperbolical em-
phasis, in these proverbs, jests, jokes, and idle tales. The
nuns of the said Poissy were good young ladies, who now
this way, now that, cheated God to the profit of the devil,
as many others did, which was but natural, because our
nature is weak; and although they were nuns, they had
their little imperfections. They found themselves barren in
a certain particular, hence the evil. But the truth of the
matter is, all these wickednesses were the deeds of an abbess
who had fourteen children, all born alive, since they had
been perfected at leisure. The fantastic amours and the wild
conduct of this woman, who was of royal blood, caused the
convent of Poissy to become fashionable; and thereafter
no pleasant adventure happened in the abbeys of France
which was not credited to these poor girls, who would have
been well satisfied with a tenth of them. Then the abbey
was reformed, and these holy sisters were deprived of the
little happiness and liberty which they had enjoyed. In an
old cartulary of the abbey of Turpenay, near Chinon, which
in these later troublous times had found a resting place
in the library of Azay, where the custodian was only too
glad to receive it, I met with a fragment under the head of
The Hours of Poissy, which had evidently been put together
by a merry abbot of Turpernay for the diversion of his
neighbours of Ussé, Azay, Mongaugar, Sacchez, and other
places of this province. I give them under the authority of
the clerical garb, but altered to my own style, because I

have been compelled to turn them from Latin into French.
I commence:—At Poissy the nuns were accustomed, when
Mademoiselle, the king's daughter, their abbess, had gone
to bed. . . . It was she who first called it *faire la petite oie,*
to stick to the preliminaries of love, the prologues, prefaces,
protocols, warnings, notices, introductions, summaries,
prospectuses, arguments, notes, epigraphs, titles, false-
titles, current titles, scholia, marginal remarks, frontispieces,
observations, gilt edges, bookmarks, reglets, vignettes, tail
pieces and engravings, without once opening the merry book
to read, re-read, and study to apprehend and comprehend
the contents. And she gathered together in a body, all these
extra-judicial little pleasures of that sweet language, which
comes indeed from the lips, yet makes no noise, and practised them so well, that she died a virgin and perfect in
shape. This gay science was afterwards deeply studied by
the ladies of the court, who took lovers for *la petite oie,*
others for honour, and at times also certain ones who had
over them the right of high and low jurisdiction, and were
masters of everything—a state of things much preferred.
But to continue: When this virtuous princess was naked and
shameless between the sheets, the said girls (those whose
cheeks were unwrinkled and their hearts gay) would steal
noislessly out of their cells, and hide themselves in that of
one of their sisters who was much liked by all of them.
There they would have cosy little chats, enlivened with
sweetmeats, pastries, liqueurs, and girlish quarrels, worry
their elders, imitating them grotesquely, innocently mocking them, telling stories that made them laugh till the tears
came, and playing a thousand pranks. At times they would
measure their feet, to see whose were the smallest, compare
the white plumpness of their arms, see whose nose had the
infirmity of blushing after supper, count their freckles,

tell each other where their skin marks were situated, dispute whose complexion was the clearest, whose hair the
prettiest colour, and whose figure the best. You can imagine
that among these figures sanctified to God there were fine
ones, stout ones, lank ones, thin ones, plump ones, supple
ones, shrunken ones, and figures of all kinds. Then they
would quarrel amongst themselves as to who took the least
stuff to make a girdle, and she who spanned the least was
pleased without knowing why. At times they would relate
their dreams, and what they had seen in them. Often one or
two, at times all of them, had dreamed they had tight hold
of the keys of the abbey. Then they would consult each
other about their little ailments. One had scratched her
finger, another had a whitlow; this one had risen in the
morning with the white of her eye bloodshot; that one had
put her finger out, telling her beads. All had some little thing
the matter with them.

"Ah! you have lied to our mother; your nails are marked
with white," said one to her neighbour.

"You stopped a long time at confession this morning,
sister," said another. "You must have a good many little
sins to confess."

As there is nothing resembles a pussy-cat so much as a
tom-cat, they would swear eternal friendship, quarrel, sulk,
dispute, and make it up again; would be jealous, laugh and
pinch, pinch and laugh, and play tricks upon the novices.

At times they would say, "Suppose a gendarme came
here one rainy day, where should we put him?"

"With Sister Ovide; her cell is so big he could get into
it with his helmet on."

"What do you mean?" cried Sister Ovide, "are not all
our cells alike?"

Thereupon my girls burst out laughing like ripe figs.

One evening they increased their council by a little novice, about seventeen years of age, who appeared innocent as a new-born babe, and would have had the host without confession. This maiden's mouth had long watered for these secret confabulations, little feasts and rejoicings by which the young nuns softened the holy captivity of their bodies, and had wept at not being admitted to them.

"Well," said Sister Ovide to her, "have you had a good night's rest, little one?"

"Oh, no!" said she, "I have been bitten by fleas."

"Ha! you have fleas in your cell? But you must get rid of them at once. Do you know how the rules of our order enjoin them to be driven out, so that never again during her conventual life shall a sister see so much as the tail of one?"

"No," replied the novice.

"Well then, I will teach you. Do you see any fleas here? do you notice any trace of fleas? do you smell an odour of fleas? Is there any appearance of fleas in my cell? Look!"

"I can't find any," said the little novice, who was Mademoiselle de Fiennes, "and smell no other odour than our own."

"Do as I am about to tell you, and be no more bitten. Directly you feel yourself pricked, you must strip yourself, lift your chemise, and be careful not to sin while looking all over your body; think only of the cursed flea, looking for it, in good faith, without paying any attention to other things; trying only to catch the flea, which is a difficult job, as you may easily be deceived by the little black spots on your skin, which you were born with. Have you any, little one?"

"Yes," cried she. "I have two dark freckles, one on

my shoulder and one on my back, rather low down, but it is hidden between the cheeks. . . ."

"How did you see it?" asked Sister Perpétue.

"I did not know it. It was Monsieur de Montresor who found it out."

"Ha! ha!" said the sister, "is that all he saw?"

"He saw everything," said she, "I was quite little; he was about nine years old, and we were playing together. . . ."

The nuns hardly being able to restrain their laughter, Sister Ovide went on—

"The above-mentioned flea will jump from your legs to your eyes, will try and hide himself in apertures and crevices, will leap from valley to mountain, endeavouring to escape you; but the rules of the house order you courageously to pursue, repeating *aves*. Ordinarily at the third *ave* the beast is taken."

"The flea?" asked the novice.

"Certainly, the flea," replied Sister Ovide; "but in order to avoid the dangers of this chase, you must be careful in whatever spot you put your finger on the beast, to touch nothing else . . . Then without regarding its cries, plaints, groans, efforts and writhings, and the rebellion which frequently it attempts, you will press it under your thumb or other finger of the hand engaged in holding it, and with the other hand you will search for a veil to bind this flea's eyes and prevent it from leaping, as the beast seeing no longer clearly will not know where to go. Nevertheless, as it will still be able to bite you, and will be getting terribly enraged, you must gently open its mouth and delicately insert therein a twig of the blessed brush that hangs over your pillow. Thus the beast will be compelled to behave properly. But, remember, that the discipline of our order allows you to retain no property, and the beast cannot belong to you. You must take into consideration that it is one of God's creatures, and strive to render it more agreeable. Therefore, before all things, it is necessary to verify three serious things—viz., if the flea be a male, if it be female, or if it be a virgin; supposing it to be a virgin, which is extremely rare, since these beasts have no morals, are all wild hussies, and yield to the first seducer who comes, you will seize her hinder feet, and drawing them under her little caparison you must bind them with one of your hairs, and carry it to the superior, who will decide upon its fate after having consulted the chapter. If it be a male——"

"How can one tell that a flea is a virgin?" asked the curious novice.

"First of all," replied Sister Ovide, "she is sad and melancholy, does not laugh like the others, does not bite so sharp, has her mouth less wide open, and blushes when touched—you know where."

"In that case," replied the novice, "I have been bitten by a male."

At this the sisters burst out laughing so heartily that one of them sounded a base note, and voided a little water; and Sister Ovide, pointing to it on the floor, said—

"You see there's never wind without rain."

The novice laughed herself, thinking that these chuckles were caused by the sister's exclamation.

"Now," went on Sister Ovide, "if it be a male flea you take your scissors, or your lover's dagger, if by chance he has given you one as a souvenir, previous to your entry into the convent. In short, furnished with a cutting instrument, you carefully slit open the flanks of the flea. Expect to hear him howl, cough, spit, beg your pardon; to see him twist about, sweat, make sheep's eyes, and anything that may come into his head to put off this operation. But be not astonished; pluck up your courage, by thinking that you are acting thus, to bring a perverted creature in to the way of salvation. Then you will dexterously take the reins, the liver, the heart, the gizzard, and noble parts, and dip them all several times into the holy water, washing and purifying them there, at the same time imploring the Holy Ghost to sanctify the interior of the beast. Afterwards you will replace all these intestinal things in the body of the flea, who will be anxious to get them back again. Being by this means baptized, the soul of the creature has become Catholic. Immediately you will get a needle and thread, and sew up the belly of the flea with great care, with such regard and attention as is due to a fellow Christian; you will even pray for it—a kindness to which you will see it is sensible by its genuflexions and the attentive glances which it will bestow upon you. In short, it will cry no more, and have no further desire to kill you; and fleas are often encountered who die from pleasure at being thus converted to our holy religion. You will do the same to all you can catch; and the others perceiving it, after staring at the convert, will go away, so perverse are they, and so terrified at the idea of becoming Christians."

"And they are therefore wicked," said the novice. "Is there any greater happiness than to be in the bosom of the church?"

"Certainly," answered Sister Ursula, "here we are sheltered from the dangers of the world and of love, in which there are so many."

"Is there any other danger than that of having a child at an unseasonable time?" asked a young sister.

"During the present reign," replied Ursula, raising her head, "love has inherited leprosy, St. Anthony's fire, the

Ardennes' sickness and the red rash, and has heaped up all the fevers, agonies, drugs, and sufferings of the lot in his pretty mortar, to draw out therefrom a terrible complaint, of which the devil has given the receipt, luckily for convents, because there are a great number of frightened ladies, who become virtuous for fear of this love."

Thereupon they all huddled up close together, alarmed at these words, but wishing to know more.

"And is it enough to love, to suffer?" asked a sister.

"Oh, yes!" cried Sister Ovide.

"You love just for one little once a pretty gentleman," replied Ursula, "and you have the chance of seeing your teeth go one by one, your hair fall off, your cheeks grow pallid, and your eyebrows drop, and the disappearance of your prized charms will cost you many a sigh. There are poor women who have scabs come upon their noses, and others who have a horrid animal with a hundred claws, which gnaws their tenderest parts. The Pope has at last been compelled to excommunicate this kind of love."

"Ah, how lucky I am to have had nothing of that sort," cried the novice.

Hearing this souvenir of love, the sisters suspected that the little one had gone astray through the heat of a *crucifix of Poissy,* and had been joking with the Sister Ovide, and drawing her out. All congratulated themselves on having so merry a jade in their company, and asked her to what adventure they were indebted for that pleasure.

"Ah!" said she, "I let myself be bitten by a big flea, who had already been baptised."

At this speech, the sister of the base note could not restrain a second sigh.

"Ah!" said Sister Ovide, "you are bound to give us the third. If you spoke that language in the choir, the abbess

would diet you like Sister Petronille; so soften the noise
of your trumpet."

"Is it true that you knew in her lifetime that Sister
Petronille, on whom God bestowed the gift of only going
twice a year to the bank of deposit?" asked Sister Ursula.

"Yes," replied Ovide. "And one evening it happened she
had to remain enthroned until matins, saying 'I am here
by the will of God.' But at the first verse, she was delivered,
in order that she should not miss the office. Nevertheless,
the late abbess would not allow that this was an especial
favour, granted from on high, and said that God did not
look so low. Here are the facts of the case. Our defunct
sister, whose canonization the order are now endeavouring
to obtain at the court of the Pope, and would have had it if
they could have paid the proper costs of the papal brief;
this Petronille, then, had an ambition to have her name
included in the Calendar of Saints, which was in no way
prejudicial to our order. She lived in prayer alone, would
remain in ecstasy before the altar of the Virgin, which is
on the side of fields, and pretend so distinctly to hear
the angels flying in Paradise, that she was able to hum the
tunes they were singing. You all know that she took from
them the chant *Adoremus,* of which no man could have
invented a note. She remained for days with her eye fixed
like a star, fasting, and putting no more nourishment into
her body than I could into my eye. She had made a vow
never to taste meat, either cooked or raw, and ate only a
crust of bread a day; but on great feast days she would
add thereto a morsel of salt fish, without any sauce. On this
diet she became dreadfully thin, yellow as saffron, and dry
as an old bone in a cemetery; for she was of an ardent disposition, and any one who had had the happiness of knocking up against her, would have drawn fire as from a flint.

However, little as she ate, she could not escape an infirmity
to which, luckily or unluckily, we are all more or less subject.
If it were otherwise, we should be very much embarrassed.
The affair in question, is the obligation of expelling after
eating, like all the animals, matter more or less agreeable,
according to constitution. Now Sister Petronille differed
from all others, because she expelled matter such as is left
by a deer, and these are the hardest substances that any
gizzard produces, as you must know, if you have ever put
your foot upon them in the forest glade, and from their
hardness they are called bullets in the language of forestry.
This peculiarity of Sister Petronille's was not unnatural,
since long fasts kept her temperament at a permanent heat.
According to the old sisters, her nature was so burning,
that when water touched her, she went *frist!* like a hot coal.
There are sisters who have accused her of secretly cooking
eggs, in the night, between her toes, in order to support her
austerities. But these were scandals, invented to tarnish this
great sanctity of which all the other nunneries were jealous.
Our sister was piloted in the way of salvation and divine
perfection by the Abbot of St. Germain-des-près de Paris
—a holy man, who always finished his injunctions with a
last one, which was to offer to God all our troubles, and
submit ourselves to His will, since nothing happened without His express commandment. This doctrine, which appears wise at first sight, has furnished matter for great
controversies, and has been finally condemned on the statement of the Cardinal of Châtillon, who declared that then
there would be no such thing as sin, which would considerably diminish the revenues of the Church. But Sister
Petronille lived imbued with this feeling, without knowing
the danger of it. After Lent, and the fasts of the great jubilee, for the first time for eight months she had need to go

to the little room, and to it she went. There bravely lifting her dress, she put herself into position to do that which we poor sinners do rather oftener. But Sister Petronille could only manage to expectorate the commencement of the thing, which kept her puffing without the remainder making up its mind to follow. In spite of every effort, pursing of lips and squeezings of body, her guest preferred to remain in her blessed body, merely putting his head out of window, like a frog taking the air, and felt no inclination to fall into the vale of misery among the others, alleging that he would not there be in the odour of sanctity. And this idea was a good one for a sample lump of dirt like himself. The good saint having used all methods of coercion, having over-stretched her muscles, and tried the nerves of her thin face till they bulged out, recognized the fact that no suffering in the world was so great, and her anguish attaining the apogee of sphincterial terrors, she exclaimed, 'O! my God, to Thee I offer it!' At this orison, the stony matter broke off short, and fell like a flint against the walls of the privy, making a croc, croc, croooc, paf! You can easily understand, my sisters, that she had no need of a torche-cul, and drew back the remainder."

"Then did she see angels?" asked one.

"Have they a behind?" asked another.

"Certainly not," said Ursula. "Do you not know that one general meeting day, God having ordered them to be seated, they answered Him that they had not the wherewithal."

Thereupon they went off to bed, some alone, others nearly alone. They were good girls, who harmed only themselves.

I cannot leave them without relating an adventure which took place in their house, when Reform was passing a sponge over it, and making them all saints, as before stated.

At that time, there was in the episcopal chair of Paris, a
veritable saint, who did not brag about what he did, and
cared for naught but the poor and suffering, whom the dear
old bishop lodged in his heart, neglecting his own interests
for theirs, and seeking out misery in order that he might
heal it with words, with help, with attentions, and with
money, according to the case: as ready to solace the rich
in their misfortunes as the poor, patching up their souls
and bringing them back to God; and tearing about hither
and thither, watching his troop, the dear shepherd! Now
the good man went about careless of the state of his cas-
socks, mantles, and breeches, so that the naked members of
his church were covered. He was so charitable that he would
have pawned himself, to save an infidel from distress. His
servants were obliged to look after him carefully. Oft-
times he would scold them when they changed unasked his
tattered vestments for new; and he used to have them
darned and patched, as long as they would hold together.
Now this good archbishop knew that the late Sieur de Poissy
had left a daughter, without a sou or a rag, after having
eaten, drunk, and gambled away her inheritance. This poor
young lady lived in a hovel, without fire in winter or cher-
ries in spring; and did needlework, not wishing either to
marry beneath her or sell her virtue. Awaiting the time
when he should be able to find a young husband for her,
the prelate took it into his head to send her the outside case
of one to mend, in the person of his old breeches, a task
which the young lady, in her present position, would be
glad to undertake. One day that the archbishop was thinking to himself that he must go to the convent of Poissy,
to see after the reformed inmates, he gave to one of his
servants, the oldest of his nether garments, which was

sorely in need of stitches, saying, "Take this, Saintot, to the young ladies of Poissy," meaning to say, "The young lady of Poissy." Thinking of affairs connected with the cloister, he did not inform his varlet of the situation of the lady's house; her desperate condition having been by him discreetly kept a secret. Saintot took the breeches and went his way towards Poissy, gay as a grasshopper, stopping to chat with friends he met on the way, slaking his thirst at the wayside inns, and showing many things to the breeches during their journey that might hereafter be useful to them. At last he arrived at the convent, and informed the abbess that his master had sent him to give her these articles. Then the varlet departed, leaving with the reverend mother, the garment accustomed to model in relief the archiepiscopal proportions of the continent nature of the good man, according to the fashion of the period, beside the image of those things of which the Eternal Father has deprived His angels, and which in the good prelate did not want for amplitude. Madame the abbess having informed the sisters of the precious message of the good archbishop they came in haste, curious and hustling, as ants into whose republic a chestnut husk has fallen. When they undid the breeches, which gaped horribly, they shrieked out, covering their eyes with one hand, in great fear of seeing the devil come out, the abbess exclaiming, "Hide yourselves, my daughters! This is the abode of mortal sin!"

The mother of the novices, giving a little look between her fingers, revived the courage of the holy troop, swearing by an Ave that no living head was domiciled in the breeches. Then they all blushed at their ease, while examining this Habitavit, thinking that perhaps the desire of the prelate was that they should discover therein some sage admonition or evangelical parable. Although this sight caused certain ravages in the hearts of these most virtuous maidens, they paid little attention to the fluttering of their reins, but sprinkling a little holy water in the bottom of the abyss, one touched it, another passed her finger through a hole, and grew bolder looking at it. It has even been pretended that, their first stir over, the abbess found a voice sufficiently firm to say, "What is there at the bottom of this? With what idea has our father sent us that which consummates the ruin of women?"

"It's fifteen years, dear mother, since I have been permitted to gaze upon the demon's den."

"Silence, my daughter. You prevent me thinking what is best to be done."

Then so much were these archiepiscopal breeches turned and twisted about, admired and re-admired, pulled here, pulled there, and turned inside out—so much were they talked about, fought about, thought about, dreamed about, night and day, that on the morrow a little sister said, after having sung the matins, to which the convent had a verse and two responses—"Sisters, I have found out the parable of the archbishop. He has sent us as a mortification his garment to mend, as a holy warning to avoid idleness, the mother abbess of all the vices."

Thereupon there was a scramble to get hold of the breeches; but the abbess, using her high authority, reserved to herself the meditation over this patchwork. She was occupied during ten days, praying, and sewing the said breeches, lining them with silk, and making double hems, well sewn, in all humility. Then the chapter being assembled, it was arranged that the convent should testify by a pretty souvenir to the said archbishop their delight that he thought of his daughters in God. Then all of them, to the very youngest, had to do some work on these blessed breeches, in order to do honour to the virtue of the good man.

Meanwhile, the prelate had had so much to attend to, that he had forgotten all about his garment. This is how it came about. He made the acquaintance of a noble of the court, who, having lost his wife—a she-fiend and sterile—said to the good priest, that he had a great ambition to meet with a virtuous woman, confiding in God, with whom he was not likely to quarrel, and was likely to have pretty children. Such a one he desired to hold by the hand, and have confidence in. Then the holy man drew such a picture of Mademoiselle de Poissy, that this fair one soon became Madame de Genoilhac. The wedding was celebrated at the archiepiscopal palace, where was a feast of the first quality, and a table bordered with ladies of the highest lineage, and the fashionable world of the court, among whom the bride appeared the most beautiful, since it was certain that she was a virgin, the archbishop guaranteeing her virtue.

When the fruits, conserves, and pastry were, with many ornaments, arranged on the cloth, Saintot said to the archbishop, "Monsigneur, your well-beloved daughters of Poissy send you a fine dish for the centre."

"Put it there," said the good man, gazing with admiration at an edifice of velvet and satin, embroidered with wire ribbon, in the shape of an ancient vase, the lid of which exhaled a thousand superfine odours.

Immediately the bride, uncovering it, found therein sweetmeats, cakes, and those delicious confections to which the ladies are so partial. But one of them—some curious devotee—seeing a little piece of silk, pulled it towards her, and exposed to view the habitation of the human compass, to the great confusion of the prelate, for laughter rang round the table like a discharge of artillery.

"Well have they made the centre dish," said the bridegroom. "These young ladies are of good understanding. Therein are all the sweets of matrimony."

Can there be any better moral than that deduced by Monsieur de Genoilhac? Then no other is needed.

HOW THE CHATEAU D'AZAY CAME
TO BE BUILT

JEHAN, son of Simon Forniez, called Simmonnin, a citizen of Tours—originally of the village of Moulinot, near to Beaune, whence, in imitation of certain persons, he took the name when he became steward to Louis the Eleventh—had to fly one day into Languedoc with his wife, having fallen into great disgrace, and left his son Jacques penniless in Touraine. This youth, who possessed nothing in the world except his good looks, his sword, and spurs, but whom worn-out old men would have considered very well off, had in his head a firm intention to save his father, and make his fortune at the court, then holden in Touraine. At early dawn this good Tourainian left his lodgings, and, enveloped in his mantle, all except his nose, which he left open to the air, and his stomach empty, walked about the town without any trouble of digestion. He entered the churches, thought them beautiful, looked into the chapels, flicked the flies from the pictures, and counted the columns all after the manner of a man who knew not what to do with his time or his money. At other times he feigned to recite his paternosters, but really made mute prayers to the ladies, offered them holy water when leaving, followed them afar off, and endeavoured by these little services to encounter some adventure, in which at the peril of his life he would find for himself a protector or a gracious mistress. He had in his girdle two doubloons which he spared far more than his skin, because that would be replaced, but the doubloons never. Each day he took from his little hoard the price of a roll and a few apples, with which he sustained life, and drank at his will and discretion of the water of the Loire. This wholesome and prudent diet, besides being good for his doubloons, kept him frisky and light as a greyhound, gave him a clear understanding and a warm heart, for the water of the Loire is of all syrups the most strengthening, because having its course afar off it is invigorated by its long run, through many strands, before it reaches Tours. So you may be sure that the poor fellow imagined a thousand and one good fortunes and lucky adventures, and what is more, almost believed them true. Oh, the good times! One evening Jacques de Beaune (he kept the name although he was not lord of Beaune), was walking along the embankment, occupied in cursing his star and everything, for his last doubloon was with scant respect upon the point of quitting him; when at the corner of a little street, he nearly ran against a veiled lady, whose sweet odour gratified his amorous senses. This fair pedestrian was bravely mounted on pretty pattens, wore a beautiful dress of Italian velvet, with wide slashed satin sleeves; while as a sign of her great fortune, through her veil a white diamond of reasonable size shone upon her forehead like the rays of the setting sun among her tresses, which were so delicately rolled, built up, and so neat, that they must have taken her maids quite three hours to arrange. She walked like a lady who was only accustomed to a litter. One of her pages followed her, well armed. She was evidently some light o' love belonging to a noble of high rank, or a lady of the court, since she held her dress high off the ground, and bent her back like a woman of quality. Lady or courtesan she pleased Jacques de Beaune, who, far from turning up his nose at her, conceived the wild idea of attaching himself to her for life. With this in view he de-

termined to follow her in order to ascertain whither she
would lead him—to Paradise or to the limbo of hell—to a
gibbet or to an abode of love. Anything was a gleam of hope
to him in the depth of his misery. The lady strolled along
the bank of the Loire toward Plessis, inhaling like a fish
the fine freshness of the water, toying, sauntering like a little
mouse who wishes to see and taste everything. When the
page perceived that Jacques de Beaune persistently followed
his mistress in all her movements, stopped when she stopped,
and watched her trifling, in a barefaced fashion, as if he had
a right so to do, he turned brusquely round with a savage
and threatening face, like that of a dog who says, "Stand
back, sir !" But the good Tourainian had his wits about him.
Believing that if a cat may look at a king, he, a baptized
Christian, might certainly look at a pretty woman, he
stepped forward, and feigning to grin at the page, he
strutted now behind and now before the lady. She said
nothing, but looked at the sky, which was putting on its
night-cap, the stars, and everything which could give her
pleasure. So things went on. At last, arrived opposite Portillon, she stood still, and in order to see better, cast her
veil back over her shoulder, and in so doing cast upon the
youth the glance of a clever woman who looks around to
see if there is any danger of being robbed. I may tell you
that Jacques de Beaune was a thorough ladies' man; he
could do the work of three husbands and walk by the side
of a princess without disgracing her, had a brave and reso-
lute air which pleased the sex, and if he was a little browned
by the sun from being so much in the open air, his skin
would look white enough under the canopy of a bed. The
glance, keen as a needle, which the lady threw him, appeared to him more animated than that with which she
would have honoured her prayer-book. Upon it he built

the hope of a windfall of love, and resolved to push the adventure to the very edge of the petticoat, risking to go still further, not only his lips, which he held of little account, but his two ears and something else besides. He followed into the town the lady, returning by the Rue des Trois-Pucelles, and led the gallant through a labyrinth of little streets, to the square in which is at the present time situated the Hôtel de la Crouzille. There she stopped at the door of a splendid mansion, at which the page knocked. A servant opened it, and the lady went in and closed the door, leaving the Sieu de Beaune open-mouthed, stupefied, and as foolish as Monsigneur St. Denis when he was trying to pick up his head. He raised his nose in the air to see if some token of favour would be thrown to him, and saw nothing except a light which went up the stairs, through the rooms, and rested before a fine window, where probably the lady was also. You can believe that the poor lover remained melancholy and dreaming, and knowing not what to do. The window gave a sudden creak and broke his reverie. Fancying that his lady was about to call him, he looked up again, and but for the friendly shelter of the balcony, which was a helmet to him, he would have received a stream of water and the utensil which contained it, since the handle only remained in the grasp of the person who delivered the deluge. Jacques de Beaune, delighted at this, did not lose the opportunity, but flung himself against the wall, crying, "I am killed," with a feeble voice. Then stretching himself upon the fragments of broken china, he lay as if dead, awaiting the issue. The servants rushed out in a state of alarm, fearing their mistress, to whom they had confessed their fault, and picked up the wounded man, who could hardly restrain his laughter at being then carried up the stairs.

"He is cold," said the page.

"He is covered with blood," said the butler, who while feeling his pulse had wetted his hand.

"If he revives," said the guilty one, "I will pay for a mass to Saint Gatien."

"Madame takes after her late father, and if she does not have thee hanged, the least mitigation of thy penalty will be that thou wilt be kicked out of her house and service," said another. "Certes, he's dead enough, he is so heavy."

"Ah! I am in the house of a very great lady," thought Jacques.

"Alas! is he really dead?" demanded the author of the calamity. While with great labour the Tourainian was being carried up the stairs, his doubtlet caught on a projection, and the dead man cried, "Ah! my doublet!"

"He groans," said the culprit, with a sigh of relief.

The Regent's servants (for this was the house of the Regent, the daughter of King Louis XI. of virtuous memory) brought Jacques de Beaune into a room, and laid him stiff and stark upon a table, not thinking for a moment that he could be saved.

"Run and fetch a surgeon," cried Madame de Beaujeu. "Run here, run there!"

The servants were down the stairs in a trice. The good lady Regent despatched her attendants for ointment, for linen to bind the wounds, for goulard-water, for so many things, that she remained alone. Gazing upon this splendid and senseless man, she cried aloud, admiring his presence and his features, handsome even in death, "Ah, God wishes to punish me. Just for one poor little time in my life has there been born in me, and taken possession of me, a naughty idea, and my patron saint is angry, and deprives me of the sweetest gentleman I have ever seen. By the rood,

and by the soul of my father, I will hang every man
who had a hand in this!"

"Madame," cried Jacques de Beaune, springing from
the table, and falling at the feet of the Regent, "I will live
to serve you, and am so little bruised that I promise you this
night as many joys as there are months in the year, in imitation of the Sieur Hercules, a pagan baron. For the last
twenty days," he went on (thinking that matters would be
smoothed by a little lying), "I have met you again and again.
I fell madly in love with you, yet dared not, by reason of
my great respect for your person, make an advance. You can
imagine how intoxicated I must have been with your royal
beauties, to have invented the trick to which I owe the happiness of being at your feet."

Thereupon he kissed her amorously, and gave her a look
that would have overcome any scruples. The Regent, by
means of time, which respects not queens, was, as every
one knows, in her middle age. In this critical and autumnal
season, women formerly virtuous and loverless desire now
here, now there, to enjoy, unknown to the world, certain
hours of love, in order that they may not arrive in the other
world with hands and heart alike empty, through having
left the fruit of the tree of knowledge untasted. The lady
of Beaujeu, without appearing to be astonished while listening to the promises of this young man, since royal personages ought to be accustomed to having them by dozens, kept
this ambitious speech in the depths of her memory, or her
registry of love, which caught fire at his words. Then she
raised the Tourainian, who still found in his misery the
courage to smile at his mistress, who had the majesty of a
full-blown rose, ears like shoes, and the complexion of a
sick cat, but was so well dressed, so fine in figure, so royal of

foot, and so queenly in carriage, that he might still find in this affair means to gain his original object.

"Who are you?" said the Regent, putting on the stern look of her father.

"I am your very faithful subject, Jacques de Beaune, son of your steward, who has fallen into disgrace in spite of his faithful services."

"Ah, well," replied the lady, "lay yourself on the table again. I hear some one coming; and it is not fit that my people should think me your accomplice in this farce and mummery."

The good fellow perceived, by the soft sound of her voice, that he was pardoned the enormity of his love. He lay down upon the table again, and remembered how certain lords had ridden to court in an old stirrup—a thought which perfectly reconciled him to his present position.

"Good," said the Regent to her maid-servants; "nothing is needed. This gentleman is better; thanks to heaven and the Holy Virgin, there will have been no murder in my house."

Thus saying, she passed her hand through the locks of the lover who had fallen to her from the skies, and taking a little reviving water she bathed his temples, undid his doublet, and, under pretence of aiding his recovery, verified better than an expert how soft and young was the skin of this young fellow and bold promiser of bliss, and all the bystanders, men and women, were amazed to see the Regent act thus. But humanity never misbecomes those of royal blood. Jacques stood up, and appeared to come to his senses, thanked the Regent most humbly, and dismissed the physicians, master surgeons, and other imps in black, saying that he had thoroughly recovered. Then he gave his name, and saluting Madame de Beaujeu, wished to depart, as though afraid of her on account of his father's disgrace, but no doubt horrified at his terrible vow.

"I cannot permit it," said she. "Persons who come to my house should not meet with such treatment as you have encountered. The Sieur de Beaune will sup here," she added to her major domo. "He who has so unduly insulted him will be at his mercy if he makes himself known immediately; otherwise, I will have him found out and hanged by the provost."

Hearing this, the page who had attended the lady during her promenade stepped forward.

"Madame," said Jacques, "at my request pray both pardon and reward him, since to him I owe the felicity of seeing you, the favour of supping in your company, and perhaps that of getting my father re-established in the office to which it pleased your glorious father to appoint him."

"Well said," replied the Regent. "D'Estouteville," said she, turning towards the page, "I give thee command of a company of archers. But for the future do not throw things out of the window."

Then she, delighted with De Beaune, offered him her hand, and led him most gallantly into her room, where they conversed freely together while supper was being prepared. There the Sieur Jacques did not fail to exhibit his talents, justify his father, and raise himself in the estimation of the lady, who, as is well known, was like her father in disposition, and did everything at random. Jacques de Beaune thought to himself that it would be rather difficult for him to remain all night with the Regent. Such matters are not so easily arranged as the amours of cats, who have always a convenient refuge upon the housetops for their moments of dalliance. So he rejoiced that he was known to the Regent without being compelled to fulfil his rash promise, since for this to be carried out it was necessary that the servants and others should be out of the way, and her reputation safe. Nevertheless, suspecting the powers of intrigue of the good lady, at times he would ask himself if he were equal to the task. But beneath the surface of conversation, the same thing was in the mind of the Regent, who had already managed affairs quite as difficult, and she began most cleverly to arrange the means. She sent for one of her secretaries, an adept in all arts necessary for the perfect government of a kingdom, and ordered him to give her secretly a false message during the supper. Then came the repast, which the lady did not touch, since her heart had swollen like a sponge, and so diminished her stomach, for she kept thinking of this handsome and desirable man, having no appetite save for him. Jacques did not fail to make a good meal for many reasons. The messenger came, Madame began to storm, to knit her brows after the manner of the late king, and to say, "Is there never to be peace in this land? Pasques Dieu! can we not have one quiet evening?" Then she arose, and strode about the room. "Ho, there! my horse! Where is Monsieur de Vieilleville, my squire? Ah, he is in Picardy. D'Estouteville, you will rejoin me with my household at the Château d'Amboise. . . ." And looking at Jacques, she said, "You shall be my squire, Sieur de Beaune. You wish to serve the State. The occasion is a good one. Pasques Dieu! come. There are rebels to subdue, and faithful knights are needed."

In less time than an old beggar would have taken to say thank you, the horses were bridled, saddled, and ready. Madame was on her mare, and the Tourainian at her side, galloping at full speed to her castle of Amboise, followed by the men-at-arms. To be brief and come to the facts without further commentary, De Beaune was lodged not

twenty yards from Madame, far from prying eyes. The
courtiers and the household, much astonished, ran about
inquiring from what quarter the danger might be expected;
but our hero, taken at his word, knew well enough where
to find it. The virtue of the Regent, well known in the kingdom, saved her from suspicion, since she was supposed to
be as impregnable as the Château de Péronne. At curfew,
when everything was shut, both ears and eyes, and the castle
silent, Madame de Beaujeu sent away her handmaid, and
called for her squire. The squire came. Then the lady and
the adventurer sat side by side upon a velvet couch, in the
shadow of a lofty fireplace, and the curious Regent, with a
tender voice, asked of Jacques, "Are you not bruised? It
was very wrong of me to make a knight, wounded by one of
my servants, ride twelve miles. I was so anxious about it that
I would not go to bed without having seen you. Do you
suffer?"

"I suffer with impatience," said he of the dozen, thinking it would not do to appear reluctant. "I see well," continued he, "my noble and beautiful mistress, that your
servant has found favour in your sight."

"There, there," replied she; "did you not tell a story
when you said——"

"What?" said he.

"Why, that you had followed me dozens of times to
churches, and other places to which I went."

"Certainly," said he.

"I am astonished," replied the Regent, "never to have
seen until to-day a noble youth whose courage is so apparent in his countenance. I am not ashamed of that which
you heard me say when I believed you dead. You are agreeable to me, you please me, and you wish to do well."

Then the hour of the dreaded sacrifice having struck,

Jacques fell at the knees of the Regent, kissed her feet, her
hands, and everything, it is said; and while kissing her,
previous to retirement, proved by many arguments to the
aged virtue of his sovereign, that a lady bearing the burden
of the state had a perfect right to enjoy herself—a theory
which was not directly admitted by the Regent, who determined to be forced, in order to throw the burden of the sin
upon her lover. This notwithstanding, you may be sure she
had highly perfumed and elegantly attired herself for the
night, and shone with desire of embraces, for desire lent
her a high colour which greatly improved her complexion;
and in spite of her feeble resistance she was, like a young
girl, carried by assault in her royal couch, where the good
lady and her young dozener conscientiously embraced each
other. Then from play to quarrel, from quarrel to riot, from
riot to ribaldry, from thread to needle, the Regent declared
that she believed more in the virginity of the Holy Mary
than in the promised dozen. Now, by chance, Jacques de
Beaune did not find this great lady so very old between the
sheets, since everything is metamorphosed by the light of
the lamps of the night. Many women of fifty by day are
twenty at midnight, as others are twenty at mid-day and a
hundred after vespers. Jacques, happier at this sight than
at that of the king on a hanging day, renewed his undertaking. Madame, herself astonished, promised every assistance on her part. The manor of Azay-le-Brulé, with good
title thereto, she undertook to confer upon her cavalier, as
well as the pardon of his father, if from this encounter she
came forth vanquished. Then the clever fellow said to himself, "This is to save my father from punishment! this for
the fief! this for the letting and selling! this for the forest
of Azay; item for the right of fishing! another for the isles
of the Indre! this for the meadows! I may as well release

from confiscation our land of La Carte, so dearly bought by my father! Once more for a place at court!" Arriving without hindrance at this point, he believed his dignity involved, and fancied that having France under him, it was a question of the honour of the crown. In short, at the cost of a vow which he made to his patron, Monsieur St. Jacques, to build him a chapel at Azay, he presented his liege homage to the Regent in eleven clear, clean, limpid, and genuine periphrases. Concerning the epilogue of this slow conversation, the Tourainian had the great self-confidence to wish excellently to regale the Regent, keeping for her on her waking the salute of an honest man, as it was necessary for the lord of Azay to thank his sovereign, which was wisely thought. But when nature is oppressed, she acts like a spirited horse, lies down, and will die under the whip sooner than move until it pleases her to rise reinvigorated. Thus, when in the morning the seignior of the castle of Azay desired to salute the daughter of King Louis XI., he was constrained, in spite of his courtesy, to make the salute as royal salutes should be made—with blank cartridge only. Therefore the Regent, after getting up, and while she was breakfasting with Jacques, who called himself the legitimate Lord of Azay, seized the occasion of this insufficiency to contradict her esquire, and pretended, that as he had not gained his wager, he had not earned the manor.

"Ventre-Saint-Paterne! I have been near enough," said Jacques. "But my dear lady and noble sovereign, it is not proper for either you or me to judge in this cause. The case being an allodial case, must be brought before your council, since the fief of Azay is held from the crown."

"Pasques Dieu!" replied the Regent with a forced laugh. "I give you the place of the Sieur de Vieilleville in my house. Don't trouble about your father. I will give you Azay, and

will place you in a royal office, if you can, without injury to
my honour, state the case in full council; but if one word
falls to the damage of my reputation as a virtuous woman,
I——"

"May I be hanged," said Jacques, turning the thing into
a joke, because there was a shade of anger in the face of
Madame de Beaujeu.

In fact, the daughter of King Louis thought more of her
royalty than of the rougish dozen, which she considered as
nothing, since fancying she had had her night's amusement
without loosening her purse-strings, she preferred the difficult recital of his claim to another dozen offered her by
the Tourainian.

"Then, my lady," replied her good companion, "I shall
certainly be your squire."

The captains, secretaries, and other persons holding office
under the regency, astonished at the sudden departure of
Madame de Beaujeu, learnt the cause of her anxiety, and
came in haste to the castle of Amboise to discover whence
proceeded the rebellion, and were in readiness to hold council when her majesty had arisen. She called them together,
not to be suspected of having deceived them, and gave them
certain falsehoods to consider, which they considered most
wisely. At the close of the sitting, came the new squire to
accompany his mistress. Seeing the councillors rising, the
bold Tourainian begged them to decide a point of law which
concerned both himself and the property of the crown.

"Listen to him," said the Regent. "He speaks truly."

Then Jacques de Beaune, without being nervous at the
sight of this august court, spoke as follows, or thereabouts:
—"Noble lords, I beg you, although I am about to speak
to you of walnut shells, to give your attention to this case,
and pardon me the trifling nature of my language. One

lord was walking with another in a fruit garden, and noticed a fine walnut tree, well planted, well grown, worth looking at, worth keeping, although a little empty; a nut tree always fresh, sweet-smelling, a tree which you would not leave if you once saw it, a tree of love which seemed the tree of good and evil, forbidden by the Lord, through which were banished our mother Eve and the gentleman her husband. Now, my lords, this said walnut tree was the subject of a slight dispute between the two, and one of those many wagers which are occasionally made between friends. The younger boasted that he could throw twelve times through it a stick which he had in his hand at the time—as many people have who walk in a garden—and with each flight of the stick he would send a nut to the ground——"

"That is, I believe, the knotty point of the case," said Jacques turning towards the Regent.

"Yes, gentlemen," replied she, surprised at the craft of her squire.

"The other wagered to the contrary," went on the pleader. "Now the first named throws his stick with such precision of aim, so gently, and so well that both derived pleasure therefrom, and by the joyous protection of the saints, who no doubt were amused spectators, with each throw there fell a nut; in fact, there fell twelve. But by chance the last of the fallen nuts was empty, and had no nourishing pulp from which could have come another nut tree, had the gardener planted it. Has the man with the stick gained his wager? Judge."

"The thing is clear enough," said Messire Adam Fumée, a Tourainian, who at that time was the keeper of the seals. "There is only one thing for the other to do."

"What is that?" said the Regent.

"To pay the wager, madame."

"He is rather too clever," said she, tapping her squire on the cheek. "He will be hanged one of these days."

She meant this as a joke. But these words were the real horoscope of the steward, who mounted the gallows by the ladder of royal favour, through the vengeance of another old woman, and the notorious treason of a man of Ballan, his secretary, whose fortune he had made, and whose name was Prévost, and not René Gentil, as certain persons have wrongly called him. This Ganelon and bad servant gave, it is said, to Madame d'Angoulême the receipt for the money which had been given him by Jacques de Beaune, then become baron of Samblançay, lord of La Carte and Azay, and one of the foremost men in the State. Of his two sons, one was Archbishop of Tours, the other Minister of Finance and Governor of Touraine. But this is not the subject of the present history.

Now that which concerns the present narrative is that Madame de Beaujeu, to whom the pleasure of love had come rather late in the day, well pleased with the great wisdom and knowledge of public affairs which her chance lover possessed, made him Lord of the Privy Purse, in which office he behaved so well, and added so much to the contents of it, that his great renown procured for him one day the handling of the revenues which he superintended and controlled most admirably, and with great profit to himself, which was but fair. The good Regent paid the bet, and handed over to her squire the manor of Azay-le-Brulé, of which the castle had long before been demolished by the first bombarders who came into Touraine, as every one knows. For this powdery miracle, but for the intervention of the king, the said engineers would have been condemned as heretics and abettors of Satan, by the ecclesiastical tribune of the chapter.

At this time there was being built with great care by Messire Bohier, Minister of Finance, the Castle of Chenonceaux, which, as a curiosity and novel design, was placed right across the river Cher.

Now the Baron de Samblançay, wishing to oppose the said Bohier, determined to lay this foundation of his at the bottom of the Indre, where it still stands, the gem of this fair green valley, so solidly was it placed upon the piles. It cost Jacques de Beaune thirty thousand crowns, not counting the work done by his vassals. You may take it for granted this castle is one of the finest, prettiest, most exquisite, and most elaborate castles of our sweet Touraine, and laves itself in the Indre like a princely creature, gaily decked with pavilions and lace-curtained windows, with fine weather-beaten soldiers on her vanes, turning which ever way the wind blows, as all soldiers do. But Samblançay was hanged before it was finished, and since that time no one has been found with sufficient money to complete it. Nevertheless, his master, King Francis the First, was once his guest, and the royal chamber is still shown there. When the king was going to bed, Samblançay, whom the king called "old fellow," in honour of his white hairs, hearing his royal master, to whom he was devotedly attached, remark, "Your clock has just struck twelve, old fellow!" replied, "Ah, sire, to twelve strokes of a hammer, an old one now, but years ago a good one, at this hour of the clock do I owe my lands, the money spent on this place, and the honour of being in your service."

The king wished to know what his minister meant by these strange words; and when his majesty was getting into bed, Jacques de Beaune narrated to him the history with which you are acquainted. Now Francis the First, who was partial to these spicy stories, thought the adventure a very droll one, and was the more amused thereat because at that time his mother, the Duchess d'Angoulême, in the decline of life, was pursuing the constable of Bourbon, in order to obtain of him one of these dozens. Wicked love of a wicked woman, for therefrom proceeded the peril of the kingdom, the capture of the king, and the death—as has been before mentioned—of poor Samblançay.

I have here endeavored to relate how the Château d'Azay came to be built, because it is certain that thus was commenced the great fortune of that Samblançay who did so much for his natal town, which he adorned; and also spent such immense sums upon the completion of the towers of the cathedral. This lucky adventure has been handed down from father to son, from lord to lord, in the said place of Azay-le-Ridel, where the story frisks still under the curtains of the king, which have been curiously respected down to the present day. It is therefore the falsest of falsities which attributes the dozen of the Tourainian to a German knight, who by this deed would have secured the domains of Austria to the House of Hapsburgh. The author of our days, who brought this history to light, although a learned man, has allowed himself to be deceived by certain chroniclers, since the archives of the Roman Empire make no mention of an acquisition of this kind. I am angry with him for having believed that a codpiece nourished with beer could have been equal to the alchemical operations of the Chinonian codpiece, so much esteemed by Rabelais. And I have for the advantage of the country, the glory of Azay, the conscience of the castle, and the renown of the House of Beaune, from which sprang the Sauves and the Noirmoutiers, re-established the facts in all their veritable, historical, and admirable beauty. Should any ladies pay a visit to the castle, there are still *dozens* to be found in the neighbourhood, but they can only be procured retail.

THE FALSE COURTESAN

THAT which certain people do not know, is the truth concerning the decease of the Duke of Orléans, brother of King Charles VI., a death which proceeded from a great number of causes, one of which will be the subject of this narrative. This prince was for certain the most lecherous of all the royal race of Monsigneur St. Louis (who was in his lifetime King of France), without even putting on one side some of the most debauched of this fine family, which was so concordant with the vices and especial qualities of our brave and pleasure-seeking nation, that you could more easily imagine Hell without Satan than France without her valorous, glorious, and jovial kings. So you can laugh as loudly at those muckworms of philosophy who go about saying, "Our fathers were better," as at the good, philanthropical old bunglers who pretend that mankind is on the right road to perfection. These are old blind bats, who observe neither the plumage of oysters nor the shells of birds, which change no more than do our ways. Hip, hip, huzzah then! make merry while you're young. Keep your throats wet and your eyes dry, since an hundredweight of melancholy is worth less than an ounce of jollity. The wrong doings of this lord, lover of Queen Isabella, whom he doted upon, brought about pleasant adventures, since he was a great wit, of an Alcibiadescal nature, and a chip of the old block. It was he who first conceived the idea of a relay of sweethearts, so that when he went from Paris to Bordeaux, every time he unsaddled his nag he found ready

for him a good meal, and a bed with as much lace inside as
out. Happy prince! who died on horseback, for he was
always across something in-doors and out. Of his comical
jokes our most excellent King Louis the Eleventh has given
a splendid sample in the book of the "Cent Nouvelles Nouvelles," written under his superintendence during his exile,
at the court of Burgundy, where, during the long evenings,
in order to amuse themselves, he and his cousin Charolois
would relate to each other the good tricks and jokes of
the period; and when they were hard up for true stories
each of the courtiers tried who could invent the best one.
But out of respect for the blood royal, the Dauphin has
credited a townsman with that which happened to the Lady
of Cany. It is given under the title of *La Medaille a revers,*
in the collection of which it is one of the brightest jewels,
and commences the hundred. But now for mine.

The Duc d'Orléans had in his suite a lord of the province of Picardy, named Raoul d'Hocquetonville, who had
taken for a wife, to the future trouble of the prince, a
young lady related to the house of Burgundy, and rich in
domains. But, an exception to the general run of heiresses,
she was of so dazzling a beauty, that all the ladies of the
court, even the queen and Madame Valentine, were thrown
into the shade; nevertheless, this was as nothing in the lady
of Hocquetonville, compared with her Burgundian consanguinity, her inheritances, her prettiness, and gentle
nature, because these rare advantages received a religious
lustre from her supreme innocence, sweet modesty, and
chaste education. The duke had not long gazed upon this
heaven-sent flower before he was seized with the fever of
love. He fell into a state of melancholy, frequented no bad
places, and only with regret now and then did he take a bite
at his royal and dainty German morsel Isabella. He became

passionate, and swore either by sorcery, by force, by trickery, or with her consent, to enjoy the favours of this gentle
lady, who, by the sight of her sweet body, forced him to the
last extremity, during his now long and weary nights. At
first, he pursued her with honied words, but he soon knew
by her untroubled air that she was determined to remain
virtuous, for without appearing astonished at his proceedings, or getting angry like certain other ladies, she replied
to him, "My lord, I must inform you that I do not desire to
trouble myself with the love of other persons, not that I
despise the joys which are therein to be experienced (and
supreme they must be, since so many ladies cast into the
abyss of love their homes, their honour, their future, and
everything), but from the love I bear my children. Never
would I be the cause of a blush upon their cheeks, for in this
idea will I bring up my daughters—that in virtue alone is
true happiness to be found. For, my lord, if the days of our
old age are more numerous than those of our youth, of them
must we think. From those who brought me up I learned to
properly estimate this life, and I know that everything
therein is transitory, except the security of the natural
affection. Thus I wish for the esteem of every one, and
above all that of my husband, who is all the world to me.
Therefore do I desire to appear honest in his sight. I have
finished, and I entreat you to allow me unmolested to attend
to my household affairs, otherwise I will unhesitatingly
refer the matter to my lord and master, who will quit your
service."

This brave reply rendered the king's brother more amorous than ever, and he endeavoured to ensnare this noble
woman in order to possess her, dead or alive, and he never
doubted a bit that he would have her in his clutches, relying
upon his dexterity at this kind of sport, the most joyous of

all, in which it is necessary to employ the weapons of all other kinds of sport, seeing that this sweet game is taken running, by taking aim, by torchlight, by night, by day, in the town, in the country, in the woods, by the waterside, in nets, with falcons, with the lance, with the horn, with the gun, with the decoy bird, in snares, in the toils, with a bird call, by the scent, on the wing, with the cornet, in slime, with a bait, with the lime-twig—indeed, by means of all the snares invented since the banishment of Adam. And gets killed in various different ways, but generally is overridden.

The artful fellow ceased to mention his desires, but had a post of honour given to the Lady of Hocquetonville in the queen's household. Now, one day that the said Isabella went to Vincennes, to visit the sick king, and left him master of the Hôtel St. Paul, he commanded the *chef* to have a delicate and royal supper prepared, and to serve it in the queen's apartments. Then he sent for his obstinate lady by express command, and by one of the pages of the household. The Countess d'Hocquetonville, believing that she was desired by Madame Isabella for some service appertaining to her post, or invited to some sudden amusement, hastened to the room. In consequence of the precautions taken by the disloyal lover, no one had been able to inform the noble dame of the princess's departure, so she hastened to the splendid chamber, which, in the Hôtel St. Paul, led into the queen's bed-chamber; there she found the Duc d'Orléans alone. Suspecting some treacherous plot, she went quickly into the other room, found no queen, but heard the prince give vent to a hearty laugh.

"I am undone!" said she. Then she endeavoured to run away.

But the good lady-killer had posted about devoted attendants, who, without knowing what was going on, closed the hotel, barricaded the doors, and in this mansion, so large that it equalled a fourth of Paris, the Lady d'Hocqueton-ville was as in a desert, with no other aid than that of her patron saint and God. Then, suspecting the truth, the poor lady trembled from head to foot, and fell into a chair; and then the working of this snare, so cleverly conceived, was, with many a hearty laugh, revealed to her by her lover. Directly the duke made a movement to approach her this woman rose and exclaimed, arming herself first with her tongue, and flashing a thousand maledictions from her eyes——

"You will possess me—but dead! Ha! my lord, do not force me to a struggle which must become known to certain people. I may yet retire, and the Sire d'Hocquetonville shall be ignorant of the sorrow with which you have for ever tinged my life. Duke, you look too often in the ladies' faces to find time to study men's, and you do not therefore know your man. The Sire d'Hocquetonville would let himself be hacked to pieces in your service, so devoted is he to you, in memory of your kindness to him, and also because he is partial to you. But as he loves so does he hate; and I believe him to be the man to bring his mace down upon your head, to take his revenge, if you but compel me to utter one cry. Do you desire both my death and your own? But be assured that, as an honest woman, whatsoever happens to me, good or evil, I shall keep no secret. Now, will you let me go?"

The bad fellow began to whistle. Hearing his whistling, the good woman went suddenly into the queen's chamber, and took from a place known to her therein, a sharp stiletto. Then, when the duke followed her to ascertain what this flight meant, "When you pass that line," cried she, pointing to a board, "I will kill myself."

My lord, without being in the least terrified, took a chair, placed it at the very edge of the plank in question, and commenced a glowing description of certain things, hoping to influence the mind of this brave woman, and work her to that point that her brain, her heart, and everything should be at his mercy. Then he commenced to say to her, in that delicate manner to which princes are accustomed, that, in the first place, virtuous women pay dearly for their virtue, since in order to gain the uncertain blessings of the future, they lose all the sweetest joys of the present, because husbands were compelled, from motives of conjugal policy, not to show them all the jewels in the shrine of love, since the said jewels would so affect their hearts, were so rapturously delicious, so titillatingly voluptuous, that a woman would no longer consent to dwell in the cold regions of domestic life; and he declared this marital abomination to be a great felony, because the least thing a man could do in recognition of the virtuous life of a good woman and her great merits, was to overwork himself, to exert, to exterminate himself, to please her in every way, with fondlings and kissings and wrestling, and all the delicacies and sweet confectionery of love; and that, if she would taste a little of the seraphic joys of these little ways to her unknown, she would believe all the other things of life as not worth a straw; and that, if such were her wish, he would for ever be as silent as the grave, and thus no scandal would besmear her virtue. And the lewd fellow, perceiving that the lady did not stop her ears, commenced to describe to her, after the fashion of arabesque pictures, which at that time were much esteemed, the wanton inventions of debauchery. Then did his eyes shoot flame, his words burn, and his voice ring, and he himself took great pleasure in calling to mind the various ways of his ladies, naming them to Madame d'Hocquetonville, and even revealing to her the tricks, caresses, and amorous ways of

Queen Isabella, and he made use of an expression so gracious and so ardently inciting, that, fancying it caused the lady to relax her hold upon the stiletto a little, he made as if to approach her. But she, ashamed to be found buried in thought, gazed proudly at the diabolical leviathan who tempted her, and said to him, "Fine sir, I thank you. You have caused me to love my husband all the more, for from your discourse I learn how much he esteems me by holding me in such respect that he does not dishonour his couch with the tricks of strumpets and harlots. I should think myself for ever disgraced, and should be contaminated to all eternity, if I put my foot in those sloughs where go these shameless hussies. A man's wife is one thing, and his mistress another."

"I will wager," said the duke, smiling, "that, nevertheless, for the future you spur the Sire d'Hocquetonville to a little sharper pace."

At this the good wife trembled, and cried, "You are a wicked man. Now I both despise and abominate you! What! unable to rob me of my honour, you attempt to soil my mind! Ah, my lord, this night's work will cost you dear :—

> If I forgive it, yet,
> God will not forget.

"Are not those verses yours?"

"Madame," said the duke, turning pale with anger, "I can have you bound——"

"Oh, no! I can free myself," replied she, brandishing the stiletto.

The rapscallion began to laugh.

"Never mind," said he. "I have a means of plunging you into the sloughs of these brazen hussies, as you call them."

"Never, while I live."

"Head and heels you shall go in—with your two feet, two hands, two ivory breasts, and two other things, white as snow—your teeth, your hair, and everything. You will go of your own accord; you shall enter into it lasciviously and in a way to crush your cavalier, as a wild horse does its rider—stamping, leaping, and snorting. I swear it by Saint Castud!"

Instantly he whistled for one of his pages. And when the page came, he secretly ordered him to go and seek the Sire d'Hocquetonville, Savoisy, Tanneguy, Cypierre, and other members of his band, asking them to these rooms to supper, not without at the same time inviting to meet his guests a pretty petticoat or two.

Then he came and sat down in his chair again, ten paces from the lady, off whom he had not taken his eye while giving his commands to the page in a whisper.

"Raoul is jealous," said he. "Now, let me give you a word of advice. In this place," he added, pointing to a secret door, "are the oils and superfine perfumes of the queen; in this other little closet she performs her ablutions and little feminine offices. I know by much experience that each one of you gentle creatures has her own special perfume, by which she is smelt and recognized. So if, as you say, Raoul is overwhelmingly jealous with the worst of all jealousies, you will use these fast hussies' scents, because your danger approaches fast."

"Ah, my lord, what do you intend to do?"

"You will know when it is necessary that you should know. I wish you no harm, and pledge you my honour, as a loyal knight, that I will most thoroughly respect you, and be for ever silent concerning my discomfiture. In short, you will know that the Duc d'Orléans has a good heart, and revenges himself nobly on ladies who treat him with disdain, by placing in their hands the key of Paradise. Only keep your ears open to the joyous words that will be handed from mouth to mouth in the next room, and cough not if you love your children."

Since there was no egress from the royal chamber, and the bars crossing hardly left room to put one's head through, the good prince closed the door of the room, certain of keeping the lady a safe prisoner there, and again impressed upon her the necessity of silence. Then came the merry blades in great haste, and found a good substantial supper smiling at them from the silver plates upon the table, and the table well arranged and well lighted, loaded with fine silver cups, and cups full of royal wine. Then said their master to them—

"Come! come! to your places, my good friends. I was becoming very weary. Thinking of you, I wished to arrange with you a merry feast after the ancient method, when the Greeks and Romans said their *Pater noster* to Master Priapus, and the learned god called in all countries Bacchus. The feast will be a proper and right hearty one, since at our libation there will be present some pretty crows with three beaks, of which I know from great experience the best one to kiss."

Then all of them recognizing their master in all things, took pleasure in this gay discourse, except Raoul d'Hocque-tonville, who advanced and said to the prince—

"My lord, I will aid you willingly in any battle but that of the petticoats, in that of spear and axe, but not of the wine flasks. My good companions here present have not wives at home, it is otherwise with me. I have a sweet wife, to whom I owe my company, and an account of all my deeds and actions."

"Then, since I am a married man I am to blame?" said the duke.

"Ah! my dear master, you are a prince, and can do as you please."

These brave speeches made, as you can imagine, the heart of the lady prisoner hot and cold.

"Ah! my Raoul," thought she, "thou art a noble man!"

"You are," said the duke, "a man whom I love, and consider more faithful and praiseworthy than any of my people. The others," said he, looking at the three lords, "are wicked men. But, Raoul," he continued, "sit thee down. When the linnets come—they are linnets of high degree—you can make your way home. S'death! I had treated thee as a virtuous man, ignorant of the extra-conjugal joys of love, and had carefully put for thee in that room the queen of raptures—a fair demon, in whom is concentrated all feminine inventions. I wished that once in thy life thou, who hast never tasted the essence of love, and dreamed but of war, should know the secret marvels of the gallant amusement, since it is shameful that one of my followers should serve a fair lady badly."

Thereupon the Sire d'Hocquetonville sat down to the table in order to please his prince as far as he could lawfully do so. Then they all commenced to laugh, joke, and talk about the ladies; and, according to their custom, they related to each other their good fortunes and their love adventures, sparing no woman except the queen of the house, and betraying the little habits of each one, to which followed horrible little confidences, which increased in treachery and lechery as the contents of the goblets grew less. The duke, gay as an universal legatee, drew the guests out, telling lies himself to learn the truth from them; and his companions ate at a trot, drank at full gallop, and their tongues rattled away faster than either.

Now, listening to them, and heating his brain with wine, the Sire d'Hocquetonville unharnessed himself little by little from his reluctance. In spite of his virtues, he indulged certain desires, and became soaked in these impurities like a saint who defiles himself while saying his prayers. Perceiving which, the prince, on the alert to satisfy his ire and his bile, began to say to him, joking him—

"By St. Castud, Raoul, we are all tarred with the same brush, all discreet away from here. Go; we will say nothing to Madame. By heaven! man, I wish thee to taste the joys of paradise. There," said he, tapping the door of the room in which was Madame Hocquetonville, "in there is a lady of the court and a friend of the queen, but the greatest priestess of Venus that ever was, and her equal is not to be found in any courtesan, harlot, dancer, doxy, or hussy. She was engendered at a moment when paradise was radiant with joy, when nature was procreating, when the planets were whispering vows of love, when the beasts were frisking and capering, and everything was aglow with desire. Although the woman to make an altar her bed, she is nevertheless too great a lady to allow herself to be seen, and too well known to utter any words but sounds of love. No light will you need, for her eyes flash fire, and attempt no conversation, since she speaks only with movements and twistings more rapid than those of a deer surprised in the forest. Only, my dear Raoul, with so merry a nag look to your stirrups, sit lightly in the saddle, since with one plunge she would hurl thee to the ceiling, if you are not careful. She burns always, and is always longing, for male society. Our poor dead friend, the young Sire de Giac, met his death through her: she drained his marrow in one springtime.

God's truth! to know such bliss as that of which she rings
the bells and lights the fires, what man would not forfeit
a third of his future happiness? and he, who has known
her once would for a second night forfeit without regret
eternity."

"But," said Raoul, "in things which should be so much
alike, how is it there is so great a difference?"

"Ha! ha! ha!"

Thereupon the company burst out laughing, and animated by the wine and a wink from their master, they all
commenced relating droll and quaint conceits, laughing,
shouting, and making a great noise. Now, knowing not that
an innocent scholar was there, these jokers, who had
drowned their sense of shame in the wine-cups, said things
to make the figures on the mantel shake, the walls and the
ceilings blush; and the duke surpassed them all, saying,
that the lady who was in bed in the next room awaiting a
gallant should be the empress of these warm imaginations,
because she practised them every night. Upon this, the
flagons being empty, the duke pushed Raoul, who let himself be pushed willingly, into the room, and by this means
the prince compelled the lady to deliberate by which dagger she would either live or die. At midnight the Sire
d'Hocquetonville came out gleefully, not without remorse
at having been false to his good wife. Then the Duc d'Orléans led Madame Hocquetonville out by a garden door,
so that she gained her residence before her husband arrived
there. "This," said she, in the prince's ear, as she passed the
postern, "will cost us all dear."

One year afterwards, in the old Rue du Temple, Raoul
d'Hocquetonville, who had quitted the service of the duke
for that of Jehan of Burgundy, gave the king's brother a
blow on the head with a club, and killed him, as every one

knows. In the same year died the Lady d'Hocquetonville,
having faded like a flower deprived of air and eaten by a
worm. Her good husband had engraved upon her marble
tomb, which is in one of the cloisters of Péronne, the following inscription:—

HERE LIES

BERTHA DE BOURGONGNE,

THE NOBLE AND COMELY WIFE

OF

RAOUL, SIRE DE HOCQUETONVILLE.

ALAS! PRAY NOT FOR HER SOUL.

SHE

BLOSSOMED AGAIN IN PARADISE,
THE ELEVENTH DAY OF JANUARY,
IN THE YEAR OF OUR LORD MCCCCVIII.,
IN THE TWENTY-THIRD YEAR OF HER AGE,
LEAVING TWO SONS AND HER LORD SPOUSE
INCONSOLABLE.

This epitaph was writen in elegant Latin, but for the
convenience of all it was necessary to translate it, although
the word *comely* is feeble beside that of *formosa,* which
signifies *beautiful in shape.* The Duke of Burgundy, called
the Fearless, to whom previous to his death the Sire d'Hocquetonville confided the troubles cemented with lime and
sand in his heart, used to say, in spite of his hard-hearted-
ness in these matters, that this epitaph plunged him into a
state of melancholy for a month, and that among all the
abominations of his cousin of Orléans, there was one for
which he would kill him over again if the deed had not
already been done, because this wicked man had villain-

ously defaced with vice the most divine virtue in the world
and had prostituted two noble hearts, the one by the other.
When saying this he would think of the lady of Hocquetonville and of his own, whose portrait had been unwarrantably
placed in the cabinet where his cousin placed the likenesses
of his wenches.

This adventure was so extremely shocking, that when
it was related by the Count de Charolois to the Dauphin,
afterwards Louis XI., the latter would not allow his secretaries to publish it in his collection, out of respect for his
great-uncle the Duke of Orléans, and for Dunois his old
comrade, the son of the same. But the person of the lady of
Hocquetonville is so sublimely virtuous, so exquisitely melancholy, that in her favour the present publication of this
narrative will be forgiven, in spite of the diabolical invention and vengeance of Monseigneur d'Orléans. The just
death of this rascal nevertheless caused many serious rebellions, which finally Louis XI., losing all patience, put down
with fire and sword.

This shows us that there is a woman at the bottom of
everything, in France as elsewhere, and that sooner or later
we must pay for our follies.

THE DANGER OF BEING TOO INNOCENT

THE lord of Moncontour was a brave soldier of Tours, who, in honour of the battle gained by the Duke of Anjou, afterwards our right glorious king, caused to be built at Vouvray the castle thus named, for he had borne himself most bravely in that affair, where he overcame the greatest of heretics, and from that was authorized to take the name. Now this said captain had two sons, good Catholics, of whom the eldest was in favour at court. After the peace, which was concluded before the stratagem arranged for St. Bartholomew's day, the good man returned to his manor, which was not ornamented as it is at the present day. There he received the sad announcement of the death of his son, slain in a duel by the lord of Villequier. The poor father was the more cut up at this, as he had arranged a capital marriage for this said son with a young lady of the male branch of Amboise. Now, by this death most piteously inopportune, vanished all the future and advantages of his family, of which he wished to make a great and noble house. With this idea, he had put his other son in a monastery, under the guidance and government of a man renowned for his holiness, who brought him up in a Christian manner, according to the desire of his father, who wished from high ambition to make of him a cardinal of renown. For this the good abbot kept the young man in a private house, had him to sleep by his side in his cell, allowed no evil weeds to grow in his mind, brought him up in purity of soul and true contrition, as all priests should be. This said clerk, when turned

nineteen years, knew no other love than the love of God,
no other nature than that of the angels who have not our
carnal properties, in order that they may live in purity, seeing that otherwise they would make good use of them. The
which the King on High, who wished to have His pages
always proper, was afraid of. He has done well, because his
good little people cannot drink in dram shops or riot in
brothels as ours do. He is divinely served; but then, remember, He is Lord of all. Now in this plight the lord of
Moncontour determined to withdraw his second son from
the cloister, and invest him with the purple of the soldier
and the courtier, in the place of the ecclesiastical purple; and
determined to give him in marriage to the maiden, affianced
to the dead man, which was wisely determined because
wrapped round with continence and sobriety in all ways as
was the little monk, the bride would be as well used and
happier than she would have been with the elder, already
well hauled over, upset, and spoilt by the ladies of the court.
The befrocked, unfrocked, and very sheepish in his ways,
followed the sacred wishes of his father, and consented to
the said marriage without knowing what a wife, and—
what is more curious—what a girl was. By chance, his journey having been hindered by the troubles and marches of
conflicting parties, this innocent—more innocent than it is
lawful for a man to be innocent—only came to the castle of
Moncontour the evening before the wedding, which was
performed with dispensations bought in the archbishopric
of Tours. It is necessary here to describe the bride. Her
mother, long time a widow, lived in the house of M. de
Braguelongne, civil lieutenant of the Chatelet de Paris,
whose wife lived with the lord of Lignieres, to the great
scandal of the period. But every one then had so many
joists in his own eye that he had no right to notice the rafters

in the eyes of others. Now, in all families people go to
perdition, without noticing their neighbours, some at an
amble, others at a gentle trot, many at a gallop, and a small
number walking, seeing that the road is all down hill. Thus
in these times the devil had many a good orgie in all things,
since that misconduct was fashionable. The poor old lady
Virtue had retired trembling, no one knew whither, but now
here, now there lived miserably in company with honest
women.

In the most noble house of Amboise there still lived the
dowager of Chaumont, an old woman of well-proved virtue, in whom had retired all the religion and good conduct
of this fine family. The said lady had taken to her bosom,
from the age of ten years, the little maiden who is concerned in this adventure, and who never caused Madame
Amboise the least anxiety, but left her free in her movements, and she came to see her daughter once a year, when
the court passed that way. In spite of this high maternal
reserve, Madame Amboise was invited to her daughter's
wedding, and also the lord of Braguelongne, by the good
old soldier, who knew his people. But the dear dowager
came not to Moncontour, because she could not obtain leave
from her sciatica, her cold, nor the state of her legs, which
gambolled no longer. Over this the good woman cried
copiously. It hurt her much to let go into the dangers of the
court and of life this gentle maiden, as pretty as it was possible for a pretty girl to be, but she was obliged to give her
her wings. But it was not without promising her many
masses and orisons every evening for her happiness. And
comforted a little, the good old lady began to think that the
staff of her old age was passing into the hands of a quasi-
saint, brought up to do good by the above-mentioned abbot,
with whom she was acquainted, the which had aided con-

siderably in the prompt exchange of spouses. At length,
embracing her with tears, the virtuous dowager made those
last recommendations to her that ladies make to young
brides, as that she ought to be respectful to his mother, and
obey her husband in everything.

Then the maid arrived with a great noise, conducted by
servants, chamberlains, grooms, gentlemen, and people of
the house of Chaumont, so that you would have imagined
her suite to be that of a cardinal legate. So arrived the
two spouses the evening before their marriage. Then, the
feasting over, they were married with great pomp on the
Lord's Day, a mass being said at the castle by the Bishop
of Blois, who was a great friend of the lord of Moncontour; in short, the feasting, the dancing, and the festivities
of all sorts lasted till the morning. But on the stroke of
midnight the bridesmaids went to put the bride to bed,
according to the custom of Touraine; and during this time
they kept quarrelling with the innocent husband, to prevent him going to this innocent wife, who sided with them
from ignorance. However, the good lord of Moncontour
interrupted the jokers and the wits, because it was necessary that his son should occupy himself in well-doing. Then
went the innocent into the chamber of his wife, whom he
thought more beautiful than the Virgin Marys painted in
Italian, Flemish, and other pictures, at whose feet he had
said his prayers. But you may be sure he felt very much
embarrassed at having so soon become a husband, because
he knew nothing of his business, and saw that certain forms
had to be gone through concerning which, from great and
modest reserve, he had not time to question even his father,
who had said sharply to him—

"You know what you have to do; be valiant therein."

Then he saw the gentle girl who was given him, comfortably tucked up in the bedclothes, terribly curious, her head buried under, but hazarding a glance as at the point of a halberd, and saying to herself—

"I must obey him."

And knowing nothing, she awaited the will of this slightly ecclesiastical gentleman, to whom, in fact, she belonged. Seeing which, the Chevalier de Moncontour came close to the bed, scratched his ear, and knelt down, a thing in which he was expert.

"Have you said your prayers?" said he.

"No," said she; "I have forgotten them. Do you wish me to say them?"

Then the young couple commenced the business of housekeeping by imploring God, which was not at all out of place. But unfortunately the devil heard, and at once replied to their requests, God being occupied at that time with the new and abominable reformed religion.

"What did they tell you to do?" said the husband.

"To love you," said she, in perfect innocence.

"That has not been told to me; but I love you, I am ashamed to say, better than I love God."

This speech did not at all alarm the bride.

"I should like," said the husband, "to repose myself in your bed, if it will not disturb you."

"I will make room for you willingly, because I am to submit myself to you."

"Well," said he, "don't look at me then. I'm going to take my clothes off, and come."

At this virtuous speech, the young damsel turned herself towards the wall in great expectation, seeing that it was for the very first time that she was about to find herself separated from a man by the confines of a shirt only. Then came the innocent, gliding into the bed, and thus they found themselves, so to speak, united, but far from you can imagine what. Did you ever see a monkey brought from across the seas, who for the first time is given a nut to crack? This ape, knowing by high apish imagination how delicious is the food hidden under the shell, sniffs and twists himself about in a thousand apish ways, saying, I know not what, between his chattering jaws. Ah! with what affection he studies it, with what study he examines it, in what examination he holds it, then throws it, rolls and tosses it about with passion, and often, when it is an ape of low extraction and intelligence, leaves the nut. As much did the poor innocent who, towards the dawn, was obliged to confess to his dear wife that, not knowing how to perform his office, or what that office was, or where to obtain the said office, it would be necessary for him to inquire concerning it, to have help and aid.

"Yes," said she; "since, unhappily, I cannot instruct you."

In fact, in spite of their efforts, essays of all kinds—in spite of a thousand things which the innocents invent, and which the wise in matters of love know nothing about—the pair dropped off to sleep, wretched at having been unable to discover the secret of marriage. But they wisely agreed to say that they had done so. When the wife got up, still a maiden, seeing that she had not been crowned, she boasted of her night, and said she had the king of husbands, and went on with her chattering and repartees as briskly as those who know nothing of these things. Then every one found the maiden a little too sharp, since for a two-edged joke a lady of Roche-Corbon having incited a young maiden, de la Bourdaisière, who knew nothing of such things, to ask the bride—

"How many loaves did your husband put in the oven?"

"Twenty-four," she replied.

Now, as the bridegrom was roaming sadly about, thereby distressing his wife, who followed him with her eyes, hoping to see his state of innocence come to an end, the ladies believed that the joy of that night had cost him dear, and that the said bride was already regretting having so quickly ruined him. And at breakfast came the bad jokes, which at that time were relished as excellent. One said that the bride had an open expression; another, that there had been some good strokes of business done that night in the castle; this one, that the oven had been burned; that one that the two families had lost something that night that they would never find again. And a thousand other jokes, stupidities and double meanings that, unfortunately, the husband did not understand. But on account of the great affluence of the relations, neighbours, and others, no one had been to bed; all had danced, rollicked, and frolicked, as is the custom at noble weddings.

At this was quite contented my said Sieur de Braguelongne, upon whom my lady of Amboise, excited by the thought of the good things which were happening to her daughter, cast the glances of a falcon in matters of gallant assignation. The poor lieutenant civil, learned in bailiffs' men and serjeants, and who nabbed all the pickpockets and scamps of Paris, pretended not to see his good fortune, although his good lady required him to. You may be sure this great lady's love weighed heavily upon him, so he only kept to her from a spirit of justice, because it was not seeming in a lieutenant criminal to change his mistresses as often as a man at court, because he had under his charge morals, the police, and religion. This notwithstanding his rebellion must come to an end. On the day after the wedding a great number of the guests departed; then Madame d'Amboise and

Monsieur de Braguelongne could go to bed, their guests having decamped. Sitting down to supper, the lieutenant received a half-verbal summons to which it was not becoming, as in legal matters, to oppose any reasons for delay.

During supper the said lady d'Amboise made more than a hundred little signs in order to draw the good Braguelongne from the room where he was with the bride, but out came instead of the lieutenant the husband, to walk about in company with the mother of his sweet wife. Now, in the mind of this innocent there had sprung up like a mushroom an expedient—namely, to interrogate this good lady, whom he considered discreet, for remembering the religious precepts of his abbot, who had told him to inquire concerning all things of old people expert in the ways of life, he thought of confiding his case to my said lady d'Amboise. But he made first awkwardly and shyly certain twists and turns, finding no terms in which to unfold his case. And the lady was also perfectly silent, since she was outrageously struck with the blindness, deafness, and voluntary paralysis of the lord of Braguelongne; and said to herself, walking by the side of this delicate morsel, a young innocent of whom she did not think, little imagining that this cap so well provided with young bacon could think of old—

"This Ho, Ho, with a beard of flies' legs, a flimsy, old, grey, ruined, shaggy beard—a beard without comprehension, beard without shame, without any feminine respect —beard which pretends neither to feel nor to hear nor to see, a pared away beard, a beaten down, disordered, gutted beard. May the Italian sickness deliver me from this vile joker with a squashed nose, fiery nose, frozen nose, nose without religion, nose dry as a lute table, pale nose, nose without a soul, nose which is nothing but a shadow; nose which sees not, nose wrinkled like the leaf of the vine;

nose that I hate, old nose, nose full of mud—dead nose.
Where have my eyes been to attach myself to this truffle
nose, to this old hulk that no longer knows his way? I
give my share to the devil of this old juiceless beard, of
this old grey beard, of this monkey face, of these old tatters,
of this old rag of a man, of this—I know not what; and
I'll take a young husband who'll marry me properly, and
... and often—every day—and well——"

In this wise train of thought was she when the innocent
began his anthem to this woman, so warmly excited, who
at the first paraphrase took fire in her understanding, like
a piece of old touchwood from the carbine of a soldier; and
finding it wise to try her son-in-law, said to herself—

"Ah! young beard, sweet scented! ah! pretty new nose
—fresh beard—innocent nose—virgin beard—nose full of
joy—beard of springtime, small key of love!"

She kept on talking the round of the garden, which was
long, and then arranged with the Innocent that, night come,
he should sally forth from his room and get into hers, where
she engaged to render him more learned than ever was his
father. And the husband was well content, and thanked
Madame d'Amboise, begging her to say nothing of this
arrangement.

During this time the good old Braguelongne had been
growling and saying to himself, "Old ha, ha; old ho, ho!
may the plague take thee! may a cancer eat thee!—worth-
less old currycomb! old slipper, too big for the foot; old
arquebus! ten-year-old codfish! old spider that spins no
more! old death with open eyes; old devil's cradle! vile
lantern of an old town-crier! old wretch whose look kills!
old moustache of an old theriacler! old wretch to make dead
men weep! old organ-pedal! old sheath with a hundred
knives; old church porch, worn out by the knees! old poor-

box in which every one has dropped. I'll give all my future to be quit of thee!" As he finished these gentle thoughts the pretty bride, who was thinking of her young husband's great sorrow at not knowing the particulars of that essential item of marriage, and not having the slightest idea what it was, thought to save him much tribulation, shame, and labour by instructing herself. And she counted upon much astonishing and rejoicing him the next night when she should say to him, teaching him his duty, "That's the thing, my love!" Brought up in great respect of old people by her dear dowager, she thought of inquiring of this good man in her sweetest manner to distil for her the sweet mysteries of the commerce. Now, the lord of Braguelongne, ashamed of being lost in sad contemplation of his evening's work, and of saying nothing to his gay companion, put this summary interrogation to the fair bride—"If she was not happy with so good a young husband——"

"He is very good," said she.

"Too good, perhaps," said the lieutenant, smiling.

To be brief, matters were so well arranged between them that the lord of Braguelongne engaged to spare no pains to enlighten the understanding of Madame d'Amboise's daughter-in-law, who promised to come and study her lesson in his room. The said lady d'Amboise pretended after supper to play terrible music in a high key to Monsieur de Braguelongne, saying that he had no gratitude for the blessings she had brought him—her position, her wealth, her fidelity, etc. In fact, she talked for half an hour without having exhausted a quarter of her ire. From this a hundred knives were drawn between them, but they kept the sheaths. Meanwhile the spouses in bed were arranging to themselves how to get away, in order to please each other. Then the innocent began to say he felt quite giddy, he knew not from what, and wanted to go into the open air. And his maiden wife told him to take a stroll in the moonlight. And then the good fellow began to pity his wife in being left alone a moment. At her desire, both of them at different times left their conjugal couch and came to their preceptors, both very impatient, as you can well believe; and good instruction was given to them. How? I cannot say, because every one has his own method and practice, and of all sciences this is the most variable in principle. You may be sure that never did scholars receive more gaily the precepts of any language, grammar, or lessons whatsoever. And the two spouses returned to their nest, delighted at being able to communicate to each other the discoveries of their scientific peregrinations.

"Ah, my dear," said the bride, "you already know more than my master."

From these curious tests came their domestic joy and perfect fidelity; because immediately after their entry into the married state they found out how much better each of them was adapted for love than any one else, their masters included. Thus for the remainder of their days they kept to the legitimate substance of their own persons; and the lord of Moncontour said in his old age to his friends—

"Do like me, be cuckolds in the blade, and not in the sheaf."

Which is the true morality of the conjugal condition.

THE DEAR NIGHT OF LOVE

In that winter when commenced that first taking up of arms by those of the religion, which was called the Riot of Amboise, an advocate, named Avenelles, lent his house, situated in the Rue des Marmousets for the interviews and conventions of the Huguenots, being one of them, without knowing, however, that the Prince of Condé, La Regnaudie, and others, intended to carry off the king.

This said Avenelles wore a nasty red beard, as shiny as a stick of liquorice, and was devilishly pale, as are all the rogues who take refuge in the darknesses of the law; in short, the most evil-minded advocate that has ever lived, laughing at the gallows, selling everybody, and a true Judas. According to certain authors of great experience in subtle rogues he was in this affair half knave, half fool, as is abundantly proved by this narrative. This *procureur* had married a very lovely lady of Paris, of whom he was jealous enough to kill her for a pleat in the sheets, for which she could not account, which would have been wrong, because honest creases are often met with. But she folded her clothes very well, so there's an end of the matter. Be sure that, knowing the murderous and evil nature of this man, his wife was faithful enough to him, always ready, like a candlestick, arranged for her duty like a chest which never moves, and opens to order. Nevertheless, the advocate had placed her under the guardianship and pursuing eye of an old servant, a duenna as ugly as a pot without a handle, who had brought up the Sieur Avenelles, and was very fond of him.

His poor wife, for all pleasure in her cold domestic life, used to go to the church of St. Jehan, on the Place de Grève, where, as every one knows, the fashionable world was accustomed to meet; and while saying her paternosters to God she feasted her eyes upon all these gallants, curled, adorned, and starched, young, comely, and flitting about like true butterflies, and finished by picking out from among the lot a good gentleman, lover of the queen-mother, and a handsome Italian, with whom she was smitten because he was in the May of his age, nobly dressed, a graceful mover, brave in mien, and was all that a lover should be to bestow a heart full of love upon an honest woman too tightly squeezed by the bonds of matrimony, which torment her, and always excite her to unharness herself from the conjugal yoke. And you can imagine that the young gentleman grew to admire Madame, whose silent love spoke secretly to him, without either the devil or themselves knowing how. Both one and the other had their correspondence of love. At first the advocate's wife adorned herself only to come to church, and always came in some new sumptuosity; and instead of thinking of God, she made God angry by thinking of her handsome gentleman, and leaving her prayers, she gave herself up to the fire which consumed her heart, and moistened her eyes, her lips, and everything, seeing that this fire always dissolves itself in water; and often said she to herself: "Ha! I would give my life for a single embrace with this pretty lover who loves me." Often, too, in place of saying her litanies to Madame the Virgin, she thought in her heart: "To feel the glorious youth of this gentle lover, to have the full joys of love, to taste all in one moment, little should I mind the flames into which the heretics are thrown." Then the gentleman gazing at the charms of this good wife, and her burning blushes when he glanced at her, came always close to her stool, and addressed to her those requests which the ladies understand so well. Then he said aside to himself : "By the double horn of my father I swear to have that woman, though it cost me my life."

And when the duenna turned her head, the two lovers squeezed, pressed, breathed, ate, devoured, and kissed each other by a look which would have set light to the match of a musketeer, if the musketeer had been there. It was certain that a love so far advanced in the heart should have an end. The gentleman, dressed as a scholar of Montaign, began to regale the clerks of the said Avenelles, and to joke in their company, in order to learn the habits of the husband, his hours of absence, his journeys, and everything, watching for an opportunity to stick his horns on. And this was how, to his injury, the opportunity occurred. The advocate, obliged to follow the course of this conspiracy, and, in case of failure, intending to revenge himself upon the Guises, determined to go to Blois, where the court then was in great danger of being carried off. Knowing this, the gentleman came first to the town of Blois, and there arranged a master-trap, into which the Sieur Avenelles should fall, in spite of his cunning, and not come out until steeped in a crimson cuckoldom. This said Italian, intoxicated with love, called together all his pages and vassals, and posted them in such a manner that on the arrival of the advocate, his wife, and her duenna, it was stated to them at all the hostelries at which they wished to put up that the hostelry being full, in consequence of the sojourn of the court, they must go elsewhere. Then the gentleman made such an arrangement with the landlord of the Soleil Royal, that he had the whole of the house, and occupied it, without any of the usual servants of the place remaining there. For greater security, my lord sent the said master and his people

into the country, and put his own in their places, so that the
advocate should know nothing of this arrangement. Behold my good gentleman who lodges his friends who come
to the court in the hostelry, and for himself keeps a room
situated above those in which he intends to put his lovely
mistress, her advocate, and the duenna, not without first
having cut a trap in the boards. And his steward being
charged to play the part of the innkeeper, his pages dressed
like guests, and his female servants like servants of the inn,
he waited for spies to convey to him the dramatis personæ
of this farce—viz., wife, husband, and duenna, none of
whom failed to come. Seeing the immense wealth of the
great lords, merchants, warriors, members of the service,
and others, brought by the sojourn of the young king, of
two queens, the Guises, and all the court, no one had a right
to be astonished or to talk of the roguish trap, or of the confusion come to the Soleil Royal. Behold, now the Sieur
Avenelles, on his arrival, bundled about, he, his wife and
the duenna from inn to inn, and thinking themselves very
fortunate in being received at the Soleil Royal, where the
gallant was getting warm, and love was burning. The advocate being lodged, the lover walked about in the courtyard,
watching and waiting for a glance from his lady ; and he did
not have to wait very long, since the fair Avenelles, looking
soon into the court, after the custom of the ladies, there
recognized, not without great throbbing of the heart, her
gallant and well-beloved gentleman. At that she was very
happy ; and if by a lucky chance both had been alone together for an ounce of time, the good gentleman would not
have had to wait for his good fortune, so burning was she
from head to foot.

"How warm it is in the rays of this lord," said she, meaning to say sun, since it was then shining fiercely.

Hearing this, the advocate sprang to the window, and beheld my gentleman.

"Ha! you want lords, my dear, do you?" said the advocate, dragging her by the arm, and throwing her like one of his bags on to the bed. "Remember that if I have a pencase at my side instead of a sword, I have a penknife in this pencase, and the penknife will go into your heart on the least suspicion of conjugal impropriety. I believe I have seen that gentleman somewhere."

The advocate was so terribly spiteful that the lady rose, and said to him—

"Well, kill me. I am afraid of deceiving you. Never touch me again, after having thus menaced me. And from to-day I shall never think of sleeping save with a lover more gentle than are you."

"There, there, my little one!" said the advocate, surprised. "We have gone a little too far. Kiss me, chick-a-biddy, and forgive me."

"I will neither kiss nor pardon you," said she. "You are a wretch!"

Avenelles, enraged, wished to take by force that which his wife denied him, and from this resulted a combat, from which the husband emerged clawed all over. But the worst of it was, that the advocate, covered with scratches, being expected by the conspirators, who were holding a council, was obliged to quit his good wife, leaving her to the care of the old woman.

The knave having departed, the gentleman putting one of his servants to keep watch at the corner of the street, mounts to his blessed trap, lifts it noiselessly, and calls the lady a gentle *psit! psit!* which was understood by the heart, which generally understands everything. The lady lifts her head, and sees her pretty lover four flea jumps above her.

Upon a sign, she takes hold of two cords of black silk, to which were attached loops, through which she passes her arms, and in the twinkling of an eye is translated by two pulleys from her bed through the ceiling into the room above, and the trap closing as it had opened, left the old duenna in a state of great flabbergastation, when, turning her head, she neither saw robe nor woman, and perceived that the woman had been robbed. How? by whom? in what way? where?—Presto! Foro! Magico! As much knew the alchemists at their furnaces reading Herr Trippa. Only the old woman knew well the crucible, and the great work—the one was cuckoldom, and the other the private property of Madame Advocate. She remained dumbfoundered, watching for the Sieur Avenelles—as well say death, for in his rage he would attack everything, and the poor duenna could not run away, because with great prudence the jealous man had taken the keys with him. At first sight, Madame Avenelles found a dainty supper, a good fire in the grate, but a better in the heart of her lover, who seized her, and kissed her, with tears of joy, on the eyes first of all, to thank them for their sweet glances during devotion at the church of St. Jehan en Grève. Nor did the glowing better half of the lawyer refuse her little mouth to his love, but allowed herself to be properly pressed, adored, caressed, delighting to be properly pressed, admirably adored, and calorously caressed after the manner of eager lovers. And both agreed to be all in all to each other the whole night long, no matter what the result might be, she counting the future as a fig in comparison with the joys of this night, he relying upon his cunning and his sword to obtain many another. In short, both of them caring little for life, because at one stroke they consummated a thousand lives, enjoyed with each other a thousand delights, giving to each other the double of their own—believing, he

and she, that they were falling into an abyss, and wishing to
roll there closely clasped, hurling all the love of their souls
with rage in one throw. Therein they loved each other well.
Thus they know not love, the poor citizens, who live
mechanically with their good wives, since they know not the
fierce beating of the heart, the hot gush of life, and the
vigorous clasp as do two young lovers, closely united and
glowing with passion, who embrace in face of the danger of
death. Now the youthful lady and the gentleman ate little
supper, but retired early to rest. Let us leave them there,
since no words, except those of paradise unknown to us,
would describe their delightful agonies, and agonizing delights. Meanwhile, the husband, so well cuckolded that all
memory of marriage had been swept away by love,—the
said Avenelles found himself in a great fix. To the council
of the Huguenots came the Prince of Condé, accompanied
by all the chiefs and bigwigs, and there it was resolved to
carry off the queen-mother, the Guises, the young king, the
young queen, and to change the government. This becoming
serious, the advocate seeing his head at stake, did not feel
the ornaments being planted there, and ran to divulge the
conspiracy to the cardinal of Lorraine, who took the rogue
to the duke his brother, and all three held a consultation
making fine promises to the Sieur Avenelles, whom with
the greatest difficulty they allowed, towards midnight, to
depart, at which hour he issued secretly from the castle.
At this moment the pages of the gentleman and all his
people were having a right jovial supper in honour of the
fortuitous wedding of their master. Now, arriving at the
height of the festivities, in the middle of the intoxication
and joyous huzzahs, he was assailed with jeers, jokes, and
laughter that turned him sick when he came into his room.
The poor servant wished to speak, but the advocate promptly

planted a blow in her stomach, and by a gesture commanded
her to be silent. Then he felt in his valise, and took therefrom
a good poniard. While he was opening and sharpening it,
a frank, naïve, joyous, amorous, pretty, celestial roar of
laughter, followed by certain words of easy comprehension,
came down through the trap. The cunning advocate, blow-
ing out his candle, saw through the cracks in the boards
caused by the shrinking of the door a light, which vaguely
explained the mystery to him, for he recognised the voice
of his wife and that of the combatant. The husband took the
duenna by the arm, and went softly up the stairs searching
for the door of the chamber in which were the lovers, and
did not fail to find it. Fancy! that like a horrid, rude advocate, he burst open the door, and with one spring was on
the bed, in which he surprised his wife, half dressed, in
the arms of the gentleman.

"Ah!" said she.

The lover having avoided the blow, tried to snatch the
poniard from the hands of the knave, who held it firmly.
Now, in this struggle of life and death, the husband finding himself hindered by his lieutenant, who clutched him
tightly with his fingers of iron, and bitten by his wife, who
tore away at him with a will, gnawing him as a dog gnaws
a bone, he thought instantly of a better way to gratify his
rage. Then this devil, newly horned, maliciously ordered, in
his patois, the servant to tie the lovers with the silken cords
of the trap, and throwing the poniard away, he helped the
duenna to make them fast. And the thing thus done in a
moment, he rammed some linen into their mouths to stop
their cries, and ran to his good poniard without saying a
word. At this moment there entered several officers of the
Duke of Guise, whom during the struggle no one had heard
turning the house upside down, looking for the Sieur Ave-

nelles. These soldiers, suddenly warned by the cries of the pages of the lord, bound, gagged and half killed, threw themselves between the man with the poniard and the lovers, disarmed him, and accomplished their mission by arresting him, and marching him off to the castle prison, he, his wife, and the duenna. At the same time the people of the Guises, recognizing one of their master's friends, with whom at this moment the queen was most anxious to consult, and whom they were enjoined to summon to the council, invited him to come with them. Then the gentleman soon untied, dressing himself, said aside to the chief of the escort, that on his account, for the love of him, he should be careful to keep the husband away from his wife, promising him his favour, good advancement, and even a few deniers, if he were careful to obey him on this point. And for greater surety he explained to him the why and the wherefore of the affair, adding that if the husband found himself within reach of this fair lady he would give her for certain a blow in the belly from which she would never recover. Finally he ordered him to place the lady in the gaol of the castle, in a pleasant place level with the gardens, and the advocate in a safe dungeon, not without chaining him hand and foot. The which the said officer promised, and arranged matters according to the wish of the gentleman, who accompanied the lady as far as the courtyard of the castle, assuring her that this business would make her a widow, and that he would perhaps espouse her in legitimate marriage. In fact, the Sieur Avenelles was thrown into a damp dungeon without air, and his pretty wife placed in a room above him, out of consideration for her lover, who was the Sieur Scipion Sardini, a noble of Lucca, exceedingly rich, and, as has before been stated, a friend of Queen Catherine de Medicis, who at that time did everything in concert with the

Guises. Then he went up quickly to the queen's apartments, where a great secret council was then being held, and there the Italian learned what was going on, and the danger of the court. Monseigneur Sardini found the privy councillors much embarrassed and surprised at this dilemma, but he made them all agree, telling them to turn it to their own advantage; and to his advice was due the clever idea of lodging the king in the castle of Amboise, in order to catch the heretics there like foxes in a bag, and there to slay them all. Indeed, every one knows how the queen-mother and the Guises dissimulated, and how the riot of Amboise terminated. This is not, however, the subject of the present narrative. When in the morning every one had quitted the chamber of the queen-mother, where everything had been arranged, Monseigneur Sardini, in no way oblivious of his love for the fair Avenelles, although he was at the time deeply smitten with the lovely Limeuil, a girl belonging to the queen-mother, and her relation by the house of La Tour de Turenne, asked why the good Judas had been caged. Then the Cardinal of Lorraine told him that his intention was not in any way to harm the rogue, but that fearing his repentance, and for greater security of his silence until the end of the affair, he had put him out of the way, and would liberate him at the proper time.

"Liberate him!" said the Luccanese. "Never! Put him in a sack, and throw the old black gown into the Loire. In the first place I know him; he is not the man to forgive you his imprisonment, and will return to the Protestant Church. Thus this will be a work pleasant to God, to rid him of a heretic. Then no one will know your secrets, and not one of his adherents will think of asking you what has become of him, because he is a traitor. Let me procure the escape of his wife and arrange the rest; I will take it off your hands."

"Ha! Ha!" said the cardinal; "you give good counsel. Now I will, before distilling your advice, have them both more securely guarded. Hi, there!"

Came an officer of police, who was ordered to let no person, whoever he might be, communicate with the two prisoners. Then the cardinal begged Sardini to say at his hotel that the said advocate had departed from Blois to return to his causes in Paris. The men charged with the arrest of the advocate, had received verbal orders to treat him as a man of importance, so they neither stripped nor robbed him. Now the advocate had kept thirty gold crowns in his purse, and resolved to lose them all to assure his vengeance, and proved by good arguments to the gaolers that it was allowable for him to see his wife, on whom he doted, and whose legitimate embrace he desired. Monseigneur Sardini, fearing for his mistress the danger of the proximity of this red learned rogue, and for her having great fear of certain evils, determined to carry her off in the night, and put her in a place of safety. Then he hired some boatmen and also their boat, placing them near the bridge, and ordered three of his most active servants to file the bars of the cell, seize the lady, and conduct her to the wall of the gardens, where he would await her.

These preparations being made, and good files bought, he obtained an interview in the morning with the queen-mother, whose apartments were situated above the stronghold in which lay the said advocate and his wife, believing that the queen would willingly lend herself to this flight. Presently he was received by her, and begged her not to think it wrong that, at the instigation of the cardinal and of the Duke of Guise, he should deliver this lady; and besides this, urged her very strongly to tell the cardinal to throw the man into the water. To which the queen said,

"Amen." Then the lover sent quickly to his lady a letter in a plate of cucumbers, to advise her of her approaching widowhood, and the hour of flight, with all of which was the fair citizen well content. Then at dusk the soldiers of the watch being got out of the way by the queen, who sent them to look at a ray of the moon, which frightened her, behold the servants raised the grating, and called the lady, who came quickly enough, and was led to the house of Monseigneur Sardini.

But the postern closed, and the Italian outside with the lady, behold the lady throw aside her mantle, see the lady change into an advocate, and see my said advocate seize his cuckolder by the collar, and half strangle him, dragging him towards the water to throw him to the bottom of the Loire; and Sardini begin to defend himself, to shout, and to struggle, without being able, in spite of his dagger, to shake off this devil in long robes. Then he was quiet, falling into a slough under the feet of the advocate, whom he recognized through the mists of this diabolical combat, and by the light of the moon, his face plashed with the blood of his wife. The enraged advocate quitted the Italian, believing him to be dead, and also because servants, armed with torches, came running up. But he had time to jump into the boat and push off in great haste.

Thus poor Madame Avenelles died alone, since Monseigneur Sardini badly strangled, was found, and revived from this murder; and later, as every one knows, married the fair Limeuil after this sweet girl had been brought to bed in the queen's cabinet—a great scandal, which from friendship the queen-mother wished to conceal, and which from great love Sardini, to whom Catherine gave the splendid estate of Chaumont-sur-Loire, and also the castle, covered with marriage.

But he had been so brutally used by the husband that he did not make old bones, and the fair Limeuil was left a widow in her spring-time. In spite of his misdeeds the advocate was not searched after. He was cunning enough eventually to get included in the number of those conspirators who were not prosecuted, and returned to the Huguenots, for whom he worked hard in Germany.

Poor Madame Avenelles, pray for her soul! for she was hurled no one knew where, and had neither the prayers of the Church nor Christian burial. Alas! shed a tear for her, ye ladies lucky in your loves.

THE SERMON OF THE
MERRY VICAR OF MEUDON

WHEN, for the last time, came Master Francis Rabelais to the court of King Henry the Second of the name, it was in that winter when the will of nature compelled him to quit for ever his fleshly garb, and live for ever in his writings resplendent with that good philosophy to which we shall always be obliged to return. The good man had, at that time, counted as nearly as possible seventy flights of the swallow. His Homeric head was but scantily ornamented with hair, but his beard was still perfect in its flowing majesty; there was still an air of spring-time in his quiet smile, and wisdom on his ample brow. He was a fine old man according to the statement of those who had the happiness to gaze upon his face, to which Socrates and Aristophanes, formerly enemies, but there become friends, contributed their features. Hearing his last hour tinkling in his ears, he determined to go and pay his respects to the King of France, because he having just at that time arrived in his castle of Tournelles, the good man's house being situated in the gardens of St. Paul, was not a stone's throw distant from the court. He soon found himself in the presence of Queen Catherine, Madame Diana, whom she received from motives of policy, the king, the constable, the cardinals of Lorraine and Bellay, Messieurs de Guise, the Sieur de Birague, and other Italians, who at that time stood well at court in consequence of the king's protection; the admiral, Montgomery, the officers of the household, and certain poets, such as Melin de St. Gelays, Philibert de l'Orme, and the Sieur Brantôme.

Perceiving the good man, the king, who knew his wit, said to him, with a smile, after a short conversation—

"Hast thou ever delivered a sermon to thy parishioners of Meudon?"

Master Rabelais, thinking that the king was joking, since he had never troubled himself further about his post than to collect the revenues accruing from it, replied—

"Sire, my listeners are in every place, and my sermons heard throughout Christendom."

Then glancing at all the courtiers, who, with the exception of Messieurs du Bellay and Chatillon, considered him to be nothing but a learned merry-andrew, while he was really the king of all wits, and a far better king than he whose crown only the courtiers venerate, there came into the good man's the malicious idea to philosophically pump over their heads, just as it pleased Gargantua to give the Parisians a bath from the turrets of Notre Dame, so he added—

"If you are in a good humour, sire, I can regale you with a capital little sermon, always appropriate, and which I have kept under the tympanum of my left ear in order to deliver it in a fit place, by way of an aulic parable."

"Gentlemen," said the king, "Master Francis Rabelais has the ear of the court, and our salvation is concerned in his speech. Be silent, I pray you, and give heed; he is fruitful in evangelical drolleries."

"Sire," said the good vicar, "I commence."

All the courtiers became silent, and arranged themselves into a circle, pliant as osiers before the father of Pantagruel, who unfolded to them the following tale, in words the illustrious eloquence of which it is impossible to equal. But since this tale has only been verbally handed down to us, the author will be pardoned if he write it after his own fashion.

"In his old age Gargantua took to strange habits, which greatly astonish his household, but the which he was forgiven since he was seven hundred and four years old, in spite of the statement of St. Clement of Alexandria in his *Stromates,* which makes out that at this time he was a quarter of a day less, which matters little to us. Now this paternal master, seeing that everything was going wrong in his house, and that every one was fleecing him, conceived a great fear that he would in his last moments be stripped of everything, and resolved to invent a more perfect system of management in his domains, and he did well. In a cellar of Gargantuan abode he hid away a fine heap of red wheat, besides twenty jars of mustard and several delicacies, such as plums and Tourainian rolls, articles of dessert, Olivet cheese, goat cheese, and others, well known between Langeais and Loches, pots of butter, hare pasties, preserved ducks, pigs' trotters in bran, boatloads and pots full of crushed peas, pretty little pots of Orleans quince preserve, hogsheads of lampreys, measures of green sauce, river game, such as francolins, teal, sheldrake, heron, and flamingo, all preserved in sea-salt, dried raisins, tongues smoked in the manner invented by Happe-Mousche, his celebrated ancestor, and sweet-stuff for Gargamelle on feast days; and a thousand other things which are detailed in the records of the Ripuary laws and in certain folios of the Capitularies, Pragmatics, royal establishments, ordinances and institutions of the period. To be brief, the good man, putting his spectacles on his nose or his nose in his spectacles, looked about for a fine flying dragon or unicorn to whom the guard of this precious treasure could be committed. With this thought in his head he strolled about the gardens. He did not desire a Coquecigrue, because the

Egyptians were afraid of them, as it appeared in the Hieroglyphics. He dismissed the idea of engaging the legions of Caucquemarres, because emperors disliked them and also the Romans according to that sulky fellow Tacitus. He rejected the Pechrocholiers in council assembled, the Magi, the Druids, the legion of Papimania, and the Massorets, who grew like quelch-grass and overran all the land, as he had been told by his son, Pantagruel, on his return from his journey. The good man calling to mind old stories, had no confidence in any race, and if it had been permissible would have implored the Creator for a new one, but not daring to trouble Him about such trifles, did not know whom to choose, and was thinking that his wealth would be a great trouble to him, when he met in his path a pretty little shrew-mouse of the noble race of shrew-mice, who bear all gules on an azure ground. By the gods! be sure that it was a splendid animal, with the finest tail of the whole family, and was strutting about in the sun like a brave shrew-mouse. It was proud of having been in this world since the Deluge, according to letters-patent of indisputable nobility, registered by the parliament of the universe, since it appears from the Ecumenical Inquiry a shrew-mouse was in Noah's ark." Here Master Alcofribas raised his cap slightly, and said, reverently, "It was Noah, my lords, who planted the vine, and first had the honour of getting drunk upon the juice of its fruit."

"For it is certain," he continued, "that a shrew-mouse was in the vessel from which we all came; but the men have made bad marriages; not so the mice, because they are more jealous of their coat of arms than any other animals, and would not receive a field-mouse among them, even though he had the especial gift of being able to convert grains of sand to fine fresh hazel nuts. This fine gentlemanly character so pleased the good Gargantua, that he decided to give the post of watching his granaries to the shrewmouse, with the most ample powers—of justice, *comittimus, missi Dominici,* clergy, men-at-arms, and all. The shrewmouse promised faithfully to accomplish his task, and to do his duty as a loyal beast, on condition that he lived on a heap of grain, which Gargantua thought perfectly fair. The shrew-mouse began to caper about in his domain as happy as a prince who is happy, reconnoitering his immense empire of mustard, countries of sugar, provinces of ham, duchies of raisins, countries of chitterlings, and baronies of all sorts, scrambling on to the heap of grain, and frisking his tail against everything. To be brief, everywhere was the shrew-mouse received with honour by the pots, which kept a respectful silence, except two golden tankards, which knocked against each other like the bells of a church ringing a tocsin, at which he was much pleased, and thanked them, right and left, by a nod of the head, while promenading in the rays of the sun, which were illuminating his domain. Therein so splendidly did the brown colour of his hair shine forth, that one would have thought him a northern king in his sable furs. After his twists, turns, jumps, and capers, he munched two grains of corn, sat upon the heap like a king in full court, and fancied himself the most illustrious of shrew-mice. At this moment there came from their accustomed holes the gentlemen of the night-prowling court, who scamper with their little feet across the floors; these gentlemen being the rats, mice, and other gnawing, thieving, and crafty animals, of whom the citizens and housewives complain. When they saw the shrew-mouse they took fright, and all remained shyly at the threshold of their dens. Among these common people, in spite of the danger, one old infidel of the trotting, nibbling race of mice, advanced a little,

and putting his nose in the air, had the courage to stare my
lord shrew-mouse full in the face, although the latter was
proudly squatted upon his rump, with his tail in the air;
and he came to the conclusion that he was a devil, from
whom nothing but scratches were to be gained. And from
these facts, Gargantua, in order that the high authority of
his lieutenant might be universally known by all the
shrew-mice, cats, weasels, martins, field-mice, mice, rats,
and other bad characters of the same kidney, had lightly
dipped his muzzle, pointed as a larding pin, in oil of musk,
which all shrew-mice have since inherited, because this one,
in spite of the sage advice of Gargantua, rubbed himself
against others of his breed. From this sprung the troubles
in Muzaraignia, of which I will give you a good account in
an historical book when I get an opportunity.

"Then an old mouse, or rat—the rabbis of the Talmud
have not yet agreed concerning the species—perceiving by
this perfume that this shrew-mouse was appointed to guard
the grain of Gargantua, and had been sprinkled with virtues, invested with full powers, and armed at all points,
was alarmed lest he should no longer be able to live, according to the custom of mice, upon the meats, morsels, crusts,
crumbs, leavings, bits, atoms, and fragments of this Canaan
of rats. In this dilemma the good mouse, artful as an old
courtier who had lived under two regencies and three kings,
resolved to try the mettle of the shrew-mouse, and devote
himself to the salvation of the jaws of his race. This would
have been a laudable thing in a man, but it was far more
so in a mouse, belonging to a tribe who live for themselves
alone, barefacedly and shamelessly, and in order to gratify
themselves would defile a consecrated wafer, gnaw a priest's
stole without shame, and would drink out of a Communion
cup, caring nothing for God. The mouse advanced with

many a bow and scrape, and the shrew-mouse let him advance rather near—for, to tell the truth, these animals are naturally short-sighted. Then this Surtius of nibblers made his little speech, not in the jargon of common mice, but in the polite language of shrew-mice :—'My lord, I have heard with much concern of your glorious family, of which I am one of the most devoted slaves. I know the legend of your ancestors, who were thought much of by the ancient Egyptians, who held them in great veneration, and adored them like other sacred birds. Nevertheless, your fur robe is so royally perfumed, and its colour is so splendiferously tanned, that I am doubtful if I recognize you as belonging to this race, since I have never seen any of them so gorgeously attired. However, you have swallowed the grain after the antique fashion. Your proboscis is a proboscis of sapience; you have kicked like a learned shrew-mouse; but if you are a true shrew-mouse, you should have in I know not what part of your ear—I know not what special auditorial channel, which I know not what wonderful door, closes I know not how, and I know not with what movements, by your secret commands to give you, I know not why, license not to listen to I know not what things, which would be displeasing to you, on account of the special and peculiar perfection of your faculty of hearing everything, which would often pain you.'"

" 'True,' said the shrew-mouse, 'the door has just fallen. I hear nothing!'

" 'Ah, I see,' said the old rogue.

"And he made for the pile of corn, from which he commenced to take his store for the winter.

" 'Do you hear anything?' asked he.

" 'I hear the pit-a-pat of my heart.'

" 'Kouick!' cried all the mice; 'we shall be able to hood-wink him.'

"The shrew-mouse, fancying that he had met with a faith-ful vassal, opened the trap of his musical orifice, and heard the noise of the grain going towards the hole. Then, with-out having recourse to forfeiture, the justice of commis-saries, he sprang upon the old mouse and squeezed him to death. Glorious death! for this hero died in the thick of the grain, and was canonized as a martyr. The shrew-mouse took him by the ears and placed him on the door of the gran-ary, after the fashion of the Ottoman Porte, where my good Panurge was within an ace of being spitted. At the cries of the dying wretch the rats, mice, and others made for their holes in great haste. When the night had fallen they came to the cellar, convoked for the purpose of holding a council to consider public affairs; to which meeting, in virtue of the Papirian and other laws, their lawful wives were admitted. The rats wished to pass before the mice, and serious quarrels about precedence nearly spoilt everything; but a big rat gave his arm to a mouse, and the gaffer rats and gammer mice being paired off in the same way, all were soon seated on their rumps, tails in air, muzzles stretched, whiskers stiff, and their eyes brilliant as those of a falcon. Then commenced a deliberation, which finished up with insults and a confusion worthy of an ecumenical council of holy fathers. One said this, and another said that, and a cat passing by took fright and ran away, hearing those strange noises: 'Bou, bou, frou, ou, ou, houic, houic, briff, briffnac, nac, nac, fouix, fouix, trr, trr, trr, trr, za, za, zaaa, brr, brrr, raaa, ra, ra, ra, ra, fouix!' so well blended together in a Babel of sound that a council ot the Hôtel de Ville could not have made a greater hubbub. During this tempest a little mouse, who was not old enough to enter parliament, thrust through a chink her inquiring snout, the hair on which was as downy as that of all mice, too downy to be caught. As the tumult increased, by degrees her body followed her nose, until she came to the hoop of a cask, against which she so dexterously squatted that she might have been mistaken for a work of art carved in antique bas-relief. Lifting his eyes to heaven to implore a remedy for the misfortunes of the State, an old rat perceived this pretty mouse, gentle and shapely, and declared that the State might be saved by her. All the muzzles turned to this Lady of Good Help, became silent, and agreed to let her loose upon the shrew-mouse, and in spite of the anger of certain envious mice, she was triumphantly marched round the cellar, where, seeing her walk mincingly, mechanically move her tail, shake her cunning little head, twitch her diaphanous ears, and lick with her little red tongue the hairs just sprouting on her cheeks, the old rats fell in love with her and wagged their wrinkled, white-whiskered jaws with delight at the sight of her, as did formerly the old men of Troy, admiring the lovely Helen returning from her bath. Then the maiden was conducted to the granary, with instructions to make a conquest of the shrew-mouse's heart, and save the fine red grain, as did formerly the fair Hebrew, Esther, for the chosen people, with the Emperor Ahasuerus, as it is written in the master-book, for *Bible* comes from the Greek word *Biblos,* as if to say the only book. The mouse promised to deliver the granaries, for by a lucky chance she was the queen of mice, a fair, plump, pretty little mouse, the most delicate little lady that ever scampered merrily across the floors, scratched between the walls, and gave utterance to little cries of joy at finding nuts, meal, and crumbs of bread in her path; a true fay, pretty and playful, with an eye clear as crystal, a little head, sleek skin, amorous body, rosy feet, and velvet tail—

a high-born mouse and polished speaker, with a natural love of bed and idleness—a merry mouse, more cunning than an old doctor of Sorbonne fed on parchment, lively, white bellied, streaked on the back, with sweetly moulded breasts, pearl-white teeth, and of a frank, open nature—in fact, a true king's morsel."

This portraiture was so bold—the mouse appearing to have been the living image of Madame Diana, then present —that the courtiers stood aghast. Queen Catherine smiled, but the king was in no laughing humor. But Rabelais went on without paying any attention to the winks of the Cardinal Bellay and de Chatillon, who were terrified for the good man.

"The pretty mouse," said he, continuing, "did not beat long about the bush, and from the first moment that she trotted before the shrew-mouse, she had enslaved him for ever by her coquetries, affectations, friskings, provocations, little refusals, piercing glances, and wiles of a maiden who desires yet dares not, amorous oglings, little caresses, preparatory tricks, pride of a mouse who knows her value, laughings and squeakings, triflings and other endearments, feminine, treacherous, and captivating ways, all traps which are abundantly used by the females of all nations. When, after many wrigglings, smacks in the face, nose lickings, gallantries of amorous shrew-mice, frowns, sighs, serenades, titbits, suppers and dinners on the pile of corn, and other attentions, the superintendent overcame the scruples of his beautiful mistress, he became the slave of this incestuous and illicit love, and the mouse, leading her lord by the snout, became queen of everything, nibbled his cheese, ate the sweets, and foraged everywhere. This the shrew-mouse permitted to the empress of his heart, although he was ill at ease, having broken his oath made to Gargantua, and betrayed the confidence placed in him. Pursuing her advantage with the pertinacity of a woman, one night that they were joking together, the mouse remembered the dear old fellow her father, and desiring that he should make his meals off the grain, she threatened to leave her lover cold and lonely in his domain if he did not allow her to indulge her filial piety. In the twinkling of a mouse's eye he had granted letters patent, sealed with a green seal, with tags of crimson silk, to his wench's father, so that the Gargantuan palace was open to him at all hours, and he was at liberty to see his good virtuous daughter, kiss her on the forehead, and eat his fill, but always in a corner. Then there arrived a venerable old rat, weighing about twenty-five ounces, with a white tail, marching like the president of a court of justice, wagging his head, and followed by fifteen or twenty nephews, all with teeth sharp as saws, who demonstrated to the shrew-mouse by little speeches and questions of all kinds that they, his relations, would soon be loyally attached to him, and would help him to count the things committed to his charge, arrange and ticket them, in order that when Gargantua came to visit them he would find everything in perfect order. There was an air of truth about these promises. The poor shrew-mouse was, however, in spite of this speech, troubled by ideas from on high, and serious pricking of his shrew-mousian conscience. Seeing that he turned up his nose at everything, went about slowly and with a careworn face, one morning the mouse, who was pregnant by him, conceived the idea of calming his doubts and easing his mind by a Sorbonnical consultation, and sent for the doctors of the tribe. During the day she introduced to him one, the Sieur Evegault, who had just stepped out of a cheese where he lived in perfect abstinence, an old confessor of high degree, a merry fellow of good appearance,

with a fine black skin, firm as a rock, and slightly tonsured
on the head by the pat of a cat's claw. He was a grave rat,
with a monastical paunch, having much studied scientific
authorities by nibbling at their works in parchments,
papers, books, and volumes of which certain fragments
had remained upon his grey beard. In honour of and great
reverence for his great virtue and wisdom, and his modest
life, he was accompanied by a black troop of black rats, all
bringing with them pretty little mice, their sweethearts, for
not having adopted the canons of the council of Chesil, it
was lawful for them to have respectable women for concu-
bines. These beneficial rats being arranged in two lines,
you might have fancied them a procession of the university
authorities going to Lendit. And they all began to sniff the
victuals.

"When the ceremony of placing them all was complete,
the old cardinal of the rats lifted up his voice, and in a good
rat-latin oration pointed out to the guardian of the grain
that no one but God was superior to him; and that to God
alone he owed obedience, and he entertained him with many
fine phrases, stuffed with evangelical quotations, to disturb
the principal and fog his flock; in fact, fine arguments interlarded with much sound sense. The discourse finished with
a peroration full of high-sounding words in honour of
shrew-mice, among whom his hearer was the most illustrious and best beneath the sun; and this oration considerably bewildered the keeper of the granaries.

"This good gentleman's head was thoroughly turned, and
he installed this fine-speaking rat and his tribe in his manor,
where night and day his praises and little songs in his honour
were sung, not forgetting his lady, whose little paw was
kissed and little tail was sniffed at by them all. Finally the
mistress, knowing that certain young rats were still fasting,

determined to finish her work. Then she kissed her lord
tenderly, loading him with love, and performing those little
endearing antics of which one alone was sufficient to send
a beast to perdition; and said to the shrew-mouse that he
wasted the precious time due to their love by travelling
about, that he was always going here or there, and that she
never had her proper share of him; that when she wanted
his society he was on the leads chasing the cats, and that she
wished him always to be ready to her hand like a lance, and
kind as a bird. Then in her great grief she tore out a grey
hair, declaring herself, weepingly, to be the most wretched
little mouse in the world. The shrew-mouse pointed out to
her that she was mistress of everything, and wished to resist,
but after the lady had shed a torrent of tears he implored
a truce and considered her request. Then instantly drying
her tears, and giving him her paw to kiss, she advised him
to arm some soldiers, trusty and tried rats, old warriors,
who would go the rounds and keep watch. Everything was
thus wisely arranged. The shrew-mouse had the rest of the
day to dance, play, and amuse himself, listen to the rounde-
lays and ballads which the poets composed in his honour,
play the lute and mandore, make acrostics, eat, drink, and be
merry. One day his mistress having just risen from her confinement, after having given birth to the sweetest little
mouse-sorex or sorex-mouse, I know not what name was
given to this mongrel fruit of love, whom you may be sure
the gentlemen of the long robe would manage to legitima-
tize" (the constable of Montmorency, who had married his
son to a legitimatized bastard of the king's, here put his hand
to his sword and clutched the handle fiercely), "a grand
feast was given in the granaries, to which no court festival
or gala can be compared, not even that of the Field of the
Cloth of Gold. In every corner mice were making merry.

Everywhere there were dances, concerts, banquets, sarabands, music, joyous songs, and epithalamia. The rats had
broken open the pots, uncovered the jars, lapped the galli-
pots, and unpacked the stores. The mustard was strewn
over the place, the hams were mangled and the corn scattered. Everything was rolling, tumbling, and falling about
the floor, and the little rats dabbled in puddles of green
sauce, the mice navigated oceans of sweetmeats, and the old
folks carried off the pasties. There were mice astride on salt
tongues. Field-mice were swimming in the pots, and the
most cunning of them were carrying the corn into their
private holes, profiting by the confusion to make ample provision for themselves. No one passed the quince confection
of Orleans without saluting it with one nibble, and oftener
with two. It was like a Roman carnival. In short, any one
with a sharp ear might have heard the frizzling frying-pans,
the cries and clamours of the kitchens, the crackling of the
furnaces, the noise of turnspits, the creaking of baskets, the
haste of the confectioners, the click of the meat-jacks, and
the noise of the little feet scampering thick as hail over the
floor. It was a bustling wedding-feast, where people come
and go, footmen, stablemen, cooks, musicians, buffoons,
where everyone pays compliments and makes a noise. In
short, so great was the delight that they all kept up a general
wagging of the head to celebrate this eventful night. But
suddenly there was heard the horrible foot-fall of Gargantua, who was ascending the stairs of his house to visit the
granaries, and made the planks, the beams, and everything
else tremble. Certain old rats asked each other what might
mean this seignorial footstep, with which they were unacquainted, and some of them decamped, and they did well,
for the lord and master entered suddenly. Perceiving the
confusion these gentlemen had made, seeing his preserves

eaten, his mustard unpacked, and everything dirtied and scratched about, he put his feet upon these lively vermin without giving them time to squeak, and thus spoiled their best clothes, satins, pearls, velvets, and rubbish, and upset the feast."

"And what became of the shrew-mouse?" said the king, waking from his reverie.

"Ah, sire!" replied Rabelais, "herein we see the injustice of the Gargantuan tribe. He was put to death, but being a gentleman he was beheaded. That was ill done, for he had been betrayed."

"You go rather far, my good man," said the king.

"No, sire," replied Rabelais, "but rather high. Have you not sunk the crown beneath the pulpit? You asked me for a sermon; I have given you one which is gospel."

"My fine vicar," said Madame Diana, in his ear, "suppose I were spiteful?"

"Madame," said Rabelais, "was it not well then of me to warn the king, your master, against the queen's Italians, who are as plentiful here as cockchafers?"

"Poor preacher," said Cardinal Odet, in his ear, "go to another country."

"Ah, monsieur," replied the old fellow, "ere long I shall be in another land."

"God's truth! Mr. Scribbler," said the constable (whose son, as every one knows, had treacherously deserted Mademoiselle de Piennes, to whom he was betrothed, to espouse Diana of France, daughter of the mistress of certain high personages and of the king), "who made thee so bold as to slander persons of quality? Ah, wretched poet, you like to raise yourself high; well, then I promise to put you in a good high place."

"We shall all go there, my lord constable," replied the old

man; "but if you are friendly to the State and to the king you will thank me for having warned him against the hordes of Lorraine, who are evils that will devour everything."

"My god man," whispered Cardinal Charles of Lorraine, "if you need a few gold crowns to publish your fifth book of Pantagruel you can come to me for them, because you have put the case clearly to this enemy, who has bewitched the king, and also to her pack."

"Well, gentlemen," said the king, "what do you think of the sermon?"

"Sire," said Mellin de Saint-Gelais, seeing that all were well pleased, "I have never heard a better pantagruelian prognostication. Much do we owe to him who made these leonine verses in the abbey of Theleme:—

> " 'Cy vous *entrez,* qui le saint Evangile
> En sens *agile* annoncez, quoy qu'on gronde,
> Céans *aurez* une refuge et bastile
> Contre *l'hostil*e erreur qui tant postille
> Par son faux *style* empoisonner le monde.' "

All the courtiers having applauded their companion, each one complimented Rabelais, who took his departure accompanied with great honour by the king's pages, who, by express command, held torches before him.

Some persons have charged Francis Rabelais, the imperial honour of our land, with spiteful tricks and apish pranks, unworthy of his Homeric philosophy, of this prince of wisdom, of this fatherly centre, from which have issued since the rising of his subterranean light a good number of marvellous works. Out upon those who would defile this divine head! All their life long may they find grit between their teeth, those who have ignored his good and moderate nourishment.

Dear drinker of pure water, faithful servant of monachal abstinence, wisest of wise men, how would thy sides ache with laughter, how wouldst thou chuckle, if thou couldst come again for a little while to Chinon, and read the idiotic mouthings, and the maniacal babble of the fools who have interpreted, commentated, torn, disgraced, misunderstood, betrayed, defiled, adulterated, and meddled with thy peerless book. As many dogs as Panurge found busy with his lady's robe at church, so many two-legged academic puppies have busied themselves with befouling the high marble pyramid in which is cemented for ever the seed of all fantastic and comic inventions, besides magnificent instruction in all things. Although rare are the pilgrims who have the breath to follow thy bark in its sublime peregrinations through the ocean of ideas, methods, varieties, religions, wisdoms, and human trickeries, at least their worship is unalloyed, pure, and unadulterated, and thine omnipotence, omniscience, and omni-language are by them bravely recognised. Therefore has a poor son of our merry Touraine here been anxious, however unworthily, to do thee homage by magnifying thine image, and glorifying thy works of eternal memory, so cherished by those who love the concentrative works wherein the universal moral is contained, wherein are found, pressed like fresh sardines in their boxes, philosophical ideas on every subject, science, art, and eloquence, as well as theatrical mummeries.

THE SUCCUBUS

A NUMBER of persons of the noble country of Touraine, considerably edified by the warm search which the author is making into the antiquities, adventures, good jokes, and pretty tales of that blessed land, and believing for certain that he should know everything, have asked him (after drinking with him of course understood), if he had discovered the etymological reason, concerning which all the ladies of the town are so curious, and from which a certain street in Tours is called the Rue Chaude. By him was it replied, that he was much astonished to see that the ancient inhabitants had forgotten the great number of convents situated in this street, where the severe continence of the monks and the nuns might have caused the walls to be made so hot that no woman of position should increase in size from walking too slowly along them to vespers. A troublesome fellow, wishing to appear learned, declared that formerly all the scandalmongers of the neighbourhood were wont to meet in this place. Another entangled himself in the minute suffrages of science, and poured forth golden words without being understood, qualifying words, harmonizing the melodies of the ancient and the modern, congregating customs, distilling verbs, alchemizing all languages since the Deluge, of the Hebrews, Chaldeans, Egyptians, Greeks, Latins, and of Turnus, the ancient founder of Tours; and the good man finished by declaring that Chaude or Chaulde, with the ex-

ception of the H and the L, came from *Cauda,* and that there
was a tail in the affair, but the ladies only understood the
end of it. An old man observed that in this same place was
formerly a source of thermal water, of which his great-
great-grandfather had drunk. In short, in less time than it
takes a fly to embrace its sweetheart, there had been a pock-
etful of etymologies, in which the truth of the matter had
been less easily found than a louse in the filthy beard of a
Capuchin friar. But a man learned and well informed,
through having left his footprint in many monasteries, consumed much midnight oil, and manured his brain with many
a volume—himself more cumbered with pieces, dyptic fragments, boxes, charters, and registers concerning the history
of Touraine than is a gleaner with stalks of straw in the
month of August—this man, old, infirm, and gouty, who had
been drinking in his corner without saying a word, smiled
the smile of a wise man and knitted his brows, the said
smile finally resolving itself in a *pish!* well articulated,
which the Author heard and understood it to be big with an
adventure historically good, the delights of which he would
be able to unfold in this sweet collection.

To be brief, on the morrow this gouty old fellow said to
him, "By your poem, which is called 'The Venial Sin,' you
have for ever gained my esteem, because everything therein
is true from head to foot,—which I believe to be a precious
superabundance in like matters. But doubtless you do not
know what became of the Moor placed in religion by the said
knight, Bruyn de la Roche-Corbon. I know very well. Now
if this etymology of the street harass you, and also the
Egyptian nun, I will lend you a curious and antique parchment, found by me in the *Olim* of the episcopal palace, of
which the libraries were a little knocked about at a period
when none of us knew if he would have the pleasure of his

head's society on the morrow. Now will not this yield you a perfect contentment?"

"Good!" said the author.

Then this worthy collector of truths gave certain rare and dusty parchments to the author, the which he has, not without great labour, translated into French, and which were fragments of a most ancient ecclesiastical process. He has believed that nothing would be more amusing than the actual resurrection of this antique affair, wherein shines forth the illiterate simplicity of the good old times. Now, then, give ear. This is the order in which were the manuscripts, of which the author has made use in his own fashion, because the language was devilishly difficult.

THE SUCCUBUS

I

WHAT THE SUCCUBUS WAS

†*In nomine Patris, et Filii, et Spiritus Sancti. Amen.*

IN the year of our Lord one thousand two hundred and seventy-one, before me, HIÉROME CORNILLE, grand inquisitor and ecclesiastical judge (thereto commissioned by the members of the chapter of Saint Maurice, the cathedral of Tours, having of this deliberated in the presence of old lord Jehan de Monsoreau, archbishop—namely, the grievances and complaints of the inhabitants of the said town, whose request is here subjoined), have appeared certain noblemen, citizens, and inhabitants of the diocese, who have stated the following facts concerning a demon suspected of having taken the features of a woman, who has much afflicted the minds of the diocese, and is at present a prisoner in the gaol of the chapter; and in order to arrive at the truth of the said charge we have opened the present court, this Monday, the eleventh day of December, after mass, to communicate the evidence of each witness to the said demon, to interrogate her upon the said crimes to her imputed, and to judge her according to the laws enforced *contra dœmonios.*

In this inquiry has assisted me to write the evidence therein given, Guillaume Tournabouche, rubrican of the chapter, a learned man.

Firstly has come before us one Jehan, surnamed Torte-

bras, a citizen of Tours, keeping by licence the hostelry of
La Cigoygne, situate on the Place du Pont, and who has
sworn by the salvation of his soul, his hand upon the holy
Evangelists, to state no other thing than that which by himself hath been seen and heard. He hath stated as here fol-
loweth :—

"I declare that about two years before the feast of St.
Jehan, upon which are the grand illuminations, a gentleman, at first unknown to me, but belonging without doubt
to our lord the King, and at that time returned into our
country from the Holy Land, came to me with the proposition that I should let to him at a rental a certain country-
house by me built, in the quit rent of the chapter over
against the place called of St. Etienne, and the which I let
to him for nine years, for the consideration of three besans
of fine gold. In the said house was placed by the said knight
a fair wench having the appearance of a woman, dressed in
the strange fashion of the Saracens and Mahommedans,
whom he would allow by none to be seen or to be approached
within a bowshot, but whom I have seen with mine own
eyes, weird feathers upon her head, and eyes so flaming
that I cannot adequately describe them, and from which
gleamed forth a fire of hell. The defunct knight having
threatened with death whoever should appear to spy about
the said house, I have by reason of great fear left the said
house, and I have until this day secretly kept in my mind
certain presumptions and doubts concerning the bad appearance of the said foreigner, who was more strange than
any woman, her equal not having as yet by me been seen.

"Many persons of all conditions having at the time believed the said knight to be dead, but kept upon his feet by
virtue of certain charms, philtres, spells, and diabolical
sorceries of this seeming woman, who wished to settle in

our country, I declare that I have always seen the said
knight so ghastly pale that I can only compare his face to the
wax of a Paschal candle, and to the knowledge of all the
people of the hostelry at La Cigoygne, this knight was interred nine days after his first coming. According to the
statement of his groom, the defunct had been chalorously
coupled with the said Moorish woman during seven whole
days shut up in my house, without coming out from her, the
which I heard him horribly avow upon his deathbed. Certain
persons at the present time have accused this she-devil of
holding the said gentleman in her clutches by her long hair,
the which was furnished with certain warm properties by
means of which are communicated to Christians the flames
of hell in the form of love, which work in them until their
souls are by this means drawn from their bodies and possessed by Satan. But I declare that I have seen nothing of
this excepting the said dead knight, bowelless, emaciated,
wishing, in spite of his confessor, still to go to this wench;
and then he has been recognised as the lord de Bueil, who
was a Crusader, and who was, according to certain persons
of the town, under the spell of a demon whom he had met
in the Asiatic country of Damascus or elsewhere.

"Afterward I have left my house to the said unknown
lady, according to the clauses of the deed of lease. The said
lord of Bueil, being defunct, I have nevertheless been into
my house in order to learn from the said foreign woman if
she wished to remain in my dwelling, and after great trouble
was led before her by a strange, half-naked black man,
whose eyes were white.

"Then I have seen the said Moorish woman in a little
room, shining with gold and jewels, lighted with strange
lights, upon an Asiatic carpet, where she was seated, lightly
attired, with another gentleman, who was there imperilling

his soul; and I had not the heart bold enough to look upon
her, seeing that her eyes would have incited me immediately
to yield myself up to her, for already her voice thrilled into
my very belly, filled my brain, and debauched my mind.
Finding this, from the fear of God, and also of hell, I have
departed with swift feet, leaving my house to her as long
as she liked to retain it, so dangerous was it to behold that
Moorish complexion from which radiated diabolical heats,
besides a foot smaller than it was lawful in a real woman to
possess; and to hear her voice, which pierced into one's
heart! And from that day I have lacked the courage to
enter my house from great fear of falling into hell. I have
said my say."

To the said Tortebras we have then shown an Abyssinian,
Nubian or Ethiopian, who, black from head to foot, had
been found wanting in certain virile properties with which
all good Christians are usually furnished, who, having persevered in his silence, after having been tormented and tortured many times, not without much moaning, has persisted
in being unable to speak the language of our country. And
the said Tortebras has recognized the said Abyssinian
heretic as having been in his house in company with the said
demoniacal spirit, and is suspected of having lent his aid to
her sorcery.

And the said Tortebras has confessed his great faith in
the Catholic religion, and declared no other things to be
within his knowledge save certain rumours which were
known to every one, of which he had been in no way a witness except in the hearing of them.

In obedience to the citation served upon him, has appeared, then, Matthew, surnamed Cognefestu, a day-
labourer of St. Etienne, who, after having sworn by the
holy Evangelists to speak the truth, has confessed to us

always to have seen a bright light in the dwelling of the said foreign woman, and heard much wild and diabolical laughter on the days and nights of feasts and fasts, notably during the days of the holy and Christmas weeks, as if a great number of people were in the house. And he has sworn to have seen by the windows of the said dwellings, green buds of all knids in the winter, growing as if by magic, especially roses in a time of frost, and other things for which there was need of great heat; but of this he was in no way astonished, seeing that the said foreigner threw out so much heat that when she walked in the evening by the side of his wall he found on the morrow his salad grown; and on certain occasions she had, by the touching of her petticoats, caused the trees to put forth leaves and hastened the buds. Finally, the said Cognefestu has declared to us to know no more, because he worked from early morning, and went to bed at the same hour as the fowls.

Afterwards the wife of the aforesaid Cognefestu has by us been required to state also upon oath the things come to her cognizance in this process, and has avowed naught save praises of the said foreigner, because since her coming her man had treated her better in consequence of the neighbourhood of this good lady, who filled the air with love as the sun did light, and other incongruous nonsense, which we have not committed to writing.

To the said Cognefestu and to his wife we have shown the said unknown African, who has been seen by them in the gardens of the house, and is stated by them for certain to belong to the said demon. In the third place, has advanced Harduin V., lord of Maillé, who being by us reverentially begged to enlighten the religion of the church, has expressed his willingness so to do, and has, moreover, engaged his word, as a gallant knight, to say no other thing

than that which he has seen. Then he has testified to have
known in the army of the Crusades the demon in question,
and in the town of Damascus to have seen the knight of
Bueil, since defunct, fight at close quarters to be her sole
possessor. The above-mentioned wench, or demon, belonged
at that time to the knight Geoffroy IV., lord of Roche-
Pozay, by whom she was said to have been brought from
Touraine, although she was a Saracen; concerning which
the knights of France marvelled much, as well as at her
beauty, which made a great noise and a thousand scandalous ravages in the camp. During the voyage this wench was
the cause of many deaths, seeing that Roche-Pozay had
already discomfited certain Crusaders, who wished to keep
her to themselves, because she shed, according to certain
knights petted by her in secret, joys around her comparable
to none others. But in the end the knight of Bueil, having
killed Geoffroy de la Roche-Pozay, became lord and master
of this young murderess, and placed her in a convent, or
harem, according to the Saracen custom. About this time
one used to see her and hear her chattering at her entertain-
ments many foreign dialects, such as the Greek of the Latin
empire, Moorish, and, above all, French better than any of
those who knew the languages of France best in the Christian host, from which sprang the belief that she was
demoniacal.

The said knight Harduin has confessed to us not to
have tilted for her in the Holy Land, not from fear, cold-
ness, or other cause, so much as that he believed the time
had arrived for him to bear away a portion of the true
cross, and also he had belonging to him a noble lady of the
Greek country, who saved him from this danger in denuding
him of love, morning and night, seeing that she took all of

it substantially from him, leaving him none in his heart or elsewhere for others.

And the said knight has assured us that the woman living in the country house of Tortebras, was really the said Saracen woman, come into the country from Syria, because he had been invited to a midnight feast at her house by the young lord of Croixmare, who expired the seventh day afterwards, according to the statement of the Dame de Croixmare, his mother, ruined at all points by the said wench, whose commerce with him had consumed his vital spirit, and whose strange phantasies had squandered his fortune.

Afterwards questioned in his quality of a man full of prudence, wisdom, and authority in this country, upon the ideas as entertained concerning the said woman, and summoned by us to open his conscience, seeing that it was a question of a most abominable case of Christian faith and divine justice, answer has been made by the said knight:—

That by certain of the host of Crusaders it has been stated to him that always this she-devil was a maid to him who embraced her, and that Mammon was for certain occupied in her, making for her a new virtue for each of her lovers, and a thousand other foolish sayings of drunken men, which were not of a nature to form a fifth Gospel. But for a fact, he, an old knight on that turn of life, and knowing nothing more of the aforesaid, felt himself again a young man in that last supper with which he had been regaled by the lord of Croixmare; then the voice of this demon went straight to his heart before flowing into his ears, and had awakened so great a love in his body that his life was ebbing from the place whence it should flow, and that eventually, but for the assistance of Cyprus wine, which he had drunk to blind his sight, and his getting under the table

in order no longer to gaze upon the fiery eyes of his diabolical hostess, and not to rend his heart for her, without
doubt he would have fought the young Croixmare, in order
to enjoy for a single moment this supernatural woman. Since
that he had had absolution from his confessor for the wicked
thought. Then, by advice from on high, he had carried back
to his spouse his portion of the true cross, and had remained
in his own manor, where, in spite of his Christian precautions, the said voice still at certain times tickled his brain, and
in the morning often had he in remembrance this demon,
warm as brimstone; and because the look of this wench was
so warm that it made him burn like a young man, he half
dead, and because it cost him then many trans-shipments of
the vital spirit, the said knight has requested us not to con-
front him with this empress of love to whom, if it were not
the devil, God the Father had granted strange liberties with
the minds of men. Afterwards, he retired, after reading
over his statement, not without having first recognised the
above-mentioned African to be the servant and page of the
lady.

In the fourth place, upon the faith pledged by us in the
name of the Chapter and of our Lord Archbishop, that he
should not be tormented, tortured, nor harassed in any manner, nor further cited after his statement, in consequence
of his commercial journeys, and upon the assurance that he
should retire in perfect freedom, has come before us a Jew,
named Salomon al Rastchild, who, in spite of the infamy
of his person and his Judaism, has been heard by us to this
one end, to know everything concerning the conduct of the
aforesaid demon. Thus he has not been required to take any
oath this Salomon, seeing that he is beyond the pale of the
Church, separated from us by the blood of our Saviour
(*trucidatus Salvator inter nos*). Interrogated by us as to

why he appeared without the green cap upon his head, and
the yellow wheel in the apparent locality of the heart in his
garment, according to the ecclesiastical and royal ordinances, the said Al Rastchild has exhibited to us letters
patent of dispensation granted by our lord the king, and
recognized by the seneschal of Touraine and Poitou. Then
the said Jew has declared to us to have done a large business for the lady dwelling in the house of the innkeeper
Tortebras, to have sold to her golden chandeliers with many
branches, minutely engraved, plates of red silver, cups en-
riched with stones, emeralds and rubies; to have brought
for her from the Levant a number of rare stuffs, Persian
carpets, silks, and fine linen; in fact, things so magnificent
that no queen in Christendom could say she was so well furnished with jewels and household goods; and that he had
for his part received from her three hundred thousand
pounds for the rarity of the purchases in which he had been
employed, such as Indian flowers, popinjays, birds' feathers,
spices, Greek wines, and diamonds. Requested by us the
judge to say if he had furnished certain ingredients of
magical conjuration, the blood of new-born children, con-
juring books, and things generally and whatsoever made use
of by sorcerers, giving him licence to state his case without
that thereupon he should be subject to any further inquest
or inquiry, the said Al Rastchild has sworn by his Hebrew
faith never to have had any such commerce; and has stated
that he was involved in too high interests to give himself
to such miseries, seeing that he was the agent of certain most
powerful lords, such as the Marquis de Montferrat, the
King of England, the King of Cyprus and Jerusalem, the
Count of Provence, the lords of Venice, and many German
gentlemen; to have belonging to him merchant galleys of all
kinds, going into Egypt with the permission of the Sultan,

and he trafficking in precious articles of silver and of gold, which took him often into the exchange of Tours. Moreover, he has declared that he considered the said lady, the subject of inquiry, to be a right loyal and natural woman, with the sweetest limbs, and the smallest he has ever seen. That in consequence of her renown for a diabolical spirit, pushed by a wild imagination, and also because that he was smitten with her, he had once that she was husbandless, proposed to her to be her gallant, to which proposition she willingly acceded. Now although from that night, he long felt his bones disjointed and his bowels crushed, he had not experienced, as certain persons say, that who once yielded was free no more; he went to his fate as lead into the crucible of the alchemist. Then the said Salomon, to whom we have granted his liberty according to the safe conduct, in spite of this statement, which proves abundantly his commerce with the devil, because he has been safely there where all Christians have succumbed, has submitted to us an agreement concerning the said demon. To make known that he made an offer to the chapter of the cathedral to give for the said semblance of a woman such a ransom, if she were condemned to be burned alive, that the highest of the towers of the church of Saint Maurice, at present in course of construction, could therewith be finished.

The which we have noted to be deliberated upon at an opportune time by the assembled chapter. And the said Salomon has taken his departure without being willing to indicate his residence, and has told us that he can be informed of the deliberation of the chapter by a Jew of the synagogue of Tours, named Tobias Nathaneus. The said Jew has before his departure been shown the African, and has recognised him as the page of the demon, and has stated the Saracens to have the custom of mutilating their slaves thus, to commit to them the task of guarding their women by an ancient usage, as it appears in the profane histories of Narsez, general of Constantinople, and others.

On the morrow after mass has appeared before us the most noble and illustrious lady of Croixmare. The same has sworn her faith in the holy Evangelists, and has related to us with tears how she had placed her eldest son beneath the earth, dead by reason of his extravagant amours with this female demon. The which noble gentleman was three-and-twenty years of age; of good complexion, very manly and well bearded, like his defunct sire. Notwithstanding his great vigour, in ninety days he had little by little withered, ruined by his commerce with the Succubus of the Rue Chaude, according to the statement of the common people; and her maternal authority over this son had been powerless. Finally, in his latter days he appeared like a poor dried up worm, such as housekeepers meet with in a corner when they clean out the dwelling-rooms. And always, so long as he had the strength to go, he went to shorten his life with this accursed woman; where, also, he emptied his cash-box. When he was in his bed, and knew his last hour to be come, he swore at, cursed, and threatened and heaped upon all—his sister, his brother, and upon her his mother—a thousand insults, rebelled in the face of his chaplain; denied God, and wished to die in damnation; at which were much afflicted the retainers of the family, who, to save his soul and pluck it from hell, have founded two annual masses in the cathedral. And, in order to have him buried in consecrated ground, the house of Croixmare has undertaken to give to the chapter, during one hundred years, the wax candles for the chapels and the church, upon the day of the Paschal feast. And, in conclusion, saying the wicked words heard by that reverend person, Dom Loys Pot, a nun of

Marmoustiers, who came to assist in his last hours the said
Baron de Croixmare, affirms never to have heard any words
offered by the defunct touching the demon who had undone
him.

And therewith has retired the noble and illustrious lady
in deep mourning.

In the sixth place has appeared before us, after adjourn-
ment, Jacquette, called Vieux-Oing, a kitchen scullion,
going to houses to wash dishes, residing at present in the
Fishmarket, who, after having pledged her word to say
nothing she did not hold to be true, has declared as here
follows:—Namely, that one day she, being come into the
kitchen of the said demon, of whom she had no fear, because
she was wont to regale herself only upon males, she had the
opportunity of seeing in the garden this female demon,
superbly attired, walking in company with a knight, with
whom she was laughing, like a natural woman. Then she had
recognised in this demon the true likeness of the Moorish
woman placed as a nun in the convent of Notre-Dame de
l'Egrignolles by the defunct senschal of Touraine and Poi-
ton, Messire Bruyn, Count of Roche-Corbon, the which
Moorish woman had been left in the situaion and place of the
image of our Lady the Virgin, the mother of our blessed
Saviour, stolen by the Egyptians about eighteen years since.
Of this time, in consequence of the troubles come about in
Touraine, no record has been kept. This girl, aged about
twelve years, was saved from the stake at which she should
have been burned by being baptized; and the said defunct
and his wife had then been godfather and godmother to this
child of hell. Being at that time laundress at the convent, she
who bears witness has remembrance of the flight which the
said Egyptian took twenty months after her entry into the
convent, so subtilely that it has never been known how or by

what means she escaped. At that time, it was thought by all, that with the devil's aid she had flown away in the air, seeing that notwithstanding much search, no trace of her flight was found in the convent, where everything remained in its accustomed order.

The African having been shown to the said scullion, she has declared not to have seen him before, although she was curious so to do, as he was commissioned to guard the place in which the Moorish woman combated with those whom she drained through the spigot.

In the seventh place has been brought before us Hugues du Fou, son of the Sieur de Bridoré, who, aged twenty years, has been placed in the hands of his father, under caution of his estates, and by him is represented in this process, whom it concerns if he should be duly attainted and convicted of having, assisted by several unknown and bad young men, laid siege to the gaol of the archbishop and of the chapter, and of having lent himself to disturb the force of ecclesiastical justice, by causing the escape of the demon now under consideration. In spite of his evil disposition we have commanded the said Hugues du Fou to testify truly, touching the things he should know concerning the said demon, with whom he is vehemently reputed to have had commerce, pointing out to him that it was a question of his salvation and of the life of the said demon. He, after having taken oath, has said:—

"I swear by my eternal salvation and by the holy Evangelists here present under my hand, to hold the woman suspected of being a demon to be an angel, a perfect woman, and even more so in mind than in body, living in all honesty, full of the migniard charms and delights of love, in no way wicked, but most generous, assisting greatly the poor and suffering. I declare that I have seen her weeping veritable tears for the death of my friend, the knight of Croixmare. And because on that day she had made a vow to our Lady the Virgin no more to receive the love of young noblemen too weak in her service; she has to me constantly and with great courage denied the enjoyment of her body, and has only granted to me love, and the possession of her heart, of which she has made me sovereign. Since this gracious gift, in spite of my increasing flame I have remained alone in her dwelling, where I have spent the greater part of my days, happy in seeing and in hearing her. Oh! I would eat near her, partaking of the air which entered into her lungs, of the lights which shone in her sweet eyes, and found in this occupation more joy than have the lords of paradise. Elected by me to be for ever my lady, chosen to be one day my dove, my wife, and only sweetheart, I, poor fool, have received from her no advances on the joys of the future, but, on the contrary, a thousand virtuous admonitions; such as that I should acquire renown as a good knight, become a strong man and a fine one, fear nothing except God; honour the ladies, serve but one and love them in memory of that one; that when I should be strengthened by the work of war, if her heart still pleased mine, at that time only would she be mine, because she would be able to wait for me, loving me so much."

So saying the young Sire Hugues wept, and weeping added :—

"That thinking of this graceful and feeble woman, whose arm seemed scarcely large enough to sustain the light weight of her golden chains, he did not know how to contain himself while fancying the irons which would wound her, and the miseries with which she would traitorously be loaded, and from this cause came his rebellion. And that he had licence to express his sorrow before justice, because his

life was so bound up with that of his delicious mistress and
sweetheart that on the day when evil came to her he would
surely die."

And the said young man has vociferated a thousand other
praises of the said demon, which bear witness to the ve-
hement sorcery practised upon him, and prove, moreover,
the abominable, unalterable, and incurable life and the
fraudulent witcheries to which he is at present subject, concerning which our lord the archbishop will judge, in order to
save by exorcisms and penitences this young soul from the
snares of hell, if the devil have not gained too strong a hold
of it.

Then we have handed back the said young nobleman into
the custody of the noble lord his father, after that by the
said Hugues, the African has been recognised as the servant
of the accused.

In the eighth place, before us, have the footguards of
our lord the archbishop led in great state the MOST HIGH
AND REVEREND LADY JACQUELINE DE CHAMPCHEVRIER,
ABBESS OF THE CONVENT OF NOTRE-DAME, under the invocation of Mount Carmel, to whose control had been submitted by the late seneschal of Touraine, father of Monseigneur the Count of Roche-Corbon, present advocate of the
said convent, the Egyptian, named at the baptismal font
Blanche Bruyn.

To the said abbess we have shortly stated the present
cause, in which is involved the holy church, the glory of
God, and the eternal future of the people of the diocese
afflicted with the demon, and also the life of a creature who
it was possible might be quite innocent. Then the cause
elaborated, we have requested the said noble abbess to testify that which was within her knowledge concerning the
magical disappearance of her daughter in God, Blanche

Bruyn, espoused by our Saviour under the name of Sister Claire.

Then has stated the very high, very noble, and very illustrious lady abbess as follows:—

"The Sister Claire, of origin to her unknown, but suspected to be of an heretic father and mother, people inimical to God, had truly been placed in religion in the convent of which the government had canonically come to her in spite of her unworthiness; that the said sister had properly concluded her novitiate, and made her vows according to the holy rule of the order. That the vows taken, she had fallen into great sadness and had much drooped. Interrogated by her, the abbess, concerning her melancholy malady, the said sister had replied with tears that she herself did not know the cause. That one thousand and one tears engendered themselves in her at feeling no more her splendid hair upon her head; that besides this she thirsted for air, and could not resist her desire to jump up into the trees, to climb and to tumble about according to her wont during her open air life; that she passed her nights in tears, dreaming of the forests under the leaves of which in other days she slept; and in remembrance of this she abhorred the quality of the air of the cloisters, which troubled her respiration; that in her inside she was filled with evil vapours; that at times she was inwardly diverted in church by thoughts which made her lose her countenance. Then I have repeated over and over again to the poor creature the holy directions of the church, have reminded her of the eternal happiness which women without sin enjoy in paradise, and how transitory was life here below, and certain the goodness of God, who for certain bitter pleasures lost, kept for us a love without end. In spite of this wise maternal advice the evil spirit has persisted in the said sister; and always would she gaze

upon the leaves of the trees and grass of the meadows
through the windows of the church during the offices and
times of prayer; and persisted in becoming as white linen
in order that she might stay in her bed, and at certain times
would run about the cloisters like a goat broken loose from
its fastening. Finally, she had grown thin, lost much of her
great beauty, and shrunk away to nothing. While in this
condition by us, the abbess her mother, was she placed in
the sick-room, we daily expecting her to die. One winter's
morning the said sister has fled, without leaving any trace
of her steps, without breaking the door, forcing of locks, or
opening of windows, nor any sign whatever of the manner
of her passage; a frightful adventure which was believed to
have taken place by the aid of the demon who had annoyed and tormented her. For the rest it was settled by the
authorities of the metropolitan church that the mission of
this daughter of hell was to divert the nuns from their holy
ways, and blinded by their perfect lives, she had returned
through the air on the wings of the sorcerer, who had left
her for mockery of our holy religion, in the place of our
Virgin Mary."

The which having said, the lady abbess was, with great
honour, and according to the command of our lord the archbishop, accompanied as far as the convent of Mount Carmel.

In the ninth place, before us has come, agreeably to the
citation served upon him, Joseph, called Leschalopier, a
money-changer, living on the bridge at the sign of the
Besant d'Or, who, after having pledged his Catholic faith
to say no other thing than the truth, and that known to
him, touching the process before the ecclesiastical tribunal,
has testified as follows:—"I am a poor father, much afflicted
by the sacred will of God. Before the coming of the Succubus of the Rue Chaude, I had, for all good, a son as

handsome as a noble, learned as a clerk and having made more than a dozen voyages into foreign lands; for the rest a good Catholic; keeping himself on guard against the needles of love, because he avoided marriage, knowing himself to be the support of my old days, the love of my eyes, and the constant delight of my heart. He was a son of whom the king of France might have been proud—a good and courageous man, the light of my commence, the joy of my roof, and, above all, an inestimable blessing, seeing that I am alone in the world, having had the misfortune to lose my wife, and being too old to take another. Now, monseigneur, this treasure without equal has been taken from me, and cast into hell by the demon. Yes, my lord judge, directly he beheld this mischievous jade, this she-devil, in whom is a whole workshop of perdition, a conjunction of pleasure and delectation, and whom nothing can satiate, my poor child stuck himself fast in the glue-pot of love, and afterward lived only between the columns of Venus, and there did not live long, because in that place lies so great a heat that nothing can satisfy the thirst of this gulf, not even should you plunge therein the germs of the entire world. Alas! then, my poor boy—his fortune, his generative hopes, his eternal future, his entire self, more than himself, have been engulfed in this sewer, like a grain of corn in the jaws of a bull. By this means become an old orphan, I, who speak, shall have no greater joy than to see burning, this demon, nourished with blood and gold. This Arachne, who has drawn out and sucked more marriages, more families in the seed, more hearts, more Christians than there are lepers in all the lazar houses of Christendom. Burn, torment this fiend—this vampire who feeds on souls, this tigrish nature that drinks blood, this amorous lamp in which burns the venom of all the vipers. Close this abyss, the bottom of which no man can find. .... I offer my deniers to the chapter for the stake, and my arm to light the fire. Watch, well, my lord judge, to surely guard this devil, seeing that she has a fire more flaming than all other terrestrial fires; she has all the fire of hell in her, the strength of Samson in her hair, and the sound of celestial music in her voice. She charms to kill the body and the soul at one stroke; she smiles to bite, she kisses to devour; in short, she would wheedle an angel, and make him deny his God. My son! my son! where is he at this hour? The flower of my life—a flower cut by this feminine needlecase as with a scissors. Ha, lord! why have I been called? Who will give me back my son, whose soul has been absorbed by a womb which gives death to all, and life to none? The devil alone copulates, and engenders not. This is my evidence, which I pray Master Tournebouche to write without omitting one iota, and to grant me a schedule, that I may tell it to God every evening in my prayer, to this end to make the blood of the innocent cry aloud into His ears, and to obtain from His infinite mercy the pardon of my son."

Here followed twenty and seven other statements, of which the transcription in their true objectivity, in all their quality of space, would be over-fastidious, would draw to a great length, and divert the thread of this curious process —a narrative which, according to ancient precepts, should go straight to the fact, like a bull to his principal office. Therefore, here is, in a few words, the substance of these testimonies.

A great number of good Christians, townsmen and townswomen, inhabitants of the noble town of Tours, testified the demon to have held every day wedding feasts and royal festivities, never to have been seen in any church, to have cursed God, to have mocked the priests, never to have crossed herself in any place; to have spoken all the languages of the earth—a gift which has only been granted by God to the blessed Apostles; to have been many times met in the fields, mounted upon an unknown animal who went before the clouds; not to grow old, and to have always a youthful face; to have received the father and the son on the same day, saying that her door sinned not; to have visible malign influences which flowed from her, for that a pastry-cook, seated on a bench at his door, having perceived her one evening, received such a gust of warm love that, going in and getting to bed, he had with great passion embraced his wife, and was found dead on the morrow, that the old men of the town went to spend the remainder of their days and of their money with her, to taste the joys of the sins of their youth, and that they died like fleas on their bellies, and that certain of them, while dying, became black as Moors; that this demon never allowed herself to be seen neither at dinner, nor at breakfast, nor at supper, but ate alone, because she lived upon human brains; that several had seen her during the night go to the cemeteries, and there embrace the young dead men, because she was not able to assuage otherwise the devil who worked in her entrails, and there raged like a tempest, and from that came the astringent biting, nitrous shooting, precipitant, and diabolical movements, squeezings, and writhings of love and voluptuousness, from which several men had emerged bruised, torn, bitten, pinched and crushed; and that since the coming of our Saviour, who had imprisoned the master devil in the bellies of the swine, no malignant beast had ever been seen in any portion of the earth so mischievous, so venomous, and so clutching; so much so that if one threw the town of Tours into this field of Venus, she would there transmute it into the grain of cities, and this demon would swallow it like a strawberry.

And a thousand other statements, sayings, and depositions, from which was evident in perfect clearness the infernal generation of this woman, daughter, sister, niece, spouse, or brother of the devil, besides abundant proofs of her evil doing, and of the calamity spread by her in all families. And if it were possible to put them here conformably with the catalogue preserved by the good man to whom is due the discovery, it would seem like a sample of the horrible cries which the Egyptians gave forth on the day of the seventh plague. Also this examination has covered with great honour Messire Guillaume Tournebouche, by whom are quoted all the memoranda. In the tenth vacation was thus closed this inquest, arrived at a maturity of proof, furnished with authentic testimony and sufficiently engrossed with the particulars, plaints, interdicts, contradictions, charges, assignments, withdrawals, confessions public and private, oaths, adjournments, appearances, and controversies, to which the said demon must reply. And the townspeople say everywhere that were she really a she-devil, and furnished with internal horns planted in her nature, with which she drank the men, and broke them, this woman might swim a long time in this sea of writing before being landed safe and sound in hell.

II

THE PROCEEDINGS TAKEN RELATIVE TO THIS FEMALE
VAMPIRE

†*In nomine Patris, et Filii, et Spiritus Sancti. Amen.*

In the year of our Lord one thousand two hundred and
seventy-one, before us, Hiérome Cornille, grand penitentiary and ecclesiastical judge to this, canonically appointed,
have appeared—

The Sire Philippe d'Idré, bailiff of the town and city of
Tours and province of Touraine, living in his hotel in the
Rue de la Rôtisserie, in Chateauneuf; Master Jehan Ribou,
provost of the brotherhood and company of drapers, residing on the Quay de Bretaingne, at the image of St. Pierre-
es-liens; Messire Antoine Jehan, alderman and chief of the
brotherhood of Changers, residing in the Place du Pont, at
the image of St. Mark—counting-tournoise-pounds; Master Martin Beaupertuys, captain of the archers of the town
residing at the castle; Jehan Rabelais, a ship's painter and
boat maker residing at the port at the isle of St. Jacques,
treasurer of the brotherhood of the mariners of the Loire;
Mark Hiérome, called Maschefer, hosier, at the sign of
Saint-Sébastien, president of the trades council; and
Jacques, called de Villedomer, master tavern-keeper and
vine-dresser, residing in the High Street, at the Pomme de
Pin; to the said Sire d'Indré, and to the said citizens we
have read the following petition by them, written, signed,
and deliberated upon, to be brought under the notice of the
ecclesiastical tribunal:—

PETITION

We, the undersigned, all citizens of Tours, are come into
the hotel of his worship the Sire d'Idré, bailiff of Touraine,
in the absence of our mayor, and have requested him to hear
our plaints and statements concerning the following facts,
which we intend to bring before the tribunal of the archbishop, the judge of ecclesiastical crimes, to whom should be
deferred the conduct of the cause which we here expose :—

A long time ago there came into this town a wicked demon
in the form of a woman, who lives in the parish of Saint-
Etienne, in the house of the innkeeper Tortebras, situated
in the quit-rent of the chapter, and under the temporal jurisdiction of the archiepiscopal domain. The which foreigner
carries on the business of a harlot in a prodigal and abusive
manner, and with such increase of infamy that she threatens
to ruin the Catholic faith in this town, because those who go
to her come back again their souls lost in every way, and
refuse the assistance of the Church with a thousand scandalous discourses.

Now whereas a great number of those who yielded to
her are dead, and whereas arrived in our town with no other
wealth than her beauty, she has, according to public clamour, infinite riches and right royal treasure, the acquisition
of which is vehemently attributed to sorcery, or at least to
robberies committed by the aid of magical attractions and
her supernaturally amorous person;

Whereas it is a question of the honour and security of
our families, and whereas never before has been seen in
this country a woman wild of body or a daughter of pleasure,
carrying on with such mischief her vocation of light o' love,
and menacing so openly and bitterly the life, the savings, the

morals, chastity, religion, and the everything of the inhabitants of this town;

Whereas there is need of an inquiry into her person, her wealth, and her deportment, in order to verify if these effects of love are legitimate, and do not proceed, as would seem indicated by her manners, from a bewitchment of Satan, who often visits Christianity under the form of a female, as appears in the holy books, in which it is stated that our blessed Saviour was carried away into a mountain, from which Lucifer or Astaroth showed him the fertile domains of Judæa, and whereas in many places have been seen succubi or demons having the faces of women, who, not wishing to return to hell, and having within them an insatiable fire, attempt to refresh and sustain themselves by sucking in souls;

Whereas in the case of the said woman a thousand proofs of *diablerie* are met with, of which certain inhabitants speak openly, and whereas it is necessary for the repose of the said woman that the matter be sifted, in order that she shall not be attacked by certain people, ruined by the result of her wickedness;

Therefore we pray that it will please you to submit to our spiritual lord, father of this diocese, the most noble and blessed Archbishop Jehan de Monsoreau, the troubles of his afflicted flock, to the end that he may advise upon them.

By so doing you will fulfil the duties of your office, as we do those of preservers of the security of this town, each one according to the things of which he has charge in his locality.

And we have signed the present, in the year of our Lord one thousand two hundred and seventy-one on All Saints' Day, after mass.

Master Tournebouche having finished the reading of this

petition, by us, Hiérome Cornille, has it been said to the petitioners—

"Gentlemen, do you, at the present time, persist in these statements? have you proofs other than those come within your own knowledge, and do you undertake to maintain the truth of this before God, before man, and before the accused?"

All, with the exception of Master Jehan Rabelais, have persisted in their belief, and the aforesaid Rabelais has withdrawn from the process, saying that he considered the said Moorish woman to be a natural woman and a good wench who had no other fault than that of keeping up a very high temperature of love.

Then we, the judge appointed, have, after mature deliberation, found matter upon which to proceed in the petition of the aforesaid citizens, and have commanded that the woman at present in the gaol of the chapter shall be proceeded against by all legal methods, as written in the canons and ordinances, *contra dæmonios*. The said ordonnance, embodied in a writ, shall be published by the town crier in all parts, and with the sound of a trumpet, in order to make it known to all, and that each witness may, according to his knowledge, be confronted with the said demon, and finally the said accused to be provided with a defender, according to custom, and the interrogations, and the process to be congruously conducted.

(Signed)   HIÉROME CORNILLE.

And, lower down,

TOURNEBOUCHE.

† *In nomine Patris, et Filii, et Spiritus Sancti. Amen.*

In the year of our Lord one thousand two hundred and seventy-one, the 10th day of February, after mass, by command of us, Hiérome Cornille, ecclesiastical judge, has been brought from the gaol of the chapter and led before us the woman taken in the house of the innkeeper Tortebras, situated in the domain of the chapter and the cathedral of St. Maurice, and thus subject to the temporal and seigneurial justice of the Archbishop of Tours; besides which, in consequence of the nature of the crimes imputed to her, she is liable to the tribunal and council of ecclesiastical justice, the which we have made known to her, to the end that she should not ignore it.

And after a serious reading, entirely and well understood by her, in the first place of the petition of the town, then of the statements, plaints, accusations, and proceedings which were written in twenty-four quires by Master Tournebouche, and are above related, we have, with the invocation and assistance of God and the Church, resolved to ascertain the truth, first by interrogatories made to the said accused.

In the first interrogation we have requested the aforesaid to inform us in what land or town she had been born. By her who speaks was it answered: "In Mauritania."

We have then inquired: "If she had a father or mother, or any relations?" By her who speaks has it been replied: "That she had never known them." By us requested to declare her name. By her who speaks has been replied: "Zulma," in Arabian tongue.

By us has it been demanded: "Why she spoke our language?" By her who speaks has it been said: "Because she had come into this country." By us it has been asked: "At what time?" By her who speaks has it been replied: "About twelve years."

By us has it been asked: "What age she then was?" By

her who speaks has it been answered: "Fifteen years, or thereabout."

By us has it been said: "Then you acknowledge yourself to be twenty-seven years of age?" By her who speaks has it been replied: "Yes."

By us has it been said to her: "That she was then the Moorish child found in the niche of Madame the Virgin, baptized by the archbishop, held at the font by the late Lord of Roche-Corbon and the Lady of Azy, his wife, afterwards by them placed in religion at the convent of Mount Carmel, where by her had been made vows of chastity, poverty, silence, and the love of God, under the divine assistance of St. Claire?" By her who speaks has it been said: "That is true."

By us has it been asked her: "If, then, she allowed to be true the declarations of the very noble and illustrious lady the abbess of Mount Carmel, also the statement of Jacquette, called Vieux-Oing, being kitchen scullion?" By the accused has it been answered: "These words are true in a great measure."

Then by us has it been said to her: "Then you are a Christian?" And by her who speaks has been answered: "Yes, my father."

Then by us has she been requested to make the sign of the cross, and to take holy water from a brush placed by Master Tournebouche in her hand; the which having done, and by us having been witnessed, it has been admitted as an indisputable fact, that Zulma, the Moorish woman, called in our country Blanche Bruyn, a nun of the convent under the invocation of Mount Carmel, there named Sister Claire, and suspected to be the false appearance of a woman under which is concealed a demon, has in our presence made act of religion and thus recognized the justice of the ecclesiastical tribunal.

Then by us have these words been said to her: "My daughter, you are vehemently suspected to have had recourse to the devil from the manner in which you left the convent, which was supernatural in every way." By her who speaks has it been stated, that she at that time gained naturally the fields by the street door after vespers, enveloped in the robes of Jehan de Marsilis, visitor of the convent, who had hidden her, the person speaking, in a little hovel belonging to him, situated in the Cupidon Lane, near a tower in the town. That there this said priest had to her then speaking, at great length, and most thoroughly taught the delights of love, of which she then speaking was before in all points ignorant, for which delights she had a great taste, finding them of good use. That the Sire d'Amboise having perceived her then speaking at the window of this retreat, had been smitten with a great love for her. Then she loving him more heartily than the monk, has fled from the hovel where she was detained for profit of his pleasure by Don Marsilis. And then she has gone in great haste to Amboise, the castle of the said lord, where she had had a thousand pastimes, hunting, and dancing, and beautiful dresses fit for a queen. One day the Sire de la Roche-Pozay having been invited by the Sire d'Amboise to come and feast and enjoy himself, the Baron d'Amboise had allowed him to see her then speaking, as she came out naked from her bath. That at this sight the said Sire de la Roche-Pozay having fallen violently in love with her, had on the morrow discomfited in single combat the Sire d'Amboise, and by great violence had, in spite of her tears, taken her to the Holy Land, where she who was speaking had led the life of a woman well beloved, and been held in great respect on account of her great beauty. That after numerous adventures, she who was speaking returned into this country in spite of her apprehensions of misfortune, because such was the will of her lord and master, the Baron de Bueil, who was dying of grief in Asiatic lands, and desired to return to his patrimonial manor. Now he had promised her who was speaking to preserve her from all peril. Now she who was speaking had faith and belief in him, the more so as she loved him very much; but on his arrival in this country the Sire de Bueil was seized with an illness, and died deplorably, without taking any remedies, in spite of the fervent requests which she who was speaking had addressed to him, but without success, because he hated physicians, master surgeons, and apothecaries; and that this was the whole truth.

Then by us has it been said to the accused that she then held to be true the statements of the good Sire Harduin and of the innkeeper Tortebras. By her who speaks has it been replied, that she recognized as evidence the greater part, and also as malicious, calumnious, and imbecile certain portions.

Then by us has the accused been required to declare if she had had pleasure and carnal commerce with all the men, nobles, citizens, and others as set forth in the plaints and declarations of the inhabitants. To which by her who speaks has it been answered with great effrontery: "Pleasure, yes! Commerce, I do not know."

By us has it been said to her, that all had died by her acts. By her who speaks has it been said that their deaths could not be the result of her acts, because she had always refused herself to them, and the more she fled from them the more they came and embraced her with infinite passion, and that when she who was speaking was taken by them she gave herself up to them with all her strength, by the grace of God, because she had in that more joy than in any other thing; and has stated, she who speaks, that she avows her secret sentiments solely because she has been requested by us to state the whole truth, and that she the speaker stood in great fear of the torments of the torturers.

Then by us has she been requested to answer, under pain of torture, in what state of mind she was when a young nobleman died in consequence of his commerce with her. Then by her speaking has it been replied, that she remained quite melancholy and wished to destroy herself; and prayed God, the Virgin, and the saints to receive her in Paradise, because never had she met with any but lovely and good hearts in which was no guile, and beholding them die she fell into great sadness, fancying herself to be an evil creature or subject to an evil fate, which she communicated like the plague.

Then by us has she been requested to state where she paid her orisons.

By her speaking has it been said that she prayed in her oratory on her knees before God, who according to the evangelist, sees and hears all things and resides in all places.

Then by us has it been demanded why she never frequented the churches, the offices, nor the feasts. To this by her speaking has it been answered, that those who came to love her had elected the feast days for that purpose, and that she speaking did all things to their liking.

By us has it been demonstrated that, by so doing, she was submissive to man rather than to the commandments of God.

Then by her speaking has it been stated, that for those who loved her well she speaking would have thrown herself into a flaming pile, never having followed in her love any course but that of nature, and that for the weight of the world in gold she would not have lent her body or her love to a king, who did not love her with his heart feet, head, hair, forehead, and all over. In short and moreover the speaker had never made an act of harlotry in selling one single grain of love to a man whom she had not chosen to be hers, and that he who had held her in his arms one hour or kissed her on the mouth a little, possessed her for the rest of her days.

Then by us has she been requested to state whence proceeded the jewels, gold plate, silver, precious stones, regal furniture, carpets, *et cetera,* worth 200,000 doubloons, according to the inventory found in her residence and placed in the custody of the treasurer of the chapter. By the speaker answer has been made, that in us she placed all her hopes, even as much as in God, but that she dare not reply to this, because it involved the sweetest things of love upon which she had always lived. And interpellated anew, the speaker has said that if we the judge knew with what fervour she held him she loved, with what obedience she followed him in good or evil ways, with what study she submitted to him, with what happiness she listened to his desires, and inhaled the sacred words with which his mouth gratified her, in what adoration she held his person, even we, an old judge, would believe with her well-beloved, that no sum could pay for this great affection which all the men ran after. And the speaker has declared never from any man loved by her, to have solicited any present or gift, and that she rested perfectly contented to live in their hearts, that she would there curl herself up with indestructible and ineffable pleasure, finding herself richer with this heart than with anything, and thinking of no other thing than to give them more pleasure and happiness than she received from them. But in spite of the iterated refusals of the speaker her lovers persisted in graciously rewarding her. At times one came to her with a necklace of pearls, saying, "This is to show my darling that the satin of her skin did not falsely appear to me whiter than pearls"; and would put it on the speaker's neck, kissing her lovingly. The speaker would be angry at these follies, but could not refuse to keep a jewel that gave them pleasure to see it there where they placed it. Each one had a different fancy. At times another liked to tear the precious garments which the speaker wore to gratify him; and another to deck out the speaker with sapphires on her arms, on her legs, on her neck, and in her hair; another to seat her on the carpet, robed in silk or black velvet, and to remain for days together in ecstasy at the perfections of the speaker to whom the things desired by her lovers gave infinite pleasure, because these things rendered them quite happy. And the speaker has said, that as we love nothing so much as our pleasure, and wish that everything should shine in beauty and harmonize, outside as well as inside the heart, so they all wished to see the place inhabited by the speaker adorned with the handsomest objects, and from this idea all her lovers were pleased as much as she was in spreading thereabout gold, silks, and flowers. Now seeing that these lovely things spoil nothing, the speaker had no force or commandment by which to prevent a knight, or even a rich citizen beloved by her, having his will, and thus found herself constrained to receive rare perfumes and other satisfactions with which the speaker was loaded, and that such was the source of the gold, plate, carpets, and jewels seized at her house by the officers of justice. This terminates the first interrogation made to the said Sister Claire, suspected to be a demon, because we the judge and Guillaume Tournebouche are greatly fatigued with having the voice of the

aforesaid in our ears, and find our understanding in every
way muddled.

By us the judge has the second interrogatory been appointed, three days from to-day, in order that the proofs
of the possession and presence of the demon in the body
of the aforesaid may be sought, and the accused, according to the order of the judge, has been taken back to the
gaol under the conduct of Master Guillaume Tournebouche.

† *In nomine Patris, et Filii, et Spiritus Sancti. Amen.*

On the thirteenth day following of the said month of
February before us, Hiérome Cornille, *et cetera,* has been
produced the Sister Claire above-mentioned, in order to
be interrogated upon the facts and deeds to her imputed,
and of them to be convicted.

By us, the judge, has it been said to the accused that,
looking at the divers responses by her given to the preceding interrogatories, it was certain that it never had
been in the power of a simple woman, even if she were
authorised, if such licence were allowed to lead the life
of a loose woman, to give pleasure to all, to cause so many
deaths, and to accomplish sorceries so perfect, without the
assistance of a special demon lodged in her body, and to
whom her soul had been sold by an especial compact. That
it had been clearly demonstrated that under her outward
appearance lies and moves a demon, the author of these
evils, and that she was now called upon to declare at what
age she had received the demon, to avow the agreement
existing between herself and him, and to tell the truth
concerning their common evil doings. By the speaker was
it replied that she would answer us, man, as to God, who
should be judge of all of us. Then has the speaker pretended

never to have seen the demon, neither to have spoken with him, nor in any way to desire to see him; never to have led the life of a courtesan, because she, the speaker, had never practised the various delights that love invents, other than those furnished by the pleasure which the Sovereign Creator has put in the thing, and to have always been incited more from the desire of being sweet and good to the dear lord loved by her, than by an incessantly raging desire. But if such had been her inclination, the speaker begged us to bear in mind that she was a poor African girl, in whom God had placed very hot blood, and in her brain so easy an understanding of the delights of love, that if a man only looked at her she felt greatly moved in her heart. That if from desire of acquaintance an amorous gentleman touched the speaker on any portion of the body, there passing his hand, she was, in spite of everything, under his power, because her heart failed her instantly. By this touch, the apprehension and remembrance of all the sweet joys of love woke again in her breast, and there caused an intense heat, which mounted up, flamed in her veins, and made her love and joy from head to foot. And since the day when Don Marsilis had first awakened the understanding of the speaker concerning these things, she had never had any other thought, and thenceforth recognised love to be a thing so perfectly concordant with her nature, that it had since been proved to the speaker that in default of love and natural relief she would have died, withered at the said convent. As evidence of which, the speaker affirms as a certainty, that after her flight from the said convent she had not passed a single day or one particle of time in melancholy and sadness, but always was she joyous, and thus followed the sacred will of God, which she believed to have been diverted during the time lost by her in the convent.

To this was it objected by us, Hiérome Cornille, to the said demon, that in this response she had openly blasphemed against God, because we had all been made to his greater glory, and placed in the world to honour and to serve Him, to have before our eyes His blessed commandments, and to live in sanctity, in order to gain eternal life, and not to be always in bed, doing that which even the beasts only do at a certain time. Then by the said sister has answer been made, that she honoured God greatly, that in all countries she had taken care of the poor and suffering, giving them both money and raiment, and that at the last judgment-day she hoped to have around her a goodly company of holy works pleasant to God, which would intercede for her. That but for her humility, a fear of being reproached and of displeasing the gentlemen of the chapter, she would with joy have spent her wealth in finishing the cathedral of St. Maurice, and there have established foundations for the welfare of her soul—would have spared therein neither her pleasure nor her person, and that with this idea she would have taken double pleasure in her nights, because each one of her amours would have added a stone to the building of this basilic. Also the more for this purpose, and for the eternal welfare of the speaker, would they have right heartily given their wealth.

Then by us has it been said to this demon that she could not justify the fact of her sterility, because in spite of so much commerce no child has been born of her, the which proved the presence of a demon in her. Moreover, Astaroth alone, or an apostle, could speak all languages, and she spoke after the manner of all countries, the which proved the presence of the devil in her. Thereupon the speaker has asked: "In what consisted the said diversity of language?"—that of Greek she knew nothing save *Kyrie eleison,* of which she made great use; of Latin, nothing, save *Amen,* which she said to God, wishing therewith to obtain her liberty. That for the rest the speaker had felt great sorrow, being without children, and if the good wives had them, she believed it was because they took so little pleasure in the business, and she, the speaker, a little too much. But that such was doubtless the will of God, who thought that from too great happiness, the world would be in danger of perishing. Taking this into consideration, and a thousand other reasons, which sufficiently establish the presence of a devil in the body of the sister, because the peculiar property of Lucifer is to be always find heretical arguments having the semblance of truth, we have ordered that in our presence the torture be applied to the said accused, and that she be well tormented, in order to reduce the said demon by suffering to submit to the authority of the Church, and have requested to render us assistance one François de Hangest, master surgeon and doctor to the chapter, charging him by a codicil hereunder written to investigate the qualities of the feminine nature (*virtutes vulvae*) of the above-mentioned woman, to enlighten our religion upon the methods employed by this demon to lay hold of souls in that way, and to see if any artifice was there apparent.

Then the said Moorish woman has wept bitterly, tortured in advance, and, in spite of her irons, has knelt down imploring with cries and clamour the revocation of this order, objecting that her limbs were in such a feeble state, and her bones so tender, that they would break like a glass; and finally, has offered to purchase her freedom from this by the gift of all her goods to the chapter, and to quit incontinently the country.

Upon this, by us has she been required to voluntarily declare herself to be, and to have always been, a demon of the nature of a Succubus, which is a female devil whose business it is to corrupt Christians by the blandishments and flagitious delights of love. To this the speaker has replied that the affirmation would be an abominable false-hood, seeing that she had always felt herself to be a most natural woman.

Then her irons being struck off by the torturer, the aforesaid has removed her dress, and has maliciously and with evil design bewildered and attacked our understand-ings with the sight of her body, the which, for a fact, exercises upon a man supernatural coercion.

Master Guillaume Tournebouche has, by reason of na-ture, quitted the pen at this period, and retired, objecting that he was unable, without incredible temptations, which worked in his brain, to be a witness of this torture, because he felt the devil violently gaining his person.

This finishes the second interrogatory; and as the ap-paritor and janitor of the chapter have stated Master François de Hangest to be in the country, the torture and interrogations are appointed for to-morrow at the hour of noon after mass.

This has been written verbally by me, Hiérome, in the absence of Master Guillaume Tournebouche, on whose be-half it is signed.

HIÉROME CORNILLE,
Grand Penitentiary.

PETITION

To-day, the fourteenth day of the month of February, in the presence of me, Hiérome Cornille, have appeared the said Masters Jehan Ribou, Antoine Jahan, Martin Beaupertuys, Hiérome Maschefer, Jacques de Ville d'Omer, and the Sire d'Idré, in place of the Mayor of the city of Tours, for the time absent. All plaintiffs designated in the act of process made at the Town Hall, to whom we have, at the request of Blanche Bruyn (now confessing herself a nun of the convent of Mount Carmel, under the name of Sister Claire), declared the appeal made to the judgment of God by the said person accused of demoniacal possession, and her offer to pass through the ordeal of water and of fire, in presence of the Chapter and of the town of Tours, in order to prove her reality as a woman and her innocence.

To this request have agreed for their parts, the said accusers, who, on condition that the town is security for it, have engaged to prepare a suitable place and a pile, to be approved by the godparents of the accused.

Then by us, the judge, has the first day of the new year been appointed for the day of ordeal—which will be next Paschal day—and we have indicated the hour of noon, after mass, each of the parties having acknowledged this delay to be sufficient.

And the present proclamation shall be cried, at the suit of each of them, in all the towns, boroughs, and castles of Touraine and the land of France, at their request and at their cost and suit.

Hiérome Cornille.

III

WHAT THE SUCCUBUS DID TO SUCK OUT THE SOUL OF THE
OLD JUDGE, AND WHAT CAME OF THE DIABOLICAL
DELECTATION.

*This is the act of extreme confession made the first day
of the month of March, in the year one thousand two hundred and seventy-one, after the coming of our blessed
Saviour, by Hiérome Cornlle, priest, canon of the chapter
of the cathedral of St. Maurice, grand penitentiary, of all
acknowledging himself unworthy, who, finding his last
hour to be come, and contrite of his sins, evil doings, for-
feits, bad deeds, and wickednesses, has desired his avowal
to be published to serve the preconisation of the truth, the
glory of God, the justice of the tribunal, and to be an alleviation to him of his punishment, in the other world.
The said Hiérome Cornille being on his deathbed, there
have been convoked to hear his declaration, Jehan de la
Haye (de Hago), vicar of the church of St. Maurice;
Pietro Guyard, treasurer of the Chapter, appointed by our
lord Jehan de Monsoreau, Archbishop, to write his words;
and Don Louis Pot, a monk of* maius MONASTERIUM
*(Marmoustier), chosen by him for a spiritual father and
confessor; all three assisted by the great and illustrious
Doctor Guillaume de Censoris, Roman Archdeacon, at
present sent into our diocese* (LEGATUS) *by our Holy
Father the Pope; and, finally, in presence of a great number of Christians come to be witnesses of the death of the
said Hiérome Cornille, upon his known wish to make act
of public repentance, seeing that he was fast sinking, and
that his words might open the eyes of Christians about to
fall into Hell.*

And before him, Hiérome, who, by reason of his great
weakness could not speak, has Don Louis Pot read the
following confession, to the great agitation of the said
company :—"My brethren, until the seventy-first year of
my age, which is the one in which I now am, with the exception of the little sins through which, all holy though
he be, a Christian renders himself culpable before God,
but which it is allowed to us to repurchase by penitence,
I believe I led a Christian life, and merited the praise and
renown bestowed upon me in this diocese, where I was
raised to the high office of grand penitentiary, of which I
am unworthy. Now, struck with the knowledge of the infinite glory of God, horrified at the agonies which await
the wicked and prevaricators in hell, I have thought to
lessen the enormity of my sins by the greatest penitence I
can show in the extreme hour at which I am. Thus I have
prayed of the Church, whom I have deceived and betrayed,
whose rights and judicial renown I have sold, to grant me
the opportunity of accusing myself publicly in the manner
of the ancient Christians. I hoped, in order to show my
great repentance, to have still enough life in me to be
reviled at the door of the cathedral by all my brethren,
to remain there an entire day on my knees, holding a candle, a cord round my neck, and my feet naked, seeing
that I had followed the ways of hell with regard to the
sacred instincts of the Church. But in this great shipwreck
of my fragile virtue, which will be to you a warning to
fly from vice and the snares of the demon, and to take
refuge in the Church, where all help is, I have been so
bewitched by Lucifer that our Saviour Jesus Christ will
take, by the intercession of all you whose help and prayers
now stream with tears. So would I have another life to
I request, pity on me, a poor abused Christian, whose eyes

spend in works of penitence. Now then listen and tremble
with great fear! Elected by the assembled Chapter to carry
out, instruct, and complete the process commenced against
a demon, who had appeared in a feminine shape, in the
person of a relapsed nun—an abominable person, denying
God, and bearing the name of Zulma in the infidel country
whence she comes; the which devil is known in the diocese
under that of Claire of the convent of Mount Carmel, and
has much afflicted the town by putting herself under an
infinite number of men to gain their souls to Mammon,
Astaroth, and Satan—princes of hell, by making them
leave this world in a state of mortal sin, and causing their
death where life has its source, I have, I the judge, fallen
in my latter days into this snare, and have lost my senses,
while acquitting myself traitorously of the functions committed with great confidence by the Chapter to my cold
senility. Hear how subtle the demon is, and stand firm
against her artifices. While listening to the first response
of the aforesaid Succubus, I saw with horror that the irons
placed upon her feet and hands left no mark there, and was
astonished at her hidden strength and at her apparent
weakness. Then my mind was troubled suddenly at the
sight of the natural perfections with which the devil was endowed. I listened to the music of her voice, which warmed
me from head to foot, and made me desire to be young, to
give myself up to this demon, thinking that for an hour
passed in her company my eternal salvation was but poor
payment for the pleasure of love tasted in those slender
arms. Then I lost that firmness with which all judges should
be furnished. This demon by me questioned, reasoned with
me in such a manner that at the second interrogatory I was
firmly persuaded I should be committing a crime in fining
and torturing a poor little creature who cried like an inno-

cent child. Then warned by a voice from on high to do
my duty, and that these golden words, this music of celestial appearance, were diabolical mummeries, that this body,
so pretty, so infatuating, would transmute itself into a
bristly beast with sharp claws, those eyes so soft into flames
of hell, her behind into a scaly tail, her pretty rosebud
mouth and gentle lips into the jaws of a crocodile, I came
back to my intention of having the said Succubus tortured
until she avowed her mission, as this practice had already
been followed in Christianity. Now when this demon
showed herself stripped to me, to be put to the torture, I
was suddenly placed in her power by magical conjurations.
I felt my old bones crack, my brain received a warm light,
my heart trans-shipped young and boiling blood. I was light
in myself, and by virtue of the magic philter thrown into
my eyes the snows of my forehead melted away. I lost all
conscience of my Christian life and found myself a schoolboy, running about the country, escaped from class and
stealing apples. I had not the power to make the sign of the
cross, neither did I remember the Church, God the Father,
nor the sweet Saviour of men. A prey to this design, I went
about the streets thinking over the delights of that voice,
the abominable, pretty body of this demon, and saying a
thousand wicked things to myself. Then pierced and drawn
by a blow of the devil's fork, who had planted himself
already in my head as a serpent in an oak, I was conducted
by this sharp prong towards the gaol, in spite of my guardian angel, who from time to time pulled me by the arm and
defended me against these temptations, but in spite of his
holy advice and his assistance I was dragged by a million
claws stuck into my heart, and soon found myself in the
gaol. As soon as the door was opened to me I saw no
longer any appearance of a prison, because the Succubus

had there, with the assistance of evil genii or fays, constructed a pavilion of purple and silk, full of perfumes
and flowers, where she was seated, superbly attired with
neither irons on her neck nor chains on her feet. I allowed
myself to be stripped of my ecclesiastical vestments, and
was put into a scent-bath. Then the demon covered me
with a Saracen robe, entertained me with a repast of rare
viands, contained in precious vases, gold cups, Asiatic
wines, songs and marvellous music, and a thousand sweet
sounds that tickled my soul by means of my ears. At my
side kept always the said Succubus, and her sweet, detestable embrace distilled new ardour into my members. My
guardian angel quitted me. Then I lived only by the terrible light of the Moorish woman's eyes, coveted the warm
embraces of the delicate body, wished always to feel her
red lips, that I believed natural, and had no fear of the bite
of those teeth which drew one to the bottom of hell. I
delighted to feel the unequalled softness of her hands
without thinking that they were unnatural claws. In short,
I acted like a husband desiring to go to his affianced without
thinking that that spouse was everlasting death. I had no
thought for the things of this world nor the interests of
God, dreaming only of love, of the sweet breasts of this
woman, who made me burn, and of the gate of hell in which
I wished to cast myself. Alas! my brethren, during three
days and three nights was I thus constrained to toil without
being able to stop the stream which flowed from my veins,
in which were plunged, like two pikes, the hands of the
Succubus, which communicated to my poor old age and to
my dried up bones, I know not what sweat of love. At first
this demon, to draw me to her, caused to flow in my inside
the softness of milk, then came poignant joys which
pricked like a hundred needles my bones, my marrow, my

brain, and my nerves. Then all this gone, all things became
inflamed, my head, my blood, my nerves, my flesh, my
bones, and then I burned with the real fire of hell, which
caused me torments in my joints, and an incredible, intolerable, tearing voluptuousness which loosened the bonds
of my life. The tresses of this demon, which enveloped my
poor body, poured upon me a stream of flame, and I felt
each lock like a bar of red iron. During this mortal delectation I saw the ardent face of the said Succubus, who laughed
and addressed to me a thousand exciting words; such as
that I was her knight, her lord, her lance, her day, her joy,
her hero, her life, her good, her rider, and that she would
like to clasp me even closer, wishing to be in my skin or
have me in hers. Hearing which, under the prick of this
tongue which sucked out my soul, I plunged and precipi-
tated myself finally into hell without finding the bottom.
And then when I had no more a drop of blood in my veins,
when my heart no longer beat in my body, and I was
ruined at all points, the demon still fresh, white, rubicund,
glowing, and laughing, said to me—

"'Poor fool, to think me a demon! Had I asked thee
to sell me thy soul for a kiss, wouldst thou not give it me
with all thy heart?'

"'Yes,' said I.

"'And if always to act thus it were necessary for thee
to nourish thyself with the blood of new-born children in
order always to have new life to spend in my arms, would
you not imbibe it willingly?'

"'Yes,' said I.

"'And to be always my gallant horseman, gay as a man
in his prime, feeling life, drinking pleasure, plunging to
the depths of joy as a swimmer into the Loire, wouldst

thou not deny God, wouldst thou not spit in the face of Jesus?'

" 'Yes,' said I.

" 'If twenty years of monastic life could yet be given thee, wouldst thou not forfeit them for two years of this love which burns thee, and to be at this sweet occupation?'

" 'Yes,' said I.

"Then I felt a hundred sharp claws which tore my diaphragm as if the beaks of a thousand birds there took their bellyfuls, shrieking. Then I was lifted suddenly above the earth upon the said Succubus, who had spread her wings, and cried to me—

" 'Ride, ride, my gallant rider! Hold yourself firmly on the back of thy mule, by her mane, by her neck; and ride, ride, my gallant rider—everything rides!' And then I saw, as a thick fog, the cities of the earth, where by a special gift I perceived each one coupled with a female demon, and tossing about, engendering in great concupiscence, all shrieking a thousand words of love and exclamations of all kinds, and all toiling away with ecstasy. Then my horse with the Moorish head pointed out to me, still flying and galloping beyond the clouds, the earth coupled with the sun in conjunction, from which proceeded a germ of stars, and there each female world was embracing a male world; but in place of the words used by creatures, the worlds were giving forth the howl of temptests, throwing out lightning and crying thunders. Then still rising, I saw overhead the female nature of all things in love with the Prince of Movement. Now, by way of mockery, the Succubus placed me in the centre of this horrible and perpetual conflict, where I was lost as a grain of sand in the sea. Then still cried my white mare to me, 'Ride, ride, my gallant rider—all things ride!' Now, thinking how little

was a priest in this torrent of the seed of worlds, nature
always clasped together, and metals, stones, waters, airs,
thunders, fish, plants, animals, men, spirits, worlds and
planets, all embracing with rage, I denied the Catholic faith.
Then the Succubus, pointing out to me the great patch of
stars seen in the heavens, said to me, 'That way is a drop
of celestial seed escaped from the great flow of the worlds
in conjunction.' Thereupon I instantly clasped the Succubus with passion by the light of a thousand million stars,
and I wished in clasping her to feel the nature of those
thousand million of creatures. Then by this great effort
of love I fell impotent in every way, and heard a great infernal laugh. Then I found myself in my bed, surrounded by
my servitors, who had had the courage to struggle with
the demon, throwing into the bed where I was stretched
a basin full of holy water, and saying fervent prayers to
God. Then had I to sustain, in spite of this assistance, a
horrible combat with the said Succubus, whose claws still
clutched my heart, causing me infinite pains; still, while
reanimated by the voice of my servitors, relations, and
friends, I tried to make the sacred sign of the cross; the
Succubus perched on my bed, on the bolster, at the foot,
everywhere occupying herself in distracting my nerves,
laughing, grimacing, putting before my eyes a thousand
obscene images, and causing me a thousand wicked desires. Nevertheless, taking pity on me, my lord the Archbishop caused the relics of St. Gatien to be brought, and
the moment the shrine had touched my bed the said Succubus was obliged to depart, leaving an odour of sulphur
and of hell, which made the throats of my servants, friends,
and others sore for a whole day. Then the celestial light
of God having enlightened my soul, I knew that I was,
through my sins and my combat with the evil spirit, in great

danger of dying. Then did I implore the especial mercy, to
live just a little time to render glory to God and to his
Church, objecting the infinite merits of Jesus dead upon the
cross for the salvation of Christians. By this prayer I
obtained the favour of recovering sufficient strength to
accuse myself of my sins, and to beg of the members of
the church of St. Maurice their aid and assistance to deliver me from purgatory, where I am about to atone for
my faults by infinite agonies. Finally, I declare that my
proclamation, wherein the said demon appeals to the judgment of God by the ordeals of holy water and of fire, is
a subterfuge due to an evil design suggested by the said
demon, who would thus have had the power to escape the
justice of the tribunal of the Archbishop and of the Chapter, seeing that she secretly confessed to me, to be able to
make another demon accustomed to the ordeal appear in
her place. And, in conclusion, I give and bequeath to the
Chapter of the church of St. Maurice my property of all
kinds, to found a Chapter in the said church, to build it
and adorn it and put it under the invocation of St. Hiérome
and St. Gatien, of whom the one is my patron and the other
the saviour of my soul."

This, heard by all the company, has been brought to the
notice of the ecclesiastical tribunal by Jehan de la Haye
(Johannes de Haga).

We, Jehan de la Haye (Johannes de Haga), elected
grand penitentiary of St. Maurice by the general assembly
of the Chapter, according to the usage and custom of that
church, and appointed to pursue afresh the trial of the
demon Succubus, at present in the gaol of the Chapter,
have ordered a new inquest, at the which will be heard all
those of this diocese having cognisance of the facts relative thereto. We declare void the other proceedings, in-

terrogations, and decrees, and annul them in the name of
the members of the Church in general and sovereign
Chapter assembled, and declare that the appeal to God,
traitorously made by the demon, shall not take place, in
consequence of the notorious treachery of the devil in this
affair. And the said judgment shall be cried by sound of
trumpet in all parts of the diocese in which have been published the false edicts of the preceding month, all notori-
ously due to the instigations of the demon, according to the
confessions of the late Hiérome Cornille.

Let all good Christians be of assistance to our Holy
Church, and to her commandments.

JEAN DE LA HAYE.

IV

HOW THE MOORISH WOMAN OF THE RUE CHAUDE TWISTED
ABOUT SO BRISKLY, THAT WITH GREAT DIFFICULTY WAS
SHE BURNED AND COOKED ALIVE, TO THE GREAT LOSS OF
THE INFERNAL REGIONS.

This was written in the month of May, of the year
1360, after the manner of a testament.

"My very dear and well-beloved son, when it shall be
lawful for thee to read this I shall be, I, thy father, reposing in the tomb, imploring thy prayers, and supplicating
thee to conduct thyself in life as it will be commanded
thee in this rescript, bequeathed for the good government
of thy family, thy future, and safety; for I have done this
at a period when I had my senses and understanding, still
recently affected by the sovereign injustice of men. In my
virile age I had a great ambition to raise myself in the
Church, and therein to attain the highest dignities, because

no life appeared to me more splendid. Now with this earnest idea, I learned to read and to write, and with great trouble became in a fit condition to enter the clergy. But because I had no protection, or good advice to superintend my training, I had an idea of becoming the writer, tabellion, and rubrician of the Chapter of St. Maurice, in which were the highest and richest personages of Christendom, since the king of France is only therein a simple canon. Now there I should be able better than elsewhere to find services to render to certain lords, and thus to find a master or gain patronage, and by this assistance enter into religion, and be mitred and ensconced in an archiepiscopal chair, somewhere or other. But this first vision was over credulous, and a little too ambitious, the which God caused me clearly to perceive by the sequel. In fact, Messire Jehan de Villedomer, who afterwards became cardinal, was given this appointment, and I was rejected, discomfited. Now in this unhappy hour I received an alleviation of my troubles, by the advice of the good old Hiérome Cornille, of whom I have often spoken to you. This dear man induced me, by his kindness, to become penman to the Chapter of St. Maurice and the archbishop of Tours, the which offer I accepted with joy, since I was reputed a good scrivener. At the time I was about to enter into the presbytery commenced the famous process against the devil of the Rue Chaude, of which the old folks still talk, and which, in its time, has been recounted in every home in France. Now, believing that it would be of great advantage to my ambition, and that for this assistance the Chapter would raise me to some dignity, my good master had me appointed for the purpose of writing all that should be in this grave cause, subject to writing. At the very outset Monseigneur Hiérome Cornille, a man approaching eighty years, of

great sense, justice, and sound understanding, suspected
some spitefulness in this cause, although he was not partial
to immodest girls, and had never been involved with a
woman in his life, and was holy and venerable, with a sanctity which had caused him to be selected as judge, all this
notwithstanding. As soon as the depositions were completed, and the poor wench heard, it remained clear that
although this merry doxy had broken her religious vows,
she was innocent of all deviltry, and that her great wealth
was coveted by her enemies, and other persons, whom I
must not name to thee for reasons of prudence. At this
time every one believed her to be so well furnished with
silver and gold that she could have bought the whole
county of Touraine, if so it had pleased her. A thousand
falsehoods and calumnious words concerning this girl,
envied by all the honest women, were circulated and believed in as gospel. At this period Master Hiérome Cornille, having ascertained that no demon other than that
of love was in this girl, made her consent to remain in a
convent for the remainder of her days. And having ascertained from certain noble knights brave in war and rich
in domains, that they would do everything to save her, he
invited her secretly to demand of her accusers the judgment of God, at the same time giving her goods to the
Chapter, in order to silence mischievous tongues. By this
means would be saved from the stake the most delicate
flower that ever heaven has allowed to fall upon our earth;
the which flower yielded only from excessive tenderness
and amiability to the malady of love, cast by her eyes into
the hearts of all her pursuers. But the real devil, under the
form of a monk, mixed himself up in this affair; in this
wise: a great enemy of the virtue, wisdom, and sanctity of
Monseigneur Hiérome Cornille, named Jehan de la Haye,

having learned that in the gaol, the poor girl was treated
like a queen, wickedly accused the grand penitentiary of
connivance with her and of being her servitor, because,
said this wicked priest, she makes him young, amorous, and
happy, from which the poor old man died of grief in one
day, knowing by this, that Jehan de la Haye had sworn
his ruin and coveted his dignities. In fact, our lord the
archbishop visited the gaol, and found the Moorish woman
in a pleasant place, reposing comfortably, and without
irons, because, having placed a diamond in a place where
none would have believed she could have held it, she had
purchased the clemency of her gaoler. At the time certain
persons said that this gaoler was smitten with her, and
that from love, or perhaps in great fear of the young
barons, lovers of this woman, he had planned her escape.
The good man Cornille, being at the point of death, through
the treachery of Jehan de la Haye, the Chapter thinking
it necessary to make null and void the proceedings taken
by the penitentiary, and also his decrees, the said Jehan
de la Haye, at that time a simple vicar of the cathedral,
pointed out that to do this it would be sufficient to obtain
a public confession from the good man on his death-bed.
Then was the moribund tortured and tormented by the
gentlemen of the Chapter, those of Saint Martin, those of
Marmoustiers, by the archbishop and also by the Pope's
legate, in order that he might recant to the advantage of
the Church, to which the good man would not consent.
But after a thousand ills, his public confession was prepared, at which the most noteworthy people of the town
assisted, and the which spread more horror and consterna-
tion than I can describe. The churches of the diocese held
public prayers for this calamity, and every one expected
to see the devil tumble into his house by the chimney. But

the truth of it is that the good Master Hiérome had the fever, and saw cows in his room, and then was his recantation obtained of him. The access passed, the poor saint wept copiously on learning this trick from me. In fact, he died in my arms, assisted by his physician, heart-broken at this mummery, telling us that he was going to the feet of God to pray him to prevent the consummation of this deplorable iniquity. This poor Moorish woman had touched him much by her tears and repentance, seeing that before making her demand for the judgment of God he had minutely confessed her, and by that means had disentangled the soul divine which was in her body, and of which he spoke as of a diamond worthy of adorning the holy crown of God, when she should have departed this life, after repenting her sins. Then, my dear son, knowing by the statements made in the town, and by the naïve responses of this unhappy wretch, all the trickery of this affair, I determined, by the advice of Master François de Hangest, physician of the Chapter, to feign an illness and quit the service of the church of St. Maurice and of the archbishopric, in order not to dip my hands in the innocent blood, which still cries and will continue to cry aloud unto God, until the day of the last judgment. Then was the gaoler dismissed, and in his place was put the second son of the torturer, who threw the Moorish woman into a dungeon, and inhumanly put upon her hands and feet irons weighing fifty pounds, besides a wooden waistband; and the gaol was watched by the crossbowmen of the town and the people of the archbishop. The wench was tormented and tortured, and her bones were broken; conquered by sorrow, she made an avowal according to the wishes of Jehan de la Haye, and was instantly condemned to be burned in the enclosure of St. Etienne, having been pre-

viously placed in the portals of the church, attired in a
chemise of sulphur, and her goods given over to the Chapter, *et cetera*. This order was the cause of great disturbances and fighting in the town, because three young knights
of Touraine swore to die in the service of the poor girl,
and to deliver her in all possible ways. Then they came into
the town, accompanied by thousands of sufferers, labouring
people, old soldiers, warriors, courtesans, and others, whom
the said girl had succoured, saved from misfortune, from
hunger and misery, and searched all the poor dwellings of
the town where lay those to whom she had done good.
Thus all were stirred up and called together to the plain
of Mont-Louis under the protection of the soldiers of the
said lords; they had for companions all the scape-graces of
twenty leagues round, and came one morning to lay siege
to the prison of the archbishop, demanding that the Moorish woman should be given up to them as though they would
put her to death, but in fact to set her free, and to place
her secretly upon a swift horse, that she might gain the
open country, seeing that she rode like a groom. Then in this
frightful tempest of men have we seen between the battle-
ments of the archiepiscopal palace and the bridges, more
than ten thousand men swarming, besides those who were
perched upon the roofs of the houses and climbing on all
the balconies to see the sedition; in short, it was easy to
hear the horrible cries of the Christians, who were terribly
in earnest, and of those who surrounded the gaol with the
intention of setting the poor girl free, across the Loire, to
the other side of Saint Symphorien. The suffocation and
squeezing of bodies was so great in this immense crowd,
blood-thirsty for the poor creature at whose knees they
would have fallen had they had the opportunity of seeing
her, that seven children, eleven women, and eight citizens

were crushed and smashed beyond all recognition, since
they were like splodges of mud; in short, so wide open
was the great mouth of this popular Leviathan, this horrible monster, that the clamour was heard at Montils-les-
Tours. All cried, 'Death to the Succubus! Throw out the
demon! Ha! I'd like a quarter! I'll have her skin! The
foot for me, the mane for thee! The head for me! The
something for me! Is it red? Shall we see? Will it be grilled?
Death to her! death!' Each one had his say. But the cry,
'Largesse to God! Death to the Succubus!' was yelled at
the same time by the crowd so hoarsely and so cruelly that
one's ears and heart bled therefrom; and the other cries
were scarcely heard in the houses. The archbishop decided,
in order to calm this storm which threatened to overthrow
everything, to come out with great pomp from the church,
bearing the host, which would deliver the Chapter from
ruin, since the wicked young men and the lords had sworn
to destroy and burn the cloisters and all the canons. Now
by this stratagem the crowd was obliged to break up, and
from lack of provisions return to their houses. Then the
monks of Touraine, the lords, and the citizens, in great
apprehension of pillage on the morrow, held a nocturnal
council, and accepted the advice of the Chapter. By their
efforts the men-at-arms, archers, knights, and citizens, in
a large number, kept watch, and killed a party of shepherds, road menders, and vagrants, who, knowing the disturbed state of Tours, came to swell the ranks of the mal-
contents. Messire Harduin de Maillé, an old nobleman,
reasoned with the young knights, who were the champions
of the Moorish woman, and argued sagely with them,
asking them if for so small a woman they wished to put
Touraine to fire and sword; that even if they were victorious they would be masters of the bad characters brought

together by them; that these said freebooters, after having
sacked the castles of their enemies, would turn to those of
their chiefs. That the rebellion commenced had had no
success in the first attack, because up to that time the place
was untouched, could they have any over the Church,
which would invoke the aid of the king? and a thousand
other arguments. To these reasons the young knights
replied, that it was easy for the Chapter to aid the girl's
escape in the night, and that thus the cause of the sedition
would be removed. To this humane and wise request
replied Monsigneur *de Censoris,* the Pope's legate, that it
was necessary that strength should remain with the religion
of the Church. And thereupon the poor wench paid for all,
since it was agreed that no inquiry should be made concerning this sedition.

"Then the Chapter had full license to proceed to the
penance of the girl, to which act and ecclesiastical ceremony the people came from twelve leagues round. So that
on the day when, after divine satisfaction, the Succubus
was to be delivered up to secular justice, in order to be
publicly burned at a stake, not for a gold pound would a
lord or even an abbot have found a lodging in the town of
Tours. The night before many camped outside the town in
tents, or slept upon straw. Provisions were lacking, and
many who came with their bellies full, returned with their
bellies empty, having seen nothing but the reflection of the
fire in the distance. And the bad characters did good strokes
of business by the way.

"The poor courtesan was half dead; her hair had
whitened. She was, to tell the truth, nothing but a skeleton,
scarcely covered with flesh, and her chains weighed more
than she did. If she had had joy in her life, she paid dearly
for it at this moment. Those who saw her pass say that she

wept and shrieked in a way that should have earned the
pity of her hardest pursuers; and in the church they were
compelled to put a piece of wood in her mouth, which
she bit as a lizard bites a stick. Then the executioner
tied her to a stake to sustain her, since she let herself roll
at times and fell for want of strength. Then she suddenly
recovered a vigorous handful, because, this notwithstanding, she was able, it is said, to break her cords and escape
into the church, where, in remembrance of her old vocation,
she climbed quickly into the galleries above, flying like a
bird along the little columns and small friezes. She was
about to escape on to the roof when a soldier perceived her,
and thrust his spear in the sole of her foot. In spite of her
foot half cut through, the poor girl still ran along the church
without noticing it, going along with her bones broken and
her blood gushing out, so great fear had she of the flames of
the stake. At last she was taken and bound, thrown into
a tumbrel and led to the stake, without being afterwards
heard to utter a cry. The account of her flight in the church
assisted in making the common people believe that she was
the devil, and some of them said that she had flown in the
air. As soon as the executioner of the town threw her into
the flames, she made two or three horrible leaps and fell
down into the bottom of the pile, which burned day and
night. On the following evening I went to see if anything
remained of this gentle girl, so sweet, so loving, but I found
nothing but a fragment of the 'os stomachal,' in which, in
spite of this, there still remained some moisture, and which
some say still trembled like a woman does in the same place.
It is impossible to tell, my dear son, the sadnesses, without
number and without equal, which for about ten years
weighed upon me; always was I thinking of this angel
burned by wicked men, and always I beheld her with her

eyes full of love. In short the supernatural gifts of this
artless child were shining day and night before me, and
I prayed for her in the church where she had been mar-
tyred. At length I had neither the strength nor the courage
to look without trembling upon the grand penitentiary
Jehan de la Haye, who died eaten up by lice. Leprosy was
his punishment. Fire burned his house and his wife; and
all those who had a hand in the burning had their own hand
singed.

"This, my well-beloved son, was the cause of a thousand
ideas, which I have here put into writing to be for ever the
rule of conduct in our family.

"I quitted the service of the Church, and espoused your
mother, from whom I received infinite blessings, and with
whom I shared my life, my goods, my soul, and all. And
she agreed with me in the following precepts—Firstly, that
to live happily, it is necessary to keep far away from
Church people, to honour them much without giving them
leave to enter your house, any more than to those who by
right, just or unjust, are supposed to be superior to us.
Secondly, to take a modest condition, and to keep oneself
in it without wishing to appear in any way rich. To have
a care to excite no envy, nor strike any onesoever in any
manner, because it is needful to be as strong as an oak,
which kills the plants at its feet, to crush envious heads,
and even then would one succumb, since human oaks are
especially rare, and that no Tournebouche should flatter
himself that he is one, granting that he be a Tournebouche.
Thirdly, never to spend more than one quarter of one's
income, conceal one's wealth, hide one's goods and chat-
tels, to undertake no office, to go to church like other people,
and always keep one's thoughts to oneself, seeing that they
belong to you and not to others, who twist them about,

turn them after their own fashion, and make calumnies therefrom. Fourthly, always to remain in the condition of the Tournebouches, who are now and for ever drapers. To marry your daughters to good drapers, to send your sons to be drapers in other towns of France furnished with these wise precepts, and to bring them up to the honour of drapery, and without leaving any dream of ambition in their minds. *A draper like a Tournebouche* should be their glory, their arms, their name, their motto, their life. Thus by being always drapers, they will be always Tourne-bouches, and rub on like the good little insects, who, once lodged in a beam, make their dens, and go on with security to the end of their ball of thread. Fifthly, never to speak any other language than that of drapery, and never to dispute concerning religion or government. And even though the government of the state, the province, religion, and God turn about, or have a fancy to go to the right or to the left, always in your quality of Tournebouche, stick to your cloth. Thus unnoticed by the others of the town, the Tour-nebouches will live in peace with their little Tour-nebouches—paying the tithes and taxes, and all that they are required by force to give, be it to God or to the king, to the town or to the parish, with all of whom it is unwise to struggle. Also it is necessary to keep the patrimonial treasure, to have peace and to buy peace, never to owe anything, to have corn in the house. and enjoy yourselves with the doors and windows shut.

"By this means none will take from the Tournebouches, neither the State, nor the Church, nor the Lords, to whom, should the case be that force is employed, you will lend a few crowns without cherishing the idea of ever seeing them again—I mean the crowns.

"Thus, in all seasons people will love the Tournebouches,

will mock the Tournebouches as poor people—as the slow
Tournebouches, as Tournebouches of no understanding.
Let the know-nothings say on. The Tournebouches will
neither be burned nor hanged, to the advantage of King or
Church, or other people; and the wise Tournebouches will
have secretly money in their pockets, and joy in their
houses, hidden from all.

"Now, my dear son, follow this the counsel of a modest
and middle-class life. Maintain this in thy family as a
county charter; and when you die, let your successor maintain it as the sacred Gospel of the Tournebouches, until
God wills it that there be no longer Tournebouches in this
world."

*This letter has been found at the time of the inventory
made in the house of François Tournebouche, lord of
Veretz, chancellor to Monseigneur the Dauphin, and condemned at the time of the rebellion of the said lord against
the King to lose his head, and have all his goods confis-
cated by order of the Parliament of Paris. The said letter
has been handed to the Governor of Touraine as an historical curiosity, and joined to the pieces of the process in the
archbishopric of Tours, by me, Pierre Gaultier, Sheriff,
President of the Trades Council.*

The author having finished the transcription and de-
ciphering of these parchments, translating them from their
strange language into French, the donor of them declared
that the Rue Chaude at Tours was so called, according to
certain people, because the sun remained there longer than
in all other parts. But in spite of this version, people of
lofty understanding will find, in the warm way of the said
Succubus, the real origin of the said name. In which acqui-
esces the author. This teaches us not to abuse our body, but
to use it wisely in view of our salvation.

DESPAIR IN LOVE

At the time when King Charles the Eighth took it into his head to decorate the castle of Amboise, there came with him certain workmen, master sculptors, good painters, and masons, or architects, who ornamented the galleries with splendid works, which, through neglect, have since been much spoiled.

At that time the court was staying in this beautiful locality, and, as every one knows, the king took great pleasure in watching his people work out their ideas. Among these foreign gentlemen was an Italian, named Angelo Cappara, a most worthy young man, and, in spite of his age, a better sculptor and engraver than any of them; and it astonished many to see one in the April of his life so clever. Indeed, there had scarcely sprouted upon his visage the hair which imprints upon a man virile majesty. To this Angelo the ladies took a great fancy because he was charming as a dream, and as melancholy as a dove left solitary in its nest by the death of its mate. And this was the reason thereof: this sculptor knew the curse of poverty, which mars and troubles all the actions of life; he lived miserably, eating little, ashamed of his pennilessness, and made use of his talents only through great despair, wishing by any means to win that idle life which is the best of all for those whose minds are occupied. The Florentine, out of bravado, came to the court gallantly attired, and from the timidity of youth and misfortune dared not ask his money from the king, who, seeing him thus dressed, believed him

well furnished with everything. The courtiers and the ladies
used all to admire his beautiful works, and also their
author; but of money he got none. All, and the ladies above
all, finding him rich by nature, esteemed him well off with
his youth, his long black hair, and bright eyes, and did not
give a thought to lucre, while thinking of these things and
the rest. Indeed, they were quite right, since these advantages gave to many a rascal of the court lands, money, and
all. In spite of his youthful appearance, Master Angelo
was twenty years of age, and no fool, had a large heart,
a head full of poetry; and more than that was a man of
lofty imaginings. But although he had little confidence in
himself, like all poor and unfortunate people, he was
astonished at the success of the ignorant. He fancied that
he was ill-fashioned, either in body or mind, and kept his
thoughts to himself. I am wrong, for he told them in the
clear starlight nights to the shadows, to God, to the devil,
and everything about him. At such times he would lament
his fate in having a heart so warm, that doubtless the ladies
avoided him as they would a red-hot iron; then he would
say to himself how he would worship a beautiful mistress,
how all his life long he would honour her, with what fidelity
he would attach himself to her, with what affection serve
her, how studiously obey her commands, with what sports
he would dispel the light clouds of her melancholy sadness
on the days when the sky should be overcast. Fashioning
himself one out of his imagination, he would throw himself
at her feet, kiss, fondle, caress, bite, and clasp her with as
much reality as a prisoner scampers over the grass when
he sees the green fields through the bars of his cell. Thus
he would appeal to her mercy; overcome with his feelings,
would stop her breath with his embraces, would become
daring in spite of his respect, and passionately bite the

clothes of his bed, seeking this celestial lady, full of courage when by himself, but abashed on the morrow if he
passed one by. Nevertheless, inflamed by these amorous
fancies, he would hammer away anew at his marble figures,
would carve beautiful breasts, to bring the water into one's
mouth at the sight of these sweet fruits of love, without
counting the other things that he raised, carved, and
caressed with his chisels, smoothed down with his file, and
fashioned in a manner that would make their use intelligible
to the mind of a greenhorn, and stain his verdure in a single
day. The ladies would criticise these beauties, and all of
them were smitten with the youthful Cappara. And the
youthful Cappara would eye them up and down, swearing
that the day one of them gave him her little finger to kiss,
he would have his desire.

Among these high-born ladies there came one day, one
by herself to the young Florentine, asking him why he
was so shy, and if none of the court ladies could make him
sociable. Then she graciously invited him to come to her
house that evening.

Master Angelo perfumes himself, purchases a velvet
mantle with a double fringe of satin, borrows from a friend
a cloak with wide sleeves, a slashed doublet, and silken
hose, arrives at the house, and ascends the stairs with hasty
feet, hope beaming from his eyes, knowing not what to do
with his heart, which leapt and bounded like a goat; and,
to sum up, so much over head and ears in love, that the
perspiration trickled down his back.

You may be sure the lady was beautiful, and Master
Cappara was the more aware of it, since in his profession
he had studied the mouldings of the arms, the lines of the
body, the secret surroundings of the sex, and other mysteries. Now this lady satisfied the especial rules of art; and

besides being fair and slender, she had a voice to disturb life in its source, to stir the fire of heart, brain and everything; in short, she put into one's imagination delicious images of love without thinking of it, which is the characteristic of these cursed women.

The sculptor found her seated by the fire in a high chair, and the lady immediately commenced to converse at her ease, although Angelo could find no other reply than "Yes" and "No," could get no other words from his throat nor idea in his brain, and would have beaten his head against the fireplace but for the happiness of gazing at and listening to his lovely mistress, who was playing there like a young fly in the sunshine. Because, with this mute admiration, both remained until the middle of the night, wandering slowly down the flowery path of love, the good sculptor went away radiant with happiness. On the road, he concluded in his own mind, that if a noble lady kept him rather close to her skirts during four hours of the night, it would not matter a straw if she kept him there the remainder. Drawing from these premises certain sweet corollaries, he resolved to ask her favours as a simple woman. Then he determined to kill everybody—the husband, the wife, or himself—rather than lose the distaff whereon to spin one hour of joy. Indeed, he was so mad with love, that he believed life to be but a small stake in the game of love, since one single day of it was worth a thousand lives.

The Florentine chiselled away at his statues, thinking of his evening, and thus spoiled many a nose thinking of something else. Noticing this, he left his work, perfumed himself, and went to listen to the sweet words of his lady, with the hope of turning them into deeds; but when he was in the presence of his sovereign, her feminine majesty made itself felt, and poor Cappara, such a lion in the street,

looked sheepish when gazing at his victim. This notwithstanding, towards the hour when desire became heated, he
was almost in the lady's lap and held her tightly clasped.
He had obtained a kiss, had taken it, much to his delight;
for, when they give it, the ladies retain the right of refusal,
but when they let it be taken, the lover may take a thousand.
This is the reason why all of them are accustomed to let it
be taken. The Florentine had stolen a good number, and
things were going on admirably, when the lady, who had
been thrifty with her favours, cried, "My husband!"

And, in fact, my lord had just returned from playing
tennis, and the sculptor had to leave the place, but not without receiving a warm glance from the lady interrupted in
her pleasure. This was all his substance, pittance, and enjoyment during a whole month, since on the brink of his
joy always came the said husband, and he always arrived
wisely between a point-blank refusal and those little caresses
with which women always season their refusals—little
things which reanimate love and render it all the stronger.
And when the sculptor, out of patience, commenced, immediately upon his arrival, the skirmish of the skirt, in
order that victory might arrive before the husband, to
whom, no doubt, these disturbances were not without profit,
his fine lady, seeing desire written in the eyes of her sculptor, commenced endless quarrels and altercations: at first
she pretended to be jealous, in order to rail against love;
then appeased the anger of the little one with the moisture
of a kiss, then kept the conversation to herself, and kept
on saying that her lover should be good, obedient to her
will, otherwise she would not yield to him her life and soul;
that a desire was a small thing to offer a mistress; that she
was more courageous, because loving more she sacrificed
more, and to his propositions she would exclaim, "Silence,

sir !" with the air of a queen, and at times she would put on
an angry look, to reply to the reproaches of Cappara : "If
you are not as I wish you to be, I will no longer love you."

The poor Italian saw, when it was too late, that this was
not a noble love, one of those which does not mete out joy
as a miser his crowns; and that this lady took delight in
letting him jump about outside the hedge and be master of
everything, provided he touched not the garden of love. At
this business Cappara became savage enough to kill any
one, and took with him trusty companions, his friends, to
whom he gave the task of attacking the husband while walking home to bed after his game of tennis with the king. He
came to his lady at the accustomed hour when the sweet
sports of love were in full swing, which sports were long,
lasting kisses, hair twisted and untwisted, hands bitten with
passion, ears as well; indeed, the whole business, with the
exception of that especial thing which good authors rightly
find abominable. The Florentine exclaims between two
hearty kisses—

"Sweet one, do you love me more than anything ?"

"Yes," said she, because words never cost anything.

"Well, then," replied the lover, "be mine in deed as in
word."

"But," said she, "my husband will be here directly."

"Is that the only reason?" said he.

"Yes."

"I have friends who will cross him, and will not let him
go unless I show a torch at this window. If he complain to
the king, my friends will say they thought they were playing
a joke on one of their own set."

"Ah, my dear," said she, "let me see if every one in the
house is gone to bed."

She rose, and held the light to the window. Seeing which

Cappara blew out the candle, seized his sword, and placing himself in front of this woman, whose scorn and evil mind he recognised.

"I will not kill you, madam," said he, "but I will mark your face in such a manner that you will never again coquette with young lovers whose lives you waste. You have deceived me shamefully, and are not a respectable woman. You must know that a kiss will never sustain life in a true lover, and that a kissed mouth needs the rest. You have made my life for ever dull and wretched; now I will make you remember for ever my death, which you have caused. You shall never again behold yourself in the glass without seeing there my face also." Then he raised his arm, and held the sword ready to cut off a good slice of the fresh fair cheek, where still all the traces of his kiss remained. And the lady exclaimed, "You wretch!"

"Hold your tongue," said he, "you told me that you loved me better than everything. Now you say otherwise; each evening have you raised me a little nearer to heaven; with one blow you cast me into hell, and you think that your petticoat can save you from a lover's wrath—No!"

"Ah, my Angelo! I am thine," said she, marvelling at this man glaring with rage.

But he, stepping three paces back, replied, "Ah, woman of the court and wicked heart, thou lovest, then, thy face better than thy lover."

She turned pale, and humbly held up her face, for she understood that at this moment her past perfidy wronged her present love. With a single blow Angelo slashed her face, then left her house, and quitted the country. The husband not having been stopped by reason of that light which was seen by the Florentines, found his wife minus her left cheek. But she spoke not a word in spite of her agony; she loved her Cappara more than life itself. Nevertheless, the husband wished to know whence proceeded this wound. No one having been there except the Florentine, he complained to the king, who had his workman hastily pursued, and ordered him to be hanged at Blois. On the day of execution a noble lady was seized with a desire to save this courageous man, whom she believed to be a lover of the right sort. She begged the king to give him to her, which he did willingly. But Cappara declaring that he belonged entirely to his lady, the memory of whom he could not banish entirely, entered the Church, became a cardinal and a great savant, and used to say in his old age that he had existed upon the remembrance of the joys tasted in those poor hours of anguish; in which he was, at the same time, both very well and very badly treated by his lady. There are authors who say that afterwards he succeeded better with his old sweetheart, whose cheek healed; but I cannot believe this, because he was a man of heart, who had a high opinion of the holy joys of love.

This teaches us nothing worth knowing, unless it be that there are unlucky meetings in life, since this tale is in every way true. If in other places the author has overshot the truth, this one will gain for him the indulgence of the conclave of lovers.

EPILOGUE

THIS second series comes in the merry month of June, when all is green and gay, because the poor muse, whose slave the author is, has been more capricious than the love of a queen, and has mysteriously wished to bring forth her fruit in the time of flowers. No one can boast himself master of this fay. At times, when grave thoughts occupy the mind and grieve the brain, comes the jade whispering her merry tales in the author's ear, tickling her lips with her feathers, dancing sarabands, and making the house echo with her laughter. If by chance the writer, abandoning science for pleasure, says to her, "Wait a moment, little one, till I come," and runs in great haste to play with the madcap, she has disappeared. She has gone back into her hole, hides herself there, rolls herself up, and retires. Take the poker, take a staff, a cudgel, a cane, raise them, strike the wench, and rave at her, she moans; strap her, she moans; caress her, fondle her, she moans; kiss her, say to her, "Here, little one," she moans. Now she's cold, now she is going to die; adieu to love, adieu to laughter, adieu to merriment, adieu to good stories. Wear mourning for her, weep and fancy her dead, groan. Then she raises her head, her merry laugh rings out again; she spreads her white wings, flies one knows not whither, turns in the air, capers, shows her impish tail, her woman's breasts, her strong loins, and her angelic face, shakes her perfumed tresses, gambols in the rays of the sun, shines forth in all her beauty, changes her colours like the breast of a dove, laughs until she cries, casts

374

the tears of her eyes into the sea, where the fishermen find them transmuted into pretty pearls, which are gathered to adorn the foreheads of queens. She twists about like a colt broken loose, exposing her virgin charms, and a thousand things so fair that a pope would peril his salvation for her at the mere sight of them. During these wild pranks of the ungovernable beast you meet fools and friends, who say to the poor poet, "Where are your tales? Where are your new volumes? You're a pagan prognosticator. Oh yes, you are known. You go to fêtes and feasts, and do nothing between your meals. Where's your work?"

Although I am by nature partial to kindness, I should like to see one of these people impaled in the Turkish fashion, and thus equipped, sent on the Love Chase. Here endeth the second series; may the devil give it a lift with his horns, and it will be well received by a smiling Christendom.

THE THIRD TEN TALES

PROLOGUE

CERTAIN persons have interrogated the author as to why there was such a demand for these tales that no year passes without his giving an instalment of them, and why he has lately taken to write commas mixed up with bad syllables, at which the ladies publicly knit their brows, and have put to him other questions of a like character. The author declares that these treacherous words, cast like pebbles in his path, have touched him in the very depths of his heart, and he is sufficiently cognizant of his duty not to fail to give to his special audience in this prologue certain reasons other than preceding ones, because it is always necessary to reason with children until they are grown up, understand things, and hold their tongues; and because he perceives many mischievous fellows among this crowd of noisy people, who ignore at pleasure the real object of these volumes. In the first place know, that if certain virtuous ladies—I say virtuous because common and low-class women do not read these stories, preferring those that are never published; on the contrary, other citizens' wives and ladies, of high respectability and godliness, although doubtless disgusted with the subject matter, read them piously to satisfy an evil spirit, and thus keep themselves virtuous. Do you understand, my good reapers of horns? It is better to be deceived by the tale of a book than cuckolded through the story of a gentleman. You are saved the damage by this, poor fools! besides which, often your lady becoming enamoured, is seized with fecund agitations to your advan-

379

tage, raised in her by the present book. Therefore do these
volumes assist to populate the land and maintain it in mirth,
honour, and health. I say mirth, because much is to be derived from these tales. I say honour, because you save your
nest from the claws of that youthful demon named cuckoldom in the language of the Celts. I say health, because this
book incites that which was prescribed by the Church of
Salerno, for the avoidance of cerebral plethora. Can you
derive a like proof in any other typographically blackened
folios? Ha! ha! where are the books that make children?
Think! Nowhere. But you will find a glut of children making books which beget nothing but weariness. But to continue. Now be it known that when ladies, of a virtuous
nature and talkative turn of mind, converse publicly on the
subject of these volumes, a great number of them, far from
reprimanding the author, confess that they like him very
much, esteeming him a valiant man, worthy to be a monk
in the Abbey of Theleme. For as many reasons as there are
stars in the heavens, he does not drop the style which he
has adopted in these said tales, but lets himself be vituperated, and keeps steadily on his way, because noble France
is a woman who refuses to yield, crying, twisting about,
and saying, "No, no; never! Oh, sir, what are you going
to do? I won't let you; you'd rumple me." And when the
volume is done and finished, all smiles, she exclaims, "Oh,
my master, are there any more to come?" You may take it
for granted that the author is a merry fellow, who troubles
himself little about the cries, tears, and tricks of the lady
you call glory, fashion, or public favour, for he knows her
to be a wanton who would put up with any violence. He
knows that in France her war-cry is, *Mount Joy!* A fine
cry, indeed, but one which certain writers have disfigured,
and which signifies, "Joy is not of the earth, it is there; seize

it, otherwise good-bye." The author has this interpretation
from Rabelais, who told it to him. If you search history,
has France ever breathed a word when she was joyously
mounted, bravely mounted, passionately mounted, mounted
and out of breath? She goes furiously at everything, and
likes this exercise better than drinking. Now, do you not
see that these volumes are French, joyfully French, wildly
French, French before, French behind, French to the backbone. Back then, curs! strike up the music; silence, bigots!
advance my merry wags, my little pages, put your soft
hands into the ladies' hands and tickle them in the middle
—of the hand of course. Ha! ha! these are high sounding
and peripatetic reasons, or the author knows nothing of
sound and the philosophy of Aristotle. He has on his side
the crown of France and the oriflamme of the king and
Monsieur St. Denis, who, having lost his head, said,
"Mount-my-Joy!" Do you mean to say, you quadrupeds,
that the word is wrong? No! It was certainly heard by a
great many people at the time; but in these days of deep
wretchedness you believe nothing concerning the good old
saints.

The author has not finished yet. Know all ye who read
these tales with eye and hand, feel them in the head alone,
and love them for the joy they bring you, and which goes
to your heart, know that the author having in an evil hour
let his ideas, *id est,* his inheritance, go astray, and being
unable to get them together again, found himself in a state
of mental nudity. Then he cried like the woodcutter in the
prologue of the book of his dear master, Rabelais, in order
to make himself heard by the gentleman on high, Lord
Paramount of all things, and obtain from Him fresh ideas.
This said Most High, still busy with the congress of the
time, threw to him through Mercury an inkstand with two

cups, on which was engraved, after the manner of a motto, these three letters, *Ave*. Then the poor fellow, perceiving no other help, took great care to turn over this said inkstand to find out the hidden meaning of it, thinking over the mysterious words and trying to find a key to them. First, he saw that God was polite, like a great Lord as He is, because the world is His, and He holds the title of it from no one. But since, in thinking over the days of his youth, he remembered no great service rendered to God, the author was in doubt concerning this hollow civility, and pondered long without finding out the real substance of this celestial utensil. By reason of turning and twisting it about, studying it, looking at it, feeling it, emptying it, knocking it in an interrogatory manner, smacking it down, standing it up straight, standing it on one side, and turning it upside down, he read backwards *Eva*. Who is Eva, if not all women in one? Therefore by the Voice Divine was it said to the author:

Think of woman; woman will heal thy wound, stop the waste-hole in thy bag of tricks. Woman is thy wealth; have but one woman, dress, undress, and fondle that woman, make use of that woman—woman is everything—woman has an inkstand of her own; dip thy pen in that bottomless inkpot. Woman lives love; make love to her with the pen only, tickle her fantasies, and sketch merrily for her a thousand pictures of love in a thousand pretty ways. Woman is generous, and all for one, or one for all, must pay the painter, and furnish the hairs of the brush. Now, muse upon that which is written there. *Ave*-hail, *Eva* woman; or *Eva*-woman, *Ave*-hail. Yes, she makes and unmakes. Heigh, then, for the inkstand! What does woman like best? What does she desire? All the special things of love; and woman is right. To have children, to produce an imitation of nature,

which is always in labour. Come to me, then, woman!—
come to me, Eva! With this the author began to dip into
that fertile inkpot, where there was a brain-fluid, concocted
by virtues from on high in a talismanic fashion. From one
cup there came serious things, which wrote themselves in
brown ink; and from the other trifling things, which merely
gave a roseate hue to the pages of the manuscript. The poor
author has often, from carelessness, mixed the inks now
here, now there; but as soon as the heavy sentences, difficult
to smooth, polish, and brighten up, of some work suitable
to the taste of the day are finished, the author, eager to
amuse himself, in spite of the small amount of merry ink
remaining in the left cup, steals and bears eagerly therefrom a few penfuls with great delight. These said penfuls
are, indeed, these same Droll Tales, the authority of which
is above suspicion, because it flows from a divine source,
as is shown in this the author's naïve confession.

Certain evil-disposed people will still cry out at this; but
can you find a man perfectly contented on this lump of
mud? Is it not a shame? In this the author has wisely comported himself in imitation of a higher power; and he
proves it by *atqui*. Listen. Is it not most clearly demonstrated to the learned that the sovereign Lord of worlds
has made an infinite number of heavy, weighty, and serious
machines with great wheels, large chains, terrible notches,
and frightfully complicated screws and weights like the
roasting-jack, but also has amused Himself with little trifles
and grotesque things light as zephyrs, and has also made
naïve and pleasant creations, at which you laugh directly
you see them. Is it not so? Then in all eccentric works, such
as the very spacious edifice undertaken by the author, in
order to model himself upon the laws of the above-named
Lord, it is necessary to fashion certain delicate flowers,

pleasant insects, fine dragons well twisted, imbricated, and coloured—nay, even gilt, although he is often short of gold —and throw them at the feet of his snow-clad mountains, piles of rocks, and other cloud-capped philosophies, long and terrible works, marble columns, real thoughts carved in porphyry. Ah! unclean beasts, who despise and repudiate the figures, phantasies, harmonies, and roulades of the fair muse of drollery, will you not pare your claws, so that you may never again scratch her white skin, all azure with veins, her amorous reins, her flanks of surpassing elegance, her feet that stay modestly in bed, her satin face, her lustrous features, her heart devoid of bitterness? Ah! wooden-heads, what will you say when you find that this merry lass springs from the heart of France, agrees with all that is womanly in nature, has been saluted with a polite *Ave!* by the angels in the person of their spokesman, Mercury, and finally, is the clearest quintessence of 'Art. In this work are to be met with necessity, virtue, whim, the desire of a woman, the votive offering of a stout Pantagruelist, all are here. Hold your peace, then, drink to the author, and let his inkstand with the double cup endow the Gay Science with a hundred glorious Droll Tales.

Stand back then, curs; strike up the music! Silence, bigots; out of the way, dunces! Step forward, my merry wags!—my little pages! give your soft hand to the ladies, and tickle theirs in the centre in a pretty manner, saying to them, "Read to laugh." And afterwards you can tell them some merry jest to make them roar, since when they are laughing their lips are apart, and they make but a faint resistance to love.

PERSEVERANCE IN LOVE

DURING the first years of the thirteenth century after the coming of our Divine Saviour there happened in the city of Paris an amorous adventure, through the deed of a man of Tours, of which the town and even the king's court was never tired of speaking. As to the clergy, you will see by that which is related below the part they played in this history, the testimony of which was by them preserved. This said man, called the Tourainian by the common people, because he had been born in our merry Touraine, had for his true name that of Anseau. In his latter days the good man returned into his own country and was mayor of St. Martin, according to the chronicles of the abbey of that town; but at Paris he was a great silversmith. But now in his prime, by his great honesty, his labours, and so forth, he became a citizen of Paris and subject of the king, whose protection he bought, according to the custom of the period. He had a house built for him free of all quit-rent, close to the church of St. Leu, in the Rue St. Denis, where his forge was well known by those in want of fine jewels. Although he was a Tourainian, and had plenty of spirit and animation, he kept himself virtuous as a true saint, in spite of the blandishments of the city, and had passed the days of his green season without once dragging his good name through the mire. Many will say this passes the bounds of that faculty of belief which God has placed in us to aid that faith due to the mysteries of our holy religion; so it is needful to demonstrate abundantly the secret cause of

385

this silversmith's chastity. And, first, remember that he came into the town on foot, poor as Job, according to the old saying; and, like all the inhabitants of our part of the country, who have but one passion, he had a character of iron, and persevered in the path he had chosen as steadily as a monk in vengeance. As a workman, he laboured from morn to night; become a master, he laboured still, always learning new secrets, seeking new receipts, and in seeking, meeting with inventions of all kinds. Late idlers, watchmen, and vagrants saw always a modest lamp shining through the silversmith's window, and the good man tapping, sculping, rounding, chiselling, modelling, and finishing, with his apprentices, his door closed and his ears open. Poverty engendered hard work, hard work engendered his wonderful virtue, and his virtue engendered his great wealth. Take this to heart, ye children of Cain who eat doubloons and micturate water. If the good silversmith felt himself possessed with wild desires, which now in one way, now in another, seize upon an unhappy bachelor when the devil tries to get hold of him, making the sign of the cross, the Tourainian hammered away at his metal, drove out the rebellious spirits from his brain by bending down over the exquisite works of art, little engravings, figures of gold and silver forms, with which he appeased the anger of his Venus. Add to this that this Tourainian was an artless man, of simple understanding, fearing God above all things, then robbers, next to that the nobles, and more than all, a disturbance. Although he had two hands, he never did more than one thing at a time. His voice was as gentle as that of a bridegroom before marriage. Although the clergy, the military, and others gave him no reputation for knowledge, he knew well his mother's Latin, and spoke it correctly without waiting to be asked. Latterly the Parisians had taught him to walk uprightly, not to beat the bush for others, to measure his passions by the rule of his revenues, not to let them take *his* leather to make others' shoes, to trust no one farther than he could see them, never to say what he did, and always to do what he said; never to spill anything but water; to have a better memory than flies usually have; to keep his hands to himself, to do the same with his purse; to avoid a crowd at the corner of a street, and sell his jewels for more than they cost him; all things, the sage observance of which gave him as much wisdom as he had need of to do business comfortably and pleasantly. And so he did, without troubling any one else. And watching this good little man unobserved, many said, "By my faith, I should like to be this jeweller, even were I obliged to splash myself up to the eyes with the mud of Paris during a hundred years of it."

They might just as well have wished to be king of France, seeing that the silversmith had great powerful nervous arms, so wonderfully strong that when he closed his fist the cleverest trick of the roughest fellow could not open it; from which you may be sure that whatever he got hold of he stuck to. More than this, he had teeth fit to masticate iron, a stomach to dissolve it, a duodenum to digest it, a sphincter to let it out again without tearing, and shoulders that would bear a universe upon them, like that pagan gentleman to whom the job was confided, and to whom the timely coming of Jesus Christ discharged from the duty. He was, in fact, a man made with one stroke, and they are the best, for those who have to be touched are worth nothing, being patched up and finished at odd times. In short, Master Anseau was a thorough man, with a lion's face, and under his eyebrows a glance that would melt his gold if the fire of his forge had gone out, but a limpid water placed in his eyes by the great Moderator of all things tempered this great ardour, without which he would have burnt up everything. Was he not a splendid specimen of a man? With such a sample of his cardinal virtues, some persist in asking why the good silversmith remained as unmarried as an oyster, seeing that these properties of nature are of good use in all places. But these opinionated critics, do they know what it is to love? Ho! Ho! Easy! The vocation of a lover is to go, to come, to listen, to watch, to hold his tongue, to talk, to stick in a corner, to make himself big, to make himself little, to agree, to play music, to drudge, to go to the devil wherever he be, to count the grey peas in the dovecot, to find flowers under the snow, to say paternosters to the moon, to pat the cat and pat the dog, to salute the friends, to flatter the gout or the cold of the aunt, to say to her at opportune moments, "You have good looks, and will yet write the epitaph of the human race." To please all the relations, to tread on no one's corns, to break no glasses, to waste no breath, to talk nonsense, to hold ice in his hand, to say, "This is good!" or, "Really, madam, you are very beautiful so." And to vary that in a hundred different ways. To keep himself cool, to bear himself like a nobleman, to have a free tongue and a modest one, to endure with a smile all the evils the devil may invent on his behalf, to smother his anger, to hold nature in control, to have the finger of God and the tail of the devil, to reward the mother, the cousin, the servant; in fact, to put a good face on everything. In default of which the female escapes and leaves you in a fix, without giving a single Christian reason. In fact, the lover of the most gentle maid that God ever created in a good-tempered moment, had he talked like a book, jumped like a flea, turned about like dice, played like King David, and built for the aforesaid woman the Corinthian

order of the columns of the devil, if he failed in the essential hidden thing which pleases his lady above all others,
which often she does not know herself and which he has
need to know, the lass leaves him like a red leper. She is
quite right. No one can blame her for so doing. When this
happens some men become ill-tempered, cross, and more
wretched than you can possibly imagine. Have not many of
them killed themselves through this petticoat tyranny? In
this matter the man distinguishes himself from the beast,
seeing that no animal ever yet lost his senses through
blighted love, which proves abundantly that animals have
no souls. The employment of a lover is that of a mountebank, of a soldier, of a quack, of a buffoon, of a prince, of
a ninny, of a king, of an idler, of a monk, of a dupe, of a
blackguard, of a liar, of a braggart, of a sycophant, of a
numskull, of a frivolous fool, of a blockhead, of a know-
nothing, of a knave. An employment from which Jesus abstained, in imitation of whom folks of great understanding
likewise disdain it; it is a vocation in which a man of
worth is required to spend above all things, his time, his
life, his blood, his best words, besides his heart, his soul,
and his brain; things to which the women are cruelly partial, because directly their tongues begin to go, they say
among themselves that if they have not the whole of a man
they have none of him. Be sure, also, that there are cats
who, knitting their eyebrows, complain that a man does
but a hundred things for them, for the purpose of finding
out if there be a hundred, and first seeing that in everything they desire the most thorough spirit of conquest and
tyranny. And this high jurisprudence has always flourished
among the customs of Paris, where the women receive more
wit at their baptism than in any other place in the world,
and thus are mischievous by birth.

But our silversmith, always busy at his work, burnishing gold and melting silver, had no time to warm his love or to burnish and make shine his fantasies, nor to show off, gad about, waste his time in mischief, or to run after she-males. Now seeing that in Paris virgins do not fall into the beds of young men any more than roast pheasants into the streets, not even when the young men are royal silversmiths, the Tourainian had the advantage of having, as I have before observed, a continent member in his shirt. However, the good man could not close his eyes to the advantages of nature with which were so amply furnished the ladies with whom he dilated upon the value of his jewels. So it was that, after listening to the gentle discourse of the ladies, who tried to wheedle and to fondle him to obtain a favour from him, the good Tourainian would return to his home, dreamy as a poet, wretched as a restless cuckoo, and would say to himself, "I must take to myself a wife. She would keep the house tidy, keep the plates hot for me, fold the clothes for me, sew my buttons on, sing merrily about the house, tease me to do everything according to her taste, would say to me as they all say to their husbands when they want a jewel, 'Oh, my own pet, look at this, is it not pretty?' And every one in the quarter will think of my wife and then of me, and say, 'There's a happy man.' Then the getting married, the bridal festivities, to fondle Madame Silversmith, to dress her superbly, give her a fine gold chain, to worship her from crown to toe, to give her the whole management of the house, except the cash, to give her a nice little room upstairs, with good windows, pretty, and hung round with tapestry, with a wonderful chest in it and a fine large bed, with twisted columns and curtains of yellow silk. He would buy her beautiful mirrors, and there would always be a dozen or so of children, his and hers, when

he came home to greet him." Then wife and children would
vanish into the clouds. He transferred his melancholy imaginings to fantastic designs, fashioned his amorous thoughts
into grotesque jewels that pleased their buyers well, they
knowing not how many wives and children were lost in the
productions of the good man, who, the more talent he threw
into his art, the more disordered he became. Now if God
had not had pity upon him, he would have quitted this
world without knowing what love was, but would have
known it in the other without that metamorphosis of the
flesh which spares it, according to Monsieur Plato, a man
of some authority, but who, not being a Christian, was
wrong. But, there! these preparatory digressions are the
idle digressions and fastidious commentaries which certain
unbelievers compel a man to wind about a tale, like swad-
dling clothes about an infant when it should run about
stark naked. May the great devil give them a clyster with
his red-hot, three-pronged fork. I am going on with my
story now without further circumlocution. This is what
happened to the silversmith in the one-and-fortieth year of
his age. One Sabbath-day, while walking on the left bank
of the Seine, led by an idle fancy, he ventured as far as
that meadow which has since been called the Pré-aux-
Clercs, and which at that time was in the domain of the
abbey of Saint Germain, and not in that of the University.
There, still strolling on, the Tourainian found himself in
the open fields, and there met a poor young girl who, seeing
that he was well dressed, curtsied to him, saying, "Heaven
preserve you, monseigneur." In saying this her voice had
such sympathetic sweetness that the silversmith felt his
soul ravished by this feminine melody, and conceived an
affection for the girl, the more so as, tormented with ideas
of marriage as he was, everything was favourable thereto.

Nevertheless, as he had passed the wench by he dared not go back, because he was as timid as a young maid who would die in her petticoats rather than raise them for her pleasure. But when he was a bow-shot off he bethought him that he was a man who for ten years had been a master silversmith, had become a citizen, and was a man of mark, and could look a woman in the face if his fancy so led him, the more so as his imagination had great power over him. So he turned suddenly back, as if he had changed the direction of his stroll, and came upon the girl, who held by an old cord her poor cow, who was munching the grass that had grown on the border of a ditch at the side of the road.

"Ah, my pretty one," said he, "you are not overburdened with the goods of this world that you thus work with your hands upon the Lord's Day. Are you not afraid of being cast into prison?"

"Monseigneur," replied the maid, casting down her eyes, "I have nothing to fear, because I belong to the abbey. The Lord Abbot has given me leave to exercise the cow after vespers."

"You love your cow, then, more than the salvation of your soul?"

"Ah, monseigneur, our beast is almost the half of our poor lives."

"I am astonished, my girl, to see you poor and in rags, clothed like a fagot, running barefoot about the fields on the Sabbath, when you carry about you more treasures than you could dig up in the grounds of the abbey. Do not the townspeople pursue you, and torment you with love?"

"Oh, never, monseigneur. I belong to the abbey," replied she, showing the jeweller a collar on her left arm like those that the beasts of the field have, but without the little bell, and at the same time casting such a deplorable glance at our townsman that he was stricken quite sad, for by the eyes are communicated contagions of the heart when they are strong.

"And what does this mean?" he said, wishing to hear all about it.

And he touched the collar, upon which was engraved the arms of the abbey very distinctly, but which he did not wish to see.

"Monseigneur, I am the daughter of an *homme de corps;* thus, whoever unites himself to me by marriage will become a bondsman, even if he were a citizen of Paris, and would belong body and goods to the abbey. If he loved me otherwise, his children would still belong to the domain. For this reason I am neglected by every one, abandoned like a poor beast of the field. But what makes me most unhappy is, that according to the pleasure of monseigneur the abbot, I shall be coupled at some time with a bondsman. And if I were less ugly than I am, at the sight of my collar the most amorous would flee from me as from the black plague."

So saying, she pulled her cow by the cord to make it follow her.

"And how old are you?" asked the silversmith.

"I do not know, monseigneur; but our master, the abbot, has kept account."

This great misery touched the heart of the good man, who had in his day eaten the bread of sorrow. He regulated his pace to the girl's, and they went together towards the water in painful silence. The good man gazed at the fine forehead, the round red arms, the queen's waist, the feet dusty, but made like those of a Virgin Mary; and the sweet physiognomy of this girl, who was the living image of St. Genevieve, the patroness of Paris, and the maidens who live in the fields. And make sure that this Joseph suspected the pretty white of the sweet girl's breasts, which were by a modest grace carefully covered with an old rag, and looked at them as a schoolboy looks at a rosy apple on a hot day. Also, may you depend upon it that these little hillocks of nature denoted a wench fashioned with delicious perfection, like everything the monks possess. Now, the more it was forbidden our silversmith to touch them, the more his mouth watered for these fruits of love. And his heart leaped almost into his mouth.

"You have a fine cow," said he.

"Would you like a little milk?" replied she. "It is so warm these early days of May. You are far from the town."

In truth, the sky was a cloudless blue, and glared like a forge. Everything was radiant with youth, the leaves, the air, the girls, the lads; everything was burning, was green, and smelt like balm. This naïve offer, made without the hope of recompense, though a byzant would not have paid for the special grace of the speech; and the modesty of the gesture with which the poor girl turned to him gained the heart of the jeweller, who would have liked to be able to put this bondswoman into the skin of a queen, and Paris at her feet.

"Nay, my child, I thirst not for milk, but for you, whom I would have leave to liberate."

"That cannot be, and I shall die the property of the abbey. For years we have lived so, from father to son, from mother to daughter. Like my poor ancestors, I shall pass my days on this land, as will also my children, because the abbot cannot legally let us go."

"What!" said the Tourainian; "has no gallant been tempted by your bright eyes to buy your liberty, as I bought mine from the king?"

"It would cost too dear; thus it is those whom at first sight I please, go as they came."

"And you have never thought of gaining another country in company with a lover on horseback on a fleet courser?"

"Oh, yes. But, monseigneur, if I were caught I should be hanged at least; and my gallant, even were he a lord, would lose more than one domain over it, beside other things. I am not worth so much; besides, the abbey has arms longer than my feet are swift. So I live on in perfect obedience to God, who has placed me in this plight."

"What is your father?"

"He tends the vines in the gardens of the abbey."

"And your mother?"

"She is a washerwoman."

"And what is your name?"

"I have no name, dear sir. My father was baptized Etienne, my mother is Etienne, and I am Tiennette, at your service."

"Sweetheart," said the jeweller, "never has woman pleased me as you please me; and I believe that your heart contains a wealth of goodness. Now, since you offered yourself to my eyes at the moment when I was firmly deliberating upon taking a companion, I believe that I see in you a sign from heaven! and if I am not displeasing to you, I beg you to accept me as your friend."

Immediately the maid lowered her eyes. These words were uttered in such a way, in so grave a tone, so penetrating a manner, that the said Tiennette burst into tears.

"No, monseigneur, I should be the cause of a thousand unpleasantness, and of your misfortune. For a poor bondsmaid, the conversation has gone far enough."

"Ho!" cried Anseau; "you do not know, my child, the man you are dealing with."

The Tourainian crossed himself, joined his hands, and said—

"I make a vow to Monsieur the Saint Eloi, under whose invocation are the silversmiths, to fashion two images of pure silver, with the best workmanship I am able to perform. One shall be a statue of Madame the Virgin, to this end, to thank her for the liberty of my dear wife; and the other for my said patron, if I am successful in my undertaking to liberate the bondswoman Tiennette here present, and for which I rely upon his assistance. Moreover, I swear by my eternal salvation, to persevere with courage in this affair, to spend therein all I possess, and only to quit it with my life. God has heard me," said he. "And you, little one," he added, turning towards the maid.

"Ha! monseigneur, look! My cow is running about the fields," cried she, sobbing at the good man's knees. "I will love you all my life; but withdraw your vow."

"Let us look after the cow," said the silversmith, raising her, without daring yet to kiss her, although the maid was well disposed to it.

"Yes," said she, "for I shall be beaten."

And behold now the silversmith, scampering after the cursed cow, who gave no heed to their amours; she was taken by the horns, and held in the grip of the Tourainian, who for a trifle could have thrown her in the air, like a straw.

"Adieu, my sweet one! If you go into the town, come to my house, over against Saint Leu's Church. I am called Master Anseau, and am silversmith to the King of France, at the sign of St. Eloi. Make me a promise to be in this field the next Lord's Day; fail not to come, even should it rain halberds."

"Yes, dear sir. For this would I leap the walls, and, in

gratitude, would I be yours without mischief, and cause you no sorrow, at the price of my everlasting future. Awaiting the happy moment, I will pray God for you with all my heart."

And then she remained standing like a stone saint, moving not, until she could see the good citizen no longer, and he went away with lagging steps turning from time to time towards her to gaze upon her. And when he was afar off, and out of her sight, she stayed on, until nightfall, lost in meditation, knowing not if she had dreamed that which had happened to her. Then went she back to the house, where she was beaten for staying out, but felt not the blows. The good silversmith could neither eat nor drink, but closed his workshop, possessed of this girl, thinking of nothing but this girl, seeing everywhere this girl; everything to him being to possess this girl. Now when the morrow was come, went he with great apprehension towards the abbey to speak to the lord abbot. On the road, however, he suddenly thought of putting himself under the protection of one of the king's people, and with this idea returned to the Court, which was then held in the town. Being esteemed by all for his prudence, and loved for his little works and kindnesses, the king's chamberlain—for whom he had once made, for a present to a lady of the Court, a golden casket set with precious stones, and unique of its kind—promised him assistance, had a horse saddled for himself, and a hack for the silversmith, with whom he set out for the abbey, and asked to see the abbot, who was Monseigneur Hugon de Sennecterre, aged ninety-three. Being come into the room with the silversmith, waiting nervously to receive his sentence, the chamberlain begged the abbot to sell him in advance a thing which was easy for him to sell, and which would be pleasant to him.

To which the abbot replied, looking at the chamberlain—

"That the canons inhibited and forbade him thus to engage his word."

"Behold, my dear father," said the chamberlain, "the jeweller of the Court, who has conceived a great love for a bondswoman belonging to your abbey, and I request you, in consideration of my obliging you in any such desire as you may wish to see accomplished, to emancipate this maid."

"Which is she?" asked the abbot of the citizen.

"Her name is Tiennette," answered the silversmith, timidly.

"Ho! ho!" said the good old Hugon, smiling. "The angler has caught us a good fish! This is a grave business, and I know not how to decide by myself."

"I know, my father, what those words mean," said the chamberlain, knitting his brow.

"Fine sir," said the abbot, "know you what this maid is worth?"

The abbot ordered Tiennette to be fetched, telling his clerk to dress her in her finest, and to make her look as nice as possible.

"Your love is in danger," said the chamberlain to the silversmith, pulling him on one side. "Dismiss this phantasy. You can meet anywhere, even at Court, with women of wealth, young and pretty, who would willingly marry you. For this, if need there be, the king would assist you by giving you some title, which in course of time would enable you to found a good family. Are you sufficiently well furnished with crowns to become the founder of a noble line?"

"I know not, monseigneur," replied Anseau. "I have put money by."

"Then see if you cannot buy the manumission of this

maid. I know the monks. With them money does everything."

"Monseigneur," said the silversmith to the abbot, coming
towards him, "you have the charge and office of represent-
ing here below the goodness of God, who is often clement
towards us, and has infinite treasures of mercy for our
sorrows. Now, I will remember you each evening and each
morning in my prayers, and never forget that I received
my happiness at your hands, if you will aid me to gain this
maid in lawful wedlock, without keeping in servitude the
children born of this union. And for this I will make you
a receptacle for the Holy Eucharist, so elaborate, so rich
with gold, precious stones, and winged angels, that no
other shall be like it in all Christendom. It shall remain
unique, it shall dazzle your eyesight, and shall be so far the
glory of your altar, that the people of the town and foreign
nobles shall rush to see it, so magnificent shall it be."

"My son," replied the abbot, "have you lost your senses?
If you are resolved to have this wench for a legal wife,
your goods and your person belong to the Chapter of the
abbey."

"Yes, monseigneur, I am passionately in love with this
girl, and more touched with her misery and her Christian
heart than even with her perfections; but I am," said he,
with tears in his eyes, "still more astonished at your harsh-
ness, and I say it although I know that my fate is in your
hands. Yes, monseigneur, I know the law; and if my
goods fall to your domain, if I become a bondsman, if I
lose my house and my citizenship, I will still keep that
engine, gained by my labours and my studies, and which lies
there," cried he, striking his forehead, "in a place of which
no one, save God, can be lord but myself. And your whole
abbey could not pay for the special creations which proceed

therefrom. You may have my body, my wife, my children, but nothing shall get you my engine; nay, not even torture, seeing that I am stronger than iron is hard, and more patient than sorrow is great."

So saying, the silversmith, enraged by the calmness of the abbot, who seemed resolved to acquire for the abbey the good man's doubloons, brought down his fist upon an oaken chair, and shivered it into fragments, for it split as under the blow of a mace.

"Behold, monseigneur, what kind of servant you will have, and of an artificer of things divine you will make a mere cart-horse."

"My son," replied the abbot, "you have wrongfully broken my chair, and lightly judged my mind. This wench belongs to the abbey, and not to me. I am the faithful servant of the rights and customs of this glorious monastery; although I might grant this woman licence to bear free children, I am responsible for this to God and to the abbey. Now, since there was here an altar, bondsmen and monks, *id est*, from time immemorial, there has never occurred the case of a citizen becoming the property of the abbey by marriage with a bondswoman. Now, therefore, is there need to exercise the right, and to make use of it that it be not lost, weakened, worn out, or fallen into disuse, which would occasion a thousand difficulties. And this is of a higher advantage to the State and to the abbey than your stones, however beautiful they be, seeing that we have treasure wherewith to buy rare jewels, and that no treasure can establish customs and laws. I call upon the king's chamberlain to bear witness to the infinite pains which his majesty takes every day to fight for the establishment of his orders."

"That is to close my mouth," said the chamberlain.

The silversmith, who was not a great scholar, remained

thoughtful. Then came Tiennette, clean as a new pin, her hair raised up, dressed in a robe of white wool with a blue sash, with tiny shoes and white stockings; in fact, so royally beautiful, so noble in her bearing was she, that the silversmith was petrified with ecstasy, and the chamberlain confessed he had never seen so perfect a creature. Thinking there was too much danger in this sight for the poor jeweller, he led him into the town and begged him to think no further of the affair, since the abbey was not likely to liberate so good a bait for the citizens and nobles of the Parisian stream. In fact, the Chapter let the poor lover know that if he married this girl he must resolve to yield up his goods and his house to the abbey, consider himself a bondsman, both he and the children of the aforesaid marriage; although, by a special grace, the abbot would let him his house on the condition of his giving an inventory of his furniture and paying a yearly rent, and coming during eight days to live in a shed adjoining the domain, thus performing an act of service. The silversmith, to whom every one spoke of the cupidity of the monks, saw clearly that the abbot would incommutably maintain this order, and his soul was filled with despair. At one time he determined to burn down the monastery; at another, he proposed to lure the abbot into a place where he could torment him until he had signed a charter for Tiennette's liberation; in fact, a thousand ideas possessed his brain, and as quickly evaporated. But after much lamentation he determined to carry off the girl, and fly with her into a sure place, from which nothing could draw him, and made his preparations accordingly; for, once out of the kingdom, his friends or the king could better tackle the monks and bring them to reason. The good man counted, however, without his abbot, for going to the meadows, he found Tiennette no more there, and learned that she was confined in the abbey, and with such rigour, that to get at her it would be necessary to lay siege to the monastery. Then Master Anseau passed his time in tears, complaints, and lamentations; and all the city, the townspeople, and the housewives, talked of his adventure, the noise of which was so great, that the king sent for the old abbot to court, and demanded of him why he did not yield under the circumstances to the great love of his silversmith, and why he did not put into practice Christian charity.

"Because, monseigneur," replied the priest, "all rights are knit together like the pieces of a coat of mail, and if one makes default, all fail. If this girl were taken from us against our wish, and if the custom were not observed, your subjects would soon take off your crown, and raise up in various places violence and sedition, in order to abolish the taxes and imposts that weigh upon the populace."

The king's mouth was closed. Every one was eager to know the end of this adventure. So great was the curiosity that certain lords wagered that the Tourainian would desist from his love, and the ladies wagered the contrary. The silversmith having complained to the queen that the monks had hidden his well-beloved from his sight, she found the deed detestable and horrible; and in consequence of her commands to the lord abbot it was permitted to the Tourainian to go every day into the parlour of the abbey, where came Tiennette, but under the control of an old monk, and she always came attired in great splendour like a lady. The two lovers had no other license than to see each other, and to speak to each other, without being able to snatch the smallest atom of pleasure, and always grew their love more powerful.

One day Tiennette discoursed thus with her lover—"My dear lord, I have determined to make you a gift of my life, in order to relieve your suffering, and in this wise: in informing myself concerning everything I have found a means to set aside the rights of the abbey, and to give you all the joy you hope for from my fruition.

"The ecclesiastical judge has ruled that as you become a bondsman only by accession, and because you were not born a bondsman, your servitude will cease with the cause that made you a serf. Now, if you love me more than all else, lose your goods to purchase our happiness, and espouse me. Then when you have had your will of me, when you have hugged me and embraced me to your heart's content, before I have offspring will I voluntarily kill myself, and thus you will become free again; at least, you will have the king on your side, who, it is said, wishes you well. And, without doubt, God will pardon me that I cause my own death, in order to deliver my lord spouse."

"My dear Tiennette," cried the jeweller, "it is finished— I will be a bondsman, and thou wilt live to make my happiness as long as my days. In thy company, the hardest chains will weigh but lightly, and little shall I reck the want of gold, when all my riches are in thy heart, and my only pleasure in thy sweet body. I place myself in the hands of St. Eloi, who will deign in this misery to look upon us with pitying eyes, and guard us from all evils. Now I shall go hence to a scrivener to have the deeds and contracts drawn up. At least, dear flower of my days, thou shalt be gorgeously attired, well housed, and served like a queen during thy lifetime, since the lord abbot leaves me the earnings of my profession."

Tiennette, crying and laughing, tried to put off her good fortune, and wished to die, rather than reduce to slavery a free man; but the good Anseau whispered such soft words to her, and threatened so firmly to follow her to the tomb,

that she agreed to the said marriage, thinking that she could
always free herself after having tasted the pleasures of love.

When the submission of the Tourainian became known
in the town, and that for his sweetheart he yielded up his
wealth and his liberty, every one wished to see him. The
ladies of the court encumbered themselves with jewels, in
order to speak with him, and there fell upon him as from
the clouds, women enough to make up for the time he had
been without them; but if any of them approached Tiennette in beauty, none had her heart. To be brief, when the
hour of slavery and love was at hand, Anseau moulded all
his gold into a royal crown, in which he fixed all his pearls
and diamonds, and went secretly to the queen, and gave it
to her, saying, "Madame, I know not how to dispose of my
fortune, which you here behold. To-morrow everything that
is found in my house will be the property of the cursed
monks, who have had no pity on me. Then deign, madame,
to accept this. It is a slight return for the joy which, through
you, I have experienced in seeing her I love; for no sum
of money is worth one of her glances. I do not know what
will become of me, but if one day my children are delivered,
I rely upon your queenly generosity."

"Well said, good man," cried the king. "The abbey will
one day need my aid, and I will not lose the remembrance
of this."

There was a vast crowd at the abbey for the nuptials of
Tiennette, to whom the queen presented the bridal dress,
and to whom the king granted a licence to wear every day
golden rings in her ears. When the charming pair came
from the abbey to the house of Anseau (now serf) over
against St. Leu, there were torches at the window to see
them pass, and a double line in the streets, as though it were
a royal entry. The poor husband had made himself a collar

of gold, which he wore on his left arm in token of his belonging to the abbey of St. Germain. But in spite of his
servitude the people cried out, "Noël! Noël!" as to a new
crowned king. And the good man bowed to them gracefully, happy as a lover, and joyful at the homage which
every one rendered to the grace and modesty of Tiennette.
Then the good Tourainian found green boughs and violets
in crowns in his honour; and the principal inhabitants of
the quarter were all there, who, as a great honour, played
music to him, and cried to him, "You will always be a noble
man in spite of the abbey." You may be sure that the
happy pair indulged in amorous conflict to their hearts'
content; that the good man's blows were vigorous; and that
his sweetheart, like a good country maiden, was of a nature
to return them. Thus they lived together a whole month,
happy as the doves, who in spring-time build their nest twig
by twig. Tiennette was delighted with the beautiful house
and the customers, who came and went away astonished at
her. This month of flowers passed, there came one day,
with great pomp, the good old Abbot Hugon, their lord and
master, who entered the house, which then belonged not to
the jeweller, but to the Chapter, and said to the two spouses:
—"My children, you are released, free and quit of everything; and I should tell you that from the first I was much
struck with the love which united you one to the other. The
rights of the abbey once recognised, I was, so far as I was
concerned, determined to restore you to perfect enjoyment,
after having proved your loyalty by the test of God. And
this manumission will cost you nothing." Having thus said,
he gave them each a little tap with his hand on the cheek.
And they fell about his knees weeping tears of joy for such
good reasons. The Tourainian informed the people of the

neighbourhood, who picked up in the streets the largesse, and received the benedictions of the good Abbot Hugon.

Then with great honour, Master Anseau held the reins of his mule, as far as the gate of Bussy. During the journey the jeweller, who had taken a bag of silver, threw the pieces to the poor and suffering, crying, "Largesse, largesse to God! God save and guard the abbot. Long live the good Lord Hugon!" And returning to his house he regaled his friends, and had fresh wedding festivities, which lasted a fortnight. You can imagine that the abbot was reproached by the Chapter, for his clemency in opening the door for such good prey to escape, so that when a year after the good man Hugon fell ill, his prior told him that it was a punishment from Heaven, because he had neglected the sacred interests of the Chapter and of God. "If I have judged that man aright," said the abbot, "he will not forget what he owes us."

In fact, this day happening by chance to be the anniversary of the marriage, a monk came to announce that the silversmith supplicated his benefactor to receive him. Soon he entered the room where the abbot was, and spread out before him two marvellous shrines, which since that time no workman has surpassed, in any portion of the Christian world, and which were named the *"Vow of a Steadfast Love."* These two treasures are, as every one knows, placed on the principal altar of the church, and are esteemed as an inestimable work, for the silversmith had spent thereon all his wealth. Nevertheless, this work, far from emptying his purse, filled it full to overflowing, because so rapidly increased his fame and his forune that he was able to buy a patent of nobility and lands, and he founded the house of Anseau, which has since been held in great honour in fair Touraine.

This teaches us to have always recourse to God and the saints in all the undertakings of life, to be steadfast in all good things, and, above all, that a great love triumphs over everything, which is an old sentence; but the author has rewritten it, because it is a most pleasant one.

CONCERNING A PROVOST WHO DID
NOT RECOGNISE THINGS

In the good town of Bourges, at the time when that lord
the king disported himself there, who afterwards abandoned
his search after pleasure to conquer the kingdom, and did
indeed conquer it, there lived a provost, entrusted by him
with the maintenance of order, and called the provost-royal.
From which came, under the glorious son of the said king,
the office of provost of the hotel, in which behaved rather
harshly my lord Tristan of Méré, of whom these tales oft
make mention, although he was by no means a merry fellow.
I give this information to the friends who pilfer from old
manuscripts to manufacture new ones, and I show thereby
how learned these Tales really are, without appearing to be
so. Very well, then, this provost was named Picot, or Picault,
of which some made *picottin, picoter,* and *picoree;* by some
Pitot, Pitaut, from which came *pitance;* by others, in
Languedoc, Pichot, from which nothing comes worth knowing; by these Petiot or Petiet; by those Petitot and Peti-
nault, or Petiniaud, which was the masonic appellation; but
at Bourges he was called Petit, a name which was eventually
adopted by the family, which has multiplied exceedingly,
for everywhere you find "des Petits," and so he will be
called Petit in this narrative. I have given this etymology
in order to throw a light on our language, and show how
our citizens have finished by acquiring names. But enough
of science. This said provost, who had as many names as
there were provinces into which the court went, was in

reality a little bit of a man, whose mother had given him so strange a hide that when he wanted to laugh he used to stretch his cheeks like a cow making water, and this smile at court was called the provost's smile. One day the king, hearing this proverbial expression used by certain lords, said, jokingly, "You are in error, gentlemen, Petit does not laugh, he's short of skin below the mouth." But with his false laugh, Petit was all the more suited to his occupation of watching and catching evil-doers. In fact, he was worth what he cost. For all malice, he was a bit of a cuckold, for all vice, he went to vespers, for all wisdom he obeyed God, when it was convenient; for all joy he had a wife in his house; and for all change in his joy he looked for a man to hang, and when he was asked to find one he never failed to meet him; but when he was between the sheets he never troubled himself about thieves. Can you find in all Christendom a more virtuous provost? No! All provosts hang too little, or too much, while this one just hanged as much as was necessary to be a provost. This good fellow had for his wife in legitimate marriage, and much to the astonishment of every one, the prettiest little woman in Bourges. So it was that often, while on his road to the execution, he would ask God the same question as several others in the town did—namely, why he, Petit, he the sheriff, he the provost-royal, had to himself, Petit, provost-royal and sheriff, a wife so exquisitely shaped, so dowered with charms, that a donkey seeing her pass by would bray with delight. To this God vouchsafed no reply, and doubtless had His reasons. But the slanderous tongues of the town replied for Him, that the young lady was by no means a maiden when she became the wife of Petit. Others said she did not keep her affections solely for him. The wags answered, that donkeys often got into fine stables. Every one had taunts ready which would have made a nice little collection had any one gathered them together. From them, however, it is necessary to take nearly four-fourths, seeing that Petit's wife was a virtuous woman, who had a lover for pleasure and a husband for duty. How many were there in the town as careful of their hearts and mouths? If you can point out one to me, I'll give you a kick or a halfpenny, whichever you like. You will find some who have neither husband nor lover. Certain females have a lover and no husband. Ugly women have a husband and no lover. But to meet with a woman who, having one husband and one lover, keeps to the deuce without trying for the trey, there is the miracle, you see, you greenheads, blockheads, and dolts! Now then, put the true character of this virtuous woman on the tablets of your memory, go your ways, and let me go mine. The good Madame Petit was not one of those ladies who are always on the move, running hither and thither, can't keep still a moment, but trot about, worrying, hurrying, chattering, and clattering, and have nothing in them to keep them steady, but are so light that they run after a gastric zephyr as after their quintessence. No; on the contrary, she was a good housewife, always sitting in her chair or sleeping in her bed, ready as a candlestick, waiting for her lover when her husband went out, receiving the husband when the lover had gone. This dear woman never thought of dressing herself only to annoy and make other wives jealous. Pish! she had found a better use for the merry time of youth, and put life into her joints in order to make the best use of it. Now you know the provost and his good wife. The provost's lieutenant in duties matrimonial, duties which are so heavy that it takes two men to execute them, was a noble lord, a landowner, who disliked the king exceedingly. You must bear this in mind, because it is one of the principal points of the story. The constable, who was a rough Scotch gentleman, had seen by chance Petit's wife, and wished to have a little conversation with her comfortably, towards the morning, just the time to tell his beads, which was Christianly honest, or honestly Christian, in order to argue with her concerning the things of science or the science of things. Thinking herself quite learned enough, Madame Petit, who was, as has been stated, a virtuous, wise, and honest wife, refused to listen to the said constable. After certain arguments, reasonings, tricks, and messages, which were of no avail, he swore by his great black *coquedouille* that he would rip up the gallant although he was a man of mark. But he swore nothing about the lady. This denotes a good Frenchman, for in such a dilemma there are certain offended persons who would upset the whole business of three persons by killing four. The constable wagered his big, black coquedouille before the king and the lady of Sorel, who were playing cards before supper ; and his majesty was well pleased, because he would be relieved of this noble, who displeased him, and that without costing him a *Thank you.*

"And how will you manage the affair ?" said Madame de Sorel to him, with a smile.

"Oh, oh !" replied the constable. "You may be sure, madame, I do not wish to lose my big black coquedouille."

"What was, then, this great coquedouille ?"

"Ha, ha ! This point is shrouded in darkness to a degree that would make you ruin your eyes in ancient books ; but it was certainly something of great importance. Nevertheless, let us put on our spectacles, and search it out. *Douille* signifies, in Brittany, a girl, and *coque* means a cook's frying pan. From this word has come into France that of *coquin*—a knave who eats, licks, laps, sucks, and fritters his money away, and gets into stews; is always in hot water, and eats up everything, leads an idle life, and doing this, becomes wicked, becomes poor, and that incites him to steal or to beg. From this it may be concluded by the learned that the great coquedouille was a household utensil in the shape of a kettle, used for cooking things."

"Well," continued the constable, who was the Sieur de Richmond, "I will have the husband ordered to go into the country for a day and a night, to arrest certain peasants suspected of plotting treacherously with the English. Thereupon my two pigeons, believing their man absent, will be as merry as soldiers off duty; and, if a certain thing takes place, I will let loose the provost, sending him, in the king's name, to search the house where the couple will be, in order that he may slay our friend, who pretends to have this good cordelier all to himself."

"What does this mean?" said the Lady of Beauté.

"Equivoque," answered the king, smiling.

"Come to supper," said Madame Agnes. "You are bad men, who with one word insult both the citizens' wives and a holy order."

Now, for a long time, Madame Petit had longed to have a night of liberty, during which she might visit the house of the said noble, where she could make as much noise as she liked without waking the neighbours, because at the provost's house she was afraid of being overheard, and had to content herself well with the pilferings of love, little tastes, and nibbles, daring at the most only to trot, while what she desired was a smart gallop. On the morrow, therefore, the lady's-maid went off about midday to the young lord's house, and told the lover—from whom she received many presents, and therefore in no way disliked him—that he might make his preparations for pleasure, and for supper, for that he might rely upon the provost's better half being with him in the evening, both hungry and thirsty.

"Good!" said he. "Tell your mistress I will not stint her in anything she desires."

The pages of the cunning constable, who were watching the house, seeing the gallant prepare for his gallantries, and set out the flagons and the meats, went and informed their master that everything had happened as he wished. Hearing this, the good constable rubbed his hands, thinking how nicely the provost would catch the pair. He instantly sent word to him, that by the king's express commands he was to return to town, in order that he might seize at the said lord's house an English nobleman, with whom he was vehemently suspected to be arranging a plot of diabolical darkness. But before he put this order into execution, he was to come to the king's hotel, in order that he might understand the courtesy to be exercised in this case. The provost, joyous at the chance of speaking to the king, used such diligence that he was in town just at the time when the two lovers were singing the first note of their evening hymn. The lord of cuckoldom and its surrounding lands, who is a strange lord, managed things so well, that madame was only conversing with her lord lover at the time that her lord spouse was talking to the constable and the king; at which he was pleased, and so was his wife—a case of concord rare in matrimony.

"I was saying to monseigneur," said the constable to the provost, as he entered the king's apartment, "that every man in the kingdom has a right to kill his wife and her lover if he find them in an act of infidelity. But his majesty, who is clement, argues that he has only a right to kill the man, and not the woman. Now what would you do, Mr. Provost, if by chance you found a gentleman taking a stroll in that

fair meadow of which laws, human and divine, enjoin you
alone to cultivate the verdure?"

"I would kill everything," said the provost; "I would
scrunch the five hundred thousand devils of nature, flower
and seed, and send them flying, the pips and the apples, the
grass and the meadow, the woman and the man."

"You would be in the wrong," said the king. "That is contrary to the laws of the Church and of the State; of the
State, because you might deprive me of a subject; of the
Church, because you would be sending an innocent to limbo
unshriven."

"Sire, I admire your profound wisdom, and I clearly
perceive you to be the centre of all justice."

"We can then only kill the knight—*Amen,*" said the constable, "kill the horseman. Now go quickly to the house of
the suspected lord, but without letting yourself be bam-
boozled, do not forget what is due to his position."

The provost, believing he would certainly be Chancellor
of France if he properly acquitted himself of his task, went
from the castle into the town, took his men, arrived at the
nobleman's residence, arranged his people outside, placed
guards at all the doors, opened noiselessly by order of the
king, climbs the stairs, asks the servants in which room
their master is, puts them under arrest, goes up alone, and
knocks at the door of the room where the two lovers are
tilting in love's tournament, and says to them—

"Open, in the name of our lord the king!"

The lady recognised her husband's voice, and could not
repress a smile, thinking that she had not waited for the
king's order to do what she had done. But after laughter
came terror. Her lover took his cloak, threw it over him,
and came to the door. There, not knowing that his life was

in peril, he declared that he belonged to the court and to the king's household.

"Bah!" said the provost. "I have strict orders from the king; and under pain of being treated as a rebel, you are bound instantly to receive me."

Then the lord went out to him, still holding the door.

"What do you want here?"

"An enemy of our lord the king, whom we command you to deliver into our hands, otherwise you must follow me with him to the castle."

This, thought the lover, is a piece of treachery on the part of the constable, whose propositions my dear mistress treated with scorn. We must get out of this scrape in some way. Then turning towards the provost, he went double or quits on the risk, reasoning thus with the cuckold:—

"My friend, you know that I consider you to be as gallant a man as it is possible for a provost to be in the discharge of his duty. Now, can I have confidence in you? I have here with me the fairest lady of the court. As for Englishmen, I have not sufficient of one to make the breakfast of the constable, M. de Richmond, who sends you here. This is (to be candid with you) the result of a bet made between myself and the constable, who shares it with the King. Both have wagered that they know who is the lady of my heart; and I have wagered to the contrary. No one more than myself hates the English, who took my estates in Picardy. Is it not a knavish trick to put justice in motion against me? Ho! ho! my lord constable, a chamberlain is worth two of you, and I will beat you yet. My dear Petit, I give you permission to search by night and by day, every nook and cranny of my house. But come in here alone, search my room, turn the bed over, do what you like. Only allow me to cover with a cloth or a handkerchief this fair lady, who is at present in the costume of an archangel, in order that you may not know to what husband she belongs."

"Willingly," said the provost. "But I am an old bird, not easily caught with chaff, and would like to be sure that it is really a lady of the court, and not an Englishman, for these English have flesh as white and soft as women, and I know it well, because I've hanged so many of them."

"Well, then," said the lord, "seeing of what crime I am suspected, from which I am bound to free myself, I will go and ask my lady-love to consent for a moment to abandon her modesty. She is too fond of me to refuse to save me from reproach. I will beg her to turn herself over and show you a physiognomy, which will in no way compromise her, and will be sufficient to enable you to recognise a noble woman, although she will be in a sense upside down."

"All right," said the provost.

The lady having heard every word, had folded up all her clothes, and put them under the pillow, had taken off her chemise, that her husband should not recognise it, had twisted her head up in a sheet, and had displayed the plump cushions which were divided by the pink line of her spine.

"Come in, my friend," said the lord.

The provost looked up the chimney, opened the cupboard, the clothes' chest, felt under the bed, in the sheets, and everywhere. Then he began to study what was on the bed.

"My lord," said he, regarding his legitimate appurtenances, "I have seen young English lads with backs like that. You must forgive me doing my duty, but I must see otherwise."

"What do you call otherwise?" said the lord.

"Well, the other physiognomy, or, if you prefer it, the physiognomy of the other."

"Then you will allow madame to cover herself and arrange to show you as little as possible of that which is our delight," said the lover, knowing that the lady had a mole or two easy to recognise. "Turn your back a moment, so that my dear lady may satisfy propriety."

The wife smiled at her lover, kissed him for his dexterity, arranged herself cunningly; and the husband seeing in full that which the jade had never let him see before, was quite convinced that no English person could be thus fashioned without being a charming Englishwoman.

"Yes, my lord," he whispered in the ear of his lieutenant, "this is certainly a lady of the court, because the townswomen are neither so well formed nor so charming."

Then the house being thoroughly searched, and no Englishman found, the provost returned, as the constable had told him, to the king's residence.

"Is he slain?" said the constable.

"Who?"

"He who grafted horns upon your forehead."

"I only saw a lady in his couch, who seemed to be greatly enjoying herself with him."

"You, with your own eyes, saw this woman, cursed cuckold, and you did not kill your rival?"

"It was not a common woman, but a lady of the court."

"You saw her?"

"And verified her in both cases."

"What do you mean by those words?" cried the king, who was bursting with laughter.

"I say with all the respect due to your majesty, that I have verified the over and the under."

"You do not, then, know the physiognomies of your own wife, you old fool without memory! You deserve to be hanged."

"I hold those features of my wife in too great respect to gaze upon them. Besides, she is so modest that she would die rather than expose an atom of her body."

"True," said the king; "it was not made to be shown."

"Old *coquedouille!* that was your wife," said the constable.

"My lord constable, she is asleep, poor girl!"

"Quick, quick then! To horse! Let us be off, and if she be in your house I'll forgive you."

Then the constable, followed by the provost, went to the latter's house in less time than it would have taken a beggar to empty the poor-box. "Hullo! there, hi!" Hearing the noise made by the men, which threatened to bring the walls about their ears, the maid-servant opened the door, yawning and stretching her arms. The constable and the provost rushed into the room, where, with great difficulty, they succeeded in waking the lady, who pretended to be terrified, and was so soundly asleep that her eyes were full of gum. At this the provost was in great glee, saying to the constable that some one had certainly deceived him, that his wife was a virtuous woman, and was more astonished than any of them at these proceedings. The constable turned on his heel and departed. The good provost began directly to undress to get to bed early, since this adventure had brought his good wife to his memory. When he was unharnessing himself, and was knocking off his nether garments, madame, astonished, said to him—

"Oh, my dear husband, what is the meaning of all this uproar—this constable and his pages, and why did he come to see if I was asleep? Is it to be henceforward part of a constable's duty to look after our . . ."

"I do not know," said the provost, interrupting her, to tell her what had happened to him.

"And you saw without my permission a lady of the court!
Ha! ha! heu! heu! hein!" Then she began to moan, to weep,
and to cry in such a deplorable manner and so loudly, that
her lord was quite aghast.

"What's the matter, my darling? What is it? What do
you want?"

"Ah, you won't love me any more after seeing how beautiful court ladies are!"

"Nonsense, my child! They are great ladies. I don't mind
telling you in confidence; they are great ladies in every respect."

"Well," said she, "am I nicer?"

"Ah," said he, "in a great measure. Yes!"

"They have, then, great happiness," said she, sighing,
"when I have so much with so little beauty."

Thereupon the provost tried a better argument to argue
with his good wife, and argued so well that she finished
by allowing herself to be convinced that Heaven has or-
dained that much pleasure may be obtained from small
things.

This shows us that nothing here below can prevail against
the Church of cuckolds.

ABOUT THE MONK AMADOR,

WHO WAS A GLORIOUS ABBOT OF TURPENAY

ONE day that it was drizzling with rain—a time when the ladies remain gleefully at home, because they love the damp, and can have at their apron-strings the men who are not disagreeable to them—the queen was in her chamber, at the castle of Amboise, against the window curtains. There, seated in her chair, she was working at a piece of tapestry to amuse herself, but was using her needle heedlessly, watching the rain fall into the Loire, and was lost in thought, where her ladies were following her example. The king was arguing with those of his Court who had accompanied him from the chapel—for it was a question of returning to dominical vespers. His arguments, statements, and reasonings finished, he looked at the queen, saw that she was melancholy, saw that the ladies were melancholy also, and noted the fact that they were all acquainted with the mysteries of matrimony.

"Did I not see the Abbot of Turpenay here just now?" said he.

Hearing these words, there advanced towards the king the monk, who, by his constant petitions, rendered himself so obnoxious to Louis the Eleventh, that that monarch seriously commanded his provost-royal to remove him from his sight; and it has been related in the first volume of these Tales, how the monk was saved through the mistake of Sieur Tristran. The monk was at this time a man whose

qualities had grown rapidly, so much so that his wit had
communicated a jovial hue to his face. He was a great
favourite with the ladies, who crammed him with wine,
confectioneries, and dainty dishes at the dinners, suppers,
and merry-makings, to which they invited him, because
every host likes those cheerful guests of God with nimble
jaws, who say as many words as they put away tit-bits.
This abbot was a pernicious fellow, who would relate to the
ladies many a merry tale, at which they were only offended
when they had heard them ; since, to judge them, things must
be heard.

"My reverend father," said the king, "behold the twi-
light hour, in which ears feminine may be regaled with
certain pleasant stories, for the ladies can laugh without
blushing, or blush without laughing, as it suits them best.
Give us a good story—a regular monk's story. I shall listen
to it, i' faith, with pleasure, because I want to be amused,
and so do the ladies."

"We only submit to this, in order to please your lordship," said the queen; "because our good friend the abbot
goes a little too far."

"Then," replied the king, turning towards the monk,
"read us some Christian admonition, holy father, to amuse
madame."

"Sire, my sight is weak, and the day is closing."

"Give us a story, then, that stops at the girdle."

"Ah, sire !" said the monk, smiling, "the one I am thinking of stops there ; but it commences at the feet."

The lords present made such gallant remonstrances and
supplications to the queen and her ladies, that, like the good
Bretonne that she was, she gave the monk a gentle smile,
and said—

"As you will, my father; but you must answer to God for our sins."

"Willingly, madame; if it be your pleasure to take mine, you will be a gainer."

Every one laughed, and so did the queen. The king went and sat by his dear wife, well beloved by him, as every one knows. The courtiers received permission to be seated— the old courtiers, of course, understood; for the young ones stood, by the ladies' permission, beside their chairs, to laugh at the same time as they did. Then the Abbot of Turpenay gracefully delivered himself of the following tale, the risky passages of which he gave in a low, soft, and flute-like voice:—

About a hundred years ago at the least, there occurred great quarrels in Christendom because there were two popes at Rome, each one pretending to be legitimately elected, which caused great annoyance to the monasteries, abbeys, and bishoprics, since, in order to be recognised by as many as possible, each of these two popes granted titles and rights to his adherents, the which made double owners every- where. Under these circumstances, the monasteries and abbeys that were at war with their neighbours would not recognise both the popes, and found themselves much em- barrassed by the others, who always gave the verdict to the enemies of the Chapter. This wicked schism brought about considerable mischief, and proved abundantly that no error is worse in Christianity than the adultery of the Church. Now at this time, when the devil was making havoc among our possessions, the most illustrious abbey of Turpenay, of which I am at present the unworthy ruler, had a heavy trial on concerning the settlement of certain rights with the redoubtable Sire de Candé, an idolatrous infidel, a re-

lapsed heretic, and most wicked lord. This devil, sent upon
earth in the shape of a nobleman, was, to tell the truth, a
good soldier, well received at Court, and a friend of the
Sieur Bureau de la Rivière, who was a person to whom
the king was exceedingly partial—King Charles the Fifth,
of glorious memory. Beneath the shelter of the favour of
this Sieur de la Rivière, the Lord of Candé did exactly as
he pleased in the valley of the Indre, where he used to be
master of everything, from Montbazon to Ussé. You may
be sure that his neighbours were terribly afraid of him,
and to save their skulls let him have his way. They would,
however, have preferred him under the ground to above it,
and heartily wished him bad luck; but he troubled himself little about that. In the whole valley the noble abbey
alone showed fight to this demon, for it has always been a
doctrine of the Church to take into her lap the weak and
suffering, and use every effort to protect the oppressed,
especially those whose rights and privileges are menaced.
For this reason this rough warrior hated monks exceedingly, especially those of Turpenay, who would not allow
themselves to be robbed of their rights either by force or
stratagem. He was well pleased at the ecclesiastical schism,
and waited the decision of our abbey, concerning which
pope they should choose, to pillage them, being quite
ready to recognise the one to whom the Abbot of Turpenay
should refuse his obedience. Since his return to his castle,
it was his custom to torment and annoy the priests whom
he encountered upon his domains in such a manner, that a
poor monk, surprised by him on his private road, which
was by the water-side, perceived no other method of safety
than to throw himself into the river, where, by a special
miracle of the Almighty, whom the good man fervently
invoked, his gown floated him on the Indre, and he made

his way comfortably to the other side, which he attained in full view of the Lord of Candé, who was not ashamed to enjoy the terrors of a servant of God. Now you see of what stuff this horrid man was made. The abbot, to whom, at that time, the care of our glorious abbey was committed, led a most holy life, and prayed to God with devotion; but he would have saved his own soul ten times, of such good quality was his religion, before finding a chance to save the abbey itself from the clutches of this wretch. Although he was very perplexed, and saw the evil hour at hand, he relied upon God for succour, saying that he would never allow the property of his Church to be touched, and that He who had raised up the Prince Judith for the Hebrews, and Queen Lucretia for the Romans, would keep his most illustrious abbey of Turpenay, and indulged in other equally sapient remarks. But his monks, who—to our shame I confess it—were unbelievers, reproached him with his happy-go-lucky way of looking at things, and declared that, to bring the chariot of Providence to the rescue in time, all the oxen in the province would have to be yoked to it; that the trumpets of Jericho were no longer made in any portion of the world; that God was disgusted with His creation, and would have nothing more to do with it; in short, a thousand and one things that were doubts and contumelies against God. At this desperate juncture there rose up a monk named Amador. This name had been given him by way of a joke, since his person offered a perfect portrait of the false god Ægipan. He was like him, strong in the stomach; like him, had crooked legs; arms hairy as those of a saddler, a back made to carry a wallet, a face as red as the phiz of a drunkard, glistening eyes, a tangled beard, was hairy faced, and so puffed out with fat and meat that you would have fancied him in an interesting condi-

tion. You may be sure that he sung his matins on the steps
of the wine-cellar, and said his vespers in the vineyards of
the Lord. He was as fond of his bed as a beggar with sores,
and would go about the valley fuddling, faddling, blessing
the bridals, plucking the grapes, and giving them to the
girls to taste, in spite of the prohibition of the abbot. In
fact, he was a pilferer, a loiterer, and a bad soldier of the
ecclesiastical militia, of whom nobody in the abbey took
any notice, but let him do as he liked from motives of Christian charity, thinking him mad. Amador, knowing that it
was a question of the ruin of the abbey, in which he was as
snug as a bug in a rug, put up his bristles, took notice of
this and of that, went into each of the cells, listened in the
refectory, shivered in his shoes, and declared that he would
attempt to save the abbey. He took cognisance of the con-
tested points, received from the abbot permission to post-
pone the case, and was promised by the whole Chapter the
vacant office of sub-prior if he succeeded in putting an end
to the litigation. Then he set off across the country, heed-
less of the cruelty and ill-treatment of the Sieur de Candé,
saying that he had that within his gown which would subdue him. He went his way with nothing but this said gown
for his viaticum; but then in it was enough fat to feed a
dwarf. He selected to go to the château, a day when it
rained hard enough to fill the tubs of all the housewives,
and arrived without meeting a soul, in sight of Candé, and
looking like a drowned dog, stepped bravely into the courtyard, and took shelter under a stye-roof to wait until the
fury of the elements had calmed down, and placed himself
boldly in front of the room where the owner of the château
should be. A servant perceiving him while laying the supper, took pity on him, and told him to make himself scarce,
otherwise his master would give him a horsewhipping, just

to open the conversation, and asked him what made him so bold as to enter a house where monks were hated more than a red leper.

"Ah!" said Amador, "I am on my way to Tours, sent thither by my lord abbot. If the Lord of Candé were not so bitter against the poor servants of God, I should not be kept during such a deluge in the courtyard, but in the house. I hope that he will find mercy in his hour of need."

The servant reported these words to his master, who at first wished to have the monk thrown into the big trough of the castle among the other filth. But the lady of Candé, who had great authority over her spouse, and was respected by him, because through her he expected a large inheritance, and because she was a little tyrannical, reprimanded him, saying, that it was possible this monk was a Christian; that in such weather thieves would succour an officer of justice; that, besides, it was necessary to treat him well to find out to what decision the brethren of Turpenay had come with regard to the schism business, and that her advice was to put an end by kindness and not by force to the difficulties arisen between the abbey and the domain of Candé, because no lord since the coming of Christ had ever been stronger than the Church, and that sooner or later the abbey would ruin the castle; finally, she gave utterance to a thousand wise arguments, such as ladies use in the height of the storms of life, when they have had about enough of them. Amador's face was so piteous, his appearance so wretched and so open to banter, that the lord, saddened by the weather, conceived the idea of enjoying a joke at his expense, tormenting him, playing tricks on him, and of giving him a lively recollection of his reception at the château. Then this gentleman, who had secret relations with his wife's maid, sent this girl, who was called Perrotte, to put an end to his ill-will towards the luckless Amador. As soon as the plot had been arranged between them, the wench, who hated monks, in order to please her master, went to the monk, who was standing under the pigstye, and assuming a courteous demeanor in order the better to please him, said—

"Holy father, the master of this house is ashamed to see a servant of God out in the rain when there is room for him in doors, a good fire in the chimney, and a table spread. I invite you in his name and that of the lady of the house to step in."

"I thank the lady and the lord, not for their hospitality, which is a Christian thing, but for having sent an ambassador to me, a poor sinner, an angel of such delicate beauty that I fancy I see the Virgin over our altar."

Saying which, Amador raised his nose in the air, and saluted with the two flakes of fire that sparkled in his bright eyes the pretty maidservant, who thought him neither so ugly nor so foul, nor so bestial; when, following Perrotte up the steps, Amador received on the nose, cheeks, and other portions of his face a slash of the whip, which made him see all the lights of the *Magnificat,* so well was the dose administered by the Sieur de Candé, who, busy chastening his greyhounds, pretended not to see the monk. He requested Amador to pardon him this accident, and ran after the dogs who had caused the mischief to his guest. The laughing servant, who knew what was coming, had dexterously kept out of the way. Noticing this business, Amador suspected the relations of Perrotte and the chevalier, concerning whom it is possible that the lasses of the valley had already whispered something into his ear. Of the people who were then in the room not one made room for the man of God, who remained right in the draught between

the door and the window, where he stood freezing until
the moment when the Sire de Candé, his wife, and his aged
sister, Mademoiselle de Candé, who had the charge of the
young heiress of the house, aged about sixteen years, came
and sat in their chairs at the head of the table, far from the
common people, according to the old custom usual among
the lords of the period, much to their discredit. The Sire
de Candé, paying no attention to the monk, let him sit at
the extreme end of the table, in a corner, where two mischievous lads had orders to squeeze and elbow him. Indeed,
these fellows worried his feet, his body, and his arms like
real torturers, poured white wine into his goblet for water,
in order to fuddle him, and the better to amuse themselves
with him; but they made him drink seven large jugfuls
without making him belch, break wind, sweat, or snort,
which horrified them exceedingly, especially as his eye remained as clear as crystal. Encouraged, however, by a
glance from their lord, they still kept on throwing, while
bowing to him, gravy into his beard, and wiping it dry in
a manner to tear every hair of it out. The varlet who served
a caudle baptized his head with it, and took care to let the
burning liquor trickle down poor Amador's backbone. All
this agony he endured with meekness, because the Spirit
of God was in him, and also the hope of finishing the litigation by holding out in the castle. Nevertheless, the mischievous lot burst into such roars of laughter at the warm
baptism given by the cook's lad to the soaked monk, even
the butler making jokes at his expense, that the lady of
Candé was compelled to notice what was going on at the
end of the table. Then she perceived Amador, who had a
look of sublime resignation upon his face, and was endeavouring to get something out of the big beef bones that had
been put upon his pewter platter. At this moment the poor

monk, who had administered a dexterous blow of the knife
to a big ugly bone, took it in his hairy hands, snapped it in
two, sucked the warm marrow out of it, and found it good.
"Truly," said she to herself, "God has put great strength
into this monk!" At the same time she seriously forbade
the pages, servants, and others to torment the poor man, to
whom out of mockery they had just given some rotten
apples and maggoty nuts. He, perceiving that the old lady
and her charge, the lady and the servants had seen him
manœuvring the bone, pushed back his sleeve, showed the
powerful muscles of his arm, placed the nuts near his wrist
on the bifurcation of the veins, and crushed them one by one
by pressing them with the palm of his hand so vigorously
that they appeared like ripe medlars. He also crunched
them between his teeth, white as the teeth of a dog, husk,
shell, fruit, and all, of which he made in a second a mash
which he swallowed like honey. He crushed them between
two fingers, which he used like scissors to cut them in two
without a moment's hesitation. You may be sure that the
women were silent, that the men believed the devil to be in
the monk; and had it not been for his wife and the darkness
of the night, the Sieur de Candé, having the fear of God
before his eyes, would have kicked him out of the house.
Every one declared that the monk was a man capable of
throwing the castle into the moat. Therefore, as soon as
every one had wiped his mouth, my lord took care to im-
prison this devil, whose strength was terrible to behold, and
had him conducted to a wretched little closet where Perrotte had arranged matters, in order to annoy him during
the night. The tom-cats of the neighbourhood had been requested to come to confess to him, invited to tell him their
sins in embryo towards the tabbies who attracted their affections, and also the little pigs, for whom fine lumps of

tripe had been placed under the bed in order to prevent them becoming monks, of which they were very desirous, by disgusting them with the style of *libera,* which the monk would sing to them. At every movement of poor Amador, who would find short horsehair in the sheets, he would bring down cold water on to the bed, and a thousand other tricks were arranged, such as are usually practised in castles. Every one went to bed in expectation of the nocturnal revels of the monk, certain that they would not be disappointed, since he had been lodged under the tiles at the top of a little tower, the guard of the door of which was committed to dogs who howled for a bit of him. In order to ascertain in what language the conversation with the cats and pigs would be carried on, the Sire came to stay with his dear Perrotte, who slept in the next room. As soon as he found himself thus treated, Amador drew from his bag a knife, and dexterously extricated himself. Then he began to listen in order to find out the ways of the place, and heard the master of the house laughing with his maidservant. Suspecting their manœuvres, he waited till the moment when the lady of the house should be alone in bed, and made his way into her room with bare feet, in order that his sandals should not be in his secrets. He appeared to her by the light of the lamp in the manner in which monks generally appear during the night—that is, in a marvellous state, which the laity find it difficult long to sustain; and the thing is an effect of the frock, which magnifies everything. Then having let her see that he was all a monk, he made the following little speech :—

"Know, madame, that I am sent by Jesus and the Virgin Mary to warn you to put an end to the improper perversities which are taking place—to the injury of your virtue, which is treacherously deprived of your husband's best attention,

which he lavishes upon your maid. What is the use of being a lady if the seigneurial dues are received elsewhere? According to this, your servant is the lady and you are the servant. Are not all the joys bestowed upon her due to you? You will find them all amassed in our Holy Church, which is the consolation of the afflicted. Behold in me the messenger, ready to pay these debts if you do not renounce them."

Saying this, the good monk gently loosened his girdle in which he was incommoded, so much did he appear affected by the sight of those beauties which the Sieur de Candé disdained.

"If you speak truly, my father, I will submit to your guidance," said she, springing lightly out of the bed. "You are, for sure, a messenger of God, because you have seen in a single day that which I have not noticed here for a long time."

Then she went, accompanied by Amador, whose holy robe she did not fail to run her hand over, and was so struck when she found it real, that she hoped to find her husband guilty; and indeed she heard him talking about the monk in her servant's bed. Perceiving this felony, she went into a furious rage, and opened her mouth to resolve it into words —which is the usual method of women—and wished to kick up the devil's delight before handing the girl over to justice. But Amador told her that it would be more sensible to avenge herself first, and cry out afterwards.

"Avenge me quickly, then, my father," said she, "that I may begin to cry out."

Thereupon the monk avenged her most monastically with a good and ample vengeance, that she indulged in as a drunkard who puts his lips to the bunghole of a barrel; for when a lady avenges herself, she should get drunk with

vengeance, or not taste it at all. And the chatelaine was re-
venged to that degree that she could not move; since nothing agitates, takes away the breath, and exhausts, like anger
and vengeance. But although she was avenged, and doubly
and trebly avenged, yet would she not forgive, in order that
she might reserve the right of avenging herself with the
monk, now here, now there. Perceiving this love for vengeance, Amador promised to aid her in it as long as her ire
lasted, for he informed her that he knew, in his quality of a
monk, constrained to meditate long on the nature of things,
an infinite number of modes, methods, and manners of
practising revenge. Then he pointed out to her canonically
what a Christian thing it is to revenge oneself, because all
through the Holy Scriptures God declares himself, above
all things, to be a God of vengeance; and, moreover, demon-
strates to us, by His establishment in the infernal regions,
how royally divine a thing vengeance is, since His vengeance is eternal. From which it followed, that women and
monks ought to revenge themselves, under pain of not being Christians and faithful servants of celestial doctrines.
This dogma pleased the lady much, and she confessed
that she had never understood the commandments of the
Church, and invited her well-beloved monk to enlighten
her thoroughly concerning them. Then the chatelaine,
whose vital spirits had been excited by the vengeance which
had refreshed them, went into the room where the jade was
amusing herself, and by chance found her with her hand
where she, the chatelaine, often had her eye—like the merchants have on their most precious articles, in order to see
that they are not stolen. They were—according to President
Lizet, when he was in a merry mood—a couple taken in
flagrant delectation, and looked dumfounded, sheepish, and
foolish. The sight that met her eyes displeased the lady be-

yond the power of words to express, as it appeared by her
discourse, of which the roughness was similar to that of
the water of her big pond when the sluice-gates were
opened. It was a sermon in three heads, accompanied with
music of a high gamut, varied in the tones, with many
sharps among the keys.

"Out upon virtue! my lord; I've had my share of it. You
have shown me that religion in conjugal faith is an abuse;
this is then the reason that I have no son. How many children have you consigned to this common oven, this poor-
box, this bottomless alms-purse, this leper's porringer, the
true cemetery of the house of Candé? I will know if I am
childless from a constitutional defect, or through your fault.
I will have handsome cavaliers, in order that I may have an
heir. You can get the bastards, I the legitimate children."

"My dear," said the bewildered lord, "don't shout so."

"But," replied the lady, "I will shout, and shout to make
myself heard, heard by the archbishop, heard by the legate,
by the king, by my brothers, who will avenge this infamy
for me."

"Do not dishonour your husband!"

"This is a dishonour, then? You are right; but, my lord,
it is not brought about by you, but by this hussy, whom I
will have sewn up in a sack and thrown into the Indre; thus
your dishonour will be washed away. Hi, there!" she called
out.

"Silence, madame!" said the sire, as shamefaced as a
blind man's dog; because this great warrior, so ready to kill
others, was like a child in the hands of his wife, a state of
affairs to which soldiers are accustomed, because in them
lies the strength and is found all the dull carnality of matter; while, on the contrary, in woman is a subtle spirit and
a scintillation of perfumed flame that lights up paradise

and dazzles the male. This is the reason that certain women govern their husbands, because mind is the master of matter.

(At this the ladies began to laugh, as did also the king.)

"I will not be silent," said the lady of Candé (said the abbot, continuing his tale) ; "I have been too grossly outraged. This, then, is the reward of the wealth I brought you, and of my virtuous conduct! Did I ever refuse to obey you even during Lent, and on fast days? Am I so cold as to freeze the sun? Do you think that I embrace by force, from duty, or pure kindness of heart? Am I too hallowed for you to touch? Am I a holy shrine? Was there need of a papal brief to kiss me? God's truth! have you had so much of me that you are tired? Am I not to your taste? Do charming wenches know more than ladies? Ha! perhaps it is so, since she has let you work in the field without sowing. Teach me the business; I will practise it with those whom I take into my service, for it is settled that I am free. That is as we should be. Your society was wearisome, and the little pleasure I derived from it cost me too dear. Thank God! I am quit of you and your whims, because I intend to retire to a monastery." . . . She meant to say a convent, but this avenging monk had perverted her tongue.

"And I shall be more comfortable in this monastery with my daughter, than in this place of abominable wickedness. You can inherit from your wench. Ha! ha! the fine lady of Candé! Look at her!"

"What is the matter?" said Amador, appearing suddenly upon the scene.

"The matter is, my father," replied she, "that my wrongs cry aloud for vengeance. To begin with, I shall have this trollop thrown into the river, sewn up in a sack, for having diverted the seed of the house of Candé from its proper

channel. It will be saving the hangman a job. For the rest
I will——"

"Abandon your anger, my daughter," said the monk. "It
is commanded us by the Church to forgive those who tres-
pass against us, if we would find favour in the sight of
Heaven, because you pardon those who also pardon others.
God avenges Himself eternally on those who have avenged
themselves, but keeps in His paradise those who have pardoned. From that comes the jubilee, which is a day of great
rejoicing, because all debts and offences are forgiven. Thus
is it a source of happiness to pardon. Pardon! pardon! to
pardon is a most holy work. Pardon Monseigneur de Candé,
who will bless you for your gracious clemency, and will
henceforward love you much. This forgiveness will restore
to you the flowers of youth; and believe, my dear sweet
young lady, that forgiveness is in certain cases the best
means of vengeance. Pardon your maid-servant, who will
pray heaven for you. Thus God, supplicated by all,
will have you in His keeping, and will bless you with male
lineage for this pardon."

Thus saying, the monk took the hand of the sire, placed
it in that of the lady, and added—

"Go and talk over the pardon."

And then he whispered into the husband's ears this sage
advice—

"My lord, use your best argument, and you will silence
her with it, because a woman's mouth is only full of words
when she is empty elsewhere. Argue continually and thus
you will always have the upper hand of your wife."

"By the body of Jupiter! there's good in this monk after
all," said the seigneur, as he went out.

As soon as Amador found himself alone with Perrotte
he spoke to her as follows—

"You are to blame, my dear, for having wished to torment a poor servant of God; therefore are you now the object of celestial wrath, which will fall upon you. To whatever place you fly it will always follow you, will seize upon you in every limb, even after your death, and will cook you like a pasty in the oven of hell, where you will simmer eternally, and every day you will receive seven hundred thousand million lashes of the whip, for the one I received through you."

"Ah, holy father," said the wench, casting herself at the monk's feet, "you alone can save me, for in your gown I should be sheltered from the anger of God."

Saying this, she raised the robe to place herself beneath it, and exclaimed—

"By my faith! monks are better than knights."

"By the sulphur of the devil! you are not acquainted with monks?"

"No," said Perrotte.

"And you don't know the service that monks sing without saying a word?"

"No."

Thereupon the monk went through this said service for her, as it is sung on great feast days, with all the grand effects used in monasteries, the psalms well chanted in F. major, the flaming tapers, and the choristers, and explained to her the *Introit,* and also the *Ite missa est,* and departed, leaving her so sanctified that the wrath of heaven would have great difficulty in discovering any portion of the girl that was not thoroughly monasticated. By his orders, Perrotte conducted him to Mademoiselle de Candé, the lord's sister, to whom he went in order to learn if it was her desire to confess to him, because monks came so rarely to the castle. The lady was delighted, as would any good Christian

have been, at such a chance of clearing out her conscience.
Amador requested her to show him her conscience, and
she having allowed him to see that which he considered the
conscience of old maids, he found it in a bad state, and
told her that the sins of women were accomplished there;
that to be for the future without sin it was necessary to
have the conscience corked up by a monk's indulgence.
The poor ignorant lady having replied that she did not know
where these indulgences were to be had, the monk informed
her that he had a relic with him which enabled him to grant
one, that nothing was more indulgent than this relic, because without saying a word it produced infinite pleasures,
which is the true, eternal and primary character of an indulgence. The poor lady was so pleased with this relic, the
virtue of which she tried in various ways, that her brain
became muddled, and she had so much faith in it that she
indulged as devoutly in indulgences as the Lady of Candé
had indulged in vengeances. This business of confession
woke up the younger Demoiselle de Candé, who came to
watch the proceedings. You may imagine that the monk had
hoped for this occurrence, since his mouth watered at the
sight of this fair blossom, whom he also confessed, because
the elder lady could not hinder him from bestowing upon the
younger one, who wished it, what remained of the indulgences. But, remember, this pleasure was due to him for
the trouble he had taken. The morning having dawned, the
pigs having eaten their tripe, and the cats having become
disenchanted with love, and having watered all the places
rubbed with herbs, Amador went to rest himself in his bed,
which Perrotte had put straight again. Every one slept,
thanks to the monk, so long that no one in the castle was up
before noon, which was the dinner hour. The servants all
believed the monk to be a devil who had carried off the cats,

the pigs, and also their masters. In spite of these ideas, however, every one was in the room at meal time.

"Come, my father," said the chatelaine, giving her arm to the monk, whom she put at her side in the baron's chair, to the great astonishment of the attendants, because the Sire de Candé said not a word. "Page, give some of this to Father Amador," said madame.

"Father Amador has need of so and so," said the Demoiselle de Candé.

"Fill up Father Amador's goblet," said the sire.

"Father Amador has no bread," said the little lady.

"What do you require, Father Amador?" said Perrotte.

It was Father Amador here, Father Amador there. He was regaled like a little maiden on her wedding night.

"Eat, father," said madame; "you made such a bad meal yesterday."

"Drink, father," said the sire. "You are, s'blood! the finest monk I ever set eyes on."

"Father Amador is a handsome monk," said Perrotte.

"An indulgent monk," said the demoiselle.

"A beneficent monk," said the little one.

"A great monk," said the lady.

"A monk who well deserves his name," said the clerk of the castle.

Amador munched and chewed, tried all the dishes, lapped up the hypocras, licked his chaps, sneezed, blew himself out, strutted and stamped about like a bull in a field. The others regarded him with great fear, believing him to be a magician. Dinner over, the Lady of Candé, the demoiselle, and the little one, besought the Sire de Candé with a thousand fine arguments, to terminate the litigation. A great deal was said to him by madame, who pointed out to him how useful a monk was in a castle; by mademoiselle, who

wished for the future to polish up her conscience every day;
by the little one, who pulled her father's beard, and asked
that this monk might always be at Candé. If ever the difference were arranged, it would be by the monk: the monk
was of a good understanding, gentle and virtuous as a
saint; it was a misfortune to be at enmity with a monastery
containing such monks. If all the monks were like him, the
abbey would always have everywhere the advantage of the
castle, and would ruin it, because this monk was very
strong. Finally, they gave utterance to a thousand reasons,
which were like a deluge of words, and were so pluvially
showered down that the sire yielded, saying, that there
would never be a moment's peace in the house until matters
were settled to the satisfaction of the women. Then he sent
for the clerk, who wrote down for him, and also for the
monk. Then Amador surprised them exceedingly by showing them the charters and letters of credit, which would
prevent the sire and his clerk delaying this agreement.
When the Lady of Candé saw them about to put an end to
this old case, she went to the linen chest to get some fine
cloth to make a new gown for her dear Amador. Every one
in the house had noticed how his old gown was worn, and it
would have been a great shame to leave such a treasure in
such a worn-out case. Every one was eager to work at the
gown. Madame cut it, the servant put the hood on, the
demoiselle sewed it, and the little demoiselle worked at the
sleeves. And all set so heartily to work to adorn the monk,
that the robe was ready by supper time, as was also the
charter of agreement prepared and sealed by the Sire de
Candé.

"Ah, my father!" said the lady, "if you love us, you will
refresh yourself after your merry labour by washing yourself in a bath that I have had heated by Perrotte."

Amador was then bathed in scented water. When he came out he found a new robe of fine linen and lovely sandals ready for him, which made him appear the most glorious monk in the world.

Meanwhile, the monks of Turpenay, fearing for Amador, had ordered two of their number to spy about the castle. These spies came round by the moat, just as Perrotte threw Amador's greasy old gown, with other rubbish into it. Seeing which, they thought that it was all over with the poor madman. They therefore returned, and announced that it was certain Amador had suffered martyrdom in the service of the abbey. Hearing which, the abbot ordered· them to assemble in the chapel and pray to God, in order to assist this devoted servant in his torments. The monk having supped, put his charter into his girdle, and wished to return to Turpenay. Then he found at the foot of the steps madame's mare, bridled and saddled, and held ready for him by a groom. The lord had ordered his men-at-arms to accompany the good monk, so that no accident might befall him. Seeing which, Amador pardoned the tricks of the night before, and bestowed his benediction upon every one before taking his departure from this converted place. Madame followed him with her eyes, and proclaimed him a splendid rider. Perrotte declared that for a monk he held himself more upright in the saddle than any of the men-at-arms. Mademoiselle de Candé sighed. The little one wished to have him for her confessor.

"He has sanctified the castle," said they, when they were in the room again.

When Amador and his suite came to the gates of the abbey a scene of terror ensued, since the guardian thought that the Sire de Candé had had his appetite for monks whetted by the blood of poor Amador, and wished to sack the abbey. But Amador shouted with his fine bass voice, and was recognised and admitted into the courtyard; and when he dismounted from madame's mare there was uproar enough to make the monks as wild as April moons. They gave vent to shouts of joy in the refectory, and all came to congratulate Amador, who waved the charter over his head. The men-at-arms were regaled with the best wine in the cellars, which was a present made to the monks of Turpenay by those of Marmoutier, to whom belonged the lands at Vouvray. The good abbot having had the document of the Sire de Candé read, went about saying—

"On these divine occasions there always appears the finger of God, to whom we should render thanks."

As the good abbot kept on at this finger of God, when thanking Amador, the monk, annoyed to see the instrument of their delivery thus diminished, said to him—

"Well, say that it was the arm, my father, and drop the subject."

The termination of this trial between the Sieur de Candé and the abbey of Turpenay was followed by a blessing which rendered him devoted to the Church, because nine months after he had a son. Two years afterwards Amador was chosen as abbot by the monks, who reckoned upon a merry government with a madcap. But Amador became an abbot, became steady and austere, because he had conquered his evil desires by his labours, and recast his nature at the female forge, in which is that fire which is the most perfecting, persevering, persistent, perdurable, permanent, perennial, and permeating fire that there ever was in the world. It is a fire to ruin everything, and it ruined so well the evil that was in Amador, that it left only that which it could not eat—that is, his wit, which was as clear as a diamond, which is, as every one knows, a residue of the great fire by which our globe was formerly carbonized. Amador was then the instrument chosen by Providence to reform our illustrious abbey, since he put everything right there, watched night and day over his monks, made them all rise at the hours appointed for prayers, counted them in chapel as a shepherd counts his sheep, kept them well in hand, and punished their faults so severely, that he made them most virtuous brethren.

This teaches us to look upon womankind more as the instruments of our salvation than of our pleasure. Besides which, this narrative teaches us that we should never attempt to struggle with the Churchmen.

The king and the queen found this tale in the best taste; the courtiers confessed that they had never heard a better; and the ladies would all willingly have been the heroines of it.

BERTHA THE PENITENT

I

HOW BERTHA REMAINED A MAIDEN IN THE MARRIED STATE

ABOUT the time of the first flight of the Dauphin, which threw our good sire, Charles the Victorious, into a state of great dejection, there happened a great misfortune to a noble house of Touraine, since extinct in every branch; and it is owing to this fact that this most deplorable history may now safely be brought to light. To aid him in this work the author calls to his assistance the holy confessors, martyrs, and other celestial dominations, who, by the commandments of God, were the promoters of good in this affair.

From some defect in his character, the Sire Imbert de Bastarnay, one of the most landed lords in our land of Touraine, had no confidence in the mind of the female of man, whom he considered much too animated, on account of her numerous vagaries, and it may be he was right. In consequence of this idea he reached his old age without a companion, which was certainly not to his advantage. Always leading a solitary life, this said man had no idea of making himself agreeable to others, having only been mixed up with wars and the orgies of bachelors, with whom he did not put himself out of the way. Thus he remained stale in his garments, sweating in his accoutrements, with dirty hands and an apish face. In short, he looked the ugliest man in Christendom. As far as regards his person only though, since so far as his heart, his head, and other secret places were concerned, he had properties which rendered him most praiseworthy. An angel (pray believe this) would have walked a long way without meeting an old warrior firmer at his post, a lord with a more spotless scutcheon, of shorter speech, and more perfect loyalty.

Certain people have stated, they have heard that he gave sound advice, and was a good and profitable man to consult. Was it not a strange freak on the part of God, who plays sometimes jokes on us, to have granted so many perfections to a man so badly apparelled? When he was sixty in appearance, though only fifty in years, he determined to take unto himself a wife, in order to obtain lineage. Then, while foraging about for a place where he might be able to find a lady to his liking, he heard much vaunted, the great merits and perfections of a daughter of the illustrious house of Rohan, which at that time had some property in the province. The young lady in question was called Bertha, that being her pet name. Imbert having been to see her at the castle of Montbazon, was, in consequence of the prettiness and innocent virtue of this said Bertha de Rohan, seized with so great a desire to possess her, that he determined to make her his wife, believing that never could a girl of such lofty descent fail in her duty. This marriage was soon celebrated, because the Sire de Rohan had seven daughters, and hardly knew how to provide for them all, at a time when people were just recovering from the late wars, and patching up their unsettled affairs. Now the good man Bastarnay happily found Bertha really a maiden, which fact bore witness to her proper bringing up and perfect maternal correction. So immediately the night arrived when it should be lawful for him to embrace her, he got her with child so roughly that he had proof of the result two months after marriage, which rendered the Sire Imbert joyful to a degree. In order that we may here finish with this portion of the story let us at once state that from this legitimate grain was born the Sire de Bastarnay, who was duke by the grace of Louis the Eleventh, his chamberlain, and, more than that, his ambassador in the countries of Europe, and well-beloved of this most redoubtable lord, to whom he was never faithless. His loyalty was an heritage from his father, who from his early youth was much attached to the Dauphin, whose fortunes he followed, even in the rebellions, since he was a man to put Christ on the cross again if he had been required by him to do so, which is the flower of friendship rarely to be found encompassing princes and great people. At first, the fair lady of Bastarnay comported herself so loyally that her society caused those thick vapours and black clouds to vanish, which obscured in the mind of this great man, the brightness of the feminine glory. Now, according to the custom of unbelievers, he passed from suspicion to confidence so thoroughly, that he yielded up the government of his house to the said Bertha, made her mistress of his deeds and actions, queen of his honour, guardian of his grey hairs, and would have slaughtered without a contest any one who had said an evil word concerning this mirror of virtue, on whom no breath had fallen save the breath issued from his conjugal and marital lips, cold and withered as they were. To speak truly on all points, it should be explained, that to this virtuous behaviour considerably aided the little boy, who, during six years occupied day and night the attention of his pretty mother, who first nourished him with her milk, and made of him a lover's lieutenant, yielding to him her sweet breasts, which he gnawed at, hungry, as often he would, and was, like a lover, always there. This good mother knew no other pleasures than those of his rosy lips, had no other caresses than those of his tiny little hands, which ran about her like the feet of playful mice, read in no other book than his clear baby eyes, in which the blue sky was reflected, and listened to no other music than his cries, which sounded in her ears as angels' whispers. You may be sure that she was always fondling him, had a desire to kiss him at dawn of day, kissed him in the evening, would rise in the night to eat him up with kisses, made herself a child as he a child, educated him in the perfect religion of maternity; finally, behaved as the best and happiest mother that ever lived, without disparagement to our lady the Virgin, who could have had little trouble in bringing up our Saviour, since he was God. This employment and the little taste which Bertha had for the blisses of matrimony much delighted the old man, since he would have been unable to return the affection of a too amorous wife, and desired to practise economy, to have the wherewithal for a second child. After six years had passed away, the mother was compelled to give her son into the hands of the grooms and other persons to whom Messire de Bastarnay committed the task to mould him properly, in order that his heir should have an heritage of the virtues, qualities, and courage of the house, as well as the domains and the name. Then did Bertha shed many tears, her happiness being gone. For the great heart of this mother it was nothing to have this well-beloved son after others, and during only certain short fleeing hours. Therefore she became sad and melancholy. Noticing her grief, the good man wished to bestow upon her another child and could not, and the poor lady was displeased thereat, because she declared that the making of a child wearied her much and cost her dear. And this is true, or no doctrine is true, and you must burn the Gospels as a

pack of stories if you have not faith in this innocent remark. This, nevertheless, to certain ladies (I do not mention men, since they have a smattering of the science), this
will still seem an untruth. The writer has taken care here
to give the mute reasons of this strange antipathy; I mean
the distaste of Bertha, because I love the ladies above all
things, knowing that for want of the pleasure of love, my
face would grow old and my heart torment me. Did you
ever meet a scribe so complaisant and so fond of the ladies
as I am? No; of course not. Therefore, do I love them devotedly, but not so often as I could wish, since I have
oftener in my hands my goose-quill than I have the barbs
with which one tickles their lips to make them laugh and be
merry in all innocence. I understand them, and in this way.

The good man Bastarnay was not a smart young fellow
of an amorous nature, and acquainted with the pranks of
the thing. He did not trouble himself much about the
fashion in which he killed a soldier so long as he killed him;
he would have killed him in all ways without saying a word,
in battle, of course, understood. This perfect heedlessness
in the matter of death was in accordance with his non-
chalance in the matter of life, the birth and manner of
begetting a child, and the ceremonies thereto appertaining.
The good sire was ignorant of the many litigious, dilatory,
interlocutory, and preparatory exploits and the little hu-
mourings of the little fagots placed in the oven to heat it; of
the sweet perfumed branches gathered little by little in the
forests of love, fondlings, coddlings, huggings, nursing,
the bites at the cherry, the cat-licking, and other little tricks
and traffic of love which ruffians know, which lovers preserve, and which the ladies love better than their salvation,
because there is more of the cat than the woman in them.
This shines forth in perfect evidence in their feminine

ways. If you think it worth while watching them, examine
them attentively while they eat; not one of them (I am
speaking of women, noble and well-educated) puts her
knife in the eatables and thrusts it into her mouth, as do
brutally the males; no, they turn over their food, pick the
pieces that please them as they would grey peas in a dovecot; they suck the sauces by mouthfuls; play with their
knife and spoon as if they only ate in consequence of a
judge's order, so much do they dislike to go straight to the
point, and make free use of variations, finesse, and little
tricks in everything, which is the especial attribute of these
creatures, and the reason that the sons of Adam delight in
them, since they do everything differently from themselves,
and they do well. You think so too. Good! I love you. Now
then, Imbert de Bastarnay, an old soldier, ignorant of the
tricks of love, entered into the sweet garden of Venus as
he would into a place taken by assault, without giving any
heed to the cries of the poor inhabitants in tears, and placed
a child as he would an arrow in the dark. Although the
gentle Bertha was not used to such treatment (poor child,
she was but fifteen), she believed in her virgin faith, that
the happiness of becoming a mother demanded this terrible, dreadful bruising and nasty business; so during this
painful task she would pray to God to assist her, and recite
Aves to our Lady, esteeming her lucky, in only having the
Holy Ghost to endure. By this means, never having experienced anything but pain in marriage, she never troubled
her husband to go through the ceremony again. Now seeing
that the old fellow was scarcely equal to it—as has been
before stated—she lived in perfect solitude, like a nun.
She hated the society of men, and never suspected that the
Author of the world had put so much joy in that from
which she had only received infinite misery. But she loved

all the more her little one, who had cost her so much before
he was born. Do not be astonished, therefore, that she held
aloof from that gallant tourney in which it is the mare who
governs her cavalier, guides him, fatigues him, and abuses
him if he stumbles. This is the true history of certain unhappy unions, according to the statement of the old men
and women, and the certain reason of the follies committed
by certain women, who too late perceive, I know not how,
that they have been deceived, and attempt to crowd into
a day more time than it will hold, to have their proper share
of life. That is philosophical, my friends. Therefore study
well this page, in order that you may wisely look to the
proper government of your wives, your sweethearts, and
all females generally, and particularly those who by chance
may be under your care, from which God preserve you.
Thus a virgin in deed, although a mother, Bertha was in
her one-and-twentieth year a castle flower, the glory of her
good man, and the honour of the province. The said Bastarnay took great pleasure in beholdinig this child come,
go, and frisk about like a willow-switch, as lively as an eel,
as innocent as her little one, and still most sensible and of
sound understanding; so much so that he never undertook
any project without consulting her about it, seeing that if
the minds of these angels have not been disturbed in their
purity, they give a sound answer to everything one asks
of them. At this time Bertha lived near the town of Loches,
in the castle of her lord, and there resided, with no desire
to do anything but look after her household duties, after
the old custom of the good housewives, from which the
ladies of France were led away when Queen Catherine and
the Italians came with their balls and merrymakings. To
these practices Francis the First and his successors, whose
easy ways did as much harm to the State of France as the

goings on of the Protestants, lent their aid. This, however, has nothing to do with my story. About this time the lord and lady of Bastarnay were invited by the king to come to his town of Loches, where for the present he was with his court, in which the beauty of the lady of Bastarnay had made a great noise. Bertha came to Loches, received many kind praises from the king, was the centre of the homage of all the young nobles, who feasted their eyes on this apple of love, and of the old ones, who warmed themselves at this sun. But you may be sure that all of them, old and young, would have suffered death a thousand times over to have at their service this instrument of joy, which dazzled their eyes and muddled their brains. Bertha was more talked about in Loches than either God or the Gospels, which enraged a great many ladies who were not so bountifully endowed with charms, and would have given all that was left of their honour to have sent back to her castle this fair gatherer of smiles. A young lady having early perceived that one of her lovers was smitten with Bertha, took such a hatred to her that from it arose all the misfortunes of the lady of Bastarnay; but also from the same source came her happiness, and her discovery of the gentle land of love, of which she was ignorant. This wicked lady had a relation who had confessed to her, directly he saw Bertha, that to be her lover he would be willing to die after a month's happiness with her. Bear in mind that this cousin was as handsome as a girl is beautiful, had no hair on his chin, would have gained his enemy's forgiveness by asking for it, so melodious was his young voice, and was scarcely twenty years of age.

"Dear cousin," said she to him, "leave the room, and go to your house; I will endeavour to give you this joy. But do not let yourself be seen by her, nor by that old baboon-face, by an error of nature on a Christian's body, and to whom belongs this beauteous fay."

The young gentleman out of the way, the lady came rubbing her treacherous nose against Bertha's, and called her "My friend, my treasure, my star of beauty"; trying in every way to be agreeable to her, to make her vengeance more certain on the poor child who, all unwittingly, had caused her lover's heart to be faithless, which, for women ambitious in love, is the worst of infidelities. After a little conversation, the plotting lady suspected that poor Bertha was a maiden in matters of love, when she saw her eyes full of limpid water, no marks on the temples, no little black speck on the point of her little nose, white as snow, where usually the marks of the amusement are visible, no wrinkle on her brow; in short, no habit of pleasure apparent on her face—clear as the face of an innocent maiden. Then this traitress put certain women's questions to her, and was perfectly assured by the replies of Bertha, that, if she had had the profit of being a mother, the pleasures of love had been denied to her. At this she rejoiced greatly on her cousin's behalf—like the good woman she was. Then she told her, that in the town of Loches there lived a young and noble lady, of the family of Rohan, who at that time had need of the assistance of a lady of position to be reconciled with the Sire Louis de Rohan; that if she had as much goodness as God had given her beauty, she would take her with her to the castle, ascertain for herself the sanctity of her life, and bring about a reconciliation with the Sire de Rohan, who refused to receive her. To this Bertha consented without hesitation, because the misfortunes of this girl were known to her, but not the poor young lady herself, whose name was Sylvia, and whom she had believed to be in a foreign land.

It is here necessary to state why the king had given this invitation to the Sire de Bastarnay. He had a suspicion of the first flight of his son the Dauphin into Burgundy, and wished to deprive him of so good a councillor as was the said Bastarnay. But the veteran, faithful to young Louis, had already, without saying a word, made up his mind. Therefore he took Bertha back to his castle; but before they set out she told him she had taken a companion and introduced her to him. It was the young lord, disguised as a girl, with the assistance of his cousin, who was jealous of Bertha, and annoyed at her virtue. Imbert drew back a little when he learnt that it was Sylvia de Rohan, but was also much affected at the kindness of Bertha, whom he thanked for her attempt to bring a little wandering lamb back to the fold. He made much of his wife, when his last night at home came, left men-at-arms about the castle, and then set out with the Dauphin for Burgundy, having a cruel enemy in his bosom without suspecting it. The face of the young lad was unknown to him, because he was a young page come to see the king's court, and who had been brought up by Cardinal Dunois, in whose service he was a knight-bachelor. The old lord, believing that he was a girl, thought him very modest and timid, because the lad, doubting the language of his eyes, kept them always cast down; and when Bertha kissed him on the mouth, he trembled lest his petticoat might be indiscreet, and would walk away to the window, so fearful was he of being recognised as a man of Bastarnay, and killed before he had made love to the lady. Therefore he was as joyful as any lover would have been in his place, when the portcullis was lowered, and the old lord galloped away across the country. He had been in such suspense that he made a vow to build a pillar at his own expense in the cathedral at Tours, because he had escaped the danger of his mad scheme. He gave, indeed, fifty gold marks to pay God for his delight. But by chance he had to pay for it over again to the devil, as it appears from the following facts if the tale pleases you well enough to induce you to follow the narrative, which will be succinct, as all good speeches should be.

II

HOW BERTHA BEHAVED, KNOWING THE BUSINESS OF LOVE

This bachelor was the young Sire Jehan de Sacchez, cousin of the Sieur de Montmorency, to whom, by the death of the said Jehan, the fiefs of Sacchez and other places would return, according to the deed of tenure. He was twenty years of age, and glowed like a burning coal; therefore you may be sure that he had a hard job to get through the first day. While old Imbert was galloping across the fields, the two cousins perched themselves under the lantern of the portcullis, in order to keep him the longer in view, and waved him signals of farewell. When the clouds of dust raised by the heels of the horses were no longer visible upon the horizon, they came down and went back into the great room of the castle.

"What shall we do, dear cousin?" said Bertha to the false Sylvia. "Do you like music? we will play together. Let us sing the lay of some sweet ancient bard. Eh? what do you say? Come to my organ; come along. As you love me, sing!"

Then she took Jehan by the hand and led him to the keyboard of the organ, at which the young fellow seated himself prettily, after the manner of women. "Ah! sweet coz," cried Bertha, as soon as the first notes tried, the lad turned his head towards her, in order that they might sing together, "ah! sweet coz, you have a wonderful glance in your eye; you move I know not what in my heart."

"Ah, cousin," replied the false Sylvia, "that it is which has been my ruin. A sweet milord of the land across the sea told me so often that I had fine eyes, and kissed them so well, that I yielded, so much pleasure did I feel in letting them be kissed."

"Cousin, does love, then, commence in the eyes?"

"In them is the forge of Cupid's bolts, my dear Bertha," said the lover, casting fire and flame at her.

"Let us go on with our singing."

Then they sang, by Jehan's desire, a lay of Christine de Pisan, every word of which breathed love.

"Ah, cousin, what a deep and powerful voice you have! It seems to pierce me."

"Where?" said the impudent Sylvia.

"There," replied Bertha, touching her little diaphragm, where the sounds of love are understood better than by ears, but the diaphragm lies nearer the heart, and that which is undoubtedly the first brain, the second heart, and the third ear of the ladies. I say this, with all respect and with all honour, for physical reasons and for no others.

"Let us leave off singing," said Bertha; "it has too great an effect upon me. Come to the window; we can do needle-work until the evening."

"Ah, dear cousin of my soul! I don't know how to hold the needle in my fingers, having been accustomed, to my perdition, to do something else with them."

"Eh? what did you do then all day long?"

"Ah, I yielded to the current of love, which makes days seem instants, months seem days, and years months; and if it could last, would gulp down eternity like a strawberry, seeing that it is all youth and fragrance, sweetness and endless joy."

Then the youth dropped his beautiful eyelids over his eyes, and remained as melancholy as a poor lady who has been abandoned by her lover, who weeps for him, wishes to kiss him, and would pardon his perfidy, if he would but seek once again the sweet path to his once-loved fold.

"Cousin, does love blossom in the married state?"

"Oh, no," said Sylvia, "because in the married state everything is duty, but in love everything is done in perfect freedom of heart. This difference communicates an indescribable soft balm to those caresses which are the flowers of love."

"Cousin, let us change the conversation; it affects me more than did the music."

She called hastily to a servant to bring her boy to her, who came, and when Sylvia saw him, she exclaimed—

"Ah, the little dear, he is as beautiful as love!"

Then she kissed him heartily upon the forehead.

"Come, my little one," said the mother, as the child clambered into her lap. "Thou art thy mother's blessing, her unclouded joy, the delight of her every hour, her crown, her jewel, her own pure pearl, her spotless soul, her treasure, her morning and evening star, her only flame, and her heart's darling. Give me thy hands, that I may eat them; give me thine ears, that I may bite them; give me thy head, that I may kiss thy curls. Be happy, sweet flower of my body, that I may be happy too."

"Ah, cousin!" said Sylvia, "you are speaking the language of love to him."

"Love is a child, then?"

"Yes, cousin; therefore the heathen always portrayed him as a little boy."

And with many other remarks fertile in the imagery of love, the two pretty cousins amused themselves until supper-time, playing with the child.

"Would you not like to have another?" whispered Jehan, at an opportune moment, into his cousin's ear, which he touched with his warm lips.

"Ah, Sylvia! for that I would endure a hundred years of purgatory, if it would only please God to give me that joy. But in spite of the work, labour, and industry of my spouse, which causes me much pain, my waist does not vary in size. Alas; it is nothing to have but one child. If I hear the sound of a cry in the castle, my heart beats ready to burst. I fear man and beast alike for this innocent darling; I dread volts, passes, and manual exercises; in fact, I dread everything. I live not in myself, but in him alone. And, alas! I like to endure these miseries, because while I fidget and tremble, it is a sign that my offspring is safe and sound. To be brief—for I am never weary of talking on this subject—I believe that my breath is in him, and not in myself."

With these words she hugged him to her breasts, as only mothers know how to hug children, with a spiritual force that is felt only in their hearts. If you doubt this, watch a cat carrying her kittens in her mouth; not one of them gives a single mew. The youthful gallant who had had certain fears about watering this fair, unfertile plain, was reassured by this speech. He thought then that it would only be following the commandments of God to win this saint to love; and he thought rightly. At night Bertha asked her cousin—according to the old custom, to which the ladies of our day object—to keep her company in her big seigneurial bed. To which request Sylvia replied—in order to keep up the rôle of a well-born maiden—that nothing would give her greater pleasure. The curfew rang, and found the two cousins in a chamber richly ornamented with carpeting, fringes, and royal tapestries, and Bertha began gracefully to disarray herself, assisted by her women. You can imagine that her companion modestly declined their services, and told her cousin, with a little blush, that she was accustomed to undress herself ever since she had lost the services of her dearly beloved, who had put her out of conceit with feminine fingers by his gentle ways; that these preparations brought back the pretty speeches he used to make, and his merry pranks while playing the lady's maid; and that to her injury, the memory of all these things brought the water into her mouth. This discourse considerably astonished the lady Bertha, who let her cousin say her prayers, and make her other preparations for the night beneath the curtains of the bed, into which my lord, inflamed with desire, soon tumbled, happy at being able to catch an occasional glimpse of the wondrous charms of the chatelaine, which were in no way injured. Bertha, believing herself to be with an experienced girl, did not omit any of her usual practices; she washed her feet, not minding whether she raised them little or much, exposed her delicate little shoulders, and did as all the ladies do when they are retiring to rest. At last she came to bed, and settled herself comfortably in it, kissing her cousin on the lips, which she found remarkably warm.

"Are you unwell, Sylvia, that you burn so?" said she.

"I always burn like that when I go to bed," replied her companion, "because at that time there comes back to my memory the pretty little tricks that he invented to please me, and which make me burn still more."

"Ah, cousin, tell me all about this *he*. Tell all the sweets of love to me, who live beneath the shadow of a hoary head, of which the snows keep me from such warm feelings. Tell me all; you are cured. It will be a good warning to me, and then your misfortunes will have been a salutary lesson to two poor weak women."

"I do not know I ought to obey you, sweet cousin," said the youth.

"Tell me why not."

"Ah, deeds are better than words," said the false maiden, heaving a sigh deep as the *ut* of an organ. "But I am afraid that this milord has encumbered me with so much joy that you may get a little of it, which would be enough to give you a daughter, since the power of engendering is weakened in me."

"But," said Bertha, "between us, would it be a sin?"

"It would be, on the contrary, a joy both here and in heaven; the angels would shed their fragrance around you, and make sweet music in your ears."

"Tell me quickly, then," said Bertha.

"Well, then, this is how my dear lord made my heart rejoice."

With these words Jehan took Bertha in his arms, and strained her hungering to his heart, for in the soft light of the lamp, and clothed with the spotless linen, she was in this tempting bed, like the pretty petals of a lily at the bottom of the virgin calyx.

"When he held me as I hold thee he said to me, with a voice far sweeter than mine, 'Ah, Bertha, thou art my eternal love, my priceless treasure, my joy by day and my joy by night; thou art fairer than the day is day; there is naught so pretty as thou art. I love thee more than God, and would endure a thousand deaths for the happiness I ask of thee!' Then he would kiss me, not after the manner of husbands, which is rough, but in a peculiar dove-like fashion."

To show her there and then how much better was the method of lovers, he sucked all the honey from Bertha's lips, and taught her how, with her pretty tongue, small and rosy as that of a cat, she could speak to the heart without saying a single word, and becoming exhausted at this game, Jehan spread the fire of his kisses from the mouth to the neck, from the neck to the sweetest forms that ever a woman gave her child to slake its thirst upon. And whoever had been in his place would have thought himself a wicked man not to imitate him.

"Ah!" said Bertha, fast bound in love without knowing it; "this is better. I must take care to tell Imbert about it."

"Are you in your proper senses, cousin? Say nothing about it to your old husband. How could he make his hands pleasant like mine? They are as hard as washer-woman's beetles, and his piebald beard would hardly please this centre of bliss, that rose in which lies our wealth, our substance, our loves, and our fortune. Do you know that it is a living flower, which should be fondled thus, and not used like a trombone, or as if it were a catapult of war? Now this was the gentle way of my beloved Englishman."

Thus saying, the handsome youth comported himself so bravely in the battle that victory crowned his efforts, and poor innocent Bertha exclaimed—

"Ah! cousin, the angels are come! but so beautiful is their music, that I hear nothing else, and so flaming are their luminous rays, that my eyes are closing."

And, indeed, she fainted under the burden of those joys of love which burst forth in her like the highest notes of the organ, which glistened like the most magnificent aurora, which flowed in her veins like the finest musk, and loosened the liens of her life in giving her a child of love, who made a great deal of confusion in taking up his quarters. Finally, Bertha imagined herself to be in Paradise, so happy did she feel; and woke from this beautiful dream in the arms of Jehan, exclaiming—

"Ah! who would not have been married in England!"

"My sweet mistress," said Jehan, whose ecstasy was sooner over, "you are married to me in France, where things are managed still better, for I am a man who would give a thousand lives for you if he had them."

Poor Bertha gave a shriek so sharp that it pierced the walls, and leaped out of the bed like a mountebank of the plains of Egypt would have done. She fell upon her knees before her Prie-Dieu, joined her hands, and wept more pearls than ever Mary Magdalene wore. "Ah, I am dead!" she cried; "I am deceived by a devil who has taken the face of an angel. I am lost; I am the mother for certain of a beautiful child, without being more guilty than you, Madame the Virgin. Implore the pardon of God for me, if I have not that of men upon earth; or let me die, so that I may not blush before my lord and master."

Hearing that she said nothing against him, Jehan rose, quite aghast to see Bertha take this charming dance for two so to heart. But the moment she heard her Gabriel moving she sprang quickly to her feet, regarded him with a tearful face, and her eyes illumined with a holy anger, which made her more lovely to look upon, exclaimed, "If you advance a single step towards me, I will make one towards death!"

And she took her stiletto in her hand.

So heartrending was the tragic spectacle of her grief that Jehan answered her—

"It is not for thee but for me to die, my dear, beautiful

mistress, more dearly loved than will ever woman be again upon this earth."

"If you had truly loved me you would not have killed me as you have, for I will die sooner than be reproached by my husband."

"Will you die?" said he.

"Assuredly," said she.

"Now, if I am here pierced with a thousand blows, you will have your husband's pardon, to whom you will say that if your innocence was surprised, you have avenged his honour by killing the man who had deceived you; and it will be the greatest happiness that could ever befall me to die for you, the moment you refuse to live for me."

Hearing this tender discourse spoken with tears, Bertha dropped the dagger; Jehan sprang upon it, and thrust it into his breast, saying—"Such happiness can be paid for but with death."

And fell stiff and stark.

Bertha, terrified, called aloud for her maid. The servant came, and terribly alarmed to see a wounded man in Madame's chamber, and Madame holding him up, crying and saying, "What have you done, my love?" because she believed he was dead, and remembered her vanished joys, and thought how beautiful Jehan must be, since every one, even Imbert, believed him to be a girl. In her sorrow she confessed all to her maid, sobbing and crying out, "that it was quite enough to have upon her mind the life of a child without having the death of a man as well." Hearing this the poor lover tried to open his eyes, and only succeeded in showing a little bit of the white of them.

"Ha! Madame, don't cry out," said the servant, "let us keep our senses together and save this pretty knight. I will go and seek La Fallotte, in order not to let any physician or surgeon into this secret, and as she is a sorceress she will, to please Madame, perform the miracle of healing this wound so that not a trace of it shall remain."

"Run!" replied Bertha. "I will love you, and will pay you well for this assistance."

But before anything else was done the lady and her maid agreed to be silent about this adventure, and hide Jehan from every eye. Then the servant went out into the night to seek La Fallotte, and was accompanied by her mistress as far as the postern, because the guard could not raise the portcullis without Bertha's special order. Bertha found on going back that her lover had fainted, for the blood was flowing from the wound. At this sight she drank a little of his blood, thinking that Jehan had shed it for her. Affected by this great love and by the danger, she kissed this pretty varlet of pleasure on the face, bound up his wound, bathing it with her tears, beseeching him not to die, and exclaiming that if he would live she would love him with all her heart. You can imagine that the chatelaine became still more enamoured while observing what a difference there was between a young knight like Jehan, white, downy, and agreeable, and an old fellow like Imbert, bristly, yellow, and wrinkled. This difference brought back to her memory that which she had found in the pleasure of love. Moved by this souvenir, her kisses became so warm that Jehan came back to his senses, his look improved, and he could see Bertha, from whom in a feeble voice he asked forgiveness. But Bertha forbade him to speak until La Fallotte had arrived. Then both of them consumed the time by loving each other with their eyes, since in those of Bertha there was nothing but compassion, and on these occasions pity is akin to love.

La Fallotte was a hunchback, vehemently suspected of

dealings in necromancy, and of riding to nocturnal orgies on a broomstick, according to the custom of witches. Certain persons had seen her putting the harness on her broom in the stable, which, as every one knows, is on the housetops. To tell the truth, she possessed certain medical secrets, and was of such great service to ladies in certain things, and to the nobles, that she lived in perfect tranquillity, without giving up the ghost on a pile of fagots, but on a feather bed, for she made a hatful of money, although the physicians tormented her by declaring that she sold poisons, which was certainly true, as will be shown in the sequel. The servant and La Fallotte came on the same ass, making such haste that they arrived at the castle before the day had fully dawned. The old hunchback exclaimed, as she entered the chamber, "Now, then, my children, what is the matter?" This was her manner, which was familiar with great people, who appeared very small to her. She put on her spectacles, and carefully examined the wound, saying, "This is fine blood, my dear; you have tasted it. That's all right, he has bled externally." Then she washed the wound with a fine sponge, under the nose of the lady and the servant, who held their breath. To be brief, Fallotte gave it as her medical opinion, that the youth would not die from this blow, "although," said she, looking at his hand, "he will come to a violent end through this night's deed." This decree of chiromancy frightened considerably both Bertha and the maid. Fallotte prescribed certain remedies, and promised to come again the following night. Indeed, she tended the wound for a whole fortnight, coming secretly at night-time. The people about the castle were told by the servant that their young lady, Sylvia de Rohan, was in danger of death, through a swelling of the stomach, which must remain a mystery for the honour of Madame, who was her cousin. Each one was satisfied with this story, of which his mouth was so full that he told it to his fellows.

The good people believed that it was the malady which was fraught with danger; but it was not! it was the convalescence, for the stronger Jehan grew, the weaker Bertha became, and so weak that she allowed herself to drift into that Paradise the gates of which Jehan had opened for her. To be brief, she loved him more and more. But in the midst of her happiness, always mingled with apprehension at the menacing words of Fallotte, and tormented by her great religion, she was in great fear of her husband, Imbert, to whom she was compelled to write that he had given her a child, who would be ready to delight him on his return. Poor Bertha avoided her lover, Jehan, during the day on which she wrote the lying letter, over which she soaked her handkerchief with tears. Finding himself avoided (for they had previously left each other no more than fire leaves the wood it has bitten) Jehan believed that she was beginning to hate him, and straightway he cried too. In the evening Bertha, touched by his tears, which had left their mark upon his eyes, although he had well dried them, told him the cause of her sorrow, mingling therewith the confession of her terrors for the future, pointing out to him how much they were both to blame, and discoursing so beautifully to him, gave utterance to such Christian sentences, ornamented with holy tears and contrite prayers, that Jehan was touched to the quick by the sincerity of his mistress. This love innocently united to repentance, this nobility in sin, this mixture of weakness and strength, would, as the old authors say, have changed the nature of a tiger, melting it to pity. You will not be astonished then, that Jehan was compelled to pledge his word as a knight-bachelor, to obey her in whatever she should command him, to save her in this world and in the next. Delighted at this confidence in her, and this goodness of heart, Bertha cast herself at Jehan's feet, and kissing them, exclaimed—

"Oh, my love! whom I am compelled to love, although it is a mortal sin to do so, thou art so good, so gentle to thy poor Bertha, if thou wouldst have her always think of thee with pleasure, and stop the torrent of her tears, whose source is so pretty and so pleasant (here, to show him that it was so, she let him steal a kiss)—Jehan, if thou wouldst that the memory of our celestial joys, angel music, and the fragrance of love should be a consolation to me in my loneliness rather than a torment, do that which the Virgin commanded me to order thee in a dream, in which I was beseeching her to direct me in the present case, for I have asked her to come to me, and she had come. Then I told her the horrible anguish I should endure, trembling for this little one, whose movements I already feel, and for the real father, who would be at the mercy of the other, and might expiate his paternity by a violent death, since it is possible that La Fallotte saw clearly into his future life. Then the beautiful Virgin told me, smiling, that the Church offered its forgiveness for our faults if we followed her commandments; that it was necessary to save one's self from the pains of hell, by reforming before Heaven became angry. Then with her finger she showed me a Jehan like thee, but dressed as thou shouldst be, and as thou wilt be, if thou dost but love thy Bertha with a love eternal."

Jehan assured her of his perfect obedience, and raised her, seating her on his knee, and kissing her. The unhappy Bertha told him then that this garment was a monk's frock, and tremblingly besought him—almost fearing a refusal —to enter the Church, and retire to Marmoutier, beyond Tours, pledging him her word that she would grant him a last night, after which she would be neither for him nor for any one else in the world again. And each year, as a reward for this, she would let him come to her one day, in order that he might see his child. Jehan, bound by his oath, promised to obey his mistress, saying that by this means he would be faithful to her, and would experience no joys of love but those tasted in her divine embrace, and would live upon the dear remembrance of them. Hearing these sweet words, Bertha declared to him that, however great might have been her sin, and whatever God reserved for her, this happiness would enable her to support it, since she believed she had not fallen through a man, but through an angel.

Then they returned to the nest which contained their love, but only to bid a final adieu to all their lovely flowers. There can be but little doubt that Seigneur Cupid had something to do with this festival, for no woman ever experienced such joy in any part of the world before, and no man ever took as much. The especial property of true love is a certain harmony which brings it about that the more one gives, the more the other receives, and vice versa, as in certain cases in mathematics, where things are multiplied by themselves without end. This problem can only be explained to unscientific people, by asking them to look into their Venetian glasses, in which are to be seen thousands of faces produced by one alone. Thus, in the hearts of two lovers, the roses of pleasure multiply within them in a manner which causes them to be astonished that so much joy can be contained, without anything bursting. Bertha and Jehan would have wished in this night to have finished their days, and thought, from the excessive languor which flowed in their veins, that love had resolved to bear them away on his wings with the kiss of death; but they held out in spite of these numerous multiplications.

On the morrow, as the return of Monsieur Imbert de Bastarnay was close at hand, the lady Sylvia was compelled to depart. The poor girl left her cousin, covering her with tears and with kisses; it was always her last, but the last lasted till evening. Then he was compelled to leave her, and he did leave her, although the blood of his heart congealed, like the fallen wax of a Paschal candle. According to his promise, he wended his way towards Marmoutier, which he entered towards the eleventh hour of the day, and was placed among the novices. Monseigneur de Bastarnay was informed that Sylvia had returned to the Lord, which is the signification of *le Seigneur* in the English language; and therefore in this Bertha did not lie.

The joy of her husband, when he saw Bertha without her waistband—she could not wear it, so much had she increased in size—commenced the martyrdom of this poor woman, who did not know how to deceive, and who, at each false word, went to her Prie-Dieu, wept her blood away from her eyes in tears, burst into prayers, and recommended herself to the graces of Messieurs the Saints in Paradise. It happened that she cried so loudly to God that He heard her, because He hears everything; He hears the stones that roll beneath the waters, the poor who groan, and the flies who wing their way through the air. It is as well that you should know this, otherwise you would not believe in what happened. God commanded the archangel Michael to make for this penitent a hell upon earth, so that she might enter without dispute into Paradise. Then St. Michael descended from the skies as far as the gate of hell, and handed over this triple soul to the devil, telling him that he had permission to torment it during the rest of her days, at the same time indicating to him Bertha, Jehan, and the child. The devil, who by the will of God is lord of all evil, told the archangel that he would obey the message. During this heavenly arrangement life went on as usual here below. The sweet lady of Bastarnay gave the most beautiful child in the world to the Sire Imbert—a boy all lilies and roses, of great intelligence, like a little Jesus, merry and arch as a pagan love. He became more beautiful day by day, while the elder was turning to an ape, like his father, whom he painfully resembled. The younger boy was as bright as a star, and resembled his father and mother, whose corporeal and spiritual perfections had produced a compound of illustrious graces and marvellous intelligence. Seeing this perpetual miracle of body and mind blended with the essential conditions, Bastarnay declared that for his eternal salvation he would like to make the younger the elder, and that he would do with the king's protection. Bertha did not know what to do, for she adored the child of Jehan, and could only feel a feeble affection for the other, whom, nevertheless, she protected against the evil intentions of the old fellow Bastarnay. Bertha, satisfied with the way things were going, quieted her conscience with falsehood, and thought that all danger was past, since twelve years had elapsed with no other alloy than the doubt which at times embittered her joy. Each year, according to her pledged faith, the monk of Marmoutier, who was unknown to every one except the servant-maid, came to pass a whole day at the Château to see his child, although Bertha had many times besought brother Jehan to yield his right. But Jehan pointed to the child, saying, "You see him every day of the year, and I only once!" And the poor mother could find no word ready to answer this speech with.

A few months before the last rebellion of the Dauphin Louis against his father, the boy was treading closely on the heels of his twelfth year, and appeared likely to become

a great savant, so learned was he in all the sciences. Old
Bastarnay had never been more delighted at having been
a father in his life, and resolved to take his son with him
to the Court of Burgundy, where Duke Charles promised
to make for this well-beloved son a position which should
be the envy of princes, for he was not at all averse to clever
people. Seeing matters thus arranged, the devil judged the
time to be ripe for his mischiefs. He took his tail and flapped
it right into the middle of this happiness, so that he could
stir it up in his own peculiar way.

III

HORRIBLE CHASTISEMENT OF BERTHA AND EXPIATION OF THE SAME, WHO DIED PARDONED

THE servant of the lady of Bastarnay, who was then
about five-and-thirty years old, fell in love with one of the
master's men-at-arms, and was silly enough to let him take
loaves out of the oven, until there resulted therefrom a
natural swelling, which certain wags in these parts call a
nine months' dropsy. The poor woman begged her mistress
to intercede for her with the master, so that he might compel this wicked man to finish at the altar that which he had
commenced elsewhere. Madame de Bastarnay had no difficulty in obtaining this favour from him, and the servant
was quite satisfied. But the old warrior, who was always
extremely rough, hastened into his pretorium, and blew
him up sky high, ordering him, under the pain of the gallows, to marry the girl; which the soldier preferred to do,
thinking more of his neck than of his peace of mind. Bastarnay sent also for the female, to whom he imagined, for
the honour of his house, he ought to sing a litany, mixed

with epithets and ornamented with extremely strong expressions, and make her think, by way of punishment, that
she was not going to be married, but flung into one of the
cells in the gaol. The girl fancied that Madame wanted to
get rid of her, in order to inter the secret of the birth of
her beloved son. With this impression, when the old ape
said such outrageous things to her—namely, that he must
have been a fool to keep a harlot in his house—she replied
that he certainly was a very big fool, seeing that for a long
time past his wife had been playing the harlot, and with a
monk too, which was the worst thing that could happen to
a warrior. Think of the greatest storm you ever saw in your
life, and you will have a weak sketch of the furious rage
into which the old man fell, when thus assailed in a portion
of his heart where was a triple life. He seized the girl by
the throat, and would have killed her there and then, but
she, to prove her story, detailed the how, the why, and the
when, and said that if he had no faith in her, he could have
the evidence of his own ears by hiding himself the day that
Father Jehan de Sacchez, the prior of Marmoutier, came.
He would then hear the words of the father, who solaced
himself for his year's fast, and in one day kissed his son for
the rest of the year. Imbert ordered this woman instantly
to leave the castle, since, if her accusation were true, he
would kill her just as though she had invented a tissue of
lies. In an instant he had given her a hundred crowns, besides her man, enjoining them not to sleep in Touraine ; and,
for greater security, they were conducted into Burgundy,
by De Bastarnay's officers. He informed his wife of their
departure, saying, that as her servant was a damaged article,
he had thought it best to get rid of her, but had given her
a hundred crowns, and found employment for the man at
the Court of Burgundy. Bertha was astonished to learn that

her maid had left the castle without receiving her dismissal from herself, her mistress; but she said nothing. Soon afterwards she had other fish to fry, for she became a prey to vague apprehensions, because her husband completely changed in his manner, commenced to notice the likeness of his first-born to himself, and could find nothing resembling his nose, or his forehead, his this, or his that, in the youngster he loved so well.

"He is my very image," replied Bertha one day that he was throwing out these hints. "Know you not that in well-regulated households, children are formed from the father and mother, each in turn, or often from both together, because the mother mingles her qualities with the vital force of the father? Some physicians declare that they have known many children born without any resemblance to either father or mother, and attribute these mysteries to the whim of the Almighty."

"You have become very learned, my dear," replied Bastarnay; "but I, who am an ignoramus, I should fancy that a child who resembled a monk——"

"Had a monk for a father!" said Bertha, looking at him with an unflinching gaze, although ice rather than blood was coursing through her veins.

The old fellow thought he was mistaken, and cursed the servant; but he was none the less determined to make sure of the affair. As the day of Father Jehan's visit was close at hand, Bertha, whose suspicions were aroused by this speech, wrote him that it was her wish that he should not come this year, without, however, telling him her reason; then she went in search of La Fallotte at Loches, who was to give her letter to Jehan, and believed everything was safe for the present. She was all the more pleased at having written to her friend the prior, when Imbert, who,

towards the time appointed for the poor monk's annual
treat, had always been accustomed to take a journey into
the province of Maine, where he had considerable property,
remained this time at home, giving as his reason the preparations for rebellion which Monseigneur Louis was then
making against his father, who, as every one knows, was
so cut up at this revolt that it caused his death. This reason
was so good an one that poor Bertha was quite satisfied
with it, and did not trouble herself. On the regular day,
however, the prior arrived as usual. Bertha seeing him,
turned pale, and asked him if he had not received her
message.

"What message?" said Jehan.

"Ah! we are lost, then; the child, thou, and I," replied
Bertha.

"Why so?" said the prior.

"I know not," said she; "but our last day has come."

She inquired of her dearly beloved son where Bastarnay
was. The young man told her that his father had been sent
for by special messenger to Loches, and would not be back
until evening. Thereupon Jehan wished, in spite of his
mistress, to remain with her and his dear son, asserting that
no harm would come of it, after the lapse of twelve years,
since the birth of their boy. The days when that adven-
turous night you wot of was celebrated, Bertha stayed in
her room with the poor monk until supper time. But on
this occasion the lovers—hastened by the apprehensions of
Bertha, which were shared by Jehan directly she had informed him of them—dined immediately, although the
prior of Marmoutier reassured Bertha by pointing out to
her the privileges of the Church, and how Bastarnay, already in bad odour at Court, would be afraid to attack a
dignitary of Marmoutier. When they were sitting down

to table their little one happened to be playing, and in spite of the reiterated prayers of his mother, would not stop his games, since he was galloping about the courtyard on a fine Spanish barb, which Duke Charles of Burgundy had presented to Bastarnay. And because young lads like to show off, varlets make themselves bachelors at arms, and bachelors wish to play the knight, this boy was delighted at being able to show the monk what a man he was becoming; he made the horse jump like a flea in the bedclothes, and sat as steady as a trooper in the saddle.

"Let him have his way, my darling," said the monk to Bertha. "Disobedient children often become great characters."

Bertha ate sparingly, for her heart was as swollen as a sponge in water. At the first mouthful, the monk, who was a great scholar, felt in his stomach a pain, and on his palate a bitter taste of poison that caused him to suspect that the Sire de Bastarnay had given them all their quietus. Before he had made this discovery Bertha had eaten. Suddenly the monk pulled off the table cloth and flung everything into the fireplace, telling Bertha his suspicion. Bertha thanked the Virgin that her son had been so taken up with his sport. Retaining his presence of mind, Jehan, who had not forgotten the lesson he had learned as a page, leaped into the courtyard, lifted his son from the horse, sprang across it himself, and flew across the country with such speed that you would have thought him a shooting-star if you had seen him digging the spurs into the horse's bleeding flanks, and he was at Loches in Fallotte's house in the same space of time that only the devil could have done the journey. He stated the case to her in two words, for the poison was already frying his marrow, and requested her to give him an antidote.

"Alas," said the sorceress, "had I known that it was for you I was giving this poison, I would have received in my breast the dagger's point, with which I was threatened, and would have sacrificed my poor life to save that of a man of God, and of the sweetest woman that ever blossomed on this earth; for, alas! my dear friend, I have only two drops of the counter-poison that you see in this phial."

"Is there enough for her?"

"Yes; but go at once," said the old hag.

The monk came back more quickly than he went, so that the horse died under him in the courtyard. He rushed into the room where Bertha, believing her last hour to be come, was kissing her son, and writhing like a lizard in the fire, uttering no cry for herself, but for the child, left to the wrath of Bastarnay, forgetting her own agony at the thought of his cruel future.

"Take this," said the monk; "my life is saved!"

Jehan had the great courage to say these words with an unmoved face, although he felt the claws of death seizing his heart. Hardly had Bertha drunk when the prior fell dead, not, however, without kissing his son, and regarding his dear lady with an eye that changed not even after his last sigh. This sight turned her cold as marble, and terrified her so much that she remained rigid before this dead man, stretched at her feet, pressing the hand of her child, who wept, although her own eye was as dry as the Red Sea when the Hebrews crossed it under the leadership of Baron Moses, for it seemed to her that she had sharp sand rolling under her eyelids. Pray for her, ye charitable souls, for never was woman so agonized, in divining that her lover had saved her life at the expense of his own. Aided by her son, she herself placed the monk in the middle of the bed, and stood by the side of it, praying with the boy, whom

she then told that the prior was his true father. In this
state she waited her evil hour, and her evil hour did not
take long in coming, for towards the eleventh hour Bastarnay arrived, and was informed at the portcullis that
the monk was dead, and not Madame and the child, and
he saw his beautiful Spanish horse lying dead. Thereupon,
seized with a furious desire to slay Bertha and the monk's
bastard, he sprang up the stairs with one bound; but at
the sight of this corpse, for whom his wife and her son
repeated incessant litanies, having no ears for his torrents
of invective, having no eyes for his writhings and threats,
he had no longer the courage to perpetrate this dark deed.
After the first fury of his rage had passed, he could not
bring himself to it, and quitted the room like a coward and
a man taken in crime, stung to the quick by those prayers
continuously said for the monk. The night was passed in
tears, groans, and prayers. By an express order from
Madame, her servant had been to Loches to purchase for
her the attire of a young lady of quality, and for her poor
child a horse and the arms of an esquire; noticing which,
the Sieur de Bastarnay was much astonished. He sent for
Madame and the monk's son, but neither mother nor child
returned any answer, but quietly put on the clothes purchased by the servant. By Madame's order this servant
made up the account of her effects, arranged her clothes,
purples, jewels, and diamonds, as the property of a widow
is arranged when she renounces her rights. Bertha ordered
even her alms-purse to be included, in order that the ceremony might be perfect. The report of these preparations
ran through the house, and every one knew then that the
mistress was about to leave it, a circumstance that filled
every heart with sorrow, even that of a little scullion, who
had only been a week in the place, but to whom Madame

had already given a kind word. Frightened at these preparations, old Bastarnay came into her chamber, and found
her weeping over the body of Jehan, for her tears had
come at last; but she dried them directly she perceived her
husband. To his numerous questions she replied briefly
by the confession of her fault, telling him how she had
been duped, how the poor page had been distressed, showing him upon the corpse the mark of the poniard wound;
how long he had been getting well; and how, in obedience
to her, and from penitence towards God and man, he had
entered the Church, abandoning the glorious career of a
knight, putting an end to his name, which was certainly
worse than death; how she, while avenging her honour,
had thought that even God Himself would not have refused the monk one day in the year to see the son for whom
he sacrificed everything; how, not wishing to live with a
murderer, she was about to quit his house, leaving all her
property behind her; because, if the honour of the Bastarnays was stained, it was not she who had brought the
shame about; because in this calamity she had arranged
matters as best she could; finally, she added a vow to go
over mountain and valley, she and her son, until all was
expiated, for she knew how to expiate all.

Having with noble mien and a pale face uttered these
beautiful words, she took her child by the hand and
went out in great mourning, more magnificently beautiful
than was Mademoiselle Hagar on her departure from the
residence of the patriarch Abraham, and so proudly, that
all the servants and retainers fell on their knees as she
passed along, imploring her with joined hands, like Notre-
Dame de la Riche. It was pitiful to see the Sieur de Bastarnay following her, ashamed, weeping, confessing him-

self to blame, and downcast and despairing, like a man being led to the gallows, there to be turned off.

Bertha turned a deaf ear to everything. The desolation was so great that she found the drawbridge lowered, and hastened to quit the castle, fearing that it might be suddenly raised again; but no one had the right or the heart to do it. She sat down on the kerb of the moat, in view of the whole castle, who begged her, with tears, to stay. The poor sire was standing with his hand upon the chain of the portcullis, as silent as the stone saints carved above the door. He saw Bertha order her son to shake the dust from his shoes at the end of the bridge, in order to have nothing belonging to Bastarnay about him; and she did likewise. Then, indicating the sire to her son with her finger, she spake to him as follows—

"Child, behold the murderer of thy father, who was, as thou art aware, the poor prior; but thou hast taken the name of this man. Give it him back here, even as thou leavest the dust taken by thy shoes from his castle. For the food that thou hast had in the castle, by God's help we will also settle."

Hearing this, Bastarnay would have let his wife receive a whole monastery of monks in order not to be abandoned by her, and by a young squire capable of becoming the honour of his house, and remained with his head sunk down against the chains.

The heart of Bertha was suddenly filled with holy solace, for the banner of the great monastery turned the corner of a road across the fields, and appeared accompanied by the chants of the Church, which burst forth like heavenly music. The monks, informed of the murder perpetrated on their well-beloved prior, came in procession, assisted by the ecclesiastical justice, to claim his body. When he saw this, the Sire de Bastarney had barely the time to make for the postern with his men, and set out towards Monseigneur Louis, leaving everything in confusion.

Poor Bertha, *en croupe* behind her son, came to Montbazon to bid her father farewell, telling him that this blow would be her death, and was consoled by those of her family, who endeavoured to raise her spirits, but were unable to do so. The old Sire de Rohan presented his grandson with a splendid suit of armour, telling him so to acquire glory and honour that he might turn his mother's faults into eternal renown. But Madame de Bastarnay had implanted in the mind of her dear son no other idea than of atoning for the harm done, in order to save her and Jehan from eternal damnation. Both then set out for the places then in a state of rebellion, in order to render such services to Bastarnay that he would receive from them more than life itself. Now the heat of the sedition was, as every one knows, in the neighborhood of Angoulême, and of Bordeaux in Guienne, and other parts of the kingdom, where great battles and severe conflicts between the rebels and the royal armies were likely to take place. The principal one which finished the war was given between Ruffec and Angoulême, where all the prisoners taken were tried and hanged. This battle, commanded by old Bastarnay, took place in the month of November, seven months after the poisoning of Jehan. Now the baron knew that his head had been strongly recommended as one to be cut off, he being the right hand of Monseigneur Louis. Directly his men began to fall back, the old fellow found himself surrounded by six men determined to seize him. Then he understood that they wished to take him alive, in order to proceed against his house, ruin his name, and confiscate his property. The poor sire preferred rather to die and save his family, and present the domains to his son. He defended himself, like the brave old lion that he was. In spite of their number, these said soldiers, seeing three of their comrades fall, were obliged to attack Bastarnay at the risk of killing him, and threw themselves together upon him, after having laid low two of his equerries and a page. In this extreme danger an esquire, wearing the arms of Rohan, fell upon the assailants like a thunderbolt, and killed two of them, crying, "God save the Bastarnays!" The third man-at-arms, who had already seized old Bastarnay, was so hard pressed by this squire, that he was obliged to leave the elder and turn against the younger, to whom he gave a thrust with his dagger through a flaw in his armour. Bastarnay was too good a comrade to fly without assisting the liberator of his house, who was badly wounded. With a blow of his mace he killed the man-at-arms, seized the squire, lifted him on to his horse, and gained the open, accompanied by a guide, who led him to the castle of Roche-Foucauld, which he entered by night, and found in the great room Bertha de Rohan, who had arranged this retreat for him. But on removing the helmet of his rescuer, he recognised the son of Jehan, who expired upon the table, by a final effort kissing his mother, and saying in a loud voice to her, "Mother, we have paid the debt we owed him!" Hearing these words, the mother clasped the body of her loved child to her heart, and separated from him never again, for she died of grief, without hearing or heeding the pardon and repentance of Bastarnay.

This strange calamity hastened the last day of the poor old man, who did not live to see the coronation of King Louis the Eleventh. He founded a daily mass in the church of Roche-Foucauld, where in the same grave he placed mother and son, with a large tombstone, upon which their lives are much honoured in the Latin language.

The morals which any one can deduce from this history are most profitable for the conduct of life, since this shows how gentlemen should be courteous with the dearly beloveds of their wives. Further, it teaches us that all children are blessings sent by God Himself, and over them fathers, whether true or false, have no right of murder, as was formerly the case at Rome, owing to a heathen and abominable law, which ill became that Christianity which makes us all sons of God.

HOW THE PRETTY MAID OF PORTILLON
CONVINCED HER JUDGE

THE maid of Portillon, who became, as every one knows, La Tascherette, was, before she became a dyer, a laundress at the said place of Portillon, from which she took her name. If any there be who do not know Tours, it may be well to state that Portillon is down the Loire, on the same side as St. Cyr, about as far from the bridge which leads to the cathedral of Tours as the said bridge is distant from Marmoutier, since the bridge is in the centre of the embankment between Portillon and Marmoutier. Do you thoroughly understand?

Yes? Good! Now the maid had there her washhouse, from which she ran to the Loire with her washing in a second, and took the ferry-boat to get to St. Martin, which was on the other side of the river, for she had to deliver the greater part of her work in Chateauneuf and other places. About Midsummer day, seven years before marrying old Taschereau, she had just reached the right age to be loved. As she was a merry girl she allowed herself to be loved, without making a choice from any of the lads who pursued her with their intentions. Although there used to come to the bench under her window the son of Rabelais, who had seven boats on the Loire, Jehan's eldest, Marchandeau the tailor, and Peccard the ecclesiastical goldsmith, she made fun of them all, because she wished to be taken to church before burthening herself with a man, which proves that she was an honest woman until she was wheedled out of her virtue. She was one of those girls who take great care not to be contaminated, but who, if by chance they get deceived, let things take their course, thinking that for one stain or for fifty a good polishing up is necessary. These characters demand our indulgence.

A young noble of the court perceived her one day when she was crossing the water in the glare of the noonday sun, which lit up her ample charms, and seeing her, asked who she was. An old man, who was working on the banks, told him she was called the Pretty Maid of Portillon, a laundress, celebrated for her merry ways and her virtue. This young lord, besides ruffles to starch, had many precious linen draperies and things; he resolved to give the custom of his house to this girl, whom he stopped on the road. He was thanked by her and heartily, because he was the Sire du Fou, the king's chamberlain. This encounter made her so joyful that her mouth was full of his name. She talked about it a great deal to the people of St. Martin, and when she got back to her washhouse was still full of it, and on the morrow at her work her tongue went nineteen to the dozen, and all on the same subject, so that as much was said concerning my Lord du Fou in Portillon as of God in a sermon; that is, a great deal too much.

"If she works like that in cold water, what will she do in warm?" said an old washerwoman. "She wants du Fou; he'll give her du Fou!"

The first time this giddy wench, with her head full of Monsieur du Fou, had to deliver the linen at his hotel, the chamberlain wished to see her, and was very profuse in praises and compliments concerning her charms, and wound up by telling her that she was not at all silly to be beautiful, and therefore he would give her more than she expected. The deed followed the word, for the moment his people were out of the room, he began to caress the maid, who thinking he was about to take out the money from his purse, dared not look at the purse, but said, like a girl ashamed to take her wages, "It will be for the first time."

"It will be soon," said he.

Some people say that he had great difficulty in forcing her to accept what he offered her, and hardly forced her at all; others that he forced her badly, because she came out, like an army flagging on the route, crying and groaning, and came to the judge. It happened that the judge was out. La Portillone awaited his return in his room, weeping and saying to the servant that she had been robbed, because Monseigneur du Fou had given her nothing but his mischief; whilst a canon of the chapter used to give her large sums for that which M. du Fou wanted for nothing. If she loved a man she would think it wise to do things for him for nothing, because it would be a pleasure to her; but the chamberlain had treated her roughly, and not kindly and gently, as he should have done, and that therefore he owed her the thousand crowns of the canon. The judge came in, saw the wench, and wished to kiss her, but she put herself on guard, and said she had come to make a complaint. The judge replied that certainly she could have the offender hanged if she liked, because he was most anxious to serve her. The injured maiden replied that she did not wish the death of her man, but that he should pay her a thousand gold crowns, because she had been robbed against her will.

"Ha! ha!" said the judge, "what he took was worth more than that."

"For the thousand crowns I'll cry quits, because I shall be able to live without washing."

"He who has robbed you, is he well off?"

"Oh, yes."

"Then he shall pay dearly for it. Who is it?"

"Monseigneur du Fou."

"Oh, that alters the case," said the judge.

"But justice?" said she.

"I said the case, not the justice of it," replied the judge. "I must know how the affair occurred."

Then the girl related naïvely how she was arranging the young lord's ruffles in his wardrobe, when he began to play with her skirts, and she turned round, saying—

"Go on with you!"

"You have no case," said the judge, "for by that speech he thought that you gave him leave to go on. Ha! ha!"

Then she declared that she had defended herself, weeping and crying out, and that that constitutes an assault.

"A wench's antics to incite him," said the judge.

Finally, La Portillone declared that against her will she had been taken around the waist and thrown, although she had kicked and cried and struggled, but that seeing no help at hand, she had lost courage.

"Good! good!" said the judge. "Did you take pleasure in the affair?"

"No," said she. "My anguish can only be paid for with a thousand crowns."

"My dear," said the judge, "I cannot receive your complaint, because I believe no girl can be thus treated against her will."

"Hi! hi! hi! Ask your servant," said the little laundress, sobbing, "and hear what she'll tell you."

The servant affirmed that there were pleasant assaults and unpleasant ones; that if La Portillone had received neither amusement nor money, either one or the other was due her. This wise counsel threw the judge into a state of great perplexity.

"Jacqueline," said he, "before I sup I'll get to the bottom of this. Now go and fetch my needle and the red thread that I sew the legal paper bags with."

Jacqueline came back with a big needle, pierced with a pretty little hole, and a big red thread, such as the judges use. Then she remained standing to see the question decided, very much disturbed, as was also the complainant at these mysterious preparations.

"My dear," said the judge, "I am going to hold the bodkin, of which the eye is sufficiently large, to put this thread into it without trouble. If you do put it in, I will take up your case, and will make Monseigneur offer you a compromise."

"What's that?" said she. "I will not allow it."

"It is a word used in justice to signify an agreement."

"A compromise is then agreeable with justice?" said La Portillone.

"My dear, this violence has also opened your mind. Are you ready?"

"Yes," said she.

The waggish judge gave the poor nymph fair play, holding the eye steady for her; but when she wished to slip in the thread that she had twisted to make straight, he moved a little, and the thread went on the other side. She suspected the judge's argument, wetted the thread, stretched it, and came back again. The judge moved, twisted about, and wriggled like a bashful maiden; still the cursed thread would not enter. The girl kept trying at the eye, and the judge kept fidgeting. The marriage of the thread could not be consummated, the bodkin remained virgin, and the servant began to laugh, saying to La Portillone that she knew better how to endure than to perform. Then the roguish judge laughed too, and the fair Portillone cried for her golden crowns.

"If you don't keep still," cried she, losing patience; "if you keep moving about I shall never be able to put the thread in."

"Then, my dear, if you had done the same, Monseigneur would have been unsuccessful too. Think, too, how easy is the one affair, and how difficult the other."

The pretty wench, who declared she had been forced, remained thoughtful, and sought to find a means to convince the judge by showing how she had been compelled to yield, since the honour of all poor girls liable to violence was at stake.

"Monseigneur, in order that the bet may be fair, I must do exactly as the young lord did. If I had only had to move I should be moving still, but he went through other performances."

"Let us hear them," replied the judge.

Then La Portillone straightens the thread; and rubs it in the wax of the candle, to make it firm and straight; then she looks towards the eye of the bodkin, held by the judge, slipping always to the right or to the left. Then she began making endearing little speeches, such as, "Ah, the pretty little bodkin! what a pretty mark to aim at! Never did I see such a little jewel! What a pretty little eye! Let me put this little thread into it! Ah! you will hurt my poor thread, my nice little thread! Keep still! Come, my love of a judge, judge of my love! Won't the thread go nicely into this iron gate, which makes good use of the thread, for it comes out very much out of order?"

Then she burst out laughing, for she was better up in this game than the judge, who laughed too, so saucy and comical and arch was she, pushing the thread backwards and forwards. She kept the poor judge with the case in his hand until seven o'clock, keeping on fidgeting and moving about like a schoolboy let loose; but as La Portillone kept on trying to put the thread in, he could not help it. As, however, his joint was burning, and his wrist was tired, he was obliged to rest himself for a minute on the side of the table; then very dexterously the fair maid of Portillon slipped the thread in, saying—

"That's how the thing occurred."

"But my joint was burning."

"So was mine," said she.

The judge, convinced, told La Portillone that he would speak to Monseigneur du Fou, and would himself carry the affair through, since it was certain the young lord has embraced her against her will, but that for valid reasons he would keep the affair dark. On the morrow the judge went to the Court and saw the Monseigneur du Fou, to whom he recounted the young woman's complaint, and how she had set forth her case. This complaint lodged in Court, tickled the king immensely. Young du Fou having said that there was some truth in it, the king asked if he had much difficulty, and as he replied, innocently, "No," the king declared the girl was quite worth a hundred gold crowns, and the chamberlain gave them to the judge, in order not to be taxed with stinginess, and said that starch would be a good income to La Portillone. The judge came back to La Portillone, and said, smiling, that he had raised a hundred gold crowns for her. But if she desired the balance of the thousand, there were at that moment in the

king's apartments certain lords who, knowing the case,
had offered to make up the sum for her with her consent.
The little hussy did not refuse this offer, saying, that in
order to do no more washing in the future she did not
mind doing a little hard work now. She gratefully acknowledged the trouble the good judge had taken, and gained
her thousand crowns in a month. From this came the falsehoods and jokes concerning her because out of these ten
lords jealousy made a hundred, whilst, differently from
young men, La Portillone settled down to a virtuous life
directly she had her thousand crowns. Even a duke, who
would have counted out five hundred crowns, would
have found this girl rebellious, which proves she was niggardly with her property. It is true that the king caused
her to be sent for to his retreat of Rue Quinquangrogne,
on the mall of Chardonneret, found her extremely pretty,
exceedingly affectionate, enjoyed her society, and forbade
the sergeants to interfere with her in any way whatever.
Seeing she was so beautiful, Nicole Beaupertuis, the king's
mistress, gave her a hundred gold crowns to go to Orlèans,
in order to see if the colour of the Loire was the same
there as at Portillon. She went there, and the more willingly because she did not care very much for the king.
When the good man came who confessed the king in his
last hour, and was afterwards canonized, La Portillone went
to him to polish up her conscience, did penance, and founded
a bed in the leper-house of St. Lazare-les-Tours. Many
ladies whom you know have been assaulted by more than
two lords, and have founded no other beds than those of
their own houses. It is well to relate this fact in order to
cleanse the reputation of this honest girl, who herself once
washed dirty things, and who afterwards became famous
for her clever tricks and her wit. She gave a proof of her

merit in marrying Taschereau, whom she cuckolded right merrily, as has been related in the story of *The Reproach*. This proves to us most satisfactorily that with strength and patience justice itself can be violated.

IN WHICH IT IS DEMONSTRATED THAT
FORTUNE IS ALWAYS FEMININE

DURING the time when knights courteously offered to each other both help and assistance in seeking their fortunes, it happened that in Sicily—which, as you are probably aware, is an island situated in the corner of the Mediterranean Sea, and formerly celebrated—one knight met in a wood another knight, who had the appearance of a Frenchman. Presumably, this Frenchman was by some chance stripped of everything, and was so wretchedly attired that but for his princely air he might have been taken for a blackguard. It was possible that his horse had died of hunger or fatigue, on disembarking from the foreign shore from which he came, on the faith of the good luck which happened to the French in Sicily, which was true in every respect. The Sicilian knight, whose name was Pezare, was a Venetian long absent from the Venetian republic, and with no desire to return there, since he had obtained a footing in the Court of the King of Sicily. Being short of funds in Venice, because he was a younger son, he had no fancy for commerce, and was for that reason eventually abandoned by his family, a most illustrious one. He therefore remained at this Court, where he was much liked by the king. This gentleman was riding a splendid Spanish horse, and thinking to himself how lonely he was in this strange Court, without trusty friends, and how in such cases fortune was harsh to helpless people and became a traitress, when he met the poor French knight, who appeared far worse off than he, who had good weapons, a fine horse, and a mansion where servants were then preparing a sumptuous supper.

"You must have come a long way to have so much dust on your feet," said the Venetian.

"My feet have not as much dust as the road was long," answered the Frenchman.

"If you have travelled so much," continued the Venetian, "you must be a learned man."

"I have learned," replied the Frenchman, "to give no heed to those who do not trouble about me. I have learned that however high a man's head was, his feet were always level with mine; more than that, I have learned to have no confidence in the warm days of winter, in the sleep of my enemies, or the words of my friends."

"You are, then, richer than I am," said the Venetian, astonished, "since you tell me things of which I never thought."

"Everyone must think for himself," said the Frenchman; "and as you have interrogated me, I can request from you the kindness of pointing to me the road to Palermo or some inn, for the night is closing in."

"Are you, then, acquainted with no French or Sicilian gentlemen at Palermo?"

"No."

"Then you are not certain of being received?"

"I am disposed to forgive those who reject me. The road, sir, if you please."

"I am lost like yourself," said the Venetian. "Let us look for it in company."

"To do that we must go together; but you are on horseback, I am on foot."

The Venetian took the French knight on his saddle behind him, and said—

"Do you know with whom you are?"

"With a man, apparently."

"Do you think you are in safety?"

"If you were a robber, you would have to take care of yourself," said the Frenchman, putting the point of his dagger to the Venetian's heart.

"Well, now, my noble Frenchman, you appear to me a man of great learning and sound sense; know that I am a noble, established at the Court of Sicily, but alone, and I seek a friend. You seem to be in the same plight, and, judging from appearances, you do not seem friendly with your lot, and have apparently need of everybody."

"Should I be happier if everybody wanted me?"

"You are a devil, who turn every one of my words against me. By St. Mark! my lord knight, can one trust you?"

"More than yourself, who commenced our federal friendship by deceiving me, since you guide your horse like a man who knows his way, and you said you were lost."

"And did you not deceive me," said the Venetian, "by making a sage of your year's walk, and giving a noble knight the appearance of a vagabond? Here is my abode; my servants have prepared supper for us."

The Frenchman jumped off the horse, and entered the house with the Venetian cavalier, accepting his supper. They both seated themselves at the table. The Frenchman fought so well with his jaws, he twisted the morsels with so much agility, that he showed himself equally learned in suppers, and showed it again in dexterously draining the wine flasks without his eye becoming dimmed or his understanding affected. Then you may be sure the Venetian thought to himself he had fallen in with a fine son of Adam, sprung from the right side and the wrong one. While they were drinking together, the Venetian endeavoured to find some joint through which to sound the secret depths of his friend's cogitations. He, however, clearly perceived that he would cast aside his shirt sooner than his prudence, and judged it opportune to gain his esteem by opening his doublet to him. Therefore he told him in what state was Sicily, where reigned Prince Leufroid and his gentle wife; how gallant was the Court, what courtesy there flourished, that there abounded many lords of Spain, Italy, France, and other countries, lords in high feather and well feathered; many princesses, as rich as noble, and as noble as rich; that this prince had the loftiest aspirations—such as to conquer Morocco, Constantinople, Jerusalem, the lands of Soudan, and other African places. Certain men of vast minds conducted his affairs, bringing together the ban and *arrière* ban of the flower of Christian chivalry, and kept up his splendour with the idea of causing to reign over the Mediterranean this Sicily, so opulent in time gone by, and of ruining Venice, which had not a foot of land. These designs had been planted in the king's mind by him, Pezare; but although he was high in that prince's favour, he felt himself weak, had no assistance from the courtiers, and desired to make a friend. In this great trouble he had gone for a little ride to turn matters over in his mind, and decide upon the course to pursue. Now, since while in this idea he had met a man of so much sense as the chevalier had proved himself to be, he proposed to fraternize with him, to open his purse to him, and give him his palace to live in. They would journey in company through life in search of honours and pleasure, without concealing one single thought, and would assist each other on all occasions as the brothers-in-arms did at the Crusades. Now, as the Frenchman was seeking his fortune, and required assistance, the Venetian did not for a moment expect that this offer of mutual consolation would be refused.

"Although I stand in need of no assistance," said the Frenchman, "because I rely upon a point which will procure me all that I desire, I should like to acknowledge your courtesy, dear Chevalier Pezare. You will soon see that you will yet be the debtor of Gauttier de Montsoreau, a gentleman of the fair land of Touraine."

"Do you possess any relic with which your fortune is wound up?" said the Venetian.

"A talisman given me by my dear mother," said the Tourainian, "with which castles and cities are built and demolished, a hammer to coin money, a remedy for every ill, a traveller's staff always ready to be tried, and worth most when in a state of readiness, a master tool, which executes wondrous works in all sorts of forges, without making the slightest noise."

"Eh! by St. Mark you have, then, a mystery concealed in your hauberk?"

"No," said the French knight; "it is a perfectly natural thing. Here it is."

And rising suddenly from the table to prepare for bed, Gauttier showed the Venetian the finest talisman to procure joy that he had ever seen.

"This," said the Frenchman, as they both got into bed together, according to the custom of the times, "overcomes every obstacle, by making itself master of female hearts; and as the ladies are the queens in this Court, your friend Gauttier will soon reign there."

The Venetian remained in great astonishment at the sight of these charms of the said Gauttier, who had indeed been bounteously endowed by his mother, and perhaps also by his father, and would thus triumph over everything, since he joined to this corporeal perfection the wit of a young page, and the wisdom of an old devil. Then they swore an eternal friendship, regarding as nothing therein a woman's heart, vowing to have one and the same idea, as if their heads had been in the same helmet; and they fell asleep on the same pillow, enchanted with this fraternity. This was a common occurrence in those days.

On the morrow the Venetian gave a fine horse to his friend Gauttier, also a purse full of money, fine silken hose, a velvet doublet fringed with gold, and an embroidered mantle, which garments set off his figure so well, and showed up his beauties, that the Venetian was certain that he would captivate all the ladies. The servants received orders to obey this Gauttier as they would himself, so that they fancied their master had been fishing, and had caught this Frenchman. Then the two friends made their entry into Palermo at the hour when the princes and princesses were taking the air. Pezare presented this French friend, speaking so highly of his merits, and obtaining such a gracious reception for him, that Leufroid kept him to supper. The knight kept a sharp eye on the Court, and noticed therein various curious little secret practices. If the king was a brave and handsome prince, the princess was a Spanish lady of high temperature, the most beautiful and most noble woman of his Court, but inclined to melancholy. Looking at her, the Tourainian believed that she was sparingly embraced by the king, for the law of Touraine is that joy in the face comes from joy elsewhere. Pezare pointed out to his friend Gauttier several ladies to whom Leufroid was exceedingly gracious and who were exceedingly jealous, and fought for him in a tournament of gallantries and

wonderful female inventions. From all this Gauttier concluded that the prince went considerably astray with his
Court, although he had the prettiest wife in the world,
and occupied himself by taxing the ladies of Sicily, in order
that he might put his horse in their stables, vary his fodder,
and learn the equestrian capabilities of many lands. Perceiving what a life Leufroid was leading, the Sire de Montsoreau, certain that no one in the Court had had the heart
to enlighten the queen, determined at one blow to plant
his halberd in the field of the fair Spaniard, by a master
stroke; and this is how. At suppertime, in order to show
courtesy to the foreign knight, the king took care to place
him near the queen, to whom the gallant Gauttier offered
his arm, to take her into the room, and conducted her there
hastily, to get ahead of those who were following, in order
to whisper, first of all, a word concerning a subject which
always pleases the ladies in whatever condition they may
be. Imagine what this word was, and how it went straight
through the stubble and weeds into the warm thicket of
love.

"I know, your majesty, what causes your paleness of
face."

"What?" said she.

"You are so loving that the king loves you night and day;
thus you abuse your advantage, for he will die of love."

"What should I do to keep him alive?" said the queen.

"Forbid him to repeat at your altar more than three
prayers a day."

"You are joking after the French fashion, Sir Knight,
seeing that the king's devotion to me does not extend beyond a short prayer a week."

"You are deceived," said Gauttier, seating himself at the
table. "I can prove to you that love should go through the

whole mass, matins, and vespers, with an *Ave* now and then, for queens as for simple women, and go through the ceremony every day, like the monks in their monastery, with fervour; but for you these litanies should never finish."

The queen cast upon the knight a glance which was far from one of displeasure, smiled at him, and shook her head.

"In this," said she, "men are great liars."

"I have with me a great truth which I will show you when you wish it," replied the knight. "I undertake to give you a queen's fare, and put you on the high road to joy; by this means you will make up for lost time, the more so as the king is ruined through other women, while I have reserved my advantages for your service."

"And if the king learns our arrangement, he will put your head on a level with your feet."

"Even if this misfortune befell me after the first night, I should believe I had lived a hundred years, from the joy therein received, for never have I seen, after visiting all Courts, a princess fit to hold a candle to your beauty. To be brief, if I die not by the sword, you will still be the cause of my death, for I am resolved to spend my life in our love, if life will depart in the place whence it comes."

Now this queen had never heard such words before, and preferred them to the most sweetly sung mass; her pleasure showed itself in her face, which became purple, for these words made her blood boil within her veins, so that the strings of her lute were moved thereat, and struck a sweet note that rang melodiously in her ears, for this lute fills with its music the brain and the body of the ladies, by a sweet artifice of their resonant nature. What a shame to be young, beautiful, Spanish, and queen, and yet neglected. She conceived an intense disdain for those of her Court who had kept their lips closed concerning this infidelity, through fear of the king, and determined to revenge herself with the aid of this handsome Frenchman, who cared so little for life that in his first words he had staked it in making a proposition to a queen, which was worthy of death, if she did her duty. Instead of this, however, she pressed his foot with her own, in a manner that admitted no misconception, and said aloud to him—

"Sir Knight, let us change the subject, for it is very wrong of you to attack a poor queen in her weak spot. Tell us the customs of the ladies of the Court of France."

Thus did the knight receive the delicate hint that the business was arranged. Then he commenced to talk of merry and pleasant things, which during supper kept the Court, the king, the queen, and all the courtiers in a good humour; so much so that when the siege was raised, Leufroid declared that he had never laughed so much in his life. Then they strolled about the gardens, which were the most beautiful in the world, and the queen made a pretext of the chevalier's sayings to walk beneath a grove of blossoming orange trees, which yielded a delicious fragrance.

"Lovely and noble queen," said Gauttier, immediately, "I have seen in all countries the perdition of love have its birth in those first attentions, which we call courtesy; if you have confidence in me, let us agree, as people of high intelligence, to love each other without standing on so much ceremony; by this means no suspicions will be aroused, our happiness will be less dangerous and more lasting. In this fashion should queens conduct their amours, if they would avoid interference."

"Well said," said she. "But as I am new at this business, I do not know what arrangements to make."

"Have you among your women one in whom you have perfect confidence?"

"Yes," said she; "I have a maid who came from Spain with me, who would put herself on a gridiron for me, like St. Lawrence did for God, but she is always poorly."

"That's good," said her companion, "because you go to see her."

"Yes," said the queen, "and sometimes at night."

"Ah!" exclaimed Gauttier, "I make a vow to St. Rosalie, patroness of Sicily, to build her a golden altar for this fortune."

"O Jesus!" cried the queen. "I am doubly blessed in having a lover so handsome and yet so religious."

"Ah, my dear, I have two sweethearts to-day, because I have a queen to love in heaven above and another one here below, and luckily these loves cannot clash one with the other."

This sweet speech so affected the queen, that for a nothing she would have fled with this cunning Frenchman.

"The Virgin Mary is very powerful in heaven," said the queen. "Love grant that I may be like her!"

"Bah! they are talking of the Virgin Mary," said the king, who by chance had come to watch them, disturbed by a gleam of jealousy, cast into his heart by a Sicilian courtier, who was furious at the sudden favour which the Frenchman had obtained.

The queen and the chevalier laid their plans, and everything was secretly arranged to furnish the helmet of the king with two invisible ornaments. The knight rejoined the Court, made himself agreeable to every one, and returned to the palace of Pezare, whom he told that their fortunes were made, because on the morrow, at night, he would sleep with the queen. This swift success astonished

the Venetian, who, like a good friend, went in search of
fine perfumes, linen of Brabant, and precious garments, to
which queens are accustomed, with all of which he loaded
his friend Gauttier, in order that the case might be worthy
the jewel.

"Ah, my friend," said he, "are you sure not to falter, but
to go vigorously to work, to serve the queen bravely, and
give her such joys in her castle of Gallardin that she may
hold on for ever to this master staff, like a drowning sailor
to a plank?"

"As for that, fear nothing, dear Pezare, because I have
the arrears of the journey, and I will deal with her as with
a simple servant, instructing her in the ways of the ladies
of Touraine, who understand love better than all others,
because they make it, remake it, and unmake it to make
it again; and having remade it, still keep on making it; and
having nothing else to do, have to do that which always
wants doing. Now let us settle our plans. This is how we
shall obtain the government of this island. I shall hold the
queen and you the king; we will play the comedy of great
enemies before the eyes of the courtiers, in order to divide
them into two parties under our command, and yet, unknown to all, we will remain friends. By this means we shall
know their plots, and will thwart them, you by listening to
my enemies and I to yours. In the course of a few days we
will pretend to quarrel, in order to strive one against the
other. This quarrel will be caused by the favour in which
I will manage to place you with the king, through the channel of the queen, and he will give you supreme power, to my
injury."

On the morrow Gauttier went to the house of the Spanish
lady whom before the courtiers he recognized as having
known in Spain, and he remained there seven whole days.

As you can imagine, the Tourainian treated the queen as a
fondly loved woman, and showed her so many *terræ in-
cognitæ* in love, French fashions, little tendernesses, etc.,
that she nearly lost her reason through it, and swore that
the French were the only people who thoroughly understood love. You see how the king was punished, who, to
keep her virtuous, had allowed weeds to grow in the garden
of love. Their supernatural festivities touched the queen
so strongly that she made a vow of eternal love to Montsoreau, who had awaked her, by revealing to her the joys
of the proceeding. It was arranged that the Spanish lady
should take care always to be ill; and that the only man to
whom the lovers would confide their secret should be the
court physician, who was much attached to the queen. By
chance this physician had in his glottis, chords exactly
similar to those of Gauttier, so that by a freak of nature
they had the same voice, which much astonished the queen.
The physician swore on his life faithfully to serve the pretty
couple, for he deplored the sad desertion of this beautiful
woman, and was delighted to know she would be served as
a queen should be—a rare thing.

A month elapsed and everything was going on to the
satisfaction of the two friends, who worked the plans laid
by the queen, in order to get the government of Sicily into
the hands of Pezare, to the detriment of Montsoreau, whom
the king loved for his great wisdom; but the queen would
not consent to have him, because he was so ungallant.
Leufroid dismissed the Duke of Cataneo, his principal follower, and put the Chevalier Pezare in his place. The Venetian took no tice of his friend the Frenchman. Then
Gauttier burst out, declaiming loudly against the treachery
and abused friendship of his former comrade, and instantly
earned the devotion of Cataneo and his friends, with whom

he made a compact to overthrow Pezare. Directly he was
in office the Venetian, who was a shrewd man, and well
suited to govern states, which was the usual employment
of Venetian gentlemen, worked wonders in Sicily, repaired
the ports, brought merchants there by the fertility of his
inventions and by granting them facilities, put bread into
the mouths of hundreds of poor people, drew thither ar-
tisans of all trades, because fêtes were always being held,
and also the idle and rich from all quarters, even from the
East. Thus harvests, the products of the earth, and other
commodities, were plentiful; and galleys and ships came
from Asia, the which made the king much envied, and the
happiest king in the Christian world, because through these
things his Court was the most renowned in the countries of
Europe. This fine political aspect was the result of the perfect agreement of two men who thoroughly understood
each other. The one looked after the pleasures, and was
himself the delight of the queen, whose face was always
bright and gay, because she was served according to the
method of Touraine, and because animated through excessive happiness; and he also took care to keep the king
amused, finding him every day new mistresses, and casting
him into a whirl of dissipation. The king was much astonished at the good temper of the queen, whom, since the
arrival of the Sire de Montsoreau in the island, he had
touched no more than a Jew touches bacon. Thus occupied,
the king and the queen abandoned the care of their kingdom
to the other friend, who conducted the affairs of government, ruled the establishment, managed the finances, and
looked to the army, and all exceedingly well, knowing
where money was to be made, enriching the treasury, and
preparing all the great enterprises above mentioned.

This state of things lasted three years, some say four,

but the monks of Saint Benoist have not wormed out the date, which remains obscure, like the reasons for the quarrel between the two friends. Probably the Venetian had the high ambition to reign without any control or dispute, and forget the services which the Frenchman had rendered him. Thus do the men who live in Courts behave, for, according to the statements of Messire Aristotle in his works, that which ages the most rapidly in this world is a kindness, although extinguished love is sometimes very rancid. Now, relying on the perfect friendship of Leufroid, who called him his crony, and would have done anything for him, the Venetian conceived the idea of getting rid of his friend by revealing to the king the mystery of his cuckoldom, and showing him the source of the queen's happiness, not doubting for a moment but that he would commence by depriving Montsoreau of his head, according to a practice common in Sicily under similar circumstances. By this means Pezare would have all the money that he and Gauttier had noiselessly conveyed to the house of a Lombard at Genes, which money was their joint property on account of their fraternity. This treasure, increased on one side by the magnificent presents made to Montsoreau by the queen, who had vast estates in Spain, and other, by inheritance in Italy; on the other, by the king's gifts to his prime minister to whom he also gave certain rights over the merchants, and other indulgences. The treacherous friend, having determined to break his vow, took care to conceal his intention from Gauttier, because the Tourainian was an awkward man to tackle. One night that Pezare knew that the queen was in bed with her lover, who loved her still as though each night were a wedding one, so skilful was she at the business, the traitor promised the king to let him take evidence in the case, through a hole which he had made in the wardrobe of the Spanish lady, who always pretended to be at death's door. In order to obtain a better view, Pezare waited until the sun had risen. The Spanish lady, who was fleet of foot, had a quick eye and a sharp ear, heard foot-steps, peeped out, and perceived the king, followed by the Venetian, through a crossbar in the closet in which she slept the nights that the queen had her lover between two sheets, which is certainly the best way to have a lover. She ran to warn the couple of this betrayal. But the king's eye was already at the cursed hole. Leufroid saw—what? That beautiful and divine lantern which burns so much oil and lights the world—a lantern adorned with the most lovely baubles, flaming brilliantly, which he thought more lovely than all the others, because he had lost sight of it for so long a time that it appeared quite new to him; but the size of the hole prevented him seeing anything else except the hand of a man, which modestly covered the lantern, and he heard the voice of Montsoreau saying, "How's the little treasure, this morning?" A playful expression which lovers use jokingly, because this lantern is in all countries the sun of love, and for this the prettiest possible names are be-stowed upon it, while comparing it to the loveliest things in nature, such as my pomegranate, my rose, my little shell, my hedgehog, my gulf of love, my treasure, my master, my little one; some even dared most heretically to say, my god! If you don't believe it, ask your friends.

At this moment the lady let them understand by a gesture that the king was there.

"Can he hear?" said the queen.

"Yes."

"Can he see?"

"Yes."

"Who brought him?"

"Pezare."

"Fetch the physician, and get Gauttier into his own room," said the queen.

In less time than it takes a beggar to say "God bless you, sir!" the queen had swathed the lantern in linen and paint, so that you would have thought it a hideous wound in a state of grievous inflammation. When the king, enraged by what he overheard, burst open the door, he found the queen lying on the bed exactly as he had seen her through the hole, and the physician, examining the lantern swathed in bandages, and saying, "How is the little treasure, this morning?" in exactly the same voice as the king had heard. A jocular and cheerful expression because physicians and surgeons use cheerful words with ladies and treat this sweet flower with flowery phrases. This sight made the king look as foolish as a fox caught in a trap. The queen sprang up, reddening with shame, and asking what man dared to intrude upon her privacy at such a moment, but perceiving the king, she said to him as follows:

"Ah! my lord, you have discovered that which I have endeavoured to conceal from you; that I am so badly treated by you that I am afflicted with a burning ailment, of which my dignity would not allow me to complain, but which needs secret dressing in order to assuage the influence of the vital forces. To save my honour and your own, I am compelled to come to my good Lady Miraflor, who consoles me in my troubles."

Then the physician commenced to treat Leufroid to an oration, interlarded with Latin quotations and precious grains from Hippocrates, Galen, the school of Salerno, and others, in which he showed him how necessary to women was the proper cultivation of the field of Venus, and that there was great danger of death to queens of Spanish tem-

perament, whose blood was excessively amorous. He delivered himself of his arguments with great solemnity of
feature, voice, and manner, in order to give the Sire de
Montsoreau time to get to bed. Then the queen took the
same text to preach the king a sermon as long as his arm,
and requested the loan of that limb, that the king might
conduct her to her apartment instead of the poor invalid,
who usually did so in order to avoid calumny. When they
were in the gallery where the Sire de Montsoreau resided,
the queen said, jokingly, "You should play a good trick on
this Frenchman, who I would wager is with some lady, and
not in his own room. All the ladies of Court are in love with
him, and there will be mischief some day through him. If
you had taken my advice he would not be in Sicily now."

Leufroid went suddenly into Gauttier's room, whom he
found in a deep sleep, and snoring like a monk in church.
The queen returned with the king, whom she took to her
apartments, and whispered to one of the guards to send to
her the lord whose place Pezare occupied. Then, while she
fondled the king, taking breakfast with him, she took the
lord directly he came, into an adjoining room.

"Erect a gallows on the bastion," said she, "then seize
the knight Pezare, and manage so that he is hanged instantly, without giving time to write or say a single word
on any subject whatsoever. Such is our good pleasure and
supreme command."

Cataneo make no remark. While Pezare was thinking
to himself that his friend Gauttier would soon be minus
his head, the Duke Cataneo came to seize and lead him on
to the bastion, from which he could see at the queen's window the Sire de Montsoreau in company with the king, the
queen, and the courtiers, and came to the conclusion that

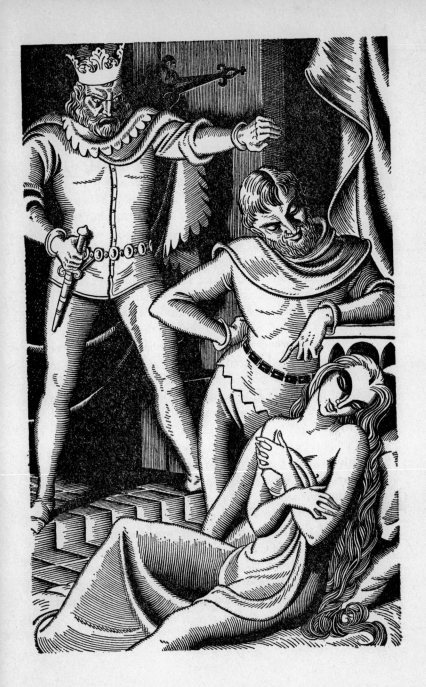

he who looked after the queen had a better chance in everything than he who looked after the king.

"My dear," said the queen to her spouse, leading him to the window, "behold a traitor, who was endeavouring to deprive you of that which you hold dearest in the world, and I will give you the proofs when you have the leisure to study them."

Montsoreau, seeing the preparations for the final ceremony, threw himself at the king's feet, to obtain the pardon of him who was his mortal enemy, at which the king was much moved.

"Sire de Montsoreau," said the queen, turning towards him with an angry look, "are you so bold as to oppose our will and pleasure?"

"You are a noble knight," said the king, "but you do not know how bitter this Venetian was against you."

Pezare was delicately strangled between the head and the shoulders, for the queen revealed his treacheries to the king, proving to him, by the declaration of a Lombard of the town, the enormous sums which Pezare had in the Bank of Genes, the whole of which were given up to Montsoreau.

This noble and lovely queen died, as related in the history of Sicily, that is, in consequence of a heavy labour, during which she gave birth to a son, who was a man as great in himself as he was unfortunate in his undertakings. The king believed the physician's statement, that the sad termination of this accouchement was caused by the too chaste life the queen had led, and believing himself responsible for it, he founded the Church of the Madonna, which is one of the finest in the town of Palermo. The Sire de Montsoreau, who was a witness of the king's remorse, told him that when a king got his wife from Spain, he ought to know that this queen would require more attention than any other, because the Spanish ladies were so lively that they equalled ten ordinary women, and that if he wished a wife for show only, he should get her from the north of Germany, where the women are cold as ice. The good knight came back to Touraine laden with wealth, and lived there many years, but never mentioned his adventures in Sicily. He returned there to aid the king's son in his principal attempt against Naples, and left Italy when this sweet prince was wounded, as is related in the Chronicle.

Besides the high moralities contained in the title of this tale, where it is said that fortune, being female, is always on the side of the ladies, and that men are quite right to serve them well, it shows us that silence is the better part of wisdom. Nevertheless, the monkish author of this narrative seems to draw this other no less learned moral therefrom, that interest which makes so many friendships, breaks them also. But from these three versions you can choose the one that best accords with your judgment and your momentary requirement.

CONCERNING A POOR MAN WHO WAS CALLED LE VIEUX PAR-CHEMINS

THE old chronicler who furnished the hemp to weave the present story, is said to have lived at the time when the affair occurred in the city of Rouen. In the environs of this fair town, where at that time dwelt Duke Richard, an old man used to beg, whose name was Tryballot, but to whom was given the nickname of *Le Vieux par-Chemins,* or Old Man of the Roads; not because he was yellow and dry as vellum, but because he was always in the high-ways and the by-ways—up hill and down dale—slept with the sky for his counterpane, and went about in rags and tatters. Notwithstanding this, he was very popular in the duchy, where every one had grown used to him, so much so that if the month went by without any one seing his cup held towards them, people would say, "Where is the old man?" and the usual answer was, "On the roads."

This said man had had for a father a Tryballot, who was in his lifetime a skilled artisan, so economical and care-ful, that he left considerable wealth to his son.

But the young lad soon frittered it away, for he was the very opposite of the old fellow, who, returning from the fields to his house, picked up, now here, now there, many a little stick of wood left right and left, saying, conscien-tiously, that one should never come home empty handed. Thus he warmed himself in winter at the expense of the careless; and he did well. Every one recognised what a good example this was for the country, since a year before his death no one left a morsel of wood on the road; he had compelled the most dissipated to be thrifty and orderly. But his son made ducks and drakes of everything, and did not follow his wise examples. The father had predicted the thing. From the boy's earliest youth, when the good Tryballot set him to watch the birds who came to eat the peas, the beans, and the grain, and to drive the thieves away, above all, the jays, who spoiled everything, he would study their habits, and took delight in watching with what grace they came and went, flew off loaded, and returned, watching with a quick eye the snares and nets; and he would laugh heartily at their cleverness in avoiding them. Tryballot senior went into a passion when he found his grain considerably less in measure. But although he pulled his son's ears whenever he caught him idling and trifling under a nut tree, the little rascal did not alter his conduct, but continued to study the habits of the blackbirds, sparrows, and other intelligent marauders. One day his father told him that he would be wise to model himself after them, for that if he continued this kind of life, he would be compelled in his old age, like them, to pilfer, and like them, would be pursued by justice. This came true; for, as has before been stated, he dissipated in a few days the crowns which his careful father had acquired in a lifetime. He dealt with men as he did with the sparrows, letting every one put a hand in his pocket, and contemplating the grace and polite demeanor of those who assisted to empty it. The end of his wealth was thus soon reached. When the devil had the empty money bag to himself, Tryballot did not appear at all cut up, saying, that he "did not wish to damn himself for this world's goods, and that he had studied philosophy in the school of the birds."

After having thoroughly enjoyed himself, of all his

goods, there only remained to him a goblet bought at
Landict, and three dice, quite sufficient furniture for drinking and gambling, so that he went about without being
encumbered, as are the great, with chariots, carpets, drip-
ping-pans, and an infinite number of varlets. Tryballot
wished to see his good friends, but they no longer knew
him, which fact gave him leave no longer to recognise any
one. Seeing this, he determined to choose a profession in
which there was nothing to do and plenty to gain. Thinking
this over, he remembered the indulgences of the blackbirds
and the sparrows. Then the good Tryballot selected for his
profession that of begging money at people's houses, and
pilfering. From the first day, charitable people gave him
something, and Tryballot was content, finding the business
good, without advance money or bad debts; on the contrary,
full of accommodation. He went about it so heartily, that
he was liked everywhere, and received a thousand consolations refused to rich people. The good man watched the
peasants planting, sowing, reaping, and making harvest,
and said to himself, that they worked a little for him as well.
He who had a pig in his larder owed him a bit of it, without
suspecting it. The man who baked a loaf in his oven often
cooked it for Tryballot without knowing it. He took nothing
by force; on the contrary, people said to him kindly, while
making him a present, "Here, Vieux par-Chemins, cheer
up, old fellow. How are you? Come, take this; the cat began
it, you can finish it."

Vieux par-Chemins was at all the weddings, baptisms,
and funerals, because he went everywhere where there was,
openly or secretly, merriment and feasting. He religiously
kept the statutes and canons of his order—namely, to do
nothing, because if he had been able to do the smallest
amount of work no one would ever give him anything

again. After having refreshed himself, this wise man would lay at full length in a ditch, or against a church wall, and think over public affairs; and then he would philosophise, like his pretty tutors, the blackbirds, jays, and sparrows, and thought a good deal while mumping; for, because his apparel was poor, was that a reason his understanding should not be rich? His philosophy amused his clients, to whom he would repeat, by way of thanks, the finest aphorisms of his science. According to him, suppers produced gout in the rich; he boasted that he had nimble feet, because his shoemaker gave him boots that did not pinch his corns. There were aching heads beneath diadems, but his never ached, because it was touched neither by luxury nor any other chaplet. And again, that jewelled rings hindered the circulation of the blood. Although he covered himself with sores after the manner of cadgers, you may be sure he was as sound as a child at the baptismal font. The good man disported himself with other rogues, playing with his three dice, which he kept to remind him to spend his coppers, in order that he might always be poor. In spite of his vow, he was, like all the order of mendicants, so wealthy that one day at the Paschal feast, another beggar wishing to rent his profit from him, Vieux par-Chemins refused ten crowns for it; in fact, the same evening he spent fourteen crowns in drinking the healths of the alms-givers, because it is in the statutes of beggary that one should show one's gratitude to donors. Although he carefully got rid of that which had been a source of anxiety to others, who having too much wealth went in search of poverty, he was happier with nothing in the world than when he had his father's money. And seeing what are the conditions of nobility, he was always on the high road to it, because he did nothing except according to his fancy, and lived nobly without la-

bour. Thirty crowns would not have got him out of a bed
when he was once in it. The morrow always dawned for
him as it did for others, while leading this happy life;
which, according to the statement of Plato, whose authority
has more than once been invoked in these narratives, certain ancient sages had led before him. At last Vieux par-
Chemins reached the age of eighty-two years, having never
been a single day without picking up money, and possessed
the healthiest colour and complexion imaginable. He believed that if he had persevered in the race for wealth he
would have been spoiled and buried years before. It is possible he was right.

In his early youth Vieux par-Chemins had the illustrious
virtue of being very partial to the ladies; and his abundance of love was, it is said, the result of his studies among
the sparrows. Thus it was that he was always ready to give
the ladies his assistance in counting the joists, and this
generosity finds its physical cause in the fact that, having
nothing to do, he was always ready to do something. His
secret virtues brought about, it is said, that popularity
which he enjoyed in the provinces. Certain people say that
the lady of Caumont had him in her castle, to learn the
truth about these qualities, and kept him there for a
week, to prevent him begging. But the good man jumped
over the hedges and fled in great terror of being rich. Ad-
vancing in age, this great quintessencer found himself disdained, although his notable faculties of loving were in no
way impaired. This unjust turning away on the part of the
female tribe caused the first trouble of Vieux par-Chemins,
and the celebrated trial of Rouen, to which it is time I came.

In the eighty-second year of his age he was compelled
to remain continent for about seven months, during which
time he met no woman kindly disposed towards him; and

he declared before the judge that that caused the greatest astonishment of his long and honourable life. In this most pitiable state he saw in the fields during the merry month of May a girl, who by chance was a maiden, and minding cows. The heat was so excessive that this cowherdess had stretched herself beneath the shadow of a beech tree, her face to the ground, after the custom of people who labour in the fields, in order to get a little nap while her animals were grazing. She was awakened by the deed of the old man, who had stolen from her that which a poor girl can only lose once. Finding herself ruined without receiving from the process either knowledge or pleasure, she cried out so loudly that the people working in the fields ran to her, and were called upon by her as witnesses, at the time when that destruction was visible in her which is appropriate only to a bridal night. She cried and groaned, saying that the old ape might just as well have played his tricks on her mother, who would have said nothing.

He made answer to the peasants, who had already raised their hoes to kill him, that he had been compelled to enjoy himself. These people objected that a man can enjoy himself very well without enjoying a maiden—a case for the provost, which would bring him straight to the gallows; and he was taken with a great clamour to the gaol at Rouen.

The girl, interrogated by the provost, declared that she was sleeping in order to do something, and that she thought she was dreaming of her lover, with whom she was then at loggerheads, because before marriage he wished to take certain liberties; and, jokingly, in this dream she let him reconnoitre to a certain extent, in order to avoid any dispute afterwards, and that in spite of her prohibition he went further than she had given him leave to go, and finding

more pain than pleasure in the affair, she had been awakened by Vieux par-Chemins, who had attacked her as a
grey-friar would a ham at the end of Lent.

This trial caused so great a commotion in the town of
Rouen that the provost was sent for by the duke, who had
an intense desire to know if the thing were true. Upon the
affirmation of the provost, he ordered Vieux par-Chemins
to be brought to his palace, in order that he might hear
what defence he had to make. The poor old fellow appeared
before the prince, and informed him naïvely of the misfortune which his impulsive nature had brought upon him,
declaring that he was like a young fellow impelled by
imperious desires; that up to the present year he had sweethearts of his own, but for the last eight months he had
been a total abstainer; that he was too poor to find favour
with girls of the town; that honest women, who once were
charitable to him, had taken a dislike to his hair, which had
feloniously turned white in spite of the green youth of his
love, and that he felt compelled to avail himself of the
chance when he saw this maiden, who, stretched at full
length under the beech tree, left visible the lining of her
dress and two hemispheres white as snow, which had deprived him of reason; that the fault was the girl's and not
his, because young maidens should be forbidden to entice
passers-by by showing them that which caused Venus to
be named *Callipyge;* finally, the prince ought to be aware
what trouble a man has to control himself at the hour of
noon, because that was the time of day at which King
David was smitten with the wife of the Sieur Uriah; that
where a Hebrew king, beloved of God, had succumbed, a
poor man, deprived of all joy, and reduced to begging his
bread, could not expect to escape; that for the matter of
that, he was quite willing to sing psalms for the remainder

of his days, and play upon the lute by way of penance, in
imitation of the said king, who had had the misfortune to
slay a husband, while he had only done a trifling injury to
a peasant girl. The duke listened to the arguments of Vieux
par-Chemins, and said that he was a man of good parts.
Then he made this memorable decree, that if, as this beggar declared, he had need of such gratifications at his age,
he gave permission to prove it at the foot of the ladder
which he would have to mount to be hanged, according to
the sentence already passed on him by the provost; that
if then, the rope being round his neck, between the priest
and the hangman, a like desire seized him he should have
a free pardon.

This decree becoming known, there was a tremendous
crowd to see the old fellow led to the gallows. There was
a line drawn up as if for a ducal entry, and in it a many
more bonnets than hats. Vieux par-Chemins was saved by
a lady curious to see how this precious violator would finish
his career. She told the duke that religion demanded that
he should have a fair chance. And she dressed herself out
as if for a ball; she brought intentionally into evidence two
hillocks of such snowy whiteness that the whitest linen
neckerchief would have paled before them; indeed, these
fruits of love stood out, without a wrinkle, over her corset,
like two beautiful apples, and made one's mouth water, so
exquisite were they. This noble lady, who was one of those
who rouse one's manhood, had a smile ready on her lips
for the old fellow. Vieux par-Chemins, dressed in garments of coarse cloth, more certain of being in the desired
state after hanging than before it, came along between the
officers of justice, with a sad countenance, glancing now
here and there, and seeing nothing but head-dresses; and
he wòǔld, he declared, have given a hundred crowns for a

girl tucked up as was the cowherdess, whose lovely plump white thighs, though they had been his ruin, he still remembered, and they might still have saved him; but, as he was old, the remembrance was not sufficiently recent. But when, at the foot of the ladder, he saw the twin charms of the lady, and the pretty delta that their confluent rotundities produced, his swelling codpiece revealed his excitement.

"Make haste and see that the required conditions are fulfilled," said he to the officers. "I have gained my pardon, but I cannot answer for my saviour."

The lady was well pleased with this homage, which, she said, was greater than his offence. The guards, whose business it was to proceed to a verification, believed the culprit to be the devil, because never in their writs had they seen an I so perpendicular as was the old man. He was marched in triumph through the town to the palace of the duke, to whom the guards and others stated the facts. In that period of ignorance, this affair was thought so much of that the town voted the erection of a column on the spot where the old fellow gained his pardon, and he was portrayed thereon in stone in the attitude he assumed at the sight of that honest and virtuous lady. The statue was still to be seen when Rouen was taken by the English, and the writers of the period have included this history among the notable events of the reign.

As the town offered to supply the old man with all he required, and see to his sustenance, clothing, and amusements, the good duke arranged matters by giving the injured maiden a thousand crowns and marrying her to her seducer, who then lost his name of Vieux par-Chemins. He was named by the duke the Sieur de Bonne-C——. This wife was confined nine months afterwards of a perfectly formed male child, alive and kicking, and born with

two teeth. From this marriage came the house of Bonne-
C——, who, from motives modest but wrong, besought
our well-beloved king Louis Eleventh to grant them letters patent to change their name into that of Bonne-Chose.
The king pointed out to the Sieur de Bonne-C—— that
there was in the State of Venice an illustrious family
named *Coglioni,* who wore three "C—— au naturel" on
their coat of arms. The gentlemen of the House of Bonne-
C—— stated to the king that their wives were ashamed to
be thus called in public assemblies; the king answered that
they would lose a good deal, because there is a good deal in
a name. Nevertheless, he granted the letters. After that
this race was known by this name, and founded families
in many provinces. The first Sieur de Bonne-C—— lived
another twenty-seven years, and had another son and two
daughters. But he grieved much at becoming rich, and no
longer being able to pick up a living in the streets.

From this you can obtain finer lessons and higher morals
than from any story you will read all your life long—of
course, excepting these hundred glorious Droll Tales—
namely, that never could adventure of this sort have happened to the impaired and ruined constitutions of court
rascals, rich people, and others who dig their graves with
their teeth by over-eating and drinking many wines that
impair the implements of happiness; which said over-fed
people were lolling luxuriously in costly draperies and on
feather beds, while the Sieur de Bonne-Chose was rough-
ing it. In a similar situation, if they had eaten cabbage, it
would have given them the diarrhœa. This may incite many
of those who read this story to change their mode of life,
in order to imitate Vieux par-Chemins in his old age.

ODD SAYINGS OF THREE PILGRIMS

WHEN the pope left his good town of Avignon to take up his residence in Rome, certain pilgrims were thrown out who had set out for this country, and would have to pass the high Alps, in order to gain this said town of Rome, where they were going to seek the *remittimus* of various sins. Then were to be seen on the roads, and in the hostelries, those who wore the collar of the order of Cain, otherwise the flower of the penitents, all wicked fellows, burthened with leprous souls, which thirsted to bathe in the papal piscina, and all carrying with them gold or precious things to purchase absolution, pay for their beds, and present to the saints. You may be sure that those who drank water going, on their return, if the landlords gave them water, wished it to be the holy water of the cellar.

At this time three pilgrims came to this said town of Avignon to their injury, seeing that it was widowed of the pope. While they were passing the Rhodane, to reach the Mediterranean coast, one of the three pilgrims, who had with him a son about ten years of age, parted company with the others, and near the town of Milan suddenly appeared again, but without the boy. Now in the evening, at supper, they had a hearty feast in order to celebrate the return of the pilgrim, who they thought had become disgusted with penitence through the pope not being in Avignon. Of these three roamers towards Rome, one had come from the city of Paris, the other from Germany, and the third, who doubtless wished to instruct his son on the journey, had his home in the duchy of Burgundy, in which he had certain fiefs, was a younger son of the house of Villers-la-Faye (*Villa in Fago*), and was named La Vaugrenand. The German baron had met the citizen of Paris just past Lyons, and both had accosted the Sire de la Vaugrenand in sight of Avignon.

Now, in this hostelry the three pilgrims loosened their tongues, and agreed to journey to Rome together, in order the better to resist the footpads, night-birds, and other malefactors, who made it their business to ease pilgrims of that which weighed upon their bodies before the pope eased them of that which weighed upon their consciences. After drinking, the three companions commenced to talk together, for the bottle is the key of conversation, and each made his confession—that the cause of his pilgrimage was a woman. The servant who watched them drinking, told them that of a hundred pilgrims who stopped in the locality, ninety-nine were travelling from the same thing. These three wise men then began to consider how pernicious is woman to man. The baron showed the heavy gold chain that he had in his hauberk to present to Saint Peter, and said his crime was such that he would not get rid of with the value of two such chains. The Parisian took off his glove and exposed a ring set with a white diamond, saying that he had a hundred like it for the pope. The Burgundian took off his hat, and exhibited two wonderful pearls, that were beautiful ear pendants for Notre-Dame-de-Lorette, and candidly confessed that he would rather have left them round his wife's neck.

Thereupon the servant exclaimed that their sins must have been as great as those of Visconti.

Then the pilgrims replied that they were such that they had each made a solemn vow in their minds never to go astray again during the remainder of their days, however beautiful the woman might be, and this in addition to the penance which the pope might impose upon them.

Then the servant expressed her astonishment that all had made the same vow. The Burgundian added, that this vow had been the cause of his lagging behind, because he had been in extreme fear that his son, in spite of his age, might go astray, and that he had made a vow to prevent people and beasts alike gratifying their passions in his house, or upon his estates. The baron having inquired the particulars of the adventure, the sire narrated the affair as follows:—

"You know that the good Countess Jeanne d'Avignon made formerly a law for the harlots, whom she compelled to live in the outskirts of the town in houses with window-shutters painted red and closed. Now passing in your company through this vile neighbourhood, my lad remarked these houses with closed window-shutters, painted red, and his curiosity being aroused—for these ten-year-old little devils have eyes for everything—he pulled me by the sleeve, and kept on pulling me until he had learned from me what these houses were. Then, to obtain peace, I told him that young lads had nothing to do with such places, and could only enter them at peril of their lives, because it was a place where men and women were manufactured, and the danger was such for any one unacquainted with the business that if a novice entered, flying chancres and other wild beasts would seize upon his face. Fear seized the lad, who then followed me to the hostelry in a state of agitation, and not daring to cast his eyes upon these said bordels. While I was in the stable, seeing to the putting up of the horses, my son went off like a robber, and the servant was unable to tell me what had become of him. Then I was in great fear of the wenches, but had confidence in the laws, which forbade them to admit such children. At supper time the rascal came back to me looking no more ashamed of himself than did our divine Saviour in the temple among the doctors. 'Whence come you?' said I to him. 'From the houses with the red shutters,' he replied. 'Little blackguard,' said I, 'I'll give you a taste of the whip.' Then he began to moan and cry. I told him that if he would confess all that had happened to him I would let him off the beating. 'Ha,' said he, 'I took good care not to go in, because of the flying chancres and other wild beasts. I only looked through the chinks of the windows, in order to see how men were manufactured.' 'And what did you see?' I asked. 'I saw,' said he, 'a fine woman just being finished, because she only wanted one peg, which a young workman was fitting in with energy. Directly she was finished she turned round, spoke to, and kissed her manufacturer.'

" 'Have your supper,' said I; and the same night I returned into Burgundy, and left him with his mother, being sorely afraid that at the first town he might want to fit a peg into some girl."

"These children often make these sort of answers," said the Parisian. "One of my neighbour's children revealed the cuckoldom of his father by a reply. One day I asked, to see if he were well instructed at school in religious matters, 'What is hope?' 'One of the king's big archers, who comes here when father goes out,' said he. Indeed, the sergeant of the archers was named Hope. My friend was dumbfounded at this, and, although to keep his countenance he looked in the mirror, he could not see his horns there."

The baron observed that the boy's remark was good in this way: that Hope is a person who comes to bed with us when the realities of life are out of the way.

"Is a cuckold made in the image of God?" asked the Burgundian.

"No," said the Parisian, "because God was wise in this respect, that he took no wife; therefore is He happy through all eternity."

"But," said the maid-servant, "cuckolds are made in the image of God before they are horned."

Then the three pilgrims began to curse the women, saying that they were the cause of all the evil in the world.

"Their heads are as empty as helmets," said the Burgundian.

"Their hearts as straight as bill-hooks," said the Parisian.

"Why are there so many men pilgrims and so few women pilgrims?" said the German baron.

"Their cursed member never sins," replied the Parisian; "it knows neither father nor mother, the commandments of God, nor those of the Church, neither laws divine nor human: their member knows no doctrine, understands no heresies, and cannot be blamed; it is innocent of all, and always on the laugh; its understanding is *nil;* and for this reason do I hold it in utter detestation."

"I also," said the Burgundian, "and I begin to understand the different reading by a learned man of the verses of the Bible, in which the account of the Creation is given. In this Commentary, which in my country we call a *Noël,* lies the reason of imperfection of this feature of women, of which, different to that of other females, no man can slake the thirst, such diabolical heat existing there. In this Noël it is stated that the Lord God, having turned his head to look at a donkey, who had brayed for the first time in his Paradise, while he was manufacturing Eve, the devil seized this moment to put his finger into this too divine creature, and made a warm wound, which the Lord took care to close with a stitch, from which comes the maid. By means of this frenum, the woman should remain closed, and children be made in the same manner in which God made the angels, by a pleasure far above carnal pleasure as the heaven is above the earth. Observing this closing, the devil, wild at being done, pinched the Sieur Adam, who was asleep, by the skin, and stretched a portion of it out in imitation of his diabolical tail; but as the father of man was on his back this appendage came out in front. Thus these two productions of the devil had a desire to reunite themselves, following the law of similarities which God had laid down for the conduct of the world. From this came the first sin and the sorrows of the human race, because God, noticing the devil's work, determined to see what would come of it."

The servant declared that they were quite correct in their statements, for that woman was a bad animal, and that she herself knew some who were better under the ground than on it. The pilgrims, noticing then how pretty the girl was, were afraid of breaking their vows, and went straight to bed. The girl went and told her mistress that she was harbouring infidels, and told her what they had said about women.

"Ah!" said the landlady, "what matters it to me the thoughts my customers have in their brains, so long as their purses are well filled."

And when the servant had told of the jewels, she exclaimed—

"Ah, these are questions which concern all women. Let us go and reason with them. I'll take the nobles, you can have the citizen."

The landlady, who was the most shameless inhabitant of the duchy of Milan, went into the chamber where the Sire de la Vaugrenand and the German baron were sleeping, and congratulated them upon their vows, saying that the women would not lose much by them; but to accomplish these said vows it was necessary they should endeavour to withstand the strongest temptation. Then she offered to lie down beside them, so anxious was she to see if she would be left unmolested, a thing which had never happened to her yet in the company of a man.

On the morrow, at breakfast, the servant had the ring on her finger, her mistress had the gold chain and the pearl earrings. The three pilgrims stayed in the town about a month, spending there all the money they had in their purses, and agreed that if they had spoken so severely of women it was because they had not known those of Milan.

On his return to Germany the baron made this observation: that he was only guilty of one sin, that of being in his castle. The citizen of Paris came back full of stories for his wife, and found her full of Hope. The Burgundian saw Madame de la Vaugrenand so troubled that he nearly died of the consolations he administered to her, in spite of his former opinions. This teaches us to hold our tongues in hostelries.

INNOCENCE

By the double crest of my fowl, and by the rose lining of my sweetheart's slipper! By all the horns of well-beloved cuckolds, and by the virtue of their blessed wives! the finest work of man is neither poetry, nor painted pictures, nor music, nor castles, nor statues, be they carved never so well, nor rowing, nor sailing galleys, but children. Understand me, children up to the age of ten years, for after that they become men or women, and cutting their wisdom teeth, are not worth what they cost: the worst are the best. Watch them playing, prettily and innocently, with slippers; above all, cancellated ones, with the household utensils, leaving that which displeases them, crying after that which pleases them, munching the sweets and confectionery in the house, nibbling at the stores, and always laughing as soon as their teeth are cut, and you will agree with me that they are in every way lovable; besides which they are flower and fruit—the fruit of love, the flower of life. Before their minds have been unsettled by the disturbances of life, there is nothing in this world more blessed or more pleasant than their sayings, which are naïve beyond description. This is as true as the double chewing machine of a cow. Do not expect a man to be innocent after the manner of children, because there is an, I know not what, ingredient of reason in the naïveté of a man, while the naïveté of children is candid, immaculate, and has all the finesse of the mother, which is plainly proved in this tale.

Queen Catherine was at that time Dauphine, and to make

herself welcome to the king, her father-in-law, who at that
time was very ill indeed, presented him, from time to time,
with Italian pictures, knowing that he liked them much,
being a friend of the Sieur Raphaël d'Urbin and of the
Sieurs Primatice and Leonardo da Vinci, to whom he sent
large sums of money. She obtained from her family—who
had the pick of these works, because at that time the Duke
of Medicis governed Tuscany—a precious picture, painted
by a Venetian named Titian (artist to the Emperor Charles,
and in very high favour), in which there were portraits
of Adam and Eve at the moment when God left them to
wander about the terrestrial Paradise, and were painted
their full height, in the costume of the period, in which it
is difficult to make a mistake, because they were attired in
their ignorance, and caparisoned with the divine grace
which enveloped them—a difficult thing to execute on account of the colour, but one in which the said Sieur Titian
excelled. The picture was put into the room of the poor
king, who was then ill with the disease of which he eventually died. It had a great success at the Court of France,
where every one wished to see it; but no one was able to
until after the king's death, since at his desire it was allowed to remain in his room as long as he lived.

One day Madame Catherine took with her to the king's
room her son Francis and little Margot, who began to talk
at random, as children will. Now here, now there, these
children had heard this picture of Adam and Eve spoken
about, and had tormented their mother to take them there.
Since the two little ones at times amused the old king,
Madame the Dauphine consented to their request.

"You wished to see Adam and Eve, who were our first
parents; there they are," said she.

Then she left them in great astonishment before Titian's

picture, and seated herself by the bedside of the king, who delighted to watch the children.

"Which of the two is Adam?" said Francis, nudging his sister Margaret's elbow.

"You silly!" replied she, "to know that, they would have to be dressed!"

This reply, which delighted the poor king and the mother, was mentioned in a letter written in Florence by Queen Catherine.

No writer having brought it to light, it will remain, like a sweet flower, in a corner of these Tales, although it is in no way droll, and there is no other moral to be drawn from it except that to hear these pretty speeches of infancy one must beget the children.

THE FAIR IMPERIA MARRIED

I

THE lovely lady Imperia, who gloriously opens these tales, because she was the glory of her time, was compelled to come into the town of Rome, after the holding of the council, for the Cardinal of Ragusa loved her more than his cardinal's hat, and wished to have her near him. This rascal was so magnificent, that he presented her with the beautiful palace that she had in the Papal capital. About this time she had the misfortune to find herself in an interesting condition by this cardinal. As every one knows, this pregnancy finished with a fine little daughter, concerning whom the Pope said jokingly that she should be named Theodora, as if to say *The Gift of God*. The girl was thus named, and was exquisitely lovely. The cardinal left his inheritance to this Theodora, whom the fair Imperia established in her hotel, for she was flying from Rome as from a pernicious place, where children were begotten, and where she had nearly spoilt her beautiful figure, her celebrated perfections, lines of the body, curves of the back, delicious breasts, and serpentine charms which placed her as much above the other women of Christendom as the Holy Father was above all other Christians. But all her lovers knew that with the assistance of eleven doctors of Padua, seven master surgeons of Pavia, and five surgeons come from all parts, who assisted at her confinement, she was preserved from all injury. Some go so far as to say that she gained therein superfineness and whiteness of skin. A famous man, of the school of Salerno, wrote a book on the subject, to show the value of a confinement for the freshness, health, preservation, and beauty of women. In this very learned book it was clearly proved to readers that that which was beautiful to see in Imperia, was that which it was permissible for lovers alone to behold; a rare case then, for she did not disarrange her attire for the petty German princes whom she called her margraves, burgraves, electors, and dukes, just as a captain ranks his soldiers.

Every one knows that when she was eighteen years of age, the lovely Theodora, to atone for her mother's gay life, wished to retire into the bosom of the Church. With this idea she placed herself in the hands of a cardinal, in order that he might instruct her in the duties of the devout. This wicked shepherd found the lamb so magnificently beautiful that he attempted to debauch. Theodora instantly stabbed herself with a stiletto, in order not to be contaminated by the evil-minded priest. This adventure, which was consigned to the history of the period, made a great commotion in Rome, and was deplored by every one, so much was the daughter of Imperia beloved.

Then this noble courtesan, much afflicted, returned to Rome, there to weep for her poor daughter. She set out in the thirty-ninth year of her age, which was, according to some authors, the summer of her magnificent beauty, because then she had attained the acme of her perfection, like ripe fruit. Sorrow made her haughty and hard with those who spoke to her of love, in order to dry her tears. The pope himself visited her in her palace, and gave her

certain words of admonition. But she refused to be comforted, saying that she would henceforward devote herself
to God, because she had never yet been satisfied by any
man, although she had ardently desired it; and all of them,
even a little priest, whom she had adored like a saint's
shrine, had deceived her. God, she was sure, would not do
so. This resolution disconcerted many, for she was the
joy of a vast number of lords. So that people ran about
the streets of Rome crying out, "Where is Madame Imperia? Is she going to deprive the world of love?" Some of
the ambassadors wrote to their masters on the subject.
The Emperor of the Romans was much cut up about it, because he loved her to distraction for eleven weeks; had left
her only to go to the wars, and loved her still as much as
his most precious member, which, according to his own
statement, was his eye, for that alone embraced the whole
of his dear Imperia. In this extremity the Pope sent for a
Spanish physician, and conducted him to the beautiful creature, to whom he proved, by various arguments, adorned
with Latin and Greek quotations, that beauty is impaired by
tears and tribulation, and that through sorrow's door wrinkles step in. This proposition, confirmed by the doctors of
the Holy College in controversy, had the effect of opening
the doors of the palace that same evening. The young cardinals, the foreign envoys, the wealthy inhabitants, and the
principal men of the town of Rome came, crowded the
rooms, and held a joyous festival; the common people
made grand illuminations, and thus the whole population
celebrated the return of the Queen of Pleasure to her occupation, for she was at that time the presiding deity of Love.
The experts in all the arts loved her much, because she spent
considerable sums of money in improving the church in
Rome, which contained poor Theodora's tomb, which was

destroyed during that pillage of Rome in which perished
the traitorous constable of Bourbon, for this holy maiden
was placed therein in a massive coffin of gold and silver,
which the cursed soldiers were anxious to obtain. The
basilic cost, it is said, more than the pyramid erected by the
Lady Rhodepa, an Egyptian courtesan, eighteen hundred
years before the coming of our divine Saviour, which
proves the antiquity of this pleasant occupation, the extravagant prices which the wise Egyptians paid for their
pleasures, and how things deteriorate, seeing that now for
a trifle you can have a chemise full of female loveliness in
the Rue du Petit-Heulen, at Paris. Is it not an abomination?

Never had Madame Imperia appeared so lovely as at
this first gala after her mourning. All the princes, cardinals,
and others declared that she was worthy the homage of the
whole world, which was there represented by a noble from
every known land, and thus was it amply demonstrated
that beauty was in every place queen of everything. The
envoy of the King of France, who was a cadet of the house
of l'Ile Adam, arrived late, although he had never yet seen
Imperia, and was most anxious to do so. He was a handsome young knight, much in favour with his sovereign, in
whose court he had a mistress, whom he loved with infinite
tenderness, and who was the daughter of Monsieur de
Montmorency, a lord whose domains bordered upon those
of the house of l'Ile Adam. To this penniless cadet the king
had given certain missions to the duchy of Milan, of which
he had acquitted himself so well that he was sent to Rome
to advance the negotiations concerning which historians
have written so much in their books. Now if he had nothing
of his own, poor little l'Ile Adam relied upon so good a beginning. He was slightly built, but upright as a column,
dark, with black, glistening eyes, and a man not easily taken

in; but concealing his finesse, he had the air of an innocent child, which made him gentle and amiable as a laughing maiden. Directly this gentleman joined her circle, and her eyes had rested upon him, Madame Imperia felt herself bitten by a strong desire, which stretched the harp strings of her nature, and produced therefrom a sound she had not heard for many a day. She was seized with such a vertigo of true love at the sight of this freshness of youth, that but for her imperial dignity she would have kissed the good cheeks which shone like little apples. Now take note of this; that so called modest women, and ladies whose skirts bear their armorial bearings, are thoroughly ignorant of the nature of a man, because they keep to one alone, like that queen of France who believed all men had ulcers in the nose because the king had; but a great courtesan, like Madame Imperia, knew man to his core, because she had handled a great many. In her retreat every one came out in his true colours, and concealed nothing, thinking to himself that he would not be long with her. Having often deplored this subjection, sometimes she would remark that she suffered from pleasure more than she suffered from pain. There was the dark shadow of her life. You may be sure that a lover was often compelled to part with a nice little heap of crowns in order to pass the night with her, and was reduced to desperation by a refusal. Now for her it was a joyful thing to feel a youthful desire, like that she had for the little priest, whose story commences this collection; but because she was older than in those merry days, love was more fully established in her, and she soon perceived that it was of a fiery nature when it began to make itself felt; indeed, she suffered in her skin like a cat that is being scorched, and so much so that she had an intense longing to spring on to this gentleman, and bear him in tri-

umph to her nest, as a kite does its prey, but with great
difficulty she restrained herself. When he came and bowed
to her, she threw back her head, and assumed a most dig-
nified attitude, as do those who have a love infatuation in
their hearts. The gravity of her demeanour to the young
ambassador caused many to think that she had work in
store for him; equivocating on the word, after the custom
of the time. L'Ile Adam, knowing himself to be dearly
loved by his mistress, troubled himself but little about Madame Imperia, grave or gay, and frisked about like a goat
let loose. The courtesan, terribly annoyed at this, changed
her tone, from being sulky became gay and lively, came to
him, softened her voice, sharpened her glance, gracefully
inclined her head, rubbed against him with her sleeve, and
called him Monseigneur, embraced him with loving words,
trifled with his hand, and finished by smiling at him most
affably. He, not imagining that so unprofitable a lover
would suit her, for her was as poor as a church mouse, and
did not know that his beauty was equal in her eyes to all
the treasures of the world, was not taken in her trap, but
continued to ride the high horse with his hands on his hips.
This disdain of her passion irritated Madame to the heart,
which by this spark was set in flame. If you doubt this, it
is because you know nothing of the profession of Madame
Imperia, who by reason of it might be compared to a chimney, in which a great number of fires had been lighted,
which had filled it with soot; in this state a match was sufficient to burn everything there, where a hundred fagots
had smoked comfortably. She burned within from top to
toe in a horrible manner, and could not be extinguished
save with the water of love. The cadet of l'Ile Adam left
the room without noticing this ardour. Madame, discon-
solate at his departure, lost her senses from her head to her

feet, and so thoroughly that she sent a messenger to him in the galleries, begging him to pass the night with her. On no other occasion of her life had she had this cowardice, either for king, pope, or emperor, since the high price of her favours came from the bondage in which she held her admirers, whom the more she humbled the more she raised herself. The disdainful hero of this history was informed by the head chamber-woman, who was a clever jade, that in all probability a great treat awaited him, for most certainly Madame would regale him with her most delicate inventions of love. L'Ile Adam returned to the salons, delighted at this lucky chance. Directly the envoy of France reappeared, as every one had seen Imperia turn pale at his departure, the general joy knew no bounds, because every one was delighted to see her return to her old life of love. An English cardinal, who had drained more than one big-bellied flagon, and wished to taste Imperia, went to l'Ile Adam and whispered to him, "Hold her fast, so that she shall never again escape us." The story of this night was told to the pope at his levée, and caused him to remark, *Laetamini, gentes, quoniam surrexit Dominnus*. A quotation which the old cardinals abominated as a profanation of sacred texts. Seeing which, the pope reprimanded them severely, and took occasion to lecture them, telling them that if they were good Christians they were bad politicians. Indeed, he relied upon the fair Imperia to reclaim the emperor, and with this idea syringed her well with flattery.

The lights of the palace being extinguished, the golden flagons on the floor, and the servants drunk and stretched about on the carpets, Madame entered her bed-chamber, leading by the hand her dear lover-elect; and she was well pleased, and has since confessed that so strongly was she bitten with love, she could hardly restrain herself from rolling at his feet like a beast of the field, begging him to crush her beneath him if he could. L'Ile Adam slipped off his garments, and tumbled into bed as if he were in his own house. Seeing which, Madame hastened her preparations, and sprang into her lover's arms with a frenzy that astonished her women, who knew her to be ordinarily one of the most modest of women on these occasions. This astonishment became general throughout the country, for the pair remained in bed for nine days, eating, drinking, and embracing in a marvellous and most masterly manner. Madame told her women that at last she had put her hand on a phœnix of love, since he revived from every attack. Nothing was talked of in Rome and Italy but the victory that had been gained over Imperia, who had boasted that she would yield to no man, and spat upon all of them, even the dukes. As to the aforesaid margraves and burgraves, she gave them the tail of her dress to hold, and said that if she did not tread them under foot, they would trample upon her. Madame confessed to her servants that, differently to all the other men she had had to put up with, the more she fondled this child of love, the more she desired to do so, and that she would never be able to part with him; nor his splendid eyes, which blinded her; nor his branch of coral, that she always hungered after. She further declared that if such were his desire, she would let him suck her blood, and eat her breasts—which were the most lovely in the world—and cut her tresses, of which she had only given a single one to the Emperor of the Romans, who kept it in his breast, like a precious relic; finally, she confessed that on that night only had life begun for her, because the embrace of Villiers de l'Ile Adam sent the blood to her in three bounds and in a brace of shakes. These expressions becoming known, made every one very miserable. Directly she went out, Imperia told the ladies of Rome that she should die if she were deserted by this gentleman, and would cause herself, like Queen Cleopatra, to be bitten by an asp. She declared openly that she had bidden an eternal adieu to her former gay life, and would show the whole world what virtue was by abandoning her empire for this Villiers de l'Ile Adam, whose servant she would rather be than reign over Christendom. The English cardinal remonstrated with the pope that this love for one, in the heart of a woman who was the joy of all, was an infamous depravity, and that he ought with a brief *in partibus,* to annul this marriage, which robbed the fashionable world of its principal attraction. But the love of this poor woman, who had confessed the miseries of her life, was so sweet a thing, and so moved the most dissipated heart, that he silenced all clamour, and every one forgave her her happiness. One day during Lent, Imperia made her people fast, and ordered them to go and confess, and return to God. She herself went and fell at the pope's feet, and there showed such penitence, that she obtained from him remission of all her sins, believing that the absolution of the pope would communicate to her soul that virginity which she was grieved at being unable to offer to her lover. It is impossible to help thinking that there was some virtue in the ecclesiastical piscina, for the poor cadet was so smothered with love that he fancied himself in Paradise, and left the negotiations of the King of France, left his love for Mademoiselle de Montmorency—in fact, left everything to marry Madame Imperia, in order that he might live and die with her. Such was the effect of the learned ways of this great lady of pleasure directly she turned her science to the profit of a virtuous love. Imperia bade adieu to her admirers at a royal feast, given in honour of her wedding, which was a won-

derful ceremony, at which all the Italian princes were present. She had, it is said, a million gold crowns; in spite of
the vastness of this sum, every one, far from blaming l'Ile
Adam, paid him many compliments, because it was evident
that neither Madame Imperia nor her young husband
thought of anything but one. The pope blessed their marriage and said that it was a fine thing to see the foolish
virgin returning to God by the road of marriage.

But during that last night in which it would be permissible
for all to behold the Queen of Beauty, who was about to
become a simple chatelaine of the kingdom of France,
there were a great number of men who mourned for the
merry nights, the suppers, the masked balls, the joyous
games, and the melting hours, when each one emptied his
heart to her. Every one regretted the ease and freedom which
had always been found in the residence of this lovely
creature, who now appeared more tempting than she had
ever done in her life, for the fervid heat of her great love
made her glisten like a summer sun. Much did they lament
the fact that she had had the sad phantasy to become a
respectable woman. To these Madame de l'Ile Adam
answered jestingly, that after twenty-four years passed in
the service of the public, she had a right to retire. Others
said to her, that however distant the sun was, people could
warm themselves in it, while she would show herself no
more. To these she replied that she would still have smiles
to bestow upon those lords who would come and see how
she played the rôle of a virtuous woman. To this the English
envoy answered, he believed her capable of pushing virtue
to its extreme point. She gave a present to each of her
friends, and large sums to the poor and suffering of Rome;
besides this, she left to the convent where her daughter was
to have been, and to the church she had built, the wealth

she had inherited from Theodora, which came from the Cardinal of Ragusa.

When the two spouses set out they were accompanied a long way by knights in mourning, and even by the common people, who wished them every happiness, because Madame Imperia had been hard on the rich only, and had always been kind and gentle with the poor. This lovely queen of love was hailed with acclamations throughout the journey in all the towns of Italy where the report of her conversion had spread, and where every one was curious to see pass, a case so rare as two such spouses. Several princes received this handsome couple at their courts, saying it was but right to show honour to this woman who had the courage to renounce her empire over the world of fashion, to become a virtuous woman. But there was an evil-minded fellow, one my lord Duke of Ferrara, who said to l'Ile Adam that his great fortune had not cost him much. At this first offence Madame Imperia showed what a good heart she had, for she gave up all the money she had received from her lovers to ornament the dome of St. Maria del Fiore, in the town of Florence, which turned the laugh against the Sire d'Este, who boasted that he had built a church in spite of the empty condition of his purse. You may be sure he was reprimanded for this joke by his brother the cardinal. The fair Imperia only kept her own wealth and that which the Emperor had bestowed upon her out of pure friendship since his departure, the amount of which was, however, considerable. The cadet of l'Ile Adam had a duel with the duke, in which he wounded him. Thus neither Madame de l'Ile Adam nor her husband could be in any way reproached. This piece of chivalry caused her to be gloriously received in all places she passed through, especially in Piedmont, where the fêtes were splendid. Verses, which the poet then composed, such as sonnets, epithalamias, and odes, have been given in certain collections; but all poetry was weak in comparison with her, who was, according to an expression of Monsieur Boccaccio, poetry itself.

The prize in this tourney of fêtes and gallantry must be awarded to the good Emperor of the Romans, who, knowing of the misbehaviour of the Duke of Ferrera, despatched an envoy to his old flame, charged with Latin manuscripts, in which he told her that he loved her so much for herself, that he was delighted to know that she was happy, but grieved to know that all her happiness was not derived from him; that he had lost the right to make her presents, but that, if the king of France received her coldly, he would think it an honour to acquire a Villiers to the holy empire, and would give him such principalities as he might choose from his domains. The fair Imperia replied that she was extremely obliged to the Emperor, but that had she to suffer contumely upon contumely in France, she still intended there to finish her days.

II

HOW THIS MARRIAGE ENDED

Not knowing if she would be received or not, the lady of l'Ile Adam would not go to Court, but lived in the country, where her husband made a fine establishment, purchasing the manor of Beaumont-le-Vicomte, which gave rise to the equivoke upon this name, made by our well-beloved Rabelais, in his most magnificent book. He acquired also the domain of Nointel, the forest of Carenelle, St. Martin, and other places in the neighbourhood of l'Ile Adam, where his brother Villiers resided. These said acqui-

sitions made him the most powerful lord in the Ile de
France and county of Paris. He built a wonderful castle
near Beaumont, which was afterwards ruined by the English, and adorned it with the furniture, foreign tapestries,
chests, pictures, statues, and curiosities of his wife, who
was a great connoisseur, which made this place equal to the
most magnificent castles known. The happy pair led a life
so envied by all, that nothing was talked about in Paris and
at Court but this marriage, the good fortune of the Sire
de Beaumont, and, above all, the perfect, loyal, gracious,
and religious life of his wife, who from habit many still
called *Madame Imperia;* who was no longer proud and
sharp as steel, but had the virtues and qualities of a respectable woman, and was an example in many things to
a queen. She was much beloved by the Church on account
of her great religion, for she had never once forgotten
God, having, as she once said, spent much of her time with
churchmen, abbots, bishops, and cardinals, who had sprinkled her well with holy water, and under the curtains
worked her eternal salvation. The praises sung in honour
of this lady had such an effect, that the king came to
Beauvoisis to gaze upon this wonder, and did the sire the
honour to sleep at Beaumont, remained there three days,
and had a royal hunt there with the queen and the whole
Court. You may be sure that he was surprised, as were
also the queen, the ladies, and the Court, at the manners
of this superb creature, who was proclaimed lady of courtesy and beauty. The king first, then the queen, and afterwards every individual member of the company, complimented l'Ile Adam on having chosen such a wife. The modesty of the chatelaine did more than pride would have accomplished ; for she was invited to Court, and everywhere,
so imperious was her great heart, so tyrannic her violent

love for her husband. You may be sure that her charms, hidden under the garments of virtue, were none the less exquisite. The king gave the vacant post of lieutenant of the Ile de France and provost of Paris to his ancient ambassador, giving him the title of Viscount of Beaumont, which established him as governor of the whole province, and put him on an excellent footing at Court. But this was the cause of a great wound in Madame's heart, because a wretch, jealous of this unclouded happiness, asked her, playfully, if Beaumont had ever spoken to her of his first love, Mademoiselle de Montmorency, who at that time was twenty-two years of age, as she was sixteen at the time the marriage took place in Rome—the which young lady loved l'Ile Adam so much that she remained a maiden, would listen to no proposals of marriage, and was dying of a broken heart, unable to banish her perfidious lover from her remembrance, and was desirous of entering the convent of Chelles. Madame Imperia, during the six years of her marriage, had never heard this name, and was sure from this fact that she was indeed beloved. You can imagine that this time had been passed as a single day, that both believed they had only been married the evening before, and that each night was as a wedding night, and that if business took the knight out of doors, he was quite melancholy, being unwilling ever to have her out of his sight, and she was the same with him. The king, who was very partial to the viscount, also made a remark to him which stung him to the quick, when he said, "You have no children?" To which Beaumont replied with the face of a man whose raw place you have touched with your finger, "Monseigneur, my brother has; thus our line is safe."

Now it happened that his brother's two children died suddenly—one from a fall from his horse at a tournament

and the other from illness. Monsieur l'Ile Adam the elder
was so stricken with grief at these two deaths that he expired soon after, so much did he love his two sons. By this
means the manor of Beaumont, the property at Carenelle,
St. Martin, Nointel, and the surrounding domains, were re-
united to the manor of l'Ile Adam, and the neighbouring
forests, and the cadet became the head of the house. At
this time Madame was forty-five, and was still fit to bear
children; but, alas! she conceived not. As soon as she saw
the lineage of l'Ile Adam destroyed, she was anxious to
obtain offspring. Now, as during the seven years which
had elapsed she had never once had the slightest symptom
of pregnancy, she believed, according to the statement of a
clever physician whom she sent for from Paris, that this
barrenness proceeded from the fact, that both she and her
husband, always more lovers than spouses, allowed pleasure
to interfere with business, and by this means engendering
was prevented. Then she endeavoured to restrain her im-
petuosity, and to take things coolly, because the physician
had explained to her that in a state of nature animals never
failed to breed, because the females employed none of those
artifices, tricks, and hanky-pankies with which women accommodate the olives of Poissy, and for this reason they
thoroughly deserved the title of *beasts*. She promised him
no longer to play with such a serious affair, and to forget
all the ingenious devices in which she had been so fertile.
But, alas! although she kept as quiet as that German woman
who lay so still that her husband embraced her to death,
and then went, poor baron, to obtain absolution from the
pope, who delivered his celebrated brief, in which he requested the ladies of Franconia to be a little more lively,
and prevent a repetition of such a crime, Madame de l'Ile
Adam did not conceive, and fell into a state of great melan-

choly. Then she began to notice how thoughtful had become her husband, l'Ile Adam, whom she watched when he thought she was not looking, and who wept that he had no fruit of his great love. Soon this pair mingled their tears, for everything was common to the two in this fine household, and as they never left each other, the thought of the one was necessarily the thought of the other. When Madame beheld a poor person's child she nearly died of grief, and it took her a whole day to recover. Seeing this great sorrow, l'Ile Adam ordered all children to be kept out of his wife's sight, and said soothing things to her, such as that children often turned out badly; to which she replied, that a child made by those who loved so passionately would be the finest child in the world. He told her that their sons might perish, like those of his poor brother; to which she replied, that she would not let them stir further from her petticoats than a hen allows her chickens. In fact, she had an answer for everything. Madame caused a woman to be sent for who dealt in magic, and who was supposed to be learned in these mysteries, who told her that she had often seen women unable to conceive in spite of every effort, but yet they had succeeded by studying the manners and customs of animals. Madame took the beasts of the field for her preceptors, but she did not increase her size; her flesh still remained firm and white as marble. She returned to the physical science of the master doctors of Paris, and sent for a celebrated Arabian physician, who had just arrived in France with a new science. Then this *savant,* brought up in the school of one Sieur Averroes, entered into certain medical details, and declared that the loose life she had formerly led had for ever ruined her chance of obtaining offspring. The physical reasons which he assigned were so contrary to the teaching of the holy books which establish the majesty of man, made in the image of his Creator, and were so contrary to the system upheld by sound sense and good doctrine, that the doctors of Paris laughed them to scorn. The Arabian physician left the school where his master, the Sieur Averroes, was unknown. The doctors told Madame, who had come to Paris, that she was to keep on as usual, since she had had during her gay life the lovely Theodora, by the cardinal of Ragusa, and that the right of having children remained with women as long as their blood circulated, and that all she had to do was to multiply the chances of conception. This advice appeared to her so good that she multiplied her victories, but it was only multiplying her defeats, since she obtained the flowers of love without its fruits. The poor afflicted woman wrote then to the pope, who loved her much, and told him of her sorrows. The good pope replied to her with a gracious homily, written with his own hand, in which he told her that when human science and things terrestrial failed, we should turn to Heaven, and implore the grace of God. Then she determined to go with naked feet, accompanied by her husband, to Notre Dame de Liesse, celebrated for her intervention in similar cases, and made a vow to build a magnificent cathedral in gratitude for the child. But she bruised and injured her pretty feet, and conceived nothing but a violent grief, which was so great that some of her lovely tresses fell off and some turned white. At last the faculty of making children was taken from her, which brought on the vapours consequent upon hypochondria, and caused her skin to turn yellow. She was then forty-nine years of age, and lived in her castle of l'Ile Adam, where she grew as thin as a leper in a lazar-house. The poor creature was all the more wretched because l'Ile Adam was still amorous, and as good as gold to her, who failed in her

duty, because she had formerly been too free with the men,
and was now, according to her own disdainful remark, only
a cauldron to cook chitterlings. "Ha!" said she, one evening when these thoughts were tormenting her. "In spite
of the Church, in spite of the king, in spite of everything,
Madame de l'Ile Adam is still the wicked Imperia!" She
fell into a violent passion when she saw this handsome
gentleman have everything man can desire, great wealth,
royal favour, unequalled love, matchless wife, pleasure such
as none other could procure, and yet fail in that which is
dearest to the head of a house—namely, lineage. With this
idea in her head, she wished to die, thinking how good and
noble he had been to her, and how much she failed in her
duty in not giving him children, and in being henceforward
unable to do so. She hid her sorrow in the secret recesses
of her heart, and conceived a devotion worthy her great
love. To put into practice this heroic design she became still
more amorous, took extreme care of her charms, and made
use of learned precepts to maintain her bodily perfections,
which threw out an incredible lustre.

About this time the Sieur de Montmorency conquered
the repulsion his daughter entertained for marriage, and
her alliance with one Sieur de Chatillon was much talked
about. Madame Imperia, who lived only three leagues distant from Montmorency, one day sent her husband out
hunting in the forest, and set out towards the castle where
the young lady lived. Arrived in the grounds she walked
about there, telling a servant to inform his mistress that
a lady had a most important communication to make to her,
and that she had come to request an audience. Much in-
terested by the account which she received of the beauty,
courtesy, and manners of the unknown lady, Mademoiselle

de Montmorency went in great haste into the gardens, and there met her rival, whom she did not know.

"My dear," said the poor woman, weeping to find the young maiden as beautiful as herself, "I know that they are trying to force you into a marriage with Monsieur de Chatillon, although you still love Monsieur de l'Ile Adam. Have confidence in the prophecy that I here make you, that he whom you have loved, and who only was false to you through a snare into which an angel might have fallen, will be free from the burden of his old wife before the leaves fall. Thus the constancy of your love will have its crown of flowers. Now have the courage to refuse this marriage they are arranging for you, and you may yet clasp your first and only love. Pledge me your word to love and cherish l'Ile Adam, who is the kindest of men; never to cause him a moment's anguish, and tell him to reveal to you all the secrets of love invented by Madame Imperia, because, in practising them, being young, you will be easily able to obliterate the remembrance of her from his mind."

Mademoiselle de Montmorency was so astonished that she could make no answer, and let this queen of beauty depart, and believed her to be a fairy, until a workman told her that the fairy was Madame de l'Ile Adam. Although the adventure was inexplicable, she told her father that she would not give her consent to the proposed marriage until after the autumn, so much is it in the nature of Love to ally itself with Hope, in spite of the bitter pills which the deceitful and gracious companion gives her to swallow like bulls' eyes. During the months when the grapes are gathered, Imperia would not let l'Ile Adam leave her, and was so amorous that one would have imagined she wished to kill him, since l'Ile Adam felt as though he had a fresh bride in his arms every night. The next morning the good woman requested him to keep the remembrance of these joys in his heart. Then, to know what her lover's real thoughts on the subject were, she said to him, "Poor l'Ile Adam, we were very silly to marry—a lad like you, with your twenty-three years, and an old woman close on forty." He answered her, that his happiness was such that he was the envy of every one, that at her age her equal did not exist among the younger women, and that if ever she grew old he would love her wrinkles, believing that even in the tomb she would be lovely, and her skeleton lovable.

To these answers, which brought the tears into her eyes, she one morning answered maliciously, that Mademoiselle Montmorency was very lovely and very faithful. This speech forced l'Ile Adam to tell her that she pained him by telling him of the only wrong he had ever committed in his life—the breaking of the troth pledged to his first sweetheart, all love for whom he had since effaced from his heart. This candid speech made her seize him and clasp him to her heart, affected at the loyalty of his discourse on a subject from which many would have shrunk.

"My dear love," said she, "for a long time past I have been suffering from a retraction of the heart, which has always since my youth been dangerous to my life, and in this opinion the Arabian physician coincides. If I die, I wish you to make the most binding oath a knight can make, to wed Mademoiselle Montmorency. I am so certain of dying, that I leave my property to you only on condition that this marriage takes place."

Hearing this l'Ile Adam turned pale, and felt faint at the mere thought of an eternal separation from his good wife.

"Yes, dear treasure of love," continued she. "I am punished by God there where my sins were committed, for the

great joys that I feel dilate my heart, and have, according
to the Arabian doctor, weakened the vessels which in a
moment of excitement will burst; but I have always implored God to take my life at the age in which I now am,
because I would not see my charms marred by the ravages
of time."

This great and noble woman saw then how well she was
beloved. This is how she obtained the greatest sacrifice of
love that ever was made upon this earth. She alone knew
what a charm existed in the embraces, fondlings, and raptures of the conjugal bed, which were such that poor l'Ile
Adam would rather have died than allow himself to be
deprived of the amorous delicacies she knew so well how
to prepare. At this confession made by her that, in the
excitement of love, her heart would burst, the chevalier cast
himself at her knees, and declared that to preserve *her* life
he would never ask her for love, but would live contented
to see her only at his side, happy at being able to touch
but the hem of her garment.

She replied, bursting into tears, "that she would rather
die than lose one iota of his love; that she would die as
she had lived, since luckily she could make a man embrace
her when such was her desire without having to put her
request into words."

Here it must be stated that the cardinal of Ragusa had
given her as a present an article, which this holy joker
called *in articulo mortis*. It was a tiny glass bottle, no big-
ger than a bean, made at Venice, and containing a poison
so subtle that by breaking it between the teeth death came
instantly and painlessly. He had received it from the Signora
Tophana, the celebrated maker of poisons of the town of
Rome.

Now this tiny bottle was under the bezel of a ring, preserved from all objects that could break it by certain plates of gold. Poor Imperia put it into her mouth several times without being able to make up her mind to bite it, so much pleasure did she take in the moment she believed to be her last. Then she would pass before her in mental review all her methods of enjoyment before breaking the glass, and determined that when she felt the most perfect of all joys she would bite the bottle.

The poor creature departed this life on the night of the first day of October. Then was there heard a great clamour in the forests and in the clouds, as if the loves had cried aloud, "The great Noc is dead!" in imitation of the pagan gods who, at the coming of the Saviour of men, fled into the skies, saying, "The great Pan is slain!" A cry which was heard by some persons navigating the Eubean Sea, and preserved by a father of the Church.

Madame Imperia died without being spoiled in shape, so much had God made her the irreproachable model of a woman. She had, it was said, a magnificent tint upon her flesh, caused by the proximity of the flaming wings of Pleasure, who cried and groaned over her corpse. Her husband mourned for her most bitterly, never suspecting that she had died to deliver him from a childless wife, for the doctor who embalmed her said not a word concerning the cause of her death. This great sacrifice was discovered six years after the marriage of l'Ile Adam with Mademoiselle de Montmorency, because she told him all about the visit of Madame Imperia. The poor gentleman immediately fell into a state of great melancholy, and finished by dying, being unable to banish the remembrance of those joys of love which it was beyond the power of a novice to restore to him; thereby did he prove the truth of that which was said at the time, that this woman would never die in a heart where she had once reigned.

This teaches us that virtue is well understood but by those who have practised vice ; for among the most modest women few would thus have sacrificed life, in whatever high state of religion you look for them.

EPILOGUE

Aн! mad little one, thou whose business it is to make the house merry, again hast thou been wallowing, in spite of a thousand prohibitions, in that slough of melancholy, whence thou hast already fished out Bertha, and come back with thy tresses dishevelled, like a girl who has been ill-treated by a regiment of soldiers! Where are thy golden aiglets and bells, thy filigree flowers of fantastic design? Where hast thou left thy crimson head-dress, ornamented with precious gewgaws that cost a minot of pearls? Why spoil with pernicious tears thy black eyes, so pleasant when therein sparkles the wit of a tale, that popes pardon thee thy sayings for the sake of thy merry laughter, feel their souls caught between the ivory of thy teeth, have their hearts drawn by the rose point of thy sweet tongue, and would barter the holy slipper for a hundred of the smiles that hover round thy vermilion lips? Laughing lassie, if thou wouldst remain always fresh and young, weep no more; think of riding the bridleless fleas, of bridling with the golden clouds thy chameleon chimeras, of metamorphosing the realties of life into figures clothed with the rainbow, caparisoned with roseate dreams, and mantled with wings blue as the eyes of the partridge. By the Body and the Blood, by the Censer and the Seal, by the Book and the Sword, by the Rag and the Gold, by the Sound and the Colour, if thou dost but return once into that hovel of elegies where eunuchs find ugly women for imbecile sul-

552

tans, I'll curse thee; I'll rave at thee; I'll make thee fast from roguery and love; I'll——

Phist! Here she is astride a sunbeam, with a volume that is ready to burst with merry meteors! She plays in their prisms, tearing about so madly, so wildly, so boldly, so contrary to good sense, so contrary to good manners, so contrary to everything, that one has to touch her with long feathers, to follow her siren's tail in the golden facets which trifle among the artifices of these new peals of laughter. Ye gods! but she is sporting herself in them like a hundred schoolboys in a hedge full of blackberries, after vespers. To the devil the magister! The volume is finished. Out upon work! What ho! my jovial friends; this way!

THE END